STORM WARNING

SECURITY SPECIALISTS INTERNATIONAL, BOOK 4

MONETTE MICHAELS

Storm Warning, Security Specialists International, Book 4

ISBN-13: 978-0-9862730-7-0
ISBN-10: 0986273074

E-Book version, published August, 2015.

Former Army helicopter pilot DJ Poe is a woman used to working in a man's world and comfortable as SSI's first female field operative. It's her instant attraction to the company's computer specialist that has her questioning her ability to overcome her past and develop an intimate relationship with a man.

Stuart "Tweeter" Walsh already admired DJ for saving his brother's life in Afghanistan, but when the tall, leggy, blonde goddess joins SSI, he falls instantly in love. All he has to do is convince the man-shy beauty to take a chance on him.

Take one alpha-male geek, add in one skittish female warrioress—throw them into close proximity, and you have the perfect conditions for storm warnings.

Note to the Reader and Acknowledgments

The year 2015 started out stormy for me. The rough weather came out of the blue, no warning at all, in the form of quintuple bypass surgery for my husband. People do not bounce back quickly from this type of surgery, and because he is my soul-mate and the love of my life, all my energy for three months was aimed at helping him get better. As of August 1st, we are six months post-surgery and beginning to see some of his energy and zest for life (and golf!) return.

So, it shouldn't surprise anyone that during this life-changing time, I had very little energy to write. *Storm Warning* was put down and picked up so many times, it should have whiplash. To get a summer release date so my fans wouldn't have to wait any longer than necessary, I decided to self-publish the book. I've been around e-publishing for a long, long time (since 1998), so I had an idea of the work it would take to get a book of this length to retailers. I also realized it could not be done without the help of a lot of wonderful, supportive friends, authors, fans, my long-time publisher, and my new distributor.

So let me thank and acknowledge those who helped or contributed to getting this book to you:

First, more thanks than I can say and much love to my primary critique partner, Cherise Sinclair. Cheri reads all my complete first drafts. She is, hands down, one of the best critique partners/first readers an author could have. I adore her, because she always makes me go that extra step to make my book the best it can be.

Thanks to my second-line-of-defense critique partner, Terri Schaefer, for giving my manuscript her eagle eye and making me do the right thing in that one scene. Yes, Terri, I fixed it.

Thanks to my beta-readers: Eran O'Donnal, Gail Northman, Debbie Kline—and especially, KaLyn Cooper for her military knowledge.

Thanks to Cherie Nicholls for sharing her British slang; to Nelle Hacking for her local Idaho knowledge, the gals would never have made it to Lewiston and the mall without you; and to Valerie Samouillan, Heather Hand, and Erin Bentley for bad guy names and Tweeter's Dark Net persona.

Thanks to Theresa Wilson for allowing me to use her middle name (Dawn) and her last name for Interpol agent Dawn Wilson,

As always, thanks to my talented cover artist April Martinez for another beautiful cover.

A second set of thanks to Gail Northman who gave me pep talks and did the formatting for the e-books.

Mega-thanks to Kelly Peterson and her staff at INscribe for taking me on so this book could make it to all the retailers my books currently reach.

And, last, but not least, thanks to Linda Eberharter, just because.

THIS BOOK IS DEDICATED TO MY HUSBAND. I LOVE YOU.

CHAPTER 1

2 a.m., January 3rd, Williamson, West Virginia

DJ Poe squinted through the windshield of the Jeep Cherokee, trying to focus on Williamson Memorial Hospital through what seemed like a blizzard of fat, fluffy snowflakes. She shivered and clasped the collar of her shearling jacket around her neck with shaking hands. The wind chill had already leached most of the warmth from the shut-off vehicle.

Not all of the cold in her bones, all of the trembling in her fingers, was due to the weather. Some could be attributed to out-and-out fear.

A little over twenty-four hours ago, she'd received an emergency text from a trusted source that read: "Your momma is dying." She hadn't been calm or warm since.

DJ swallowed hard, the taste of dread acrid in her mouth. God, she hadn't been this scared since one muggy, West Virginian summer night ten years ago.

She'd deal better if she was doing something. Instead, she sat here on her ass, waiting for an all-clear, while somewhere in that building her mother could be dying. "Could be" being the operative term—because the whole situation smelled like an elaborate trap.

Her mother's health and safety were the only reasons DJ would come back to Mingo County, one of the most morally corrupt places in the world—and the site of DJ's own personal hell on Earth, Red Bone. Since she'd served several tours in Afghanistan as an Army helicopter pilot, she recognized hell when she saw it.

Face it, Dahlia Jane, the fear is worse because of the guilt.

Yeah, that nailed it. While DJ had tried to get her mother away from her abusive husband, she'd failed, miserably. When DJ had gone to the legal system, justice failed both her and her mother. Physical evidence of abuse, it seemed, wasn't enough; which demonstrated her father and his friend Ed Varney had too much clout and her mother, a typical abuse victim, had refused to file charges.

DJ had been too far away to change any of the outcomes, but once she received her discharge, "Operation: Rescue Nancy Poe" had become DJ's top priority. She'd just finalized her solo plan to sneak her mother out of Red Bone when she'd received the alarming text.

Guilt, thy name is Dahlia Jane Poe.

Yeah, DJ should've gone against her mother's express wishes to forget about her and Red Bone and tried something more drastic sooner. Something along the lines of what she and her friends Andy and Devin Walsh were doing tonight. Of course, at the moment she wasn't doing a damn thing but taking up space and worrying like an old woman. The guys, typical macho Marines, had also smelled a trap and convinced her they needed to surveil first.

DJ pounded the steering wheel with her fist. Dammit! What the fuck was taking them so long? They'd been gone fifteen minutes. How long could it take to find one room when they already had the number and knew the layout of the building? This was a small county hospital, not a large city medical center. She could've been in and out five times already.

Frustrated, worried, and just generally pissed at the whole effin' situation, she pounded the steering wheel again. It didn't help.

Hold on, Momma. I'm here.

"She's not here, DJ." Andy's husky baritone came over the headset she wore under her wool watch cap. "She never was."

Relief swept over her. For the first time in over a day, she relaxed. She unclenched and wiggled her tension-cramped fingers even as she slumped into her seat. Her mother wasn't dying all alone in a hospital bed.

The whole emergency text had been a ruse, a trap loaded with the perfect bait. Only her father and the Varneys would know just what enticement was needed—and only they had reasons to lure her back to their turf.

"Roger that. Not totally surprised," she replied. Obviously, the source of the text message, Mrs. Binkley, her high school English teacher, had been misled or maybe even forced to send the message. She'd have to follow up that line of inquiry once she and the guys had found her mother and secured her safety. They might have to rescue more than one woman tonight.

Then it hit her, this *had been* a trap, so—

Swallowing hard past the boulder-sized lump in her throat, she asked, "Who did you find?"

"Three men waiting by the elevator and a woman in the room," said Andy.

Woman? Had her father and the Varneys hurt Mrs. Binkley? Used her as a decoy?

"Let me see the woman's picture," she gritted out.

"Sending image," Andy said. "But she's not an innocent."

"Got that right, brother," Dev said. "We're bugging out, DJ."

"Roger that." She stared at the image on her smart phone. While the situation wasn't funny, her lips twitched at the sight.

Donna Barstow—Red Bone's resident slut.

Donna had done anything for money ten years ago, and it looked as if the skunk hadn't changed her scent.

"What did she tell you," DJ asked, "before you gagged her."

"She knows nothing." Dev's low growl was filled with distaste. "She was shocked—just shocked, mind you—that we thought Nancy Poe would be in that bed." He huffed. "Of course, the medical chart inside the room says 'Nancy Poe,' and the hospital computer system we hacked into gives Room 420 as Nancy Poe's private room."

"DJ," Andy interjected, "we'll give a full report once we're away from the hospital. Things are quiet and under control—for now." He paused and added, "But either the hospital security is really lax or purposely MIA."

Someone had messed with the hospital's security? More likely, someone in security was in on the trap. The Varneys owned a lot of people in Mingo County.

"Roger that." DJ started the Jeep, put the defrosters on high, and then got out to clear the snow off the headlights and windows. The snow was coming down more heavily, maybe an inch an hour. The winds had picked up slightly and the wind chill could freeze extremities in less than five minutes. She pulled her balaclava up around her nose, so she wouldn't inhale the cold air directly.

"We going to Red Bone?" Andy's voice came across the headset as clear as if he'd been standing right next to her. She heard the clang of a metal door shutting and then the thudding of the two men's boots as they descended stairs.

Red Bone was where she'd been born, raised, and lived for the first eighteen years of her life. It was a mining town— well, not even a town, but a population district—south of Williamson, on U.S. 52. The godforsaken bump in the road had become a place to loathe as soon as she'd developed breasts, mostly because of Sean Varney.

Sean was two years older than her. He was a spoiled brat, a bully—her nemesis—and the reason she hadn't been back to West Virginia since the morning after she'd graduated high school.

DJ shuddered and clenched her teeth against the anguished moan threatening to claw its way out of her throat. The memories of that time had never faded, but had gone stealthy like a predatory beast waiting to attack her when she was at her weakest.

She'd made it her business never to be weak. But that might be impossible here and now. The memories—the pain—were far too close to the surface.

"DJ? You copy?" Dev's voice held a hint of impatience.

Get your head out of your ass, Dahlia Jane.

DJ shook off the tentacles of the sly past—for now.

"Yeah—and yeah, Red Bone," DJ replied, happy her voice didn't reflect her unease. "If my momma's at the cabin, then we're going to get her out of that fricking hellhole."

If her mother wasn't at the old homestead, then DJ would happily beat the information out of her bastard of a father. He deserved to get a taste of his own medicine. The man had beaten her and her mother whenever he felt like it—didn't need a reason. He was just plain mean.

The memories of years of abuse at her old man's hands slithered through her mind's eye. She shook her head—*Not now.* Remembering him and Sean would do her absolutely no good. She couldn't allow anything to distract her from the mission at hand.

But it's all a part of what's going on now, isn't it? If you'd dealt with your pa and the Varneys all those years ago, now wouldn't be happening.

Yeah, she'd been a coward, the proverbial ostrich with her neck buried halfway to China. Because of her lack of guts, her mother, and maybe even Mrs. Binkley, could be hurt or worse.

No, she couldn't think that way. Her mother was fine. Mrs. Binkley, also. She refused to allow the past and a mixed bag of negative emotions to tank the mission; it was too important, maybe the most important mission of her whole life.

DJ pulled her Beretta pistol and double-checked the magazine. The routine maneuver served to calm her nerves. The only better routine would've been performing a pre-flight check on a Black Hawk, the airframe to which she'd been assigned after finishing Army flight school.

Gun in hand, she checked the surroundings for potential danger.

No one was out. But why would they be? It was the middle of the fricking night, colder than the ice lakes of Hell, and snowing as if the next Ice Age had arrived. Shift change at the hospital wouldn't be for several more hours. All the other fine citizens of Williamson were home, tucked in their beds.

Worry gnawed at her control once again. Was her mother safe and warm? Was she hurt? Was she even alive?—*Stop it.*— All she could do was move forward one step at a time.

Assured the area was secure for the men's return, she holstered her weapon, then climbed back into the driver's seat and waited for her teammates.

DJ couldn't have asked for better partners than Andy and Dev. The men had dropped everything, sacrificed their last few days of leave from their Marine Special Operations Command teams, and driven straight through from the North Carolina coast to help with the rescue of her mother.

She'd only known the two Marines for about six months, but Andy and Dev had become closer to her than her blood kin—with the exception of her mother. They'd met when Dev had asked a room full of Army helicopter pilots for a volunteer to fly a risky rescue mission to pick up a MARSOC team led by his brother Andy. All the pilots had offered, but DJ had been chosen since she was the best pilot for the job. The risky mission had been a success.

That one small act, something she would've done for anyone, led to the Walsh family adopting her as one of their own. They'd even gotten her an interview which had led to a job with the private security firm Security Specialists

International, owned by Ren Maddox, the husband of the Walsh's only daughter, Keely. DJ would be SSI's first female operative.

With a job waiting for her, she left the Army after ten years. She'd arrived in the States and stayed with the Walshes at Camp Lejeune while she'd finalized her plans to get her mother away from her father.

Then Mrs. Binkley's text had arrived. It had been Andy and Dev's mother Molly who'd noticed DJ's distress. The woman had gently, but determinedly, pried the information out of DJ—and then called a family meeting where DJ had given the Walshes the Cliff's Notes version about her family situation.

Andy and Dev had insisted on coming along as her backup. They wouldn't take "no" for an answer. Their—the whole Walsh family's—unqualified support had filled a place in her heart that had been empty for far too long.

A low whistle over the headset alerted her to the brothers' approach. She unlocked all the doors. The two men piled in.

DJ turned toward Dev. "Tell me about—"

"Later. Get us away from here," Dev said. "If someone discovers the four people we left trussed up in that suspiciously vacant ward, a cluster of cosmic proportions will rain down on us."

"Why? What did you do?" As the men buckled up, DJ pulled smoothly out of the alley into which she'd backed. Driving at an appropriate speed for the weather, she headed for the outskirts of Williamson; her destination, an all-night truck stop right off U.S. 52.

"*Who* is the correct question. One of the three men was the Mingo County Sheriff."

Dev delivered the statement in the same calm tone and manner he'd use to order a coffee. But the impact on her nerves was like that of a surface-to-air-missile taking down a chopper. She lost the cool facade she'd forcibly donned before the men had reached the Jeep and shrieked, "Sheriff? God, what did you—"

Dev grasped her shoulder, then gently squeezed. "Chill, DJ. They're tied up, but unharmed. They can't identify us. We had ski masks on and wore gloves. Just get us to a place so we can fully debrief." He looked in the side mirror. "I haven't spotted a tail. Andy?"

"Nada. I keep telling you, no one saw us, bro," Andy chimed in from the back seat. "That wing was deserted. Old technology security cameras, shut down. I checked them as we went in and out. That hospital doesn't have the budget to do anything super-high-tech small. Face it, the Sheriff was being a bad boy. He didn't want DJ's capture to be seen. Kidnapping charges definitely wouldn't look good for his re-election chances."

Andy was making light of the situation, but it was serious. From the beginning, the whole situation had stunk to high heaven. She should've anticipated the potential of crooked law enforcement participation. She hadn't warned the Walshes about the Varneys—so they hadn't had all the facts about how things worked in Mingo County. She'd only told them about her low-life father and that had been bad enough. Now, it looked as if the minute details she'd skimmed over in her back story might bite them all on their asses.

"Sweet Jesus, what have I gotten you guys into?" This wasn't their fight. Guilt, fear, and worry—of late, her close emotional companions—ate at her gut. "Maybe you guys should—"

"Shut it, DJ. Do *not* finish that sentence," Dev gritted out. "We aren't leaving until we get your mom and *you* away from here."

"Yeah, we're a team, and a team member doesn't leave a teammate behind. You know that," Andy scolded.

Yeah, she did, but that was in the military—this was personal. However, she wasn't surprised at their response, but was still leery of risking their lives and reputations.

Dev added, "Plus ... you're family now. We'd go to war for you."

And it might come to that.

Tears of gratitude formed in her eyes. *Not the time, Dahlia Jane.* She furiously blinked the wetness away as she carefully negotiated the curvy, snow-covered road. The mountain road was tricky on dry days, but on snowy days, it was downright treacherous. One wrong move and they'd slide off the icy pavement into the Tug River.

With all the potential dangers, her gaze never ceased moving back and forth from the road to the rearview mirror. No one on the road, but them and a few truckers who had to make deliveries or lose money. Most importantly, no county sheriff's car in high-speed pursuit.

And who was the Sheriff now?

She'd find out once they stopped. Chances were she might not even know the man, but she'd bet he was firmly in Ed Varney's back pocket.

To distract her mind from chasing the unknowns like a hamster running a wheel, she said, "So ... Donna sure looked scared. What did you do or say to her? The Donna I knew could skin a person with the sharp edge of her tongue."

DJ chanced a quick glance at Dev. His lips twisted with disgust. Yeah, that was how a lot of decent people felt about old Donna.

Before Dev could open his mouth, Andy laughed. "Ole Dev told her that if she made a single peep before morning that he knew where she lived and he'd come back and personally give her a facelift with a dull knife."

"Facelift?" DJ bit her lip, stifling an inappropriate snicker, as she carefully steered through a series of S-curves that hadn't seen a plow or salt.

Dev snorted. "That's what she said she was in the hospital for."

"Nothing's changed with that bitch," she said on a sigh as she pulled out of the last curve with only a slight skid. Donna had regularly had tune-ups even when DJ lived in Red Bone. She was fairly sure her father and Ed Varney paid for most of the body work.

The Walshes hummed in a way she'd quickly come to recognize meant they wanted her to share—but only if she wanted to. Their patient silence filled the confines of the Jeep until she couldn't stand it any longer.

DJ grimaced. "Donna was—and probably still is—the town slut. She spread her legs for most of Red Bone's and the surrounding area's male population over the age of sixteen including my father and my two brothers. She's quite the femme fatale."

She could still remember the one time her mother had put her foot down about her husband "visiting" Donna. Her father had beaten her mother, beaten DJ when she tried to stop him, and then had still gone to see the fat-assed bitch. His regular nights had been Tuesday and Saturday. On Saturdays, he'd shared Donna with his boss Ed Varney in a threesome.

Everyone in Red Bone knew about her father's philandering. Her mother had tried to shelter DJ from the salacious knowledge, but there were always people who liked to gossip. *Bless their hearts.*

"Not seeing that. Not my type." Dev looked over the seat at his brother. "Yours, Andy?"

"Only if I was blind, deaf, dumb, criminally stupid—and so crippled I couldn't run the other way."

DJ's lips twisted upwards before thinning into a tight tense line as she struggled to keep the Jeep on the road when a particularly vicious gust of wind hit the vehicle sideways. "Thanks, guys. I needed a good laugh. I always thought she looked too … too…"

"Tarted up? Cheap? Skanky?" Dev suggested.

"Rode hard and put away wet," Andy muttered. "She smelled like it, too."

"Eeuw, thanks for putting that image in my brain." DJ shook her head as the brothers chuckled. The laughter relieved some of the tension in the vehicle. "I bet Donna had sex in the hospital bed. She told me once … well, never mind. I'd never take sex advice from the likes of her. My momma raised me better."

Worry for her mother rose to swamp her once again. She choked up on the steering wheel until her fingers ached. When the vehicle began to drift, she realized what she was doing and deliberately loosened her grip and steered the Jeep back on her side of the center line. Now was not the time to have an accident because she'd become distracted.

With a sigh of relief, DJ spotted the bright lights of the truck stop. She pulled into the parking lot and backed into a spot between a darkened pickup truck and an equally empty SUV.

"We can talk here without being noticed." Besides the two vehicles and theirs, there were at least twenty semis and quite a few cars. They'd be just three among many snow weary travelers.

After she turned off the vehicle, she turned to face Dev and so that she could see Andy in the seat behind his brother. "Okay, show me the damn pictures."

Andy hung over the seat and pulled up the first picture on his phone. "Here's the Sheriff."

The picture was of a large, dark-haired male. He lay on his side, hog-tied with zip ties, and had gauze bandaging and tape over his mouth. He wore an eye patch, but his other flame-blue eye glared into the camera.

God help them all. His daddy bought Sean the Sheriff's job.

DJ swallowed the threatening nausea and fought against being sucked into the black hole of her past. The guys needed more intel—part of which would include what had happened between Sean and her on the night she graduated from high school. The events of that night were why they were here now.

She managed to gasp out, "That's Sean Varney. His father Ed is my father's boss."

Both men's body postures tensed. Their gazes sharpened as they glanced from the image on the cell phone to her face and then back again.

Could they sense her fear of Sean? Her distaste? Her horror? Probably.

For a few seconds, she ignored their questioning looks and took a couple of slow breaths in an attempt to regain control of her emotions. She wasn't sure she could talk about what Sean had done to her. Didn't want to see the pity on their faces, if she could.

Denial, thy name is Dahlia Jane.

DJ swept a shaky finger across the cell phone's screen and shuddered at the next image—Sean standing against the wall next to the elevator, his hands behind his neck. He'd bulked up even more over the last ten years. But the feral look promising pain and eventually death in the one good eye—the one she hadn't damaged—hadn't changed at all. It still chilled her to the bone. He'd aimed the same expression at her on graduation night right after she managed to get away.

Seeing that look in Sean's eye was the tipping factor. She could no longer hold back the tsunami of dark memories.—*It was a hot summer night. A good night for a swim in the creek by her family's cabin. Sean followed her—made crude remarks and sexual overtures. She refused him. Tried to leave. He pounced on her like a hungry bobcat on a rabbit.*

Nothing she did stopped him. She scratched and kicked. Screamed until her throat was raw and only mewling sounds emerged.

Sean beat her until she lay, gasping, half in, half out of the creek. Then he stripped her with rough, pinching fingers. Raped her—taking her virginity—and beat her some more. Time blurred as he raped her again. She fell unconscious then. She only roused when dawn broke. Sean must have fallen asleep, but the sun awakened him, too—and he raped her yet again. But this time, she managed to find a rock near her hand. In her fear and pain, she hit him in the face, in his eye.

He screamed, roared, cursed—and threatened, "I'll cut you to pieces, you fucking bitch. You'll beg for death."

As he rolled on the ground, covering his damaged eye with his hands, she struggled to her feet and then stumbled away. She fell many times, but kept getting up until she could no longer manage it. Then she crawled. Anything to put distance between her and the animal who'd hurt her.

Relaxing her clenched jaw and taking several deep breaths, DJ beat back the nightmarish images. That brutalized girl no longer existed. She couldn't. The Army had made DJ strong, strong enough that no man could ever hurt her in such a way again.

Maybe if she told herself that often enough, she might even begin to believe it, might be able to live a normal life and be more than good buddies with men.

"DJ … come back to us, please." Dev's voice broke through the miasma inside her mind.

She blinked and then looked at Dev and Andy. How long had she been lost in the past? It must've been awhile since their expressions had switched from questioning to concerned.

Then it hit her.

"Sweet Jesus," DJ whispered, a sick feeling in her stomach. "Sean as a law enforcement officer would have access to databases most citizens wouldn't. Maybe not the classified stuff, but my regular Army records. He could've come after me at any time."

"It's awfully hard to kidnap a Chief Warrant Officer off a military base stateside or on deployment. That would cause a ruckus," Dev pointed out. "He waited to set his trap until you were out. He and his buddies might not have even been aware of your plan to take your mom away."

"Yeah, that makes more sense than Momma or Mrs. Binkley screwing the pooch." DJ laid her head back against the headrest, willing her stomach to stop churning.

"If it bothers you, we can have Tweeter and Keely look into who's accessed your Army records. They can also check to see if your classified records were hacked." Andy patted her shoulder. "The fucker could've also hired a private investigator and gotten the info about you and your discharge date that way."

She nodded. "Show me the other two."

Andy held his phone up with another picture.

"That's Ed Varney." She shivered. If she'd been Catholic, she might've crossed herself. The devil hadn't changed at all. He was still big, ugly, and mean-looking. She was surprised he hadn't had a heart attack since his bulk looked to be all fat, concentrated in his middle.

"And here's the last guy," Andy said. "Looks like he eats small pets and children for breakfast. His vocabulary was … impressive."

DJ frowned as she looked at the picture of the last man. Andy had also taken closeups of the man's tattoos. He could be militia, an outlaw biker, or an ex-con. He looked very rough. "I don't know him. Um, where did y'all get the restraints you used to hog tie them? I didn't see you take in any."

Dev's face darkened with repressed rage. "The bastards had them. We also found a couple of syringes on them. We gave each of them a little dose of whatever they'd planned for you. We kept part of one, and we'll have Dad get it analyzed on base. It's evidence they'd planned to take you by force. We have lots of lovely pictures before and after our take-down of them."

DJ shuddered. No matter how strong she was, how well she fought, or how heavily armed she'd have been, the three men could've easily overpowered her. God, she was glad she'd come with backup.

"Dev opted to drug them." Andy let out a disappointed sigh. "I wanted to beat the shit out of them."

"Glad you restrained yourself," she said.

"They're alive, but won't be real happy. They don't dare come after us, even if they could discover who we are. What they were doing was illegal," Andy said. "We took the pictures to show you—but also to turn over to the Feds when we report the attempted kidnapping."

"If I'd only reported Sean … ten years ago…"

But you didn't and here you are.

Yeah, here she was. Her mother missing. Two decent men involved in the filth that was her past. All of a sudden she was that eighteen-year-old girl again and nothing had changed. She choked back the sob threatening to escape. The view outside the Jeep's windshield blurred, not because of the heavy snow, but because of the tears welling in her eyes.

Again with the crying? God bless it, Dahlia Jane, man the fuck up. You aren't alone. You have a team. Share the load.

Dev wiped away a tear streaking down her cheek with his gloved thumb. "Talk to us."

DJ blinked away the tears and sniffed. "Yeah … you need to know the whole, sordid story—need to know what you could be walking into and why."

Also, they needed to learn she wasn't the hero they thought she was. She'd run away all those years ago and stayed away. She'd failed in her attempts to free her mother, thus leaving her in the hands of an abusive man.

Cut yourself some slack. You tried. Your momma has to share some of the blame. She never grabbed the safety lines you threw out.

With her head resting against the seat back, she inhaled and then slowly exhaled, several times. Her vision finally clear, she stared at the roof of the Jeep.

Jesus, she'd rather face a horde of Taliban terrorists than talk about this crap. She sniffled and immediately resented the weakness in her that still allowed the past to bother her this way.

Andy handed her a handkerchief over the back of the seat. "Here ya go. You know, anything you tell us will stay with us, if that's what you want."

Get a fucking spine, Dahlia Jane. Just spit it out.

"The night I graduated high school ... Sean Varney beat and raped me."

Silence met the stark statement, which said it all without having to relive the gory details. Been there. Done that once this evening. Walking an emotional tightrope without a safety net as a result.

The energy pouring off the two men had gone from cool and calm to nuclear in a split second. She sensed their stares, their concern. She couldn't look at them. Because if she found pity in their eyes, she'd fall right off the thin line she was walking and then be of no use to her mother.

DJ inhaled, then let out a harsh, shaky breath. "My momma found me ... I was too hurt, too weak, to make it all the way home ... after I got away from him."

Echoes of Sean bellowing in pain from the hurt she'd managed to mete out—screaming he'd cut her to pieces and use her as fish bait—rang in her head again.

Dammit! No! She slammed a mental door, shutting out the cacophony from the past.

"She'd come to find me, because..." She gasped for breath.

Why wasn't there enough oxygen all of a sudden?

"Breathe." Dev rubbed her arm. "Take your time."

The sound of his calm voice, the warmth of his hand through her coat helped. She took several breaths, then continued, "My father and Sean's had made a deal..."

"What kind of deal?" Dev's voice now had a darker, more feral edge. His hand squeezed her arm, but that was okay since he was angry on her behalf. While Andy's curses sizzled in the cold air, he gently laid a warm hand on her shoulder, adding his support to his brother's.

A devil's deal.

"That Sean could now have me since I'd graduated high school. I guess they'd been making plans for a while."

DJ looked at her lap and pleated and unpleated Andy's handkerchief. She was embarrassed. Her father had bartered her away like a piece of property to curry favor with his boss. Dev and Andy had been raised by a decent man who loved his only daughter and would emasculate any man who threatened her well-being. They had to be disgusted. She was disgusted.

"You didn't report the rape." Andy's voice was harsh. "Why not?"

She looked up. Even with all her training and years in the Army, she felt as helpless now as she had ten years ago. "Nothing would've been done. The three of them would've made me out to be a lying harlot."

At their looks of shocked disbelief, she reached out a hand, pleading. "You have to understand. The Varneys had—still have—clout in Mingo County, both in money and power. They owned the then-Sheriff," she let out a hysterical laugh, "just as much as they currently own the office of sheriff."

She held her breath and clamped her lips shut. If she gave into hysteria now, she didn't think she could stop and there were still things that needed to be explained … and done tonight.

Several seconds passed, then Dev asked, "What happened after your mom found you?"

She could tell he kept his tone, gentle, calm, to help her settle down. She looked at him and then Andy. "It's okay, guys. I won't go all crazy-woman hysterical on you." Maybe.

"Jesus H. Christ, DJ." Andy shook his head. "You don't have to tell us that." Yeah, she did since she was a flea's whisker away from losing control. "But, hell, I wouldn't blame you even if you did. You've got cause."

Dev nodded. "You know you don't have to face any of this alone any longer, right? We're here ... hell, the whole Walsh family would be here, if needed, to support you."

And that was why she'd count her blessings every damn day that she'd been present when Dev needed a pilot.

"Now, tell us the rest. How did you get away?" Dev said.

"My father was visiting Donna that night. We were afraid Ed and his men would come looking for me. So, my momma hid me in an out-building and then called my English teacher Mrs. Binkley who got me out of town." DJ shuddered and pulled her collar up around her neck. "She drove me to her nurse friend in Williamson and got me basic medical treatment. Then Mrs. Binkley had her cousin drive me to Cincinnati and I received more treatment. I lived at the YWCA until I'd healed enough to enlist in the Army and ... that's it."

A pregnant silence settled over the vehicle.

DJ stared out the window. The snow had slowed a bit, but was swirling in the gusty winds. There was no traffic on the highway. No movement in the parking lot. It was as if she and the two men were alone in a snow-globe-universe of white and cold and dark.

Dev grunted then blew out a breath. "Besides being an employee, what's your father's relationship to the Varneys that he'd pimp his only daughter?"

Yeah, that was what her father had done all right. Could it be uglier or dirtier?

DJ couldn't shake the shame of it all—had tried for years to figure out why her father hated her so much. Fathers were supposed to love and cherish their daughters. Or, at least, that was what she'd learned once she'd escaped from Red Bone.

She looked at the now horribly wrinkled handkerchief and twisted it even more. "My father is Ed's right-hand man. Ed was ... is..."

She shook her head and concentrated on swallowing and breathing past the lump in her throat. Until now, she'd been the victim of her past. What would they think of her when they learned the truth?—That half her DNA came from a degenerate crook.

And the other half comes from an angel incarnate.

"I'm such a wuss."

"DJ," Dev rubbed her arm, "you aren't a wuss." He leaned over and gave her a brotherly kiss on her cold cheek, his lips so warm she shivered at the difference in temperature.

Andy leaned forward and rubbed her shoulder through her thick shearling coat. "Give yourself a break. You were traumatized at an early age. You received no justice. No counseling. So, you've never fully processed the attack. You have post-traumatic stress disorder, not a thing to be ashamed of, but something that must be dealt with."

"Once you get to Idaho, talk to Keely or Vanko's wife Elana. Both of them have had similar traumas and deal with PTSD. They'll listen … help you get you counseling, if you need it."

Dev slid a finger along her cheek and then tapped the tip of her nose before sitting back in his seat. "So, to review the cluster to this point, your asshat of a father wanted to suck up to his boss and decided to gift his only daughter to the man's scum-sucking rapist of a son to accomplish that."

"Yeah, that sums it up." DJ tilted her head back and frowned at the Jeep's roof. "When Sean wanted something, his daddy got it for him. For some reason, Sean decided he wanted me all those years ago. Now, he wants revenge … and his daddy and my father will help him get it."

"Why does fucktard Sean want revenge?" Andy asked.

She laughed, a harsh sound. "Because I'm the reason he wears an eye patch. I managed to hit him in the face with a rock after he…" She couldn't say the words again. Once was enough. As it was, she'd be sure to have nightmares later, if this godforsaken night ever ended.

"Good for you," Dev purred the words as Andy muttered, "Serves the fuckwit right."

"Now, tell us exactly what the Varneys do that provides all their money and clout?" Dev asked.

She snorted. "If it's illegal, Ed Varney does it." At Dev's raised eyebrow and Andy's gimme-more grunt, she added, "When I lived in Mingo County, Ed ran guns, drugs, and moonshine. I've been told he's expanded his criminal empire to include human trafficking to brothels in the Midwest."

Her stomach lurched and she swallowed hard at the thought her father could be involved in something so evil and sick as selling humans. Yeah, her paternal genes sucked big time. "No matter who the elected officials might've been, Ed oversaw his little part of the world like a *Posse Comitatus*. Do you know what that means?"

"Yeah," Dev said. "It means some elected official, or any asshat who has lots of political pull, runs roughshod over the area where he lives. Militias tend to be involved most of the time."

"Exactly. Ed held most of the power in Mingo County while I was growing up," DJ said. "With Sean as the elected Sheriff, he has solidified his control."

"Do the Varneys have militia ties?" asked Andy.

"Oh hell yeah. Their unit is an offshoot of Christian Identity, one of the Aryan Nation militias. The unit has reciprocal trading agreements and vows of mutual support with other militias across the United States, including a few in Idaho, Washington State, and Montana."

DJ eyed the two men. Their expressions were grim. "So, I'm not holding my breath that Sean and my father will never track me and Momma down even after we move to Idaho—if I still have a job after all this comes out. I never told Ren the details of why I left West Virginia and about my family's criminal ties."

"Fuck, DJ," Andy drawled. "Ren won't hold the Varneys' and your father's backgrounds against you. He was happy to get you. Your military training is just what he was looking for in a female operative."

Andy was being nice. She had no doubt the Walshes had lobbied hard to get Ren to hire her on the basis of her Army record and after a few Skype interviews. She'd never be able to pay them back, but she'd work hard for SSI—and to make a new life for her and her mother in Idaho.

"Is there anything else we need to know before we go and get your mom?" Dev asked.

"No—that's the whole mess." She scanned the two men's faces. Both wore the calm expressions of the highly trained Marines they were. But what was behind those facades now that they knew the mess they might be wading into? "You don't need to come with me…"

Dev growled and Andy frowned. Okay, maybe that was insulting, but she had to give them an out. She had no clue who her father might have backing him up at the cabin. She needed to approach this from a different angle, one they'd understand from a military viewpoint.

"Guys, the mission has changed. This is more than getting my momma out of a lightly secured hospital…"

Now, both men glared. Okay, that approach was probably even more insulting.

"Dev … Andy … with Sean being the law in Mingo County, this could turn into a real goat rope…"

"Jesus," Dev turned to Andy, "can you believe this?"

Andy shook his head. "Nope, she must not have processed the part about her being our new sister." Then he turned, his gaze fierce. "Let me spell this out. Me and Dev would kill for you, bury the bodies, and lie like bandits about it. No militia or a fucking rapist bastard wearing a tin badge will make one bit of difference—we're staying."

Dev used his finger to turn her face toward him. "So, soldier … stop trying to protect us. We're here. We'll do what we need to do to rescue your mom and then take these assholes down once and for all. End. Of. Story."

DJ let out the breath she'd been holding. The sense of relief knowing she wouldn't have to go it alone was much bigger than she would've thought. She might've left her crew when she left the Army, but she now had a new crew, a new team, in the Walshes. It was a damn good feeling.

She turned on the Jeep and drove out of the parking lot onto the snow-covered highway. "Okay, here's the layout of my family's property and cabin…"

As she drove back to where her life had begun twenty-eight-years ago, she briefed her team and gave them as many details as she could about what to expect.

CHAPTER 2

3:00 a.m., in the hills outside of Red Bone

The three of them hunkered down in a copse of snow-laden trees off to the side of her family's cabin. A cold chill had settled in her belly. The area echoed with bad memories of arguments and abuse, diluted only by her mother's love and sacrifice for her only daughter.

Please be here and unharmed, Momma.

DJ shook off the fear fileting her insides and fixed her attention on the target they needed to breach. As far as she could tell not much had changed since she'd left home, in either the surroundings or the character of the people who lived there.

The cabin built by her great-great-grandfather with hand-hewn logs and cement-sand-lime chinking still looked as if it would fall down any second. The fieldstone fireplace had giant cracks and tilted toward the back of the building. The wooden porch sagged, and the window to her attic bedroom was still boarded up from the time she tried to escape in her junior year in the middle of the night. Her father had never seen any need to "gussy up" the exterior.

There were some concessions to the twenty-first century—two satellite dishes hung precariously on the rickety eaves. Her father had probably justified those expenses as a cost of doing business.

"How do you want to do this, DJ?" Dev spoke in a low monotone.

After she'd briefed the guys on the way here as to the physical layout of the property, she'd offered the mission lead to Dev or Andy. Both men had declined in favor of her home field knowledge. Their continued faith in her went a long way in calming her nerves and tamping down the bad memories that coming home had brought to the surface. The images were still there, lurking under the surface of her consciousness, but for now she was in control.

DJ surveyed the surroundings once more, looking for anything she might've overlooked during her first go-round. No matter how focused she was, she could always miss some detail that might bite her or her teammates in the ass.

Several pickup trucks were parked in the side yard. Since several inches of snow had accumulated on the vehicles, they'd been there for a while. Lights were on in the cabin. Tendrils of smoke with an occasional flickering of bright red sparks rose lazily from the chimney. Her not-so-loving father was up with his drinking buddies, or maybe some of Varney's militia men, keeping him company while waiting on Varney to call and report on her abduction.

"I'll knock on the door," DJ said. "While I distract father-dearest and whoever else is inside, you can go around to the backdoor. My parents' bedroom is located at the back of the house on the main level. Find my momma and get her the hell out of there. Once she's clear, I'll bid my father a not-so-fond farewell."

"One of us will get your mom," Andy muttered. "The other will back you up and make sure you're clear. You aren't confronting that bastard and his buddies alone."

She cast both men a look her helicopter crew would've recognized as her don't-argue-with-me expression and found them looking mulish. How could she have forgotten that while Dev and Andy had ceded her the lead, they were still Special Ops and would argue with authority if they didn't see things her way?

DJ shook her head and blew out a frosty breath. In the short time she'd known the two men, she'd discovered they were far more stubborn than she was—and bigger and meaner. Truth be told, confronting her father would be distressing—because deep inside, she was still the little girl who wanted her father to love and cherish her.

Plus, Andy and Dev were correct—she needed backup. Her emotional issues could rise up at anytime and throw her off the game plan.

"Okay … thanks." She stood, brushed snow off her legs and butt. Then she pulled her weapon and flicked off the safety, just in case, and placed it in her jacket pocket. She felt for the switchblade in her other pocket. She was as ready as she'd ever be.

"Com check," she spoke under her breath into the headset mostly hidden under her watch cap.

"All clear," Dev said.

"Ditto," Andy replied. "Don't do anything stupid, DJ. Keep your com unit on so we can hear everything."

DJ shot Andy the finger over her shoulder as she walked away and grinned as the men's chuckles came over the headset. Her long legs made an easy and quick trip through the shin-high snow. When she was within a few meters of the front door, motion sensors activated exterior lights on the front corners of the cabin. Something else new since she'd been here last. Bet the local critters set those puppies off on a regular basis—and they'd be just as regularly ignored.

Unless they have cameras attached to them, Dahlia Jane.

Nah, her father was too cheap to pay for that kind of upgrade.

DJ paused and let her eyes adjust. She shoved her hand in her pocket and lightly gripped her pistol, just in case. Once her vision was clear, she mounted three steps, which had been half-assed repaired, crossed the small expanse of porch decking, and then knocked on the roughly hewn door.

"That you, Ed?"

Her father's irritating whine came through the wood door. Her gut clenched at the all-too-familiar sound; it brought back too many memories of bare-assed strappings with his belt as he'd whined about what an ungrateful brat she was. She still carried faint scars from when he'd gotten carried away.

"Didn't hear ya drive up. What the fuck took ya so long? Did you get the little bitch?"

Little bitch?

Her heart stuttered. Yeah, nothing had changed. But then why would it? The man was rotten to the core. Her only value in his worldview was as barter for more money and power in the Varney empire, and she'd deprived him of potential ownership in the Varneys' dirty empire when she'd left. She wondered what her barter value was currently?

Too bad, Pa. I ain't playing.

"We're in. Shit locks—so no problem." Dev's voice came over the headset. "Your mom isn't in the first floor bedroom. Andy's searching the attic."

Shit. Was her mother even here?

DJ snarled as the sound of multiple locks being undone echoed in the snow-filled night air.

"Stop growling, DJ. It's distracting." Dev continued, "Someone's been cooking meth in the kitchen. Front room—there's three men on a couch to your left as you enter. They look drunk. Too out of it to be on meth. Guy opening the door, on the other hand, is practically bouncing. Watch him—he could get violent."

"Roger that," she muttered right before the door opened. She pulled her hand from her gun pocket and slid her other hand into the pocket with the knife. It was better not to shoot guns inside a meth house.

And then she was face-to-face with her father for the first time in ten years.

Her stomach curdled, and she swallowed the bile threatening to come up—fought the Pavlovian response to back away and cower.

The bastard was shorter than she remembered, or, maybe it was because she'd grown taller. He had a comb-over on the top of his balding head and a ragged, salt-and-pepper mullet elsewhere. Sort of a Billy Ray Cyrus meets Bruce Willis look.

She smelled booze wafting off his dirty flannel shirt. His breath could fell a bear. Yeah, he was twitching—bouncing just as Dev had said. His pupils were so dilated she could barely detect the pale blue of his irises. His facial skin was pasty and hung loose on his bones. His teeth were rotten and some missing.

Christ Jesus, he's the frickin' poster boy for meth addiction.

"You're using meth? I knew you were rotten to the core. Never thought you were stump stupid." She scanned his body and felt only disgust. "You look like shit, old man."

"Dahlia Jane." Her father looked over her—twice—then leered. The gaps in his teeth made him look like a sick jack o'lantern. She'd need a long, hot shower after this just to scrub the icky feeling off her skin. He was her effin' father and he eyed her as if she were a hooker.

"My, my, my, you grew up good." He smacked his lips. "Look just like your momma did at your age. Built like a brick outhouse, but you got my daddy's family's height. Damn girl. Sean might keep you alive for a while before he offs you. He do you yet? That why it took y'all so long to get here?" He craned his neck to look past her. "Where is Sean and his daddy?"

"Um, they're tied up." DJ walked toward her father and forced him to move out of her way. She spotted the other three men … all strangers. Her brothers weren't here. Why that fact relieved her? She didn't know. The fact they weren't present didn't mean they'd straightened up; it just meant they were elsewhere.

She wrinkled her nose. The place smelled like unwashed men and fresh moonshine overlaid by the sharp smell of the acetone used in the meth cooking.

A loud snort and then a buzz-saw sound came from one of the men on the couch. As if on cue, the other two began to snore. Yeah, they were drunk out of their puny minds.

Dev was a shadow among the shadows of the back hall. Knife in hand, he never took his eyes off the men on the couch.

DJ turned her gaze back to her father who blinked like an owl and whose meth-fried brain cells had finally processed her previous words. "Whatcha mean *tied up*?"

"As in hog-tied and gagged. They ain't coming. I'll be leaving once I get Momma."

"Now see here, girl." Her father lurched toward her, his fist raised.

As a young girl, she'd pleaded with him not to hurt her. As she'd grown older, she'd tried to run away from the violence. Now, she moved into him, blocked his arm, grabbed his other arm, and then used it to turn him around, twisting his arm up behind his back. She pulled her switchblade with her left hand. The snick of the blade sounded like a gunshot in the silent room. She placed the knife under his chin, the blade flat against his throat—for now.

"Where's my momma, you disgusting freak of nature," she gritted out over his ear.

"We got her, DJ." Dev preceded his brother into the room, his focus, on the men on the couch who hadn't moved and were still snoring in stereo. Andy followed with her mother cradled against his chest. He'd bundled her in a thick, fleecy blanket. She didn't move. Didn't make a sound. Andy's expression was dark and ugly as he eyed her father.

"Momma…" DJ's voice was a strangled whisper. What had the fucker done to her? As she was about to ask, her father began to struggle in an attempt to get away. She pulled the knife away so she didn't accidentally slice his throat, while simultaneously jerking his arm up higher to stop his bid for freedom. He groaned at the pressure she placed on his joints. "Don't fricking move. I really … really want to slit your throat right now."

The Walshes joined her by the door. She could barely see her mother's face, but what she could see was pale and bruised.

Fucking abusive asshole! DJ couldn't stand the foul creature being anywhere near her mother. She shoved her father toward the couch. He stumbled and fell to the floor, landing like a pile of pick-up-sticks, his legs and arms askew.

"You'll fucking regret this, you little she-bitch. Sean and I will find you and my cunt of a wife. We'll make you both bleed and beg for mercy."

DJ saw red. Her asshole father could threaten and call her anything he wanted—but not her mother. She growled and started forward.

"DJ…" Dev sounded worried and moved as if to place himself between her and her father.

"I won't kill him." She waved Dev off as she strode over and lifted the waste of a carbon life form off the ground by his filthy shirt. "Shut the hell up, old man." Then she shook him. "Never…"

She shook him again and then shoved him away. He stumbled, regained his balance, and came at her. She punched him in the gut as hard as she could. His pained expulsion of breath satisfied a bit of her need for retribution. "Ever…"

Proving just how dumb he really was, he came at her yet again. She easily avoided him and hit him on the jaw this time. "Call my momma a cunt again."

DJ then kicked his legs out from under him and he landed on his ass. This time, he stayed down and glared at her. His rapid, wheezing breaths harmonized with the loud snores of the men.

She backed away until she reached Andy and Dev, who'd remained to guard her. Would they have stopped her from killing the piece of shit who'd fathered her? Yeah, they would've. They would've protected her from herself—that's what teammates did for one another.

Gawd! She mentally cringed. They'd seen where she'd come from—seen who'd fathered her. Their father was a damn hero, and hers was a piece of scum-sucking, drug-addicted shit.

He was never your father, Dahlia Jane, just a sperm donor.

"We done here?" Dev asked, his voice even and impassive.

She inhaled sharply and shook her head. "Got a few more words to say to my ex-father."

"I'll take your mom to the vehicle," Andy said. "Short clock, DJ. I want to get your mom checked over by a doctor."

"What?" She looked away from her father who now glowered at her as if he wanted to kill her. "Momma..."

"She's been beaten pretty badly." Andy peeled back the blanket.

DJ snarled under her breath as she could now see the full extent of the beating her mother had endured. She swept a lock of hair off her mother's bruised forehead. Both her eyes were swollen shut; her jaw, red and purple. Her lips were split and had dried blood on them. Her breathing, shallow.

Sweet Jesus, her mother had to be in horrible pain. She wasn't making a sound—was she even conscious?

"God, I'm so, so sorry I didn't get here before," DJ whispered, tears leaking from the corners of her eyes, down her cheeks, and then dripping onto her mother's bruised face. "Forgive me, Momma."

"No ... baby girl ... not your..." Her mother gasped, then moaned.

"Shh, Momma." DJ stroked her mother's hair. "Where else is she hurt?" she asked Andy. The words ground out of her mouth like stone scraping over stone.

"Everywhere. I'm mostly concerned about her ribs. Finish this up, or let Dev do it." Andy walked out of the cabin, his words carried back to her on the wind.

DJ turned to find Dev standing over her father, who'd enough brain power left to process the danger the larger, younger man posed.

"Maybe I should kick you while you're down, you fucking worthless piece of dog crap. Beating women make you feel manly?" Dev moved his foot as if he'd follow through with his threat.

"Dev, no." DJ moved and grabbed his arm, tugging him away. "We'll tie them up and leave them. We need to get my momma to a hospital."

Not the one in Williamson either. Someone there had colluded with the Varneys to clear that wing and faked the medical records to lure DJ in to be abducted.

Dev snorted with disgust, but nodded. As she stood guard, he hog-tied all four men with zip ties and left them on the drafty floor.

"Go on, Dev. I have some final words for the fucker who sired me."

Dev scrutinized her closely for several seconds. He must've found what he needed in her face, because he nodded and stalked out of the room, pulling the door almost closed behind him.

DJ knelt next to her father's head. "Listen up, old man. Me and those boys with me are your worst effin' nightmare. I've got more friends just like them. So, you keep that in your sick, feeble brain when you're plotting your revenge. Which you will, 'cause you're thick as a post. My advice? Forget about me and Momma. Tell that fucker Sean and his daddy to forget about me, too."

"Dahlia Jane, you done just fucked up, girl," her father sneered, though it lost some effect since his words were slurred. "You don't know who you're messing with."

DJ shook her head and sighed. "Yep, dumber than shit." She stood and kicked him in the ribs with her Army-booted foot. "That's for my momma."

Then she turned and walked out of the cabin to find Dev, still on the porch, still covering her ass. God, she loved the Walsh men.

"You going to close the door?"asked Dev.

"Nah, maybe the old bastard will do me a favor and catch pneumonia and die."

"Works for me." Dev joined her as she walked down the wobbly steps and never looked back.

CHAPTER 3

February 1st, Grangeville, Idaho

At the far east end of Grangeville, Idaho, DJ pulled into the parking lot of Ma's Bar and Grill. The lot was shared with the Fill'er Up Gas Station and Pantry and Ted's Taxidermy. The group of businesses was the last bit of civilization between here and Sanctuary which was almost an hour further to the east. All the rest of this part of Idaho was dominated by the Nez Perce National Forest, a vast wilderness area of mountains, forests, and rivers.

DJ stopped next to a gas pump to fill the bottomless pit of a tank in the late model Hummer she'd bought for a bargain price off a friend of Colonel Walsh's. She now understood why the Marine captain sold the vehicle dirt cheap—it was a gas hog. But it also was a rugged, high-off-the-ground, armored gas hog. Some things were more important than money.

Money was replaceable. Safety was priceless.

"Are we here?" A yawn accompanied her mother's soft-voiced question.

DJ glanced at her mother and smiled. Her mother's eyes shone bright blue-green and were filled with happiness and love. It just showed what less stress, good food, and excellent care could do for a person.

After DJ and the Walshes had taken her mother to a twenty-four-hour emergency medical care facility and it was discovered her ribs were merely bruised—and after they ascertained that Mrs. Binkley was safe—they'd driven to the Walsh home on Camp Lejeune. Molly Walsh had treated Nancy Poe as if she were a long-lost sister. Her mother had blossomed under Molly's tender loving care until it was time for them to leave for Idaho so DJ could begin her SSI employment.

DJ had managed the cross-country car trip in easy stages so her mother wouldn't get overly tired—and so she could see some of the country. Prior to her rescue, her mother had never been more than two hours away from Red Bone.

The car trip had been both a healing and bonding time for the two of them.

"Not yet, Momma. Maybe another hour depending on the weather and road conditions." DJ looked at the gray sky. They hadn't seen the sun since Boise.

The weather forecast had predicted heavy snow with accumulations anywhere between twelve and twenty-four inches for the higher elevations of the Bitteroots. From the looks of the clouds, the heavier snow would begin sooner rather than later. They needed to get to Sanctuary, which was at a much higher elevation than Grangeville, *before* the snow set in for real.

"If you need to use the bathroom, now would be a good time," DJ said. "I'll fill the tank. You stay inside where it's warm until I come and get you."

"Should we buy groceries?" Her mother unbuckled her seat belt and grabbed her purse off the floor.

"Not necessary. We'll be staying in the main lodge. We'll eat our meals with the operatives and trainees who also live in the lodge. It'll be like living in a ritzy hotel. Should be fun. All you have to do is relax."

Her mother reached over the center console and stroked her face. "I love you, Dahlia Jane. I know you want to make my life easier, but not sure I know how to relax."

"Learn." DJ stared into the aquamarine eyes so like her own. "I love you, too. So much." Lingering guilt made her sick to her stomach over what her mother must've endured for the years DJ had been gone. "I'm so … so sorry I didn't get you away from that bastard sooner. When I think of what you…"

"Hush, baby girl. It's over." She pulled her hand away from DJ's face. "I was young and stupid. I loved the bastard and married him. Then he gave me you, the most wonderful gift I've ever received. The day you were born I vowed you'd be free to make your own choices. I wanted you away from Al Poe and his low-life militia cronies. So, as I have told you time and time again, none of what happened to me is your fault."

"But, Momma … I should've—"

"Not another word, Dahlia Jane Poe." Her mother placed her finger on DJ's lips. "I told you to leave. You did, and I'm so damn proud of what you've accomplished. Besides, you tried to get me out several times … not your fault the earlier plans failed."

Her mother was far too forgiving.

DJ should've taken some of her flight crew, gone to Red Bone, and stolen her away in the dark of night years ago. But her mother—and Mrs. Binkley—had assured her, and DJ had wanted to believe, that her father had been more talk than action after DJ left Red Bone. Mostly, he'd ignored or humiliated his wife, treated her like a servant—or, at least, he had until recently. His actions had become more physical and more erratic over the last six months. Her mother hadn't provided specific details, which allowed DJ to imagine the worst.

DJ blamed the new level of her father's violence on his meth use. She fisted her hands and could almost feel the steam coming out of her ears, recalling the damage from the last beating her mother had endured. She forced her fingers to relax and took a slow breath to regain control.

Time to change the subject. They'd had this discussion several times since the night of the rescue, but despite all her mother's love and assurances, DJ hadn't been able to let go of her guilt. The only thing giving DJ some peace of mind was the fact the attorney she'd retained had already served divorce papers on her bastard of a father and had obtained a permanent restraining order against him. Her mother would soon be legally free of the man once and for all.

She picked up her mother's delicate hand and kissed the back of it. "Momma, if you love me, please don't call me baby girl ... or Dahlia Jane. I'm DJ now. I have to gain the respect of my SSI colleagues. Dahlia Jane isn't the kick-ass name of a personal security operative."

Her mother giggled and, suddenly, looked so beautiful, carefree, and far younger than her forty-four years of age. She'd married at fifteen and given birth to DJ at sixteen. DJ's maternal grandparents had pushed the marriage, seeing that their daughter had the sense to fall in love with Al Poe, an up-and-comer in the county power structure. Her grandparents had died before Al had become an abusive criminal. Though from what her mother had told her, DJ's grandparents wouldn't have lifted a finger even if they'd lived. They were of the old school of thought that a husband ruled his home and outside interference need not come knocking on the door.

"Come on, pretty lady." DJ unlocked the doors and used the inside release to pop the gas tank cover. "Let's get hopping so we can see what our new home looks like before those dark snow clouds start dumpin'."

DJ exited the driver's side and jogged around to help her mother out of the high-off-the-ground Hummer. Once on the slush-covered cement pad surrounding the gas pumps, the top of her mother's head came to the middle of DJ's chest.

DJ was just shy of six feet tall. She might've gotten her mother's curly blonde hair and aquamarine eyes, but she'd gotten the Poe men's height. Her womanly curves came from both sides of the family. She loved the height; she was uncomfortable with the attention the curves drew from the male part of the population.

"Go inside, Momma. Get yourself something to drink and a snack. Not sure when the lodge meal times are scheduled, but I imagine we'll be a little early for the evening meal." DJ handed her mother some money. "Grab me a large fountain Diet Pepsi."

"You and that Diet Pepsi. Shoulda bought stock in that company when you were a toddler. I'd be a rich woman." Her mother winked.

DJ laughed.

Her mother then practically skipped through the slushy puddles into the store. She'd treated everything that had happened since the night DJ and the Walsh brothers had rescued her like a trip to Disney World—and that particular experience would also happen one day since her mother had wistfully admitted she'd seen a TV special and wanted to go visit Mickey and friends.

DJ could easily afford to give her mother the full Disney experience. She'd had very few expenses while in the Army and saved most of her pay. Now, she also had the fabulous salary SSI would pay her. So, if her mother wanted something, she'd damn well get it. DJ was so gonna spoil that woman.

As the huge tank filled, DJ walked around the vehicle, checking the tires to make sure they were properly inflated. She'd put the chains on only if the road conditions necessitated it. She expected to make it to Sanctuary before the weather worsened that badly. Then she cleaned the salt and other road grit from the windows and lights.

As she worked, two identical extended cab trucks roared into the lot and pulled up to the pumps on the other side of hers. The drivers got out of the trucks and began to fill the tanks. A man jogged from the diner and began a conversation with a passenger from one of the vehicles. The two men, who obviously knew each other, stood less than three feet away and spoke loudly with no concern about being overheard. Probably because they spoke colloquial Spanish in one of the Central American dialects—Salvadoran.

DJ recognized the dialect from a two-year deployment in Central America where she'd flown missions in conjunction with the DEA and local drug enforcement. Very early in her Army career, she'd discovered she had an affinity for languages. She could fluently speak and read Spanish, French, and German. She was less fluent in Russian and Farsi. Her language aptitude had given her the opportunity to be trained in personal security and designated as a chopper pilot for escorting VIPs in war zones and eventually transporting Special Operations Command teams on classified missions.

When the two Hispanic men mentioned SSI, her neck began to itch just as it always did right before someone fired upon her helicopter. She concentrated more intently on their conversation.

The man who'd exited the truck asked the man from the diner, "Juan, is Keely Maddox inside?"

"Yes, Cervantes." Juan responded, but avoided looking directly in Cervantes' eyes.

Cervantes was obviously the alpha-dog and running the show, whatever in the hell the show was. He was also armed; the wind had blown open his jacket for a second or two, revealing a holstered pistol.

"She is there," Juan swept his arm back toward the diner, "along with her son and several other SSI women. They are eating still."

Cervantes swore and looked at the sky. "Weather report says high winds. Heavy snow. Can't wait too long for the women to leave, or we'll never make base before the roads get bad." He paused and then said, "If the snow begins to get heavy before they are ready to leave, we'll go in and get them."

"And the others inside?" Juan asked.

"We'll kill them." Cervantes' tone was as flat and cold as his ebony-eyed gaze. "We can leave no witnesses."

Not. Gonna. Happen. No one was hurting anyone from SSI on her watch and especially not the Walsh's only daughter and only grandchild.

"But, Cervantes, there are too many inside," Juan protested. "We are outnumbered."

"We will have surprise on our side. They are civilians. It will be easy. We need to take the woman before she reaches the safety of SSI's property." Cervantes pointed to the diner. "Now go and check on their progress with their meal and report back to me."

Juan nodded and walked casually toward the restaurant as Cervantes began to clean off the truck's headlamps and then the windows. When he rounded the back to clean the side windows, he noticed her. Slowly, he looked up and down her body—twice—then smiled. "*Hola, Senorita.*"

Typical leering Hispanic machismo *bullshit.*

DJ shot him the icy glare that had stopped many an unwanted Lothario in his tracks, then turned her back and focused on dispensing the last few gallons into the Hummer's tank—slowly. She needed to hear more about what they'd planned. More importantly, she needed to try to figure out who'd sent them and what their ultimate agenda might be. Since she didn't intend to allow them to take Keely and the baby, she wanted to have some answers for her employer Ren Maddox.

Cervantes's gaze lingered on her body her for a few more seconds, then he muttered, "*Ai yi yi*, a ball buster." He loudly joked to one of the other men in his local dialect. "It is too bad I don't have the time to take the giant blonde whore down a peg or two. She'd look good on her knees sucking my cock."

Never. Never again. Dark, debasing memories of Sean forcing her to her knees and—*NO!*

DJ swallowed hard and forced the hot, oily, queasy feeling away. After several breaths of cold, crisp, clean-smelling air, she had her control back and then replaced the latent fear the past always brought with icy rage for the fucktard Cervantes and his crew.

The other man laughed. "I would help, Cervantes."

Both men would be singing soprano in an Idahoan prison if they tried anything on with her. But they wouldn't. Cervantes had a mission and was on a short clock.

Juan jogged back to his boss. She spotted a gun on his hip. "They are near the end of their meal."

Shit. The countdown clock to FUBAR had just gotten even shorter.

"That is good. We'll pull to the far side of the gas station building and wait." Cervantes tossed the windshield squeegee into the bucket of soapy water. "We'll follow our original plan and follow them once they drive away from here and take them farther down the road."

Like hell they will.

Cervantes moved away to address the man fueling the lead truck and spoke so softly she couldn't hear what was said.

DJ scanned the ominous, dark clouds rolling in over the mountain peaks. She could smell … feel the heavier snow approach. The wind had already picked up. For now, the clouds merely dropped intermittent, large, fluffy flakes that were taken away on the wind. Any snow that managed to hit the ground created lacy, swirling, geometric patterns on the cleared dark asphalt.

The bad weather clock was also winding down fast. One way or the other, the mercenaries, because that is what they had to be, would make a move soon. Too soon to get the local law here, she was sure.

DJ prayed the stories the Walshes told about Keely and her fighting abilities were true, since it looked as if she and her boss's wife would be defending themselves, innocent civilians—and DJ's mother—holed up in a diner.

Move your ass, Dahlia Jane. Worry won't win the battle. Planning will.

She replaced the nozzle and snatched her receipt as she put the gas cap back on. Then she hoofed it toward the gas station storefront. She didn't look back as the Latino men coarsely commented on her ass and legs and speculated on the size of her tits hidden by her thick shearling jacket.

She would've liked to knee them in their nuts, but that pleasurable experience would have to be forfeited. She had to de-escalate the looming, bad-ass situation.

Entering the gas station/convenience store, DJ found her mother talking and laughing with the burly clerk. She placed a hand on her mother's shoulder and squeezed gently. "Momma, hate to interrupt, but we have a change in plans. There's trouble a-brewin'." She turned toward the clerk whose name tag read *Bud*. "What kind of law enforcement coverage do y'all have in this area?"

"Sheriff and State Police. But both are spread pretty thin. Idaho County is huge." Bud frowned. "What's wrong?"

Shit. She'd been afraid of that. Idaho County was a sparsely populated area. So less tax dollars meant less law enforcement.

"Call them. The four men at the gas pumps plan on kidnapping Keely Maddox and her son. Two confirmed as armed. Have to assume the other two are also. Anyone caught in the crossfire is gonna get hurt. We need the law here … fast."

"Dahlia Jane…" Her mother's voice wobbled with fear.

DJ took her mother's hand and rubbed a thumb over the back of it. "It'll be all right. Trust me. Nothing will happen to you, Keely, her baby, or anyone else."

"Motherfuckers." Bud snarled and slapped a hand on the counter. Her mother startled and gripped DJ's hand. "Excuse my language, ladies. But someone's always trying to hurt Keely and the other SSI gals." He pulled a cell phone from under the counter. "You go warn them. I'll call out all the troops including SSI."

Yeah, that would be good. Ren would pull out all stops to protect his wife and child. A little bit of the tension left her body, but not enough to decry the urgency of the situation. It would get worse before it got better, every battle sense she'd developed over the years of flying in war zones told her that.

Bud snorted. "Knowing Keely, that little gal has a fu–, um, fricking arsenal in the back of her Hummer."

DJ was counting on it.

"Bud," DJ called.

"Yeah?" His head came up and his dark brown eyes glittered with a fierce light.

"You might want to lock up and take cover if the bastards decide to take the fight to the restaurant."

"Yeah, me and my rifle will be locked down in the back in the walk-in refrigerator. Don't worry about the civilians in the diner. Nick has a safe place for them. Since I don't expect you'll be taking advantage of it, you take care, ya hear?"

"You, too." DJ turned toward her mother whose face had grown pale; the apprehension in her aqua-colored eyes was unacceptable. Yet, the situation couldn't be avoided. "It's gonna be okay, Momma. I promise. Right now, I need to move my vehicle away from the pumps and to the front of the restaurant."

She gripped her mother's arm and led her to the door. "Act natural. We're two ladies who stopped for gas and a bite to eat. Don't stare at the men across from our vehicle."

"Baby girl," her mother spoke under her breath as DJ practically carried her to the Hummer. "Why can't we wait on the law or the SSI men to get here?"

"Because these men won't wait. They're real bad asses. Hired guns. When they attack, innocent people die. That isn't happening on my watch."

Low whistles and crude comments in Spanish followed her as she boosted her mother into the passenger seat. She ignored the men as she quick-stepped around to the driver's side, got in, and started the Hummer. Then she slowly circled the pump and parked next to the only other Hummer in front of the restaurant; it had to be the SSI vehicle Bud had spoken of.

DJ looked at her mother. "Ready?"

"What are you gonna do?" Her mother's soft voice was even shakier than before. Seeing and hearing the men had emphasized the situation was real and not an over-reaction on DJ's part. DJ grimaced. *Way to go, Dahlia Jane. You've already broken your promise to keep her life stress-free.*

But she refused to lie or sugarcoat anything. Her mother needed honesty, not deception. She'd had more than enough of that crap from DJ's cheating, criminal bastard of a father.

"Not sure yet. Flying by the seat of my pants for the moment." DJ unbuckled her seat belt and unlocked the doors. In the rearview mirror, she noted the two trucks pulling away. She followed them with her peripheral vision as they circled around to the far side of the gas station, just as Cervantes had planned. "But I'll think of something ... or Keely will, that gal is smart, lethal—and this is her turf."

DJ took in a deep breath, exhaled, then took her mother's small hands between hers. "This is what I'm trained for. I'll do all that is within my power to make sure nothing happens to you or anyone inside that restaurant." Or die trying.

"I know that." Her mother pulled her hands away and then tucked a curl under DJ's cap. "I'm worried about you. Just be careful."

"I'm always careful." Sometimes, however, careful—or being well-trained—wasn't always enough.

DJ hurried her mother into the restaurant and then looked around the main dining area. There were tables in the middle, booths around the sides, and a eat-at-counter opposite the entrance. She heaved a sigh of relief. The place wasn't that crowded—Juan had exaggerated. There hadn't been all that many vehicles in the parking lot. Any townsfolk who might've walked had probably been kept away by the cold and the blizzard threat.

Ma's current clientele was comprised of five men—rough-looking, outdoor types. She wouldn't be surprised if some of them were armed since this part of Idaho was isolated and a lot of survivalists lived in this part of the state.

Two waitresses moved about the room. Loud, male voices came from the kitchen area through the pass-through window which was behind the eat-at-counter.

The only women customers—thus, by default, the SSI contingent—sat in a booth at the rear left-hand corner of the restaurant. A great strategic position. From their vantage point, they could see everyone in the place and watch the main entrance. Exactly the booth she would've chosen.

DJ took her mother's hand and began to wend their way through the tables in the center of the dining area. There was also a barroom, off to the left side, through a double-wide doorway. It was dark this early in the day. So, no worries about anymore civilians in there.

As she approached the booth, she easily identified Keely and Riley. The Colonel and Molly had lots of pictures of their daughter and grandchild on their mantel. She also recognized Calista, a famous cover model who'd recently married SSI operative Risto Smith. The woman next to Calista, or Callie as she was called, was a dark-haired woman holding Riley Maddox. Next to them was an older woman.

The women were smiling and laughing—and she really hated to ruin their day.

DJ let go of her mother's hand and urged her forward until they stopped at the edge of the table. The women ceased talking and looked up with welcoming smiles on their faces even though they didn't know DJ or her mother from Adam.

DJ's Skype interviews had only been with Ren Maddox and his brother Trey.

DJ cleared her throat. "Ladies, I'm DJ Poe."

Keely's eyes lit up even more. She scooted out of the booth, jumped up, and gave DJ a hug.

DJ wasn't sure how to react. So, she gently patted the smaller woman on the back two times and stepped out of the eager woman's embrace.

"You're early!" Keely seemed to take DJ's stiffness in stride and turned to DJ's mother. "This must be Nancy." The petite blonde hugged DJ's equally petite mother, who hugged right back. No awkwardness there.

The blonde dynamo stepped back and looked between the two of them. "We weren't expecting you until late tomorrow. But no worries, Scotty has everything ready for you. We're excited to have you with us. We've heard so much about you from Andy and Dev and the rest of my family."

"Hate to be rude." DJ's tone was grim. "We have a situation."

"What's wrong?" Keely frowned and scrutinized DJ's face. "What's happened?"

"Hasn't happened yet—and we're running out of time." DJ's bluntly spoken words wiped the smiles off the other women's faces. She glanced at the window and groaned. It had started to snow harder. "A really short clock now. Four men. Two confirmed armed. Hispanics from El Salvador. Most likely mercs. Planning on kidnapping you and Riley."

"Frick-fracking hell!" Keely yelled. The restaurant went silent at her shout. "Ren will have a cow." Then she called out, "Nick! Prepare to repel attackers."

A bass voice from the back bellowed, "Goddammit, Keely. You're a trouble magnet."

DJ jumped, and her mother gasped as the screech of metal rang around the room as what looked to be blast shutters rolled down over the plate glass windows. Gas Station Bud hadn't mentioned blast shutters when he'd said Nick had a safe place.

"Someone needs to lock and bar the front door," Nick yelled. "I've got the back covered."

A man closest to the front door hollered, "On it!"

"Um, wait! Weapons?" DJ said. "Bud said y'all might have weapons in the Hummer. FYI, Bud's calling the cops and SSI."

"Go ahead and shut the door, Zeke!" Keely said. The man ran to do her bidding.

Keely pulled a Bren Ten from a tote bag on the booth seat. Callie pulled a Ladies' Ruger from a bag by her feet. And, confirming her earlier supposition, several of the customers pulled hand guns.

DJ's lips twisted, and she pulled her Beretta from the shoulder holster under her coat. "Well, we've got hand guns covered, but I was hoping for some assault rifles, maybe a sniper rifle."

Keely held up a finger. "Just a sec." Then she yelled, "Nick!"

"What!"

"You pull out my weapon bags?"

"Already did." A huge man dressed in a chef's apron, a Sammy Hagar T-shirt, and jeans with a gun belt strapped around his waist lumbered into the dining room. He carried two large bags which he dumped by the booth. "Safe room's open and ready for anyone who wants to join me and my Smith and Wesson." He patted the holstered gun with a grim smile on his face.

Keely glanced at the other women, who'd gotten up from the table. "Lacey, take Elana, Riley, and Nancy to the back and introduce them to Earl's safe room. Callie, DJ, and I will go on the roof to keep an eye on the situation and repel the frick-fracking douchebags, if necessary, until our backup arrives."

DJ snorted back a laugh at Keely's description of the mercenaries. She couldn't have said it better herself.

"Baby girl?" DJ's mother tugged on her jacket sleeve. "Why the roof?"

"Gives us tactical advantage." She rubbed her mother's back. "Go with the other women. Help take care of the baby, okay? Molly would want that."

Her mother's lips firmed. "Molly loves that baby. Nothin' will happen to him. They gotta get through me first."

Or Nick's Smith and Wesson.

DJ gently shoved her mother toward the older woman in Keely's group. Now that Keely had named the women, DJ knew that Lacey was the wife of Quinn Jones, who was third in command at SSI behind Ren and Trey Maddox. The dark-haired woman, Elana, had recently married another SSI operative, Vanko Petriv. Andy had told her how he, Dev, and the Colonel had helped rescue Elana from a Russian mobster just before the beginning of the new year.

"Dahlia Jane Poe…" DJ winced at her mother's full use of her name, but noted no one was really paying attention to them as they prepared for the attack. "Don't get killed."

DJ mentally sighed. It would take her mother a long time to get used to her only daughter being a trained warrior. So, if she needed to continue to worry, then DJ would take the time to reassure her. God knew her mother had been DJ's emotional and, all too often, physical bulwark throughout her childhood.

"Momma"—DJ attempted a cocky grin—"if the Taliban, al Qaeda, and lots of narcotrafficantes couldn't kill me, a bunch of frick-fracking douchebag mercenaries damn well won't. Plus," she added in a gentle, but firm, tone, "this *is* the kind of work I'll be doing for SSI. Protecting people."

Her mother frowned, then sighed and went with Lacey who mouthed at DJ, "She'll be fine."

DJ nodded her thanks and turned toward her boss's wife who'd taken control of the restaurant like a military officer and had gotten the customers organized. The men turned the metal tables on their sides, checked over their weapons, and talked quietly among themselves—preparing to fight, to defend the unarmed civilians from whoever tried to get into the restaurant.

Keely, like every single Walsh she'd met so far—and she'd met them all but one, Tweeter, the computer geek son—had true command presence. But command presence didn't mean shit when the woman was also the wife of an over-protective, alpha-male as was evidenced by Keely's much put-upon tone as she spoke to what had to be Ren on the phone. "Listen, big guy. I don't plan this shit."

DJ snorted back a laugh as Keely held her phone at arm's length and crossed her eyes at it, then glanced at the ceiling and mouthed, "Lord, save me."

Placing the phone back at her ear, Keely muttered, "Just get here. Callie, DJ, and I can hold them off until you bring in the troops. The bastards won't be leaving. I promise." She swiped a finger over the phone's screen to end the call and looked up. "Ren's pissed, in case you couldn't tell. He and the guys are already on their way. They're thirty or so minutes out by road. Vanko and Tweeter will get here sooner in the chopper."

Chopper.

The mere word hit her happy spot deep inside. She loved flying helicopters and knew SSI had a Black Hawk for SARs and operations and a Bell jet helicopter for ferrying SSI personnel around the rough terrain of Idaho. She was jonesing to fly again. Hadn't flown since the Colonel had gotten her permission to fly one of the Marine's Black Hawks—that had been well over two weeks ago.

Keely clapped her hands. The low rumble of conversations ceased. "Gentleman and ladies." She smiled at the two waitresses, who also were armed and stood behind the counter. "The doors and window shields should hold. If they don't, do what you feel you need to do. Earl has room for all of you in the safe room. Don't be heroes on my account."

"Keely, we haven't had a good fight around here in a coon's age," one burly man who looked like a lumberjack yelled back. "You gals do your thing. We'll defend Nick's booze supply."

"And his ma's baked goods," another man who had biker patches on his leather jacket added. "No thieving assholes are stealing her cupcakes and cookies."

"Or her sour cream cake," a red-haired giant also in biker leathers added. "Love that cake. I'd fucking marry that cake."

The other men laughed, and one guy punched the cake-loving man in the arm.

DJ chuckled, then looked at Callie, who stood behind Keely. "Are they for real?"

Callie nodded, a wry twist to her lips. "Nick's mom's baked goods are worth killing for. I'm especially fond of her carrot cake."

The former model's expression turned dark. "Unfortunately, SSI makes a lot of enemies. So, since Ma's is a place we're known to visit, Nick and the locals have gotten used to the attacks. Ren paid for the security upgrades on this building after Keely had frequent cravings for Ma's food during her pregnancy."

"Nick makes some damn good chili, but don't tell Scotty. I love his chili, too." Keely handed DJ a headset, an AK-47 assault rifle, and a smaller zippered bag. "The locals really like the action. Says we keep their survivalist skill sets up to snuff. You know, in case there's a zombie apocalypse or an alien invasion." She nodded at the zippered bag. "Extra mags for the rifle, and there's some ammo in there for your Beretta. Let's get to the roof and assess the situation."

CHAPTER 4

DJ put on her headset as she followed the other two women and then pulled her wool cap over it. She clicked it on. "What channel we using?"

"Channel 9, for now," Keely said.

DJ set the channel and then checked over the rifle as she kept pace. Clean, well-oiled, and a full magazine—exactly what she'd expect from a woman who was taught to shoot and care for a weapon by a Marine.

At the end of the hallway, Keely stopped to unbolt a door. Callie turned to the side to give Keely more room and DJ caught a side view of Callie's profile. "You're pregnant. Maybe you should stay in the safe room."

"You'll need my sharp-shooting skills." Callie's voice was matter-of-fact, as if taking part in a potential gun battle with mercenaries was business as usual. "I'm good—better than good. Trust me."

"I know you're expert-rated with long and hand guns." When Callie raised a perfectly groomed eyebrow, DJ added, "Loren and Paul told me. I was just … concerned."

"DJ … pregnancy isn't a handicap," said Keely as she held the door open and waved first Callie, then DJ up the stairs. "Our men know that also."

"Maybe Ren does, but Risto is still balky some days," muttered Callie as she climbed. "But he'll get over it. Plus, he's on an op, and what he doesn't know won't hurt him." She shot a glare at DJ over her shoulder. "And you'll never tell him any details."

DJ frowned. "No ma'am. But I won't have to, will I? The other SSI operatives will."

"Yes, dammit," Callie responded. "But we gals stick together. Got me?"

"Got it." *Don't ask. Don't tell. Female solidarity.*

As Callie opened the door, the all-familiar buzz of adrenaline swept over DJ's body at the thought of seeing action again. Yeah, shit could happen, but she and these two exceptional women would do what they could to avoid such a consequence. She and Keely followed Callie out onto a wind-swept and snow-covered roof.

DJ looked around. The roof was basically flat, but from what she could tell, under all the snow, it angled slightly downward from the center toward the roof edge. There would have to be drains that dumped the water runoff into the building's gutters and down spouts. There was a four-foot-high wall which edged all four sides of the roof with cut-outs every meter or so. The gaps would make perfect shooting positions without sky-lining the shooter.

"SSI suggested the wall around the roof, right?" she asked.

"Yep. Ren wanted us to be able to lock down Ma's and defend until help came." Keely sighed. "The bad guys seem to think we women are the weak links at SSI."

DJ snorted. "Not from the stories I've heard from your family."

Keely grinned. "Eventually, the word will spread and the smarter asshats will stay away."

"But there's so many more dumb ones," Callie said, "that we'll probably more than get SSI's money's worth out of these security add-ons."

Keely nodded, then hunched over and moved to the front of the roof. Once there, she dropped to her stomach and aimed her rifle through the gap. "So, where were the mercs going to wait for us? There's no one at the pumps."

The snow came down steadily, the wind blowing the flakes around. Visibility was about two hundred meters, give or take a meter. DJ knee-walked through several inches of accumulated snow to come up on Keely's right side and then dropped to her stomach. Callie mirrored her movements on the left.

"They pulled to the far side of the gas station," DJ glanced at Keely and found a mostly composed facade. The only sign of tension on the younger woman's face was the tightness in her jaw as if she clenched her teeth. "I expect they'll make a move to attack the restaurant soon, since you haven't hit the road. They wanted to reach their base before the roads got bad."

Keely muttered, "We're on the wrong frick-fracking roof." She wiggled backwards on her stomach like a snake, then shoved up to her knees, all the while cradling her rifle. "We need to disable their vehicles. I promised Ren he'd have people to question."

DJ voiced her thought. "If they used their GPS to get here…"

"…then we can get coordinates to their local hidey-hole," Callie finished.

"And grab whoever might be at the base," Keely added. "Whatever intel we gain, Tweetie and I can use to track back to the big boss, if the pecker-headed asswipe isn't in Idaho."

DJ eyed the gas station roof. The buildings weren't far apart, maybe a bit less than two meters. The other roof was also flat, but didn't have a wall around the perimeter. "I can jump the gap. Y'all stay here. Once I take out the trucks from above, the mercs aren't gonna be happy. If they attack…"

"We'll handle it." Keely frowned. "You sure … about the jump…"

"I'm sure." DJ grinned. "I've got longer legs than you. Plus, I've jumped gaps bigger than that on ops in Afghanistan." Then she bit her lip. Keely would have the clearance to know all about her SOCOM missions, but did Callie?

Loose lips, Dahlia Jane!

"Forget I said that, okay?" DJ directed the words at Callie.

"No need. I've seen your classified files, so has Elana." Callie patted DJ's arm. "All analysts at SSI have the same clearance as Keely and Tweeter. Most of our work is NSA, NCS/CIA, and Defense Intelligence Agency related."

Well, that's a relief, but—

"My momma doesn't know about the classified ops. She thinks I only flew VIPs and search-and-rescue missions." DJ looked at both women. "And I don't want her to know."

"She won't hear it from us," Keely promised. Callie nodded.

"Thanks." DJ stood, then turned and eyed the gap between the two roofs once more. She slung the rifle over her back and hooked the ammo bag onto the rifle strap, then moved to the back edge of Ma's roof. She took several breaths then ran. She used the wall to launch and then propelled herself, using the techniques she was taught in mountaineering school to jump crevices. She cleared the space with a half a meter to spare. Her landing, while not picture perfect since she lost her balance and ended up on her ass, was good enough. She wasn't injured and her equipment all survived the leap. She sat in the snow for a second and caught her breath as adrenaline galloped through her bloodstream.

She grinned. Damn, she'd missed the rush—the living on the edge her service in the Army had provided. Working for SSI would be a blessing in more ways than one.

"DJ…" Keely's voice came over the headset. "You okay?"

"Fine." She chuckled softly. "More than fine." She rose to her knees and repositioned her rifle more comfortably across her back, then she got onto her stomach. She belly-crawled to the far side of the gas station's roof. Removing her rifle, she cradled it in her arms and took a look over the side, then quickly pulled her head back.

"In place," she muttered into the headset microphone. "Three men still in trucks with engines running. They're fricking listening to some kind of salsa music. One guy, stationed at the front corner of the building, is armed with an assault rifle. Have me some easy engine shots. Is it a go?"

"Go to Channel 6. The guys want to join the party. You might hear some bossy-assed comments. Ignore them."

"Roger that." She reset her headset. "What's their ETA?" DJ repositioned her rifle and looked over the side to sight both shots, then pulled back and played them out in her head.

"Tweeter and Vanko were already in the air on they way home from Lewiston, so ten to fifteen minutes," Keely said. "Ren, Trey, and Price are coming by road from Sanctuary and are still a half hour out."

"Sit rep." A deep, unruffled baritone came over the headset. The background noise was the familiar and welcome sound of a Black Hawk.

The copter noise settled in her belly, making her happy. The male voice shot a tingling awareness straight to her core.

Now, what was the question?

Head in the game, Dahlia Jane. Sit rep.

"In position to disable two vehicles belonging to four armed Hispanic men. Trucks are parked too close to the building to take out the tires from my position. Waiting on the go ahead to take out the engines instead."

"Are they armored?" The same male voice asked.

"Plain old Dodge trucks," DJ replied more calmly than she felt. "Who's this?"

"Tweeter Walsh. Welcome to Idaho, DJ."

Andy and Dev's baby brother's voice was as smooth as the finest Kentucky Bourbon. But its kick was like that of moonshine straight out of the still—it threatened her composure in ways she'd never experienced with any other man before.

She shoved the disconcerting fact to a dark corner of her mind and packed it in ice. She'd pull out the strange reaction later and examine the singularity when shit wasn't about to explode all around her.

"Vanko Petriv here, DJ." She could detect his slight accent. He was Ukrainian, if she recollected correctly. "Take out the engines. We want to talk to these men." In other words, wound, not wipe, if they retaliate. "Sounds as if you ladies have it under control."

"Not handled yet." All back-to-business, DJ went to her knees and aimed the rifle over the roof's edge. Guy at the corner had his back to her. So, she took the extra time to eye her shots once more.

Taking in a breath, then letting it out, she placed three shots in each engine. On the next full breath, she placed a second set of three-shot bursts right next to the first—as insurance. She then shifted away from the edge, dropped, cradled her rifle in her arms, and belly-crawled as fast as she could away from the side and toward the front of the gas station.

Less than two full breaths later, a barrage of automatic rifle fire tore up the edge of the roof where she'd been. Probably the guy at the corner; the others wouldn't have had the time to get out and shoot that fast. A flying chip of cement block hit the side of her face. Ignoring the sting, she crawled even farther out of range, then swiped some snow over the small cut, numbing the pain for the time being.

"DJ?" Keely sounded worried, but her brother's "Sit rep, DJ" sounded as if he were spitting out nails.

"I'm fine. They're shooting at ghosts." DJ propped herself up on her elbows and looked over at Ma's roof and found Keely and Callie peering through a toothed gap in the wall. She gave them a thumb's up.

The wild shooting continued along the far side of the station's roof.

"Go ahead. Waste ammo, you dumb fuckers," DJ muttered as she kept her head down and turned away from the odd, stray piece of flying roof.

Male grunts and chuckles came over the headset.

"Stay down," Callie said. "Keely and I will do our job and keep the assclowns away from the restaurant and the vehicles in the parking lot."

"Roger that." She brushed some snow away and then rested her head on her gloved hands. "Let me know if I can help."

"Will do," Callie said.

DJ turned her head and propped her chin on her folded hands. While eyeing the front parking lot, she took a mental inventory of her physical status. This was her first action in a while.

Breathing?—Controlled.

Pulse?—About fifteen beats over her resting heart rate, due to adrenaline mostly, and recovering with each breath.

Senses?—Fully engaged, not fuzzy. Her Army trainers had always taught the recruits to make the stress hormonal cocktail your friend. *Use it, don't succumb to it.*

No flashbacks to any war zones. Nice to know that four mercs in pickup trucks didn't trigger her PTSD. Eventually something would and she'd deal with it.

Right now, she was fully in the zone and operational.

Ramping her battle readiness up another notch, she focused her senses on her surroundings. The mercs had ceased shooting. Tweeter and Vanko spoke only to relay ETA and flight approach. The only other sound was the wind whistling over the roof and through the forest that backed up on the two buildings. Her only physical sensations were the cold of the snow beneath her body, the gelid wind and icy flakes hitting her face, and the familiar solidity of the rifle in her hands. She smelled her own light sweat, the damp musk of her shearling coat, and the smell of gun oil. Nothing moved in the front parking lot but snow devils scurrying across the surface.

Then a familiar voice carried on the wind, so amplified she would've sworn the speaker—Cervantes—was next to her. "Get the woman and the child. We'll take her vehicle."

"Heads up, ladies," DJ whispered into the headset. "They're making their move on the front of the restaurant."

"About frick-fracking time. It's damn cold up here," Keely muttered.

DJ smiled. She really liked Dev and Andy's little sister.

"Blast shutters engaged on all window and doors bolted at Ma's?" Keely's brother's deep voice rumbled over the headset.

DJ's pulse jumped and her breathing hitched before she could wrestle both back under control.

"First thing we did, Tweetie," Keely replied. "Civilians not looking for a break in the tedium of their day are in the safe room."

Tweetie. Tweeter. No one who had a voice like his should be called Tweeter. His given name was Stuart Allen Walsh. She didn't think she could call him Tweeter and keep a straight face. Stuart didn't seem right either, but it was better than a cartoon character name.

The crunch of snow indicated movement on the ground.

"They're on the move." DJ angled herself so she had a view of the front corner of the gas station. Since she had no wall to hide behind, she had to be careful not to skyline herself.

"Ready." The response was so soft and low it could've been either Callie or Keely speaking.

The first man around the corner led with his rifle. He moved along the front of the gas station. Just before she was about to lose sight of him, one shot rang out. He was down, hit in the hip.

"He's down. Still armed and dangerous," DJ said. "Good shot."

"Thanks. I love Keely's Lapua. I'll keep him and the others pinned down," Callie said. "They're not leaving this parking lot."

Two shots rang out. "Took off some brick, right above another guy's head. Just keeping them honest." She sounded amused.

It wasn't a surprise that no one else attempted to come around the front corner.

DJ strained to hear the men's conversation, but the wind had whipped around and was now blowing snow and sound in the other direction. But they only had one move—

"They'll head around back," DJ muttered just as Keely said, "I'll cover the back."

Keely laughed. "It's their only other choice with Callie covering the front so well."

"Exactly." DJ belly-crawled toward the back of the gas station roof and positioned herself so she had a view of the back corner.

"I'm in position," Keely said. "Be prepared for anything. They're stranded and desperate."

"In place." DJ muttered, "Let's hope they make stupid moves and make it easier for us to take them down."

"I love mean women," Vanko muttered.

DJ heard Keely's brother snort and mutter, "Yeah. I practically raised one of them."

"You did good, big brother," Keely replied.

There was a lot of affection in the siblings' voices. A pang of envy cut through DJ like a knife. Her brothers despised her and would pimp her out in an instant.

"DJ…"

Head in the now, Dahlia Jane.

"…don't make your move until at least one more of them is down," Keely said. "Then you can get off the roof to cover the others."

"Am I that easy to read?" DJ asked.

"It's what I'd want to do," Keely said. "I frick-fracking hate waiting around, especially in the snow and the cold."

"But I'd beat your sweet ass if you did, sprite. DJ…" This was a new male voice. His tone was rougher, more of a low growl. "Wait for Tweeter and Vanko to arrive. Let them handle it."

"Ren…" Keely spoke.

DJ cut her off. "No time. They're on the move again. I hear them." She placed her eye on her scope and zeroed in on the corner of the building about where an average height man's hip would be. "They'll shoot at the chopper. Why take that chance? Keep the Hawk back until we secure the scene."

Just as she finished countermanding her boss's order—*I am so fired*—the barrel of a gun peeked around the corner.

"Wait for it," whispered DJ.

"Oh heck yeah," Keely muttered back.

When no shots rang out, the gun's owner followed.

DJ aimed lower, going for the man's legs. Just as she took her shot, Keely's rang out from behind her. Both shots hit—hers in a thigh; Keely's low on the man's torso as he went down.

"Another one down." Keely's voice was eerily atonal. There wasn't even a hint of emotion to indicate she'd just shot a man. "Two more to go."

Another shot rang out from the front of the building. It was the Lapua. "Nicked one on the arm. He's still mobile. Sorry, girls," Callie said.

"No worries," said DJ. "Once I get off this roof, consider the rest of the assholes immobilized."

She chanced a bigger look over the edge of the roof, exposing her upper torso for a few seconds. No one shot at her, so she took her time and looked all along the rear of the building to find her roof exit strategy. When she spotted the closed trash bin, she dropped back to her stomach and belly-crawled toward the back corner of the station, closer to Ma's.

Once there, DJ looked over the side again and did the mental math—approximate height of the building minus the approximate height of the bin equaled approximately her almost six feet height plus or minus half a foot. "Easy drop."

Before she exited the roof, she ejected the old magazine from her rifle and put in a fresh one and then slung the rifle over her back. She pulled her Beretta and made sure it was in ready position then slid it down the front of her jeans, leaving her jacket unbuttoned. She took several deep breaths and then held one to listen for sounds of movement from the other side of the station.

Hearing nothing but the wind, she whispered, "Evacing the roof."

Rumbles of male pissed-off cursing were white noise. The only thing that pierced DJ's focus was Keely's calm, "Go, DJ. Your ass is covered."

DJ lay on her stomach, close to the edge. Then she swung one, then the other leg over the edge. She wiggled back until her upper body was braced on her forearms at the edge of the roof with her legs dangling down the back wall. She then slowly shimmied off the roof, allowing her body to slide down the wall until the only thing holding her to the building were her hands gripping the roof's edge.

"Looking good, DJ. Drop." Keely's encouraging words were all she needed.

DJ let go and took the impact of landing on the bin's lid with bent knees. The *boom* when she hit the bin sounded as if a cannon had gone off. Heart racing, mouth dry as a desert, she didn't mess around and dropped to her ass and scooched off the lid. She wouldn't get any points for grace, but it was effective. The deep snow behind the trash bin absorbed most of the shock to her legs and butt. She stood up and shook the snow off then checked over her rifle.

"You okay, DJ?" Keely asked.

"Yep, other than feeling like a human snow cone. See anything? They had to hear me hitting the bin." DJ had her rifle in the ready position as she peeked around the edge of the thick metal of the trash container.

"Nada. What's your plan?" Keely asked.

Before she could answer, a man crept around the back corner of the gas station.

DJ took a quick shot. It chipped some brick off the building at the man's shoulder height. He dove back around the corner. "Dammit. Missed him."

"Bad angle. But you scared the hell out of him." Keely snickered. "He won't be popping around the corner again anytime soon."

"Good," DJ said, "'cause I'm heading into the trees to get closer and above the last two bastards."

"Good plan," Keely said. "I'll keep them pinned down."

"Me, too," Callie said.

DJ had spotted the tree she wanted from the roof. It was huge and had excellent climbing limbs. She slipped silently through the spindly, new growth trees at the edge of the forest. Her gaze kept touching the corner of the gas station where the two mercs were trapped and the one she and Keely had shot lay, alive and still armed.

When she reached the tree, she muttered, "Climbing."

"Anyone so much as twitches. I'll shoot." Keely sounded as if she wanted them to twitch.

DJ licked her dry lips, then slung her rifle across her back, grabbed a branch, and pulled herself up. Once on the lower branch, she began climbing swiftly—reminiscent of the innocent and eager tomboy she'd been for the early years of her life before she'd "blossomed" as he mother had called it. Her teen years had been hell and a constant battle to keep hormonal teen boys—and other male predators—at arm's length. She paused in climbing as dark images of the one time she'd failed threatened to—

Shove that shit away. It's over.

Then the sound of a chopper came on the breeze, bringing her fully back to the present.

She spoke in a low, savage tone. "Keep that Hawk back. I'll put these fuckers out of commission once I'm set."

"You have two minutes." Keely's brother's tone matched hers. "Then I'm bringing this bird in with guns blazing."

"Shit. Roger that." DJ swung up the last two branches in less time it took to think about it. She lay along a thick branch and inched farther out. Using a convenient notch, she braced her rifle and sighted her shots. The two men stood between one truck and the side of the building. She eyed first one merc, then the one called Cervantes.

"Targets in my sights." She never took her eyes off the men who were arguing. Her finger was on the rifle's trigger.

An exasperated, macho-male sigh over the headset was followed by the low growling voice of her boss, "DJ, just wound. Understood?"

"Affirmative, that was my plan." DJ shot at the man closest to her. She hit him in the leg and then his shoulder as he went down. This opened up her next shot. The merc leader Cervantes turned to run, she placed two shots at his legs, both hitting his thigh, as he twisted away. She prayed she missed anything vital since he'd be the one who'd have most of Ren's answers.

"Both men are down with shots to the legs. Approach with caution. Both are moving and still armed. I'll be there by the time the chopper lands." DJ set the safety on her rifle, slung it over her shoulder, and began the climb down.

The SSI chopper swooped in over the parking lot and hovered perfectly over the two trucks, even with the fierce swirling winds. Stuart held the bird level as if he were flying on a calm sunny day.

Steady hands—as good as any Army rotor pilot she'd served with. Hell, the computer geek handles that Hawk like an ace.

His older brothers had never mentioned their baby brother had skills other than communing with computers and riding herd on Keely through M.I.T.

"Shove the guns away from you and remain lying flat." Vanko's voice came over the Hawk's speakers.

DJ looked up after she reached the ground. A leanly muscled blond man was strapped in and stood in the open cabin door, an automatic rifle aimed at the two men she'd just taken down. Okay, so she wouldn't have to take control of the situation. No skin off her nose. She'd back the man-who-had-to-be-Vanko's play.

The chopper moved to the side of the trucks and, in a feat of some damn fine flying, hovered even lower to allow Vanko to jump to the ground. The chopper then rose smoothly and swooped off to land farther away from the building.

"DJ…" Keely's voice came over the headset. "Callie and I are going into the restaurant to give the all-clear, then we'll disarm the man in the front. Paramedics are en route. "

"Tell my momma, I'll come to her as soon as the scene's cleared. She doesn't need to see this. I'll check on the guy at the back of the station, then move to assist where needed."

While DJ was sure her mother knew that her daughter shot people while in the military, she sure didn't want her mother to view the end results up-close-and-personal. DJ planned to buffer her mother from the realities of what SSI did as much as possible. Her mother had already experienced her share of violence in the world; she didn't need to live through DJ's share, also.

"Roger that," Keely replied.

DJ pulled her Beretta and moved toward Juan, the man she and Keely had shot. She approached with caution. Old Juan was unconscious. He'd bled a lot. One of the bullets must have nicked an artery. She took his rifle, two knives, and pistol and threw them several feet into a stand of new-growth trees, leaving them for whatever law enforcement crime scene crew showed up to work the scene. She then used Juan's belt and applied a tourniquet to his leg. She checked his pulse and respirations.

She clicked her headset. "Ren?"

"Yes, DJ?"

"Tell the paramedics the guy behind the gas station has a suspected nicked femoral artery. I've applied a tourniquet. He's unconscious. Vitals aren't great, but he's holding his own. He's disarmed."

"Roger that," Ren replied. "See you soon."

"Roger that." After cleaning Juan's blood off her gloves in the snow, she headed for the side of the building where Vanko stood watch over the other two men she'd shot.

The chopper's rotors had wound down and once again she could hear the fiercely blowing wind whistling through the thicket of trees behind the buildings.

So, she shouldn't have been surprised to find the man who had to be Stuart Walsh checking the two downed mercs for other weapons while Vanko covered him.

Looks as if he is also a full member of the SSI team.

She paused for a second taking in the picture he made. Damn, Stuart was nothing like what his brothers had described. Just proved, she should never make assumptions about a person—or even a situation—until she'd observed both for herself. From mere hearsay—albeit, in her defense, from his family's own lovingly shared and often humorous stories—she'd labeled Stuart a pencil-necked, pasty, less-than-physically-fit computer geek. In the flesh, he sure as hell didn't look like a nerd who spent all his time communing in a virtual world.

Stuart Allen Walsh was what some of the women in her pilot classes would've called a hunk. He was tall—taller than her six feet by maybe four or five inches—with broad shoulders and long, leanly muscled legs as outlined by tight, well-worn jeans. Dirty-blond, slightly long, shaggy hair flew around his hatless head. His facial skin was darkened by exposure to the out-of-doors, and he had sculpted facial features accented by a five o'clock shadow.

Her nipples tightened. Her core clenched. Her clit throbbed—and her panties dampened uncomfortably. *Holy shit!* What a time for her latent libido to awaken.

DJ had never had an immediate sexual attraction to any male since being raped by Sean. Yeah, she could objectively admire a guy's good looks and even understand why some women lusted after them, but she hadn't lusted—ever. The men she'd served with were her teammates; they had her respect and that was that. She'd fully expected the same attitude to carry over to the SSI team.

It's a fluke. Really. She didn't even know him. He could be a total jerk.

But, in point of fact, she did know him in an indirect way. His parents and brothers had praised his—and Keely's—attributes to the skies. Stuart wasn't a jerk. He was smart, loyal, a good brother—a responsible, decent human being. He looked and sounded as if he'd be a perfect match for any woman.

But DJ wasn't one of those women—couldn't be. She'd never intended to find a mate—or even succumb to desire for a man. Just look at where love and desire had landed her mother. DJ's father had taken everything her mother had offered and abused it until the love died.

Button it up, Dahlia Jane. He's a team member. Think of him like your Army chopper crew. He's just one of the guys.

Yeah, she could do that. Had to do that. This SSI job was far too important for her to piss it away by being attracted to her employer's brother-in-law.

DJ moved closer to where the two mercs lay on the ground. She'd automatically aimed her gun at the man lying on the ground closest to her as Stuart checked both men out. She took several deep breaths and absently noted that upon her arrival on scene, Vanko had switched his full attention to the other merc.

She sighed with satisfaction. Already she worked in tandem with the well-trained SSI operatives. But she wasn't happy to discover—even after her internal pep talk—she was still somewhat breathless at the sight of Stuart.

Keely came around the front of the building and joined Vanko and her brother. She spotted DJ and waved, a big smile on her face. "Hey, DJ, come closer and meet Vanko and Tweeter."

Meet Stuart? Actually talk to him?

She'd sooner have nails driven into her skull.

Gut it up, Dahlia Jane. You'll probably never see him most of the time. You can be pleasant.

DJ plastered what she hoped was an interested, friendly expression on her face and strode through the snow to meet the two men. And damn, if her panties didn't get wetter at just the thought of shaking hands with Stuart.

Gawd, why now? Why this man?

The cause of her angst eyed her with a gleam in what turned out to be ice blue eyes—wolf eyes—set off by long, thick dark lashes any woman would lust after.

Shit. She had to shut this attraction down—and fast.

CHAPTER 5

When Keely shouted, Tweeter looked up.

DJ Poe walked toward them. She was tall. She was armed—and carried herself like the baddest bad ass in all of Idaho. Sweet blonde curls escaped a dark watch cap. She had the face of an angel and eyes the color of a tropical sea.

Her expression reminded him of the one Keely had worn as a thirteen-year-old entering her first class at M.I.T; it was a mixture of fear and tenacity. DJ was scared, but wasn't about to let it rule her.

A potent combination of tenderness and lust stormed through his body as ferociously as the winds raging around them. He willed his ill-timed sexual desire to subside. DJ didn't need to see the evidence of his instant attraction. He was well aware of her background prior to entering the Army. Dev and Andy had given him, Ren, and Keely a heads up about her early years in Red Bone. He knew all about DJ's bastard of an abusive father and about the sexual attack she'd endured at the hands of Sean Varney. He definitely didn't want DJ to think of him as a sexual predator like the man who'd raped her.

Tweeter had been predisposed to like DJ—she'd saved his brother and his MARSOC team's lives at the risk of her own. He recognized what an asset she'd be for SSI—her classified files indicated she had an impressive skill set and a high IQ.

But all his brothers' mission anecdotes, the details of her early years in West Virginia, the dry vital statistics, and the two-dimensional military photos hadn't prepared him for the in-the-flesh DJ Poe. There was no way he could've prepared for the fiery lust she'd ignite in him—and, probably, in every unattached male within the sight of her sexy body and sound of her low, honeyed tone of voice.

Fuck! Was DJ already beyond his reach? All four of his horn-dog brothers had seen her first. Had any of them staked a claim? The Walsh brothers had a no-poaching rule after two dates.

That was a definite need-to-know. ASAP.

And if she wasn't claimed by one of his brothers, then he'd work carefully to gain her trust. He never wanted to be the man to put fear in her eyes.

When DJ stopped opposite him, she avoided looking at him or the others. Instead, she glared at the merc at Tweeter's feet who spat out a stream of colloquial Spanish at DJ's approach.

"What did he say, DJ?" He had a fairly good guess— Spanish profanity was similar in most dialects. "That wasn't the Mexican Spanish I'm used to."

Tweeter was interested in how she'd respond, but he also wanted to shift her attention to him.

DJ looked up. Her aquamarine-colored eyes were beautiful. For several breaths, she said nothing. Her mouth thinned and her gaze grew fierce ... then wary ... then afraid ... and, finally, back to fierce.

Why all the conflicting emotions? She was among friends. The danger was over. The civilians were safe. The bad guys taken down with dispatch and a lot of skill by her, Callie, and Keely.

The fierceness didn't bother him; he liked strong women. The fear could be chalked up to a new job, meeting new people. But the wariness seemed to be aimed at him in particular. What in the fuck had his family told her that would make her so watchful where he was concerned? Or was she like this with all men?

She finally replied, "Nothing my crew hasn't ever called me before. It's nothing."

The merc let loose with another spate of angry Spanish.

Tweeter nudged the merc with his boot and said in his fluent Mexican Spanish, "Shut the fuck up." Then he looked at DJ's now studiously blank face. "What did the *pendejo* say to you? What I managed to catch wasn't nothing, and if your crew ever said such to you, they should've had their asses kicked out of the Army."

DJ's brow creased and then she shot him a quizzical look as if she were surprised he cared. "Let it go, Ace. They're just words from a loser." She then fixed her gaze on anything but him.

Okay, she was definitely uncomfortable with him. That was puzzling and unacceptable if for no other reason than they had to work together.

Then it hit him—"You called me Ace. You know you can call me, Tweeter," he said, drawing her gaze back to him.

DJ worried her lush, lower lip. Her trigger finger rubbed the barrel of her Beretta. Nervous tics. "No, I can't. Sorry."

"Why?" Tweeter needed to figure a way to get her past being nervous around him. He wanted her to like him—trust him—because without those two things, she'd never allow him to get closer.

"Stuart's your given name. It's a fine name and a very proper Southern one, but too formal for co-workers." She teethed her lower lip for the space of several breaths and then exhaled on a sigh. "You handled the Black Hawk like a pro ... an Ace. From what your brothers told me, you're also a computer ace."

She gave him a firm look. "What you aren't is a Tweeter or a Tweetie. So, Ace it is, unless you object."

"Ace is fine." She could call him anything she liked as long as she stopped being nervous around him.

DJ had turned her attention back to the mercs.

The merc at his feet groaned and uttered something in a snarling, nasty tone. Tweeter was just about to teach the asshole to clean his language up around the ladies when DJ leaned over and rattled off a few sentences in, what sounded to Tweeter's ear, the same Spanish dialect as the merc's.

"What did you say to the *govnyuk*?" Vanko asked.

DJ looked Vanko in the eyes; her lips twisted in a feral smile. "I told Cervantes to keep his filthy mouth shut or my next shot would be in his pencil dick."

Okay, she didn't seem to have a problem relating to Vanko. Was it because she knew Vanko was happily married and thus not a threat?

"Cervantes?" Keely asked.

DJ turned toward Keely. "One of his men called him that. I suspect he's the leader. He's lucky Ren wanted him alive. I had a head shot." She looked at Cervantes. "Right between his beady eyes."

Vanko barked out a laugh. "That's just mean. I think I like you, DJ." Vanko turned, his attention caught by something behind them. "Elana!" He moved to his wife, gathered her into his arms, and kissed her.

In that instant, Tweeter wanted what Vanko and Elana had. What Ren and his sister had. What his parents had. He cast a glance at DJ who stared at the affectionate couple, a look of longing on her face. DJ probably didn't realize it—but her expression indicated she wanted it, too.

"I like ornery." Tweeter was happy to see DJ cast him a shy, questioning look. He added, "Keely was always ornery." His sister stuck out her tongue, proving his point. "So, I expect we'll get along just fine. Welcome to SSI, DJ." He held out his hand and waited to see what she'd do.

Tweeter let out the breath he'd been holding when DJ moved closer and offered her ungloved hand. Her hand trembled slightly.

Okay, she was still watchful, but not avoiding him. He could work with that.

Tweeter gently gripped her fine-boned hand and stared into the depths of her beautiful eyes. Their Siren call could lure him in and hold him forever—and he'd be a very willing victim.

"Thanks, Ace." She shook his hand once, then pulled away quickly as if his touch burned her skin.

And maybe it had. The minimal contact had sent another tingle of heated awareness down his spine. He inhaled sharply. This close, her scent was something sweet, musky, and warm intermingled with the crisp smell of snow, the green scent of the tree she'd climbed, and the smoky residue of gunfire.

Everything in him shouted that DJ was meant to be his. Yet, she reacted like a small wild creature around him. If he came on too strongly, he'd scare her off.

DJ turned away from Tweeter and called out, "Elana?"

Elana walked over with Vanko glued to her side. His friend had a besotted look on his face and a possessive hand over his wife's stomach. She must be pregnant. He was pleased for Vanko—and again envious. Tweeter loved kids and enjoyed being a doting uncle to his nephew Riley. Coming from a large family, he'd always planned on adding to the Walsh clan—and sooner sounded better than later.

"Yes, DJ?" Elana asked.

"Where's my momma?"

"She's sitting in the restaurant with Callie and Lacey and holding Riley." Elana laughed. "Your mother likes Riley very much, and Riley adores her."

"Good, that's good." DJ looked around and then fixed her gaze on his sister sitting in the driver's seat of one of mercenaries' trucks. "Keely, you get a position on their base camp yet?"

"Yeah," Keely shouted. "Tweeter, get your ass over here. I need your portable GPS so I can transfer these coordinates. We need to move out. Who knows when these yahoos were supposed to check in? With no word, their friends could up and leave at any time."

Tweeter ran over and climbed into the passenger side of the truck in which his sister sat. DJ followed on his heels, but detoured to the driver's side.

"Where's their base camp?" DJ leaned into the driver's side. "Is it close?"

"It's not too far away," Tweeter replied before Keely could while he programmed his portable GPS and sent the coordinates to the chopper's on-board computer. "Looks like Morrissey's rental cabins, not too far from Fire Tower 9."

Sirens sounded in the distance. "The law's here," he said. "They can block off the access road at the base of the mountain. The chopper will get us on scene faster."

"Ren's here, also," Keely noted as one of the SSI Hummers pulled into the lot ahead of an Idaho State Trooper's car and Sheriff Dan Morgan's Jeep.

Ren, Ren's brother Trey, and Price Teague exited the Hummer, guns in hand.

Now was the time to make his first move in gaining DJ's trust and friendship—before Price or anyone else set eyes on DJ.

"DJ, you want to fly the Hawk? The coordinates are already locked into the chopper's nav system." As Ren closed in, his brother-in-law's eyebrow arched, but he didn't countermand Tweeter's offer. "I'll ride second seat," Tweeter added to make sure he was in close proximity to DJ at all times.

Ren grunted and shot Tweeter a "we'll talk later" look.

"Sure." DJ's whole face lit up with her enthusiasm at the chance to fly. She leaned into the driver's side even more and scanned the truck's nav system which highlighted the area around Morrissey's property. "Even without the specific coordinates, I know exactly where those cabins are." She smiled at him. "Thanks, Ace."

Ren caught his eye and mouthed, "Ace?"

Tweeter ignored the smirk on his brother-in-law's face and drew DJ's attention back to him and away from the nav maps.

"No need to thank me." Tweeter winked. "You're part of the team."

DJ's reaction was to grin and nod. "Damn right I am."

He'd guessed correctly—one key to winning DJ's trust and friendship: Her love of flying.

A second key: She wanted to be a part of the team ... to be needed.

DJ shoved away from the truck and strode toward the SSI's Black Hawk, sitting like an exotic, black behemoth in the snow-covered parking lot. Her long, skin-tight-jeans-covered legs ate up the yards away from the truck.

Tweeter and Ren hurried to catch up and then paced her.

"How do you know the Morrissey place?" Ren asked.

Like a flash, the excitement Tweeter had seen in DJ's eyes vanished. She was back to the expressionless mask she'd used when he'd first seen her. She turned toward Ren and held out her hand. As with Vanko, there was no trembling or any signs of guardedness.

So ... most men—well, at least, married men—didn't bother her. *Interesting.* Since she had no reason to fear or hate Tweeter—after all he was darn sure his mom had sung his praises and his brothers would never make him out to be a bad guy—the only other reason for her nervousness around him had to be she was attracted, albeit reluctantly.

One step at a time, Walsh. Stick with the slow-and-easy-wins-the-race approach.

"Hi, Ren. Nice to finally meet you outside of cyberspace." She shook Ren's hand several times. "To answer your question, I studied all the maps of this area I could get my hands on—and memorized all the places of interest and topographical oddities."

DJ walked around the helicopter, checking caps, intakes, and hose lines. Tweeter approved, and he could tell Ren did also.

"Those cabins are about a mile from that particular fire tower," DJ said. "As the crow flies, the location is northwest of our current position. Elevation is around eight thousand feet."

Ren whistled. "Dev and Andy told me you were detail-oriented. Glad to know they hadn't exaggerated. Welcome to the team."

"Thanks." DJ's cheeks flushed a darker rose as if she were embarrassed by the compliment. She looked down and kicked at some snow that had accumulated on the wheels.

Third key to DJ: Praising her for her skills and work ethic.

"Well, then," Ren angled his head at the chopper, "get in the Hawk and get situated. Tweeter's already volunteered to be co-pilot." He turned to yell at Dan Morgan who was checking over the merc at the back corner of the gas station. "Yo, Dan, you okay with taking over the prisoners?"

Dan jogged over. "Yeah." He scowled at Keely who'd come to join them at the helicopter. "All this carnage your work?"

His little sister scrunched her nose. "Um, Callie got the one in front. I helped DJ with the guy in back. Those two," Keely pointed to the men by the truck, "are all DJ's handiwork. Give us credit, Dan. They're still alive."

Dan snorted, then asked, "Who the fuck is DJ?" He looked around with a perplexed look on his face and finally focused on DJ as she was about to enter the chopper's cockpit. Her bulky jacket rode up her back and displayed her top-notch ass covered by the practically painted on jeans as she stepped inside. The all-too-single cop, and Tweeter and Price's frequent drinking and trolling buddy, smiled and looked DJ up and down, taking in all her feminine attributes. His gaze lingered on her firm, heart-shaped bottom for several seconds. The gleam in Dan's eyes had Tweeter clenching and unclenching his fists.

This was exactly what he'd feared would happen. Tweeter growled low in his throat. Keely smothered a giggle and Ren threw him a "what the fuck" look.

Tweeter ignored them both and kept his eye on Dan. No fucking way was Dan—or any other man—making a move on DJ.

Possessive much?

Fuck yeah. The Walshes had seen her first.

"Well, hello there. You must be DJ." Dan's voice was low and way-out-of-line sexy under the circumstances. "We need to talk."

"Nice to meet you, Sheriff. Sorta busy here." DJ barely looked at Dan as she stepped back to the ground. She shook his hand—and pulled it away quickly. "Your questions will have to wait. It's been almost three-quarters of an hour since we began the take down of the mercs. We have an op to finish."

Thank fuck, she treated Dan in a distant, but professional manner.

That still didn't mean Dan wouldn't attempt to make a move on her. Dan and Price hit on all the single females who visited or lived in the area.

Vanko cut off whatever Dan would've said next. "I'll stay here and help Dan make sure these men get medical care and then are locked down in the hospital and placed under guard."

"That'll work," Ren said. "Dan, could you handle getting the troopers to block off the access road to Fire Tower 9? We need to investigate a report of mercenaries headquartered at the Morrissey rentals."

"More mercenaries?" When Ren nodded, Dan grimaced. "I'd really like a month or two to go by without some asshats coming into my county and targeting your wife."

Then the man sighed. "We'll handle it. Since you all are still special deputies, let's try to arrest them, okay? And make some time to come into the station as soon as possible and make a full report about this cluster."

"Will do," Ren said.

After one more lingering and, to Tweeter's eye, lascivious glance at DJ who sat in the helicopter doing a pre-flight check, Dan jogged toward the state troopers and his own men who'd just pulled in with two paramedic units on their bumpers.

"I forgot all about my momma!" DJ stood at the open cockpit door, shooting an anxious glance at the restaurant. "She doesn't drive. My Hummer—"

Elana walked to the chopper and touched DJ's leg, halting her words. "Don't worry. One of us will drive your mom to Sanctuary in your vehicle. Give me your keys."

"Thanks, Elana." DJ handed her the keys. She looked at Ren and said, "I'm ready to take off as soon as y'all get on board."

"Fire her up," Ren said as he turned to listen to something Keely had to say.

As DJ strapped in and set the rotors to turning, Tweeter strapped himself in. "There are some computer upgrades, but on the whole this Hawk should be similar to the ones you flew in the Army."

"You'll clue me in on those differences before I need them, right?" He nodded. DJ then shot him a look from under her lashes as she checked the gauges and hummed with satisfaction. "Looking good here. Um, thanks again for including me."

"Hey, no problem." Tweeter handled her thanks casually, one peer to another. She needed to feel comfortable working alongside him. He planned on partnering her a lot during her new employee training period—part of his slow-and-steady approach to gaining her trust. "Be prepared to fly and report at the same time. Ren will want to hear everything that happened today before Dan hears it."

"Ren's my boss." DJ looked over at him as she adjusted the headset. "Of course, he has the right to hear what went down from me first. I recall every word the mercs said. I'll type it up as soon as we get to Sanctuary."

Tweeter grinned. "Ren's going to love you. Some of the operatives hate preparing written reports after giving them verbally."

DJ laughed. "Hey, bitching is okay as long as they do the job."

After Ren, Trey, Price, and two state troopers piled into the cabin of the chopper and shut the door, DJ smoothly took the Hawk up.

Tweeter shot a questioning look over his shoulder at Ren. "Troopers?" he mouthed, then switched to a private channel on the chopper's com system and reached over to change DJ's to the same channel so she could listen in as well. She didn't jerk away when he touched her headset, just turned and arched one golden-brown brow at him before concentrating on the white world outside of the Black Hawk.

He considered that a small victory.

"Troopers?" he asked Ren again, this time out loud.

"Dan wanted someone from law enforcement along as 'witnesses'. Since we could be facing another gun battle, he wanted their objective statements in case he needed to get the state prosecutor off his back. The political asshats in Boise still haven't gotten over the death toll from that one time two different sets of mercenaries came after Keely."

"Understandable," Tweeter said.

"Is SSI in trouble because me and the gals shot the bastards?" DJ asked as she handled the chopper as if it were a calm, sunny day with low winds. In fact, the visibility was down to less than a quarter mile. The bitch winds were swirling. And DJ still managed to push the air speed. Her face reflected a fierce concentration, but her posture, her hands, were relaxed.

God, the way she handled the Hawk was sexy.

When she looked over after no response from him, he could see only concern about her earlier actions against the mercs. There was absolutely no fear on her face about the flying conditions or what might lie ahead at the rental cabins. "Did I get SSI in trouble?" she asked again.

"No." Tweeter shook his head. "Absolutely not."

Ren leaned in between them. "You did the right thing. You heard shit about to go down. The men were armed. You called the law and realized they were too far away to make a difference in a fucked up situation. You took action to protect my wife, my child, and other innocents. You did everything right. If something similar happens again—and I hope the fuck it doesn't—I want you to follow through on your gut and situational awareness again." He squeezed her shoulder. "Dev and Andy told me you'd be coming on board fully operational. They were right. Welcome to SSI."

DJ sighed. Her aquamarine eyes glistened like sunny, sparkling Caribbean waters. Yeah, he'd read her correctly—she needed to be needed, a part of a team.

"I promise, you won't regret hiring me, Ren." The tone in her voice was that of a solemn oath.

"I know I won't," Ren replied. "You've already proven your worth in my eyes."

"Thanks." DJ's gaze sharpened and her expression smoothed out as she checked the nav map. "ETA at target is less than two minutes. How do you want to handle this?" She teethed her lower lip.

Nerves? Now? Worried about impressing the boss, maybe?

"How do *you* think we should handle it," Tweeter prompted, gaining him a quick, grateful look from her before she turned her attention to what lay ahead.

"There's a parking area about half a klick from the cabins. I can land there … or hover and drop y'all and then fly protection over the area until you tell me to land."

Ren grunted. "Drop us in the parking lot and fly protection. If the fuckers try to escape, you can stay on top of them. I don't want these fuckballs to get away. Someone is gonna pay for targeting my wife and son." He turned to Tweeter. "Stay with DJ and give us some cover from the air."

Tweeter nodded and caught the uncertain look DJ cast his way before focusing her attention to the radar and constantly changing conditions. What? She didn't realize he was a full member of the team? She'd learn it soon enough once her training began.

"DJ, will you have any problem handling the chopper in these weather conditions with the cabin door open?" Ren asked.

DJ stiffened and her face tightened at Ren's words. "Sir…"

"It's Ren, DJ. We're not military."

"Ren … if I could handle the conditions in Afghanistan—" she snorted. Her tone had been clipped and icy. Her snort filled with disdain.

Yeah, she was pissed at someone questioning her ability. Tweeter frowned at Ren who shook his head slightly. Fuck it, Ren was testing her. Tweeter bit the inside of his cheek to keep from leaping to defend her. She wouldn't want to appear weak in front of the boss.

"—then this is a piece of cake." She sighed. "Sorry. That was rude. Let me rephrase. If I couldn't do it, Ren, I wouldn't have offered."

"Your first response was fine." Ren winked at Tweeter. "Never be afraid to tell me things straight out. If you go too far, I'll let you know. I'm not a tyrant."

"Since when?" muttered Trey over the private channel.

"I heard that, little brother," Ren said.

DJ's lips twisted into a small grin which she shared with Tweeter. He smiled back. She was already starting to relax around him. Thank God for the bonding power of the Black Hawk.

"We're here, Ren." DJ took the chopper in over the parking lot.

The howling winds blew snow from every direction. Without the radar, it would've been difficult to tell up from down. But DJ didn't seem to notice as she smoothly made adjustments as she took the chopper into a low hover. The strain in holding the position was only obvious in her hands as she gripped the cyclic stick.

Tweeter kept a close eye on her, his hand lightly resting on the co-pilot's stick, just in case she needed some extra muscle. She didn't read as a hot dog to him, just confident, which meant she knew her limits. If she needed help, she'd ask.

He also kept an ear on what Ren and the others were doing over the now-shared channel.

"DJ, take her up as soon as you drop us," Ren ordered. "If we need you, we'll call."

"Roger that." DJ held the Hawk steady. "Watch your step, gentlemen. Three to four feet to the ground."

The wind jostled the helicopter and DJ made adjustments accordingly to keep the helicopter steady as the men jumped out.

"We're away," said Ren.

"Roger that. Stay safe." DJ took the chopper to a safe elevation and began a figure-eight flight pattern over the more rugged area where the cabins were located. Morrissey had nestled the cabins among the tree-covered slopes for the illusion of privacy. Only the parking lot and the main lodge were in a level, cleared area.

"Can you see anything moving down there, Ace?" She inhaled sharply.

He turned to her, concerned she was in trouble, and then noticed her gaze was glued on the nav map. Ahh, she'd discovered one of his additions to the comp's programming.

"What in the hell are those little yellow blips?" she asked.

"That's part of the software upgrades I told you about. All SSI operatives wear sub-dermal locator chips. It's part of our three-dimensional security system bubble over Sanctuary."

Tweeter pointed to the numbers below the yellow dots moving on the screen. "That one's Ren. Trey. Price. Those two," he tapped at them in turn, "are temporary ones pinned on the troopers' coats."

"Cool." Her voice held real interest. "So, can you also track SSI operatives during missions?"

"Yeah."

"With what?" She never wavered in her flight pattern, adjusting for weather conditions as if it were ingrained in her DNA. He'd let Ren know she multi-tasked well.

"Special hand-held computers I designed which also serve as encrypted satellite phones." Damn, he liked the admiration in her eyes when she looked at him. "Wait until you see the hologram map of Sanctuary."

"A hologram? That's fairly advanced technology." She sounded impressed.

"Yeah, Keely and I are refining and testing it for military use. We can track anything with a heat signature entering our property. Human bogies show up as red blips since they don't have the locator chips under their skin or a guest badge. Vehicles and large projectiles show up as blue blips. Keely and I are working on a program to identify inanimate objects that don't put off heat, but it requires—"

DJ cut him off. "Red blips? Something like those?" She pointed.

"Yeah. Exactly like them." Tweeter unbuckled from his seat. "Ren, five bogies outside of the sixth cabin back on the west side. Moving to cover y'all from the air."

"Roger that," Ren replied.

Tweeter picked up his assault rifle and moved to the cabin door. He hooked a cable onto his flight harness and opened the door and sat so he could lean out. The change in air pressure caused the chopper to wobble, but DJ adjusted and had it steady within seconds.

"I'm in position," Tweeter said. "Snow's let up some. I can see them. Yeah, they're definitely bugging out."

"Roger that," Ren replied. "If they start shooting at the chopper—"

"I'll take evasive action, boss," DJ interjected. "I'm not letting anything happen to this bird. Never lost a chopper, and I don't plan to start now with some jumped-up hired killers."

Tweeter laughed. "She told you, buddy. Take care of your asses. DJ and I have you covered from up top."

"Roger that," DJ responded. "Changing flight pattern. Hold onto your stomach, Ace. It's gonna be a bumpy ride."

"Yee-haw," Tweeter shouted as DJ placed the Hawk into a wide turn.

CHAPTER 6

Later that night, The Lodge, Sanctuary

Tweeter sat back in his chair at the dining table, his gaze fixed on DJ who sat across from him and next to her mother. A slight smile twisted his lips at her blush of embarrassment as Price praised her skills. Of course, if Price didn't stop looking at DJ as if she were his favorite dessert, friend or not, he'd have to kill the son of a bitch.

"Scotty, I kid you not," Price said. "DJ piloted that chopper and herded those asshats—pardon my language, Nancy—as if they were sheep and she and that chopper were a collie."

Nancy Poe glanced at her daughter with a mixture of pride and shock on her face. Then she turned to Price. "I knew my baby girl—"

"Momma, please—" DJ muttered.

"You are my baby girl and nothing will change that." DJ's mother caressed her daughter's cheek before turning back to Price who sat on Nancy's other side. "As I was saying, I knew she flew helicopters and took important people around and saved soldiers like Andy from enemy territory, but I never realized she could help catch bad guys with one."

Price grinned. "Ma'am, your daughter along with Keely and Callie took down—"

91

"Shut it, Price." Tweeter growled the words and cut the man off before he told Nancy how DJ had shot the mercs at the gas station.

The look DJ gave him was so filled with gratitude he swore he could burst into flames from the glow in her aquamarine gaze.

"But … but—" Price sputtered.

"Why don't we state that DJ has already proven what an important member of the team she'll be," Keely suggested, "and leave it at that. Okay?"

"Momma…" DJ kissed her mother's cheek. "I'll explain later. Price, thank you for the compliments and making me feel appreciated. But she doesn't need to know what I do … exactly."

"But I want to know," Nancy said.

"Some things I won't be able to tell you, because they're confidential." DJ's calm, firm tone brooked no arguments. "And other things I just plain don't want you to know. I'm a former soldier. Trust me, you don't really want to know."

Nancy frowned, then she shook her head and sighed. "Okay, but if you're going into danger, I do need to know. That way, I can have a heart-to-heart with God and let him know to keep an eye on you and your team."

"Prayers are always appreciated," Ren said. "We also want you to feel part of the SSI family, Nancy. So, if you have questions or concerns, you can always come to me or Keely. We'll tell you what we can, but as DJ said, some things will be on a need-to-know basis."

"Thank you, Ren. I already feel very welcome here." Nancy looked over her shoulder at Scotty who'd gone to the kitchen to plate dessert. Throughout the meal, the older man's appreciative gaze had often found DJ's attractive mother. "Scotty has made me feel right at home. He even welcomed me into his kitchen and told me I could bake and cook anytime I had a hankering."

"Nancy," Ren began gently. "You don't need to—"

"Ren, please … I want to help." Nancy gestured with a sweep of her arm. "You've provided this wonderful home for my daughter and me. Told me I don't have to lift a finger to help, but I want to. I can cook and help Scotty take care of all y'all. Please I want to do this. I *need* to do this."

DJ was definitely her mother's daughter—both women liked to be needed.

"Fine," Ren said. "But please don't feel that you have to. We're glad to have you and DJ—and room-and-board are part of the salary package for all operatives and their families."

"No one asked me, but I'll tell you I'm glad to have Nancy in my kitchen." Scotty began serving plates of pecan pie with whipped topping. "She baked this pie. She's going to teach me some of her Southern specialties, beginning tomorrow morning with biscuits and red eye gravy on the breakfast buffet."

"Oh, yum, my favorite." DJ closed her eyes and licked her lips. "Can't wait for breakfast."

"Her biscuits and red eye gravy are that good?" Tweeter asked as he swept his gaze between DJ and her mother. They looked more like sisters than mother and daughter.

Keely giggled and whispered something to Ren who narrowed his gaze and looked between DJ and Tweeter. Yeah, his sister knew him too well. She and her hubby would both be confronting him. Ren because of Tweeter's allowing DJ to fly the Black Hawk on the mission to round up the rest of the mercs, and Keely, for his personal attention in getting DJ and her mother settled since they'd arrived at Sanctuary.

Keely's fond expression told him she approved. Ren, not so much. Not that his brother-in-law would be able to change his mind. Tweeter was Walsh-stubborn—and Ren, more than anybody, knew just how stubborn that was. The man also understood intense attraction at first sight, because it had happened between him and Keely.

"Yeah, Ace—" DJ grinned at him across the table, dragging him back to the present. "The best. I really missed her cooking while in the Army."

"Not much chance for red eye gravy in Afghanistan, huh?" Tweeter replied.

DJ threw back her head and laughed. "Um, that would be correct. Not sure I'd call anything we had in Afghanistan as home cooking."

Her laugh went straight to his heart. He'd enjoy hearing that laugh every damn day for the rest of his life.

He turned his attention toward Nancy, who smiled at her daughter, sharing in the happiness. "Nancy, ma'am—"

"Yes, Stuart?" Nancy turned her smiling face toward him. Like her daughter, she'd refused to call him Tweeter.

"What time do I need to be downstairs to be first in line for your cooking?" he asked. He hadn't had a real southern breakfast since his last visit home to North Carolina. Plus, if he were early enough he could snag a seat next to DJ so he could engage her in general conversation. Get to know her better. Let her get to know him outside of the upcoming training and apart from what his parents and brothers had told her about him.

"0700 hours, boy," Scotty growled. "I couldn't convince the woman to sleep in."

"Are you sayin' I look haggard, Scotty?" Nancy's voice was almost a purr.

Whoa! What was going on here? Nancy and Scotty had only know each other for less than four hours and they were already ... acting flirtatious around one another?

As if you can talk, Walsh. You've already claimed DJ as yours.

Tweeter shot a look at DJ. Her eyes were narrowed as she looked between her mother and Scotty. What she saw had her inhale sharply and then look across the table at him. She widened her eyes and hitched a shoulder as if to say "what's up with that?"

He shrugged and shook his head. Inside he was thrilled that she'd immediately turned to him. The silent gesture demonstrated she valued and trusted his opinion, an important stepping stone on the path toward the relationship he wanted with her.

"You don't look haggard," Scotty said, a male's exasperation coloring his tone of voice. "You're beautiful. But, dammit, woman, you just rode clear across country. Got tangled with mercs terrorizing Ma's. And before that, your fuckwad of a husband hurt you. You're still healing. You need to take a break … rest up. Let me … us take care of you. The kitchen ain't goin' anywhere."

"Uh, Momma?" A frown creasing her forehead, DJ tugged on Nancy's arm. "Just what have you been telling Scotty while the rest of us were chasing down bad guys and talking to the Sheriff?"

Nancy fluttered her lashes at Scotty. "Everything. I told him everything as I baked pies and helped prep the vegetables for tomorrow's vegetable soup. He's a very nice man and a good listener." The older woman turned a piercing look on her daughter. "You have a problem with that?"

"No." DJ's tone was appeasing as if she were afraid to upset Nancy. "I'm glad you've made a new friend. But I agree with Scotty, you've had a lot on your plate lately, so resting—"

Nancy covered DJ's mouth with her hand. "I can rest when I'm dead. I like it here. I wanna live free, do what I want for once in my life. I love to cook. The kitchen is a dream kitchen, and Scotty is nice enough to share it with me. So, tomorrow morning at 0700, whatever time that is—"

"7:00 a. m., ma'am" Tweeter interjected before anyone else could.

Nancy shot him a grateful look. "Thank you, Stuart. At 7:00 a.m, there will be my momma's special red eye gravy and my West Virginia State Fair winning biscuits on the menu."

"Okay, Momma, but if I think you're doing too much, I'll—"

"I'll make sure she doesn't overdo, DJ." Scotty stood behind and between the two women. He gave DJ's shoulder a squeeze, but his warm gaze was on Nancy. "And if you see something I need to know about her health or welfare, you tell me. I'll make sure she sees Lacey and does as she's told."

Tweeter smiled. He wasn't the only Sanctuary male captivated by a Poe woman. Good to know. He and Scotty needed to talk later, over a beer or two. Maybe they could share intel on how to win the trust and affections of the ladies in question.

DJ studied Scotty with a narrow-eyed stare. Something she saw in the crusty old Navy man's face must've convinced her he meant her mother no harm, because then she smiled. "Thanks, Scotty. Between the two of us, we'll ride herd on her."

Nancy's inelegant snort had everyone at the table laughing.

Later that night, Tweeter's house

"Hey, Dev." Tweeter sat in his leather recliner in the den of his home.

"Hey, little brother." Dev's voice came across the crystal-clear satellite connection. The transmission was so sharp, Tweeter could hear the sounds of other men in the background … playing poker. "DJ and Nancy get to Sanctuary okay?"

Tweeter took a few short minutes to detail what had gone down and how DJ had already won over the rest of the team, the State troopers, Dan and his deputies, and all the locals at Ma's and Bud, the gas station clerk. Then he added a shorter description of the Scotty-and-Nancy show at dinner.

"Man, Scotty's moving fast." Dev chuckled. "Nancy is far nicer than that flight attendant he was engaged to. And for a woman her age, Nancy is still a looker, even after all the crap her fucker of a husband put her through."

"Yeah." Tweeter hesitated and then switched to the issue for which he'd made the call. "Did you or the other brothers declare an interest in DJ while she stayed with Mom and Dad?"

Silence reigned for several seconds, so many seconds, that if Tweeter hadn't heard the men laughing and cursing at each other in the background he would've thought he'd lost the connection.

"No ... not exactly. Why?" Dev's voice was low and harsh with a growl mixed in.

Tweeter stiffened. "What the fuck does not exactly mean?" Had one of his brothers already taken her out on two dates? God, he hoped to hell not.

"It means, little brother," Dev said. "That she was asked and declined. Now, tell me why you're asking."

Relief swept over him like a brush fire through a wheat field, and he relaxed into the chair. "I'm invoking the Walsh no-poaching rule." That was as straightforward as he could be.

"You've already been on two dates with DJ?" Dev asked, demonstrating he got Tweeter's message, but his tone indicated he didn't believe it.

"Not yet, but I'll get there." Tweeter inhaled and then let it out. "DJ needs to get to know me first. To trust me. So, I'm stealth courting."

Dev's shout of laughter was so loud Tweeter had to hold the phone away from his ear. "What's so fucking funny?"

"Because Loren and Paul came on really strong, as in full-court-press strong, while she was at Mom and Dad's. She shut them the fuck down ... in a firm, but nice way." Dev snickered. "You should've seen the looks on their faces when they'd crapped out."

Tweeter smiled at the image of his hot shot SEAL brothers being shot down by a woman. Women usually fell all over themselves to catch the twins' attentions.

Dev continued, "Andy and I thought about pursuing her right after she risked her ass in Afghanistan to rescue him, but we realized she kept men at arm's length. Later, while rescuing Nancy and after we met her douchebag of a father and the fucker who raped her, we realized she had issues. Serious emotional issues."

Tweeter heard the not-so-subtle warning in his brother's tone. "I won't hurt her."

"Hell, little brother, I know that." Dev snorted. "You might be the only Walsh male who could bring her fully into the family fold. You're a typical over-protective Walsh male, plus you know how to handle traumatized women because of Keely and all she went through. I know Andy will join me in wishing you luck. If you haven't won her over by the time we're out of the Marines and situated at Sanctuary, we'll aid the cause. I'm betting Loren and Paul will help also."

Tweeter never loved his big brother more than in that moment. "I'm curious, other than being shocked she'd turned them down, how did Loren and Paul act toward her after she rejected them?"

"They were fine. Told her no hard feelings. She agreed. Then they told her she was their sister by choice, no matter what.—Tweeter, she cried when they said that."

His heart swelled with love for his siblings. Loren and Paul had given her what she'd needed at that moment—acceptance after she'd rejected them. He had a gut feeling other men— aside from her ass of a father and the fucker who raped her— hadn't been as accepting when she'd turned them down.

Dev's voice softened. "That girl's had a hard life. Her mom tried to soften it, but Nancy told me one night that DJ even before the rape had taken things too seriously. She never had a real childhood like we had. Even Keely had more of a normal childhood than DJ. Nancy cried when she talked about the aftermath of DJ's rape. Told me she sent her daughter away and encouraged her to stay away so Sean Varney wouldn't hurt her again."

"Shit." DJ had been sent away and deprived of the only person who loved her. Tweeter really wanted to beat the crap out of Sean Varney and DJ's father.

"Exactly. If we'd known the guy we'd tied up when we went in after Nancy was DJ's rapist, the fucking pissant would've been a dead man. There's lots of mine shafts in that part of West Virginia. The body would never have been found."

"That fucker's mine." Tweeter warned his brother off. "Tell Andy, Loren, and Paul. Sean Varney will deal with me for what he did to DJ—and what he's still trying to do."

No one would avenge the wrongs done to DJ, but him.

"We'll back you up, little brother." A voice in the background shouted Dev's name. "Gotta go. It's my turn to beat the shit out of some guys at poker. See you all later this spring. Call if you need us to do anything prior to then. Andy and I still have leave time we can use up."

"Thanks, Dev. Tell Andy I said hi. Stay safe."

"Planning on it. Out."

Tweeter swept his finger to cut the call, then rested his head on the chair back and closed his eyes. It was clear in his mind he'd been training his whole life to be with a woman with DJ's background. But convincing her they were *meant* to be together wouldn't be easy.

He'd read her files, all of them—both unclassified and classified. Her classified file showed stellar service on ops she'd never be allowed to acknowledge. She'd turned down Officer's Candidate School and Army Intelligence. She'd also turned down an offer to join the CIA to do on-the-ground intelligence gathering.

DJ was a war hero. She had skill sets most men would envy. She was intelligent and courageous, but underneath she was an inexperienced innocent when it came to dealing with the opposite sex. What experience she did have was bad.

Her psych evaluation described her as having a "poorly differentiated sense of self"; she'd work her heart-shaped ass to the bone to get her superior officers, or an employer, the results they desired. She'd care for everyone around her, but would demand nothing for herself.

If he had anything to say about it, that extreme self-sacrifice would change. He'd make it his life's goal to take care of her for a change, make her see she deserved more than to exist for others, to be used as a token to win her father perks and privileges with his employer. She was more than a possession.

Soon, DJ would realize she was born to be his partner, his mate, the love of his life, and the center of his existence.

CHAPTER 7

February 8th, the Main Lodge

DJ sat on the cushioned bench in the kitchen nook. Her back was to the gorgeous snow-covered mountain scenery. Instead of taking in the glory of nature, she eyed her mother shyly flirting with Scotty. The connection between the two had blossomed over the week since they'd arrived at Sanctuary, much to the amusement of the Sanctuary inhabitants.

With each day that passed, her mother shed more and more of the protective layers she'd developed over the years of living with her abusive, soon-to-be-ex-husband. Yeah, there were still times when her mother startled at a loud noise or voice or jumped when someone came up behind her suddenly. But those times were growing fewer and farther apart—mostly due to Scotty's attention. With a light hand and a soft grumbly-bear-tone-of-voice, the former sailor was slowly but surely helping her mother put her old life in Red Bone behind her.

For that reason alone, Scotty had moved to near the top of her favorite SSI employee list.

"He won't hurt her."

And there was her number one favorite SSI employee.

DJ turned as Ace slid onto the bench seat next to her. He'd set his plate filled with her mother's made-from-scratch buttermilk biscuits, her mother's cheesy grits, and some egg concoction Scotty had called a frittata on the table. She was shocked she hadn't even noticed his approach. DJ was normally highly attuned to her surroundings, especially where men were concerned. Maybe it was because after working alongside Ace since the day she'd arrived, she'd gotten used to his presence. Her unconscious mind must not consider him a threat, which could be a huge mistake. Because under Stuart Walsh's easy-going, friendly exterior and all that intelligence lay a deeply complex man.

Her breath hitched and her heart pounded at his sudden appearance, at his nearness. Then the heat from his body and his intoxicating scent, a combination of fresh mountain air, pine woods, clean wool flannel shirt, and his unique male musk, enveloped her like a protective force field. She took several slow breaths, breathing in even more of him. Her heart rate slowed just as fast as it had escalated.

Had it been his scent or the deep breathing that had calmed her? Her gut response to that question both scared and excited her.

Uncomfortable with Ace's effect on her equilibrium, DJ said the first thing that came into her head. "My momma's still married."

DJ winced. She sounded like a whiny little girl. "Forget I said that. She deserves to be happy, and…" She inhaled sharply to ease past the lump in her throat. "If Scotty makes her happy, I need to suck it up and let her be." She stabbed at a piece of sausage patty, shoved it in her mouth, and chewed.

"Sounds like a plan." Ace buttered a biscuit and then slathered honey on it.

DJ shifted to see his face. He'd sounded amused, and if he had a grin on his face, she … she … well, she didn't know what she'd do.

Yes, she did. She'd challenge him to another fricking kick-boxing match. The computer wizard had put her on her butt every day of training, which had led her to conclude he was a macho-man in geek's clothing. She'd also learned he didn't make any accommodations for her or anyone else. The man liked to win.

She respected that … she liked to win also, but wanted to win because she was the best, not because someone let her.

Ace turned to look at her, his handsome face, expressionless. "Is there a problem?"

Yeah, he might not be smiling on the outside over her rant about her mother and Scotty, but deep inside, he was laughing like a loon. She'd learned to read him very well in a short period of time. His light blue eyes were very expressive. They could glitter coolly with amusement one minute or turn fiery with anger the next.—As they had when Ben Crawley, one of a group of corporate security guards taking advanced personal security training at SSI, had called her a stone cold bitch after she'd rejected the man's verbal and physical advances during a training session a few days earlier.

A warm feeling spread through her at the memory of how Ace had backed her up while she'd handled the cocky douchebag. Said douchebag and every other male who'd been present now understood she wasn't a frail, delicate flower and that she'd defend herself verbally and physically to get her point across. The fact that Ace could've taken over at any time and handled the situation for her, but hadn't, said a lot about how much he respected her and her abilities. She had no doubt if for some lame reason Crawley had gotten the advantage over her that Ace would've cleaned the forest floor with the moron.

She shivered, a sensual awareness that lit her core and made her heart pound, as she recalled how Ace had stood between her and the other men, giving her the ability to concentrate on handing Crawley his ass.

Crawley was now gone. Ren had overheard most of the encounter over her and Ace's headsets—and hadn't liked the fact the mental defective wouldn't take "no" for an answer.

Ren, after personally escorting Crawley to Grangeville, had called the man's bosses and given them a detailed report as to why, in Ren's opinion, Crawley was a lawsuit waiting to happen. Crawley was now unemployed as Keely had gleefully informed DJ last night as they headed, along with Callie, to the indoor shooting range.

"Earth to DJ," Ace said. "I'll repeat ... is there a problem?"

"Nope." She turned back and decimated her last piece of sausage patty into pea-sized pieces and then mixed them into the veggie frittata and took a bite.

Ace leaned in until his hot breath whispered across her cheek. "DJ ... it's okay to worry about your mother. She's gone through a lot. I expect your parents' marriage had been ... bad for a while."

"Bad?" She snorted. "Try more like a freaking disaster of epic proportions." She turned toward him and all she saw in his light blue eyes this time was genuine concern. "And the marriage was over a long time ago."

"There ya go." He shoulder-bumped her. "She's grabbing onto this new life with both hands. She's strong and resilient ... a lot like her daughter. She deserves to have fun. And Scotty's a good man. When his fiancée called off their engagement, it was as if a thundercloud settled over him. Your mom's new zest for life has broken through those clouds. I'm thinking that's a good thing."

"Yeah, it is." DJ sighed. "You won't tell anyone about my..."

"Nope."

"Thanks." DJ shoulder-bumped him back and heard his low chuckle. The knot in her stomach unwound.

Ace was an easy person to be around, even with the hidden depths and his odd effect on her pulse. She picked up the honey bear he'd just finished using and drowned her biscuit in the sweet goo, then began to eat the sticky-sweet mess with a fork. She needed all the carbs she could get. With the higher altitude, she burned up calories like a bunny on speed. "What's on the schedule for today? More physical testing?"

"Ren and Trey signed off on your physical readiness yesterday. Your oxygen uptake is well within normal range. They feel you're ready to be tested on your mountaineering skills."

Ace pulled out his ever-present computer tablet and pulled up the interactive map of Sanctuary.

DJ had been assigned her own tablet yesterday. While not the techno-wizard Ace and Keely were, she was good with map apps and GPS programs because of all her flight training. She'd played with her tablet last night before she'd gone to bed. It had almost been as fun as a video game. But the Bat Cave's hologram map was even better than a game—the 3-D security map was like something out of a sci-fi movie.

Ace and Keely had a lot of fun high-tech toys. Not that DJ knew exactly how they worked, but she liked what they did.

"We'll test your climbing skills while we check the perimeter security installations. You up for that?"

"Hell, yeah. I've been chomping at the bit to do some climbing." She'd excelled at mountaineering training at the Army Mountaineering School, as part of a test program for Army pilots assigned to support Special Operations Command missions.

He nodded. "Good. Not everyone takes to climbing especially at this altitude and these conditions. We'll take the snow mobiles to get from one set of arrays to the next. But we'll be snow-shoeing and climbing to actually do the inspections. Some of the security installations have registered as erratic."

"Erratic? Is someone testing your security?"

"Could be. But most of the ones that are blinking in and out are situated on highly exposed and rugged terrain. So they could've loosened up from high winds, rock fall, or an avalanche—all of which has happened at one time or another. I try to check the arrays routinely whether they need it or not."

"When was the last time you checked them?" she asked.

"Right before you arrived." A fierce frown tightened his lips.

"Then you suspect something."

"At this point, I don't suspect anything other than several arrays aren't working properly." Ace blanked out his expression once more and shrugged. "We have redundant systems, so we haven't lost our security perimeter."

"No red blinkie lights of strangers on the holo-map?" She began piling empty plates to carry to the sink.

Ace laughed, a low, raspy rumble that did strange things to her insides and raised goose bumps on her skin. "Nope, no red blinkie lights."

DJ slid out and carried the plates to the sink where Scotty was doing clean up. The older man smiled at her. "Heard you aced your weapons' test on the range last night. Keely and Callie wondered why you never tried to qualify as a sniper?"

"I liked flying helicopters more." DJ placed the dishes in the sink. "Plus, I had a choice of special programs and figured the extra training at the Army Mountaineering school would be more useful for my tours."

And it had. The one time she had a "hard landing," she'd found all the climbing and survival skills she'd learned had kept her, her crew, and her V.I.P. passengers alive until help arrived to extract them.

Scotty placed a hand on her arm as she began to rinse the plates to load in the dishwasher. "I can do that. You go weapon up with Tweeter. Never know what you two might find out there. Your momma and I got this."

The older man must've overheard their plans for the day.

"Thanks, Scotty." DJ turned to join Ace, who waited for her by the back exit from the kitchen. She hesitated and then turned back to Scotty. "Don't hurt my momma, please," she spoke in a tone that only the two of them could hear. "She's been hurt enough."

Scotty's expression turned hard, but his tone was gentle. "I swear I won't hurt a hair on that precious woman's head. And if I ever meet up with your pa, well, he won't be the one walking away from the confrontation."

"Good. And I'll cover your ass if and when that ever happens." She patted him on the arm and walked over to the counter where her mother spoke with Keely who was feeding Riley.

DJ hugged her mother. "Love you. I'm going out with Ace. I expect we'll be gone for most of the day."

"Be careful." Her mother returned the hug and then looked at Ace. "I'm making fried chicken for dinner, my bacon-flavored green beans, mashed red-skin potatoes and gravy, with sugar cream pie for dessert. So, y'all might want to be back in time to get some."

"Ma'am. Consider that a date." Ace eyed DJ. "Ready, partner?"

The way he said "partner" and the look in his eyes shot straight to the heart of her so fast and so hard she swore her insides had been struck by lightning. She took a second and breathed through the sizzling sensation before responding.

"Hell, yeah. Let's go. I want to check *you* out on *your* mountaineering skills." She walked over and punched him on the arm, a very solidly muscled arm. "I perfected my skills in Army Mountaineering School and in a war zone. Where'd you polish yours?"

Ace snorted as he took her arm and gently urged her into the back hallway. "The school of Walsh when I was really small. Then later, Dad sent me and Keely, when she was old enough, to a mountaineering school in Colorado run by an ex-Army mountaineering specialist. My only getting-shot-at-while-climbing experiences, I had here. Lots of bad asses think they can come onto Sanctuary and take whatever in the hell they want."

DJ had heard some of those local war stories. Dan Morgan, the Sheriff, had shared some of them after a few beers at Ma's.

He wanted her to know what she'd gotten herself into by joining SSI. Then the man had asked her out. She'd turned him down. The Sheriff was a player as was Price Teague. She'd turned Price down the first night she'd spent on Sanctuary. Besides Crawley, several other males taking SSI's corporate personal security programs and other male SSI recruits and operatives had asked her out. She'd turned them down also.

The only man who hadn't asked her out ... was Ace—and, dammit, that bothered her. A lot.

CHAPTER 8

Hours later, Sanctuary's far northern perimeter

"Sabotage?" DJ looked at Ace whose light blue eyes had turned dark with anger.

"Looks like."

She frowned and watched him work over the cable, his hands steady even though his body practically pulsed with his rage. "Wouldn't you or someone have seen red blinkie lights?"

"No red lights. No outside intruders set off any alarms."

The only conclusion was—"That means someone had a badge or an implant."

"Yeah," Ace growled the word, his expression dark. "Keely and I will figure out who it was. Process of elimination. It sure as hell won't fucking happen again."

DJ wanted to pat him on the back, tell him it wasn't his fault. But he wasn't ready to hear that. The system had been created to reveal intruders, not point fingers at authorized personnel.

Ace finished splicing the cable back together. "That'll hold until I can lay new cable between the arrays." He looked toward the west. "Can't do much more today. A front is coming in."

"The weather report didn't mention one." DJ helped Ace pack up his tools.

"Weather changes fast up here."

The gusts of wind on the leading edge of the frontal system came on suddenly, strong enough to blow the both of them off the precarious ledge. While they had on climbing harnesses and had tied off on the pitons mounted in the rock wall, even an unexpected, short fall could dash them against the jagged rocks and hurt them severely.

After one particularly potent blast of wind, Ace placed himself between DJ and the edge. "Definitely time to go." He spoke into his headset to be heard over the howling winds. "You rappel down first. I'll be right behind you."

"See ya at the bottom." DJ turned her back to the ledge, gathered her line in her gloved hands, and took a little jump backwards. As she descended, she kicked off the side of the mountain in three-to-four foot sections. She only had to walk her way laterally across the mountain wall to avoid sharp crags twice.

Even with the increasingly bad weather, the descent was straightforward for someone with her expertise. Ace had picked great locations for all the arrays, making the job of checking on the perimeter security system lifelines easy enough even for even a moderately experienced climber.

When she reached the bottom, something tugged on the sleeve of her jacket. She looked down and spotted the jagged tear from a bullet even before she heard a crack of a gunfire muffled somewhat by the snow. She unhooked the lines and began to run. "Ace. Shots. Get to cover."

"You hit?" His normally smooth baritone had turned gritty.

"Caught my sleeve. Can't tell how bad." DJ moved away from the base of the mountain and toward the shelter of the trees where the snowmobiles were parked. "You okay?"

Several more cracks of gunfire sounded. The bullets hit around her, sending up snow and chips of rock flying. She ran a zig-zag pattern but still felt several pieces of rock hit her body hard enough to feel through her snow gear.

The snow started to fall more heavily. *Thank you, Jesus.* With the lower visibility, DJ's white snow gear would blend more easily into the terrain, but Ace was a sitting duck on the side of the mountain.

"Ace? Answer me. You okay?" As she moved from rock to shrub to rock, she stopped and let off several shots in the general direction from which the sniper's shots had come. There was no way she could hit a target she couldn't see, but maybe the fucker would concentrate on her position and leave Ace alone. "Ace, answer me." Her breathing was choppy from exertion and, yes, fear for him.

"He's not shooting at me." Ace's voice was a low snarl filed with anger, frustration, and worry—for her. "You're his target."

Then what sounded like a small explosion boomed in the narrow pass between the two mountain peaks. As the echoes of the blast were carried away on the wind, a loud roar filled the air.

She'd heard that sound before—

Shots hit all around her crew and Andy's MARSOC team like a vicious hail storm. The Taliban snipers had them pinned down. Men shouted, screamed, cursed, and fired at the enemy they couldn't see, but who could see them. Then the rumble and roar of the massive snow overhang letting loose. Avalanche! The shooting had triggered it. Snow, trees, and rocks barreled down the mountain at more than a hundred miles an hour. Turning, she shouted—

"Avalanche." The voice wasn't hers this time and it pulled her out of the nightmarish flashback which had frozen her in place. "Move that sweet ass, DJ."

Reacting instantly to the command in Ace's voice, DJ left the cover of the rock she'd hid behind and zig-zagged through the knee-high snow. She still had someone shooting at her. She had to make him work for the kill.

Two more shots pinged off rocks around her. She spotted, then dove for a crevice in the mountain that looked to be large enough to take her body—barely.

Just as she wiggled inside the narrow opening, the first deluge of rocks, debris, and snow hit, pummeling the side of her still a bit exposed. She gasped as pain shot up and down the arm that had been tagged by the sniper's bullet—grunted when something hard and sharp hit her hip. Sucking in a frantic breath, she managed to thrust herself completely into protective bosom of the mountain.

Sandwiched on three sides by rock, she turned her face away from the crashing snow and detritus, toward the back of her rock shelter. This gave her a little bit of breathing space. The avalanche quickly walled her into the mountain just as effectively as the brick wall had trapped the poor soul in Poe's *The Cask of Amontillado.*

It was cold and dark in the cave. Andy had shoved her inside and pulled Dev in with him. Others in Andy's team must've made it, because she heard men calling out names. Then—

"DJ! Where the fuck are you?"Ace barked into her ear; his voice, a mixture of authority and apprehension.

She shuddered and tried to shove her memories into the "done and over" file in her mind, but sensed them hovering in the periphery. The past would take her over again before she was out of this mess. This was one of her worst fucking nightmares resurrected—right behind the night she'd been raped.

"Dahlia Jane, answer me!" There was alarm in his voice now.

"Um … in the mountain?" God, was that meek, wimpy voice hers? She turned her face toward the way out—praying she'd been wrong about the wall of snow. Nope. It was there, maybe a small hole near the top, but she was effectively trapped with no room to maneuver or to dig herself out. She coughed and cleared her throat. "Snowed into the side of the mountain. In a crevice. I have air … sort of." She went light-headed for a split-second when she couldn't seem to catch her next breath.

Stop panicking, Dahlia Jane. Ace will get you out.

She forced herself to take a deep breath and let it out slowly. The dizziness dissipated.

"Stop talking. Calm your breathing." He should talk. His breaths came fast and loud over the headset. God bless technology. The earpiece and mic were her connection to her partner, her anchor ... to the now and not the past. "The avalanche is over. I'm coming down to get you out."

Hot tears streamed down her cheeks. She shivered, the wetness made her feel colder than she already was. "The sh-shooter?" She clenched her teeth so they wouldn't chatter.

"Stop talking." He let out a breathy curse. "Fuck. Sorry, not swearing at you, just the situation. God, sugar, I never would've brought you—"

"Shut it, Ace." She shook her head at the amount of responsibility these Walsh men took upon their shoulders for actions not wholly under their control. Dev must've apologized a hundred times as they'd dug out of that cave in Afghanistan. "It's not your—"

"Hush. Conserve your air. For now, tap the mic once for *yes*, and twice for *no*." He paused. "Shooter's gone. When I catch the mother-fucker, he's dead."

He'd do it, too. She'd learned a lot about Stuart Allen Walsh in the past week and quadrupled that knowledge working alongside him today. He was just as much of an alpha-male as his brothers. When men like the Walshes were pissed and worried, their protectiveness shot into the stratosphere. She had no doubt Ace would get her out of the mountain and then he'd find and go after the man or men who'd put her in danger.

Of course, she'd be right there with him, covering his ass. They were partners.

The whole day had been a continuation of the partnership dance he'd initiated between the two of them from the first day they'd met. Over the last week, he'd tested her skill sets while subtly taking care of her.

What he may or may not have realized was she'd been doing the same with him ever since the Crawley incident.

Their flying skill sets and physical fitness were superior. Their mountaineering and climbing skills were about equal. Her abilities as a security system technician were rotten, but she was a good assistant and learned fast—and he'd told her as much.

Today, they'd worked as a team from the moment they'd mounted the snow mobiles. By the end of the day, they'd anticipated each other's moves before they made them. Yeah, today had placed the seal on them as partners, as good friends. She'd trust Ace with her life.

"Sugar, you still doing good?" The wind shrieked over their connection. The sound of his breaths as he exerted himself to get to her was punctuated by the clanking of metal on his rope and harness as he rappelled.

She tapped once.

"Good girl. I'm down on top of the avalanche snow. Shit, what a clusterfuck. Thank God, your subdermal transponder is working. I know exactly where you are."

"Good."

She smiled as a Doberman-Pinscher type-snarl came out of his mouth and he muttered, "Hush, Dahlia Jane."

She frowned. They'd be having words about the use of her full name after they were safe and warm—and after she assessed how his use of her full name—and *sugar*—made her heart stutter.

Normally, she'd chalk the endearment usage as being a Southern thing. Ace's mother called everyone "sweetie" or "honey."

But Ace's *sugar* didn't sound casual. His voice went softer when he said it. Even when he'd used her full name, there'd been an underlayment of an emotion that touched her in a way no other man had ever managed.

"...can you dig out from the inside? Answer me. Tap yes or no. Now!"

Ace sounded frantic. He must've been trying to get a response while she was off wool-gathering.

Head in the game, Dahlia Jane. Snow. Buried alive. Freaking dangerous situation.

DJ tried to maneuver her body to face the outside, but the space could only accommodate her sideways—and it was a tighter fit than she liked. Her round butt and big boobs were smooshed. She'd have bruises and scrapes where her outerwear had been ripped as she'd scrambled to get into the crevice.

Now she knew what canned sardines must feel like.

"I hear you breathing. Give me a yes or no." His voice pleaded. "Can you dig out from your side?"

Blowing out a frustrated breath, she tapped twice.

"Fucking hell. Okay, I see the beginning of the crack above where your signal says you are. I'm digging." He panted between words. "You'll soon see more light. Have more air. Just hold on."

She tapped once and then rested her head back against the cold rock and closed her eyes. She'd lost her cap somewhere and was losing heat through the top of her head at a rapid rate. She couldn't even move her arms to put her jacket's hood up.

Shit. Shit. Shit.

She focused on breathing slowly. She wiggled her toes in her boots and shook her hands in order to keep her extremities warm and ready to move when called upon. A pain in her left arm made itself known as a throbbing ache. In the good news-bad news columns, the hole the bullet had made in her outerwear let in just enough cold, damp air to numb the wound. The bad news was, it let in the cold, damp air and set her to shivering.

For now, she was okay. But if Ace didn't get her out soon, she'd be in danger of hypothermia and eventually shock.

Behind her closed lids, images streamed on an infinite loop, dragging her back once again—

Two Marines dead. Crushed or suffocated by the snow and rocks. Those who survived finally dug out of the snowy tomb. Then a shooting battle ensued as the cold, tired, bruised survivors fought and clawed their way back to the place she and her crew had hidden the Hawk. Then she got them in the air. A strafing run to take out the terrorist snipers' nests. Dodging surface-to-air missiles. Snow and death.

DJ stifled a moan. No use upsetting Ace. She wasn't in that kind of danger now, not even close. All she had to do was stay calm and wait. Ace would get her out.

Even behind her closed lids, she sensed the area around her becoming lighter. A wisp of air over her cheek had her turning her head to see Ace's gloved hand digging from the top down.

Relief and something else, something more intimate, swept through her. She blinked tears out of her eyes. "Hey, Ace." She took a deep breath to get past the lump of emotion clogging her throat. "I see your hand."

His hand disappeared and was replaced by his eyes peering through the small opening he'd made. His glacier blue eyes were filled with too many emotions to name. "Hey there. This is going to take a bit. You okay?" His voice was level and matter of fact.

"I'm super." Changing the subject, she asked, "Have you called in the attack?" She turned her head to face the rock wall so she wouldn't get a permanent crick in her neck.

"Yeah. Price was in the Bat Cave. He spotted the bogey. He was about to call us…" Ace's breathing was only slightly elevated as he dug at her snow prison at a pace that would kill a less physically fit man. "…I reported the shots and the avalanche as they happened. Price and Trey went after the motherfucker. But the bastard had already left Sanctuary land, and he lost them in the national forest lands."

Ace had to be tired, but never slowed once in his digging. It had been a long day of physically grueling work in cold, high-altitude conditions for both of them. Then this had happened.

"Take your time." She chuckled. "I'm not going anywhere."

"You said you were hit." He peered inside. "You're hurt. I need to get you out. I can rest later, once I have you somewhere safe and warm."

The driving need to place her welfare above his own was clear in his voice and his eyes. It was then she recognized Ace had deep feelings for her. Surprisingly enough, she was good with that thought.

Something inside her cracked and warmth filled places which had been frozen for far too long—

Since the night Sean raped you.

DJ's whole body buzzed with what could only be described as happiness.

"I'm good—"

Or maybe not. Blood was seeping—enough that she could feel it saturate her clothing along her arm and hip.

"Don't kill yourself on my account. The guys coming to get us?"

"They would, but the front's here." He angled back so she could see past his head and broad shoulders. "The chopper can't fly in this shit."

Blowing white bands of snow swirled backed by a dark grey sky. She had no clue how much time had gone by since the shots and the avalanche, but it had to be getting near sundown.

"No, they shouldn't risk it. We can make a snow cave." She let out a weak chuckle. "We have a good start on one with all the digging you're doing."

Ace stopped and stared at her. Then he shook his head.

"What's that look?" she asked.

"You're amazing." His lips twisted slightly. "No need to put all that SERE training to use. We won't have to make a snow cave. There are survival facilities set up all over Sanctuary with heat, light, food, water, and sleeping accommodations. We're about one klick away from the closest one. We'll ride out the storm there."

"Cool." She wiggled toward the front of her crevice until her left side touched the snow. She could now see his full upper body. He'd dug enough. "If you reach in and get your arms around my upper torso, I think I can shove off the back of this crevice with my feet and wiggle out over the opening you made."

"Sounds like a plan." Lying on his stomach, he reached in and circled his arms around her body just under her arms. "Got you, sugar. On the count of three, you push and I'll tug."

Distracted by the feel of his arms anchored so close to her breasts and the little squeeze he'd given her, DJ didn't answer right away.

"DJ?" He gave her another squeeze that caused her nipples to bud and kept her motionless, staring at the rock wall in front of her.

Was this arousal she felt? She wouldn't know. She hadn't felt anything since her last date had gotten to second base in the front seat of his daddy's Ford truck. That had been one week before Sean had raped her.

"Sugar—"

She shook her head, erasing the memories. Damn the past. Would it ever leave her alone?

"On three, it is." She turned her head and caught a look in Ace's eyes that had her trembling from head to toe. It looked like love shining from his eyes. She'd seen a similar look on Colonel Walsh's face when he looked at Ace's mother.

Suddenly, as if by wizardry or some force of magic, the memories of her lost innocence faded to black and all she saw was Ace's face and the deep affection in his eyes. She wasn't sure how it had happened, but it was there … had been there, if truth were told, from the day they'd met. She also wasn't sure how to react, or even if she should, because no one had ever looked at her as if she'd hung the moon and the stars.

"One, two…"

Just let Ace take the lead. Right now, get ready to wiggle your ass, Dahlia Jane.

"…three!" Ace pulled, using his upper body strength as he moved to his knees to get more leverage on top of the pile of snow.

DJ pushed with her legs and wiggled like a worm on uppers across the top of the snow until she was half in and half out of the opening. At this point, she could no longer use her legs to shove off the wall of rock. She lay there panting and wheezing with Ace on his knees, hovering over her, massaging her back and shoulders.

"Give … a sec … need second … wind." She weakly patted one of his arms.

"Just lie there. We'll rest a bit."

That sounded nice. Resting was just about her top speed right now. She was dizzy again. Cold. Altitude. Adrenaline drop. Plus, she might've bled more than she'd realized.

Ace stroked her head with a gloved hand before putting his wool cap on her so it covered her ears. It was warm from his body heat and smelled like him; it made her feel better almost immediately.

He muttered against her ear. "All you have to do is relax into my hold. Let me do the work."

She gave him a thumb's up as she lay on the snow, working for each breath. The cold air threatened to freeze her lungs. She managed to raise her uninjured arm and pull her neck gaiter over her lower face so she could breathe through the wool. Even the action of moving her arm was a labor befitting Hercules.

Ace adjusted his kneeling stance until he was about two feet away from her head. He grabbed her under the arms and leaned back. She slid a foot or so. He continued to move backwards on his knees, then leaned and pulled every couple of feet or so. It took a while but with the unstable snow and debris pile underneath them, he couldn't stand without sinking into the mess.

Finally, after what seemed like hours, she was out, her whole almost six feet lying flat on her stomach on top of the snow. Ace checked her neck and then patted over her body, checking her for breaks most likely.

A wave of nausea hit DJ. Her left side while not a happy camper had been blessedly numb to that point. Now, it blazed like the fires of hell. She moaned piteously and then gagged, but managed not to throw up.

"What the fuck?"

"Sorry. Hip. Left. Hurts." She buried her face against her non-sore arm and breathed through the pain.

"You told me you were only tagged on your arm." He pulled out a small Maglite and shined it on the area of her left hip which pounded to the beat of a heavy metal band. "Motherfuckingsonofabitch."

She glanced up. Ace looked like an avenging angel with no one to take his vengeance out upon. His obvious concern warmed her heart and soul; too bad it didn't work quite the same way on her freezing body.

"Ace…" She patted his muscled thigh, soothing him in the only way she could at the moment. "My arm was the only place the sniper caught me. The hip injury's from some debris in the avalanche. I'm not dying, just cold. You did promise me a warm place."

"Yeah." He inhaled and exhaled roughly for several seconds, then ground out, "But once there, I'll determine if you're fine or not. Try not to move around. I'll pull you over the snow surface until we get to more solid ground. This is gonna hurt, sugar. Tell me when it gets to be too much, and I'll stop and let you rest for a bit."

Hell, yeah, it would hurt. But the end was in sight. She wanted to be in that cave and its promised amenities more than she wanted her next breath—and after Afghanistan, she'd vowed never to go into a cave ever again. How time and circumstances changed a person's perceptions.

"Maybe I should try to crawl on my stomach." She would've said more, but he growled like a rabid wolf. "Or maybe not."

"Good call."

DJ lifted her head and watched as Ace dug in once more and reached for her. Then he repeated his earlier maneuver, sliding her along the top of the snow.

For the most part, the sliding motion was bearable. Then her sore hip hit some submerged rock or tree part. It was as if a blacksmith from hell had pounded on her body with a molten hot hammer. She screamed.

"Fuck me." Ace added a string of curses she was fairly sure he'd learned from a long line of Marines as he'd grown up on various bases. "I'm so sorry—"

"It's okay." She didn't want him blaming himself. None of this was his fault.

"It's not fucking okay." Ace began to slide her over the snow pile once more. "Bear with me. Once I get you off this snow pile, I'll be able to carry you to the snowmobiles."

Still with every single foot they traversed, he swore and rained curses down on the heads of the man who'd gotten away.

DJ couldn't help but find him funny, sweet, and absolutely wonderful. The warm feeling that had filled her earlier grew and grew with each curse word and foot of movement over the avalanche snow. Even her pain was thrust out of her mind by her growing feelings for this man. When they found the asshat who'd shot at her and caused the avalanche, she'd thank the man for waking her up to the possibilities of a future with Ace, then she'd let Ace kill him. He deserved the honors.

When Ace stopped to readjust his tugging position for the umpteenth time, DJ raised her head and looked around. The wind and snow were at blizzard levels; if there were a tenth of a kilometer visibility, she'd be surprised.

"Will the snowmobiles be buried?" Ace had made it sound as if the one kilometer to the SSI safe place would be as easy as a walk in the park, or rather a short snowmobile ride in the park.

"I saw them as I rappelled down. The avalanche never reached the trees where we parked them." Ace leaned over and brushed his lips over her frozen cheeks.

The kiss was brief and a total surprise. His mouth had been warm. The touch, gentle. After she got over the initial shock, she wanted him to do it again. It had felt good … right.

"We're almost at the edge of the avalanche's reach," Ace said. "After that, we have a short walk to the snowmobiles and then we're outta here."

She gave him a tired smile. "Knowing I can ride has given me a second wind. I should be able to walk once you get me off this pile of crap."

"We'll see. Plus, I planned on us riding double. You can't handle a snowmobile with your injuries." Then he dug in and pulled her several more times.

Finally, he stopped and stood. "Okay, got footing. Up you go." He lifted her to her feet as if she weighed less than nothing. If he hadn't been holding her, she would've collapsed. "Dammit. Hold onto me, sugar."

She placed her arms around his neck, and he swung her into his arms with her uninjured side next to his body. He began to walk toward the tree line.

"I can walk if you put your arm around my waist."

"No, you can't." His glare was the blue of a gas flame.

"Ace, darlin'… I'm heavy. You did all the work." She was about to build on her so logical argument when he stopped abruptly and stared at her.

"You called me darlin'." She nodded even though it hadn't been a question. He inhaled sharply, muttered "thank fuck," and then took control of her mouth and kissed her breathless.

This kiss was as different from his first as day was to night. And she liked it way the hell more. This kiss was lush … hungry. His mouth ate at hers gently, but insistently, until she gasped and opened to him. His tongue surged inside and tasted her until her body seemed to burst into flames pushing the cold and her pain aside and replacing them with sheer pleasure.

When he pulled his lips from hers, he rasped, "I'm carrying you. End of argument." He began walking again.

"Okay." DJ couldn't put together a sentence to save her life. She was darn sure she couldn't walk. Her knees were weak from the emotion conveyed through his kiss. She tightened her hold on his neck, nestled her head on his shoulder, and breathed in his clean masculine aroma. God, she'd buy this scent if they bottled it.

When they reached the snowmobiles, which had been covered to protect them from the weather, he muttered "shit" under his breath. She looked to see what the problem was now.

Shit was right. Their transportation was buried under a foot of snow.

"Put me down. I'll lean on one of the snowmobiles while you dig the other out."

"Sure?"

"Yes." But when he set her down, she stumbled as one of her feet slid off the top of a hidden rock. Her left side hit a snowmobile.

Hellacious pain shot up and down the injured side. The pain combined with exhaustion, loss of blood, and exposure finally ganged up on her. Stars floated across her field of vision. The world spun. And, finally, her shaky knees gave way as blackness claimed her.

The last thing she heard was Ace swearing up a storm—and that made her smile.

CHAPTER 9

Sanctuary Cave A8

After a hellish snowmobile ride with a semi-conscious DJ riding in front of him, followed by a hike up the steep path, carrying her against his chest, he was more than happy to see the entrance to Cave A8, the northeastern-most of their survival shelters. It wasn't as fancy as some of the others, but it had the basics, courtesy of a solar-powered generator and routine re-supplying.

"We here?"

DJ's slurred tones worried him. She had to be in the early stages of hypothermia. The current temperature was well below zero with the wind-chill factored in. Her protective outer gear had large tears which had allowed cold air and moisture inside. She'd been missing her hat when he'd pulled her out almost an hour after the avalanche. It was a wonder she was still conscious.

"Yeah, we are."

"Good." DJ lay limply against his body. She wasn't shivering and that wasn't a good sign. "What do you need me to do?"

God, she was barely conscious and still wanted to help.

"Nothing." He lowered her so he could free up a hand. Her knees gave way as soon as her feet touched the ground. He scrambled to hold onto her. "Dammit. Hold on, sugar."

"'kay."

DJ struggled to put her arms around his torso, but he could tell that wouldn't work. So, he braced her tightly against his body with an arm around her waist, then he entered the security code with his free hand.

When the door slid open, he swung her back into his arms and carried her into the entry cave. The automatic LED-floor lighting came on and the outer door swooshed closed behind him. He walked to the retinal scan beside the door to the inner chamber and placed his eye to it. Then he spoke into the intercom for voice recognition. "Tweeter Walsh." The door to the inner cave slid open.

"Lights, fifty percent. Heat, sixty-eight degrees."

The lights came on and the thermostat clicked, indicating the geothermal heating system was working.

"Neat." Sighing, DJ snuggled her head on his shoulder.

DJ still hadn't begun shivering. But his first priority was to make sure she wasn't actively bleeding, then he could get her warm.

The cave was simply laid out. One rock wall held a row of storage cabinets and lockers containing survival gear. Off to one side of the cabinets was a glass-brick wall behind which was a simple bathroom. On the other side was a small kitchen stocked with non-perishable foods and a refrigerator and microwave.

Tweeter placed DJ on a bench in front of the storage cabinets and opened her jacket and unzipped her snowsuit. The warmer air of the cave, relative to the outside sub-freezing temps, had already begun to do its job—DJ was shivering.

"Hang in there." He stroked a hand lightly over her injured arm and was happy to note the bullet wound was merely a gouge and wasn't bleeding. He stripped her thermal leggings down enough to check out the damage to her left hip.

DJ inhaled sharply as he peeled away the fabric which had stuck to her skin where she'd bled. "B-b-bleeding?" Her teeth chattered.

"Not now." After he cleaned it, it would bleed again. He regretted that, but wanted to make sure no rock grit, dirt, tree material, or cloth was in the wound.

"G-g-good. C-c-cold."

"Will do something about that now. Just hang in there. You're doing well." Especially, considering she'd been walled into a cold, damp rock prison for sixty minutes before he'd dug her out.

Tweeter opened one of the cabinets and pulled out towels, a couple of sleeping bags, and a down-filled comforter, then made her a place to lie down. He placed an extra blanket on the bedding to protect it from her damp clothing. Shifting her off the hard bench, he laid her on the makeshift bed and then pulled off her boots.

DJ blinked liked an owlet, never taking her gaze off him.

He gave her an encouraging smile. "Going to get you dry now so you can get warmer. That means I need to cut off the ski underwear. Can you handle that?"

God only knew he didn't want to trip any emotional triggers that might throw her into a PTSD meltdown.

She nodded and tried to smile, but an intense round of shivering had her biting down on her lip.

If she freaked, he'd handle it. But so far she'd dealt with all his touching and exposing of skin without a single complaint.

Keeping an eye on her body language, he used his knife to cut off her thermal underwear which was soaked from sweat and bloody from the two wounded areas.

As a one-hundred-percent, card-carrying dominant male, he couldn't help but notice her body. She was very female with her full breasts and a slender waist that flowed into lush hips. He grimaced at the bloody wounds marring her creamy skin and scowled at the evidence of older wounds.

Use the big brain, Walsh. She's hurting and cold.

Tweeter shoved his visceral reactions aside and pulled the extra, now damp, blanket from under her, so she lay against only dry bedding. He covered her nudity with another blanket and then layered on the comforter.

"Feeling warmer yet?" He tucked the covers around her shoulders.

"S-s-so c-c-cold." She whimpered as another wave of shudders swept over her.

She needs body heat, dumbass.

Tweeter pulled off his outerwear, took off his boots, and shed his sweaty thermal underwear. "DJ?" He never took his gaze off her as he pulled on a dry pair of thermal leggings.

"Hmmm?" She didn't open her eyes. Her teeth chattered and the sound had him clenching his jaw.

"I'm gonna share my body warmth. Can you handle me cuddling you?"

"Pl-l-ease." She nodded.

Tweeter lifted the comforter and quickly scooted in next to her and then recovered them both. He pulled off the hat he'd put on her earlier and swept damp blonde ringlets off her forehead. Her too cold and clammy forehead. Snagging a towel, he wrapped it around her head, then pulled her body closer to his. He couldn't resist nuzzling her neck and inhaling her sweet and citrus scent.

"That feel better?"

"Mmm, yeah." She turned into his touch and inhaled. "Warm. Feels g-good."

The fear, which had clawed at his guts when he'd realized she was being shot at and later trapped by the avalanche, released its hold. He hated she'd been hurt on his watch, but was proud of how she'd handled the whole situation. Most of all he was thankful she wasn't hurt worse than she was and that he'd been there to get her out.

"Cold. Hurt. Sorry." She moved restlessly against him. He pulled her closer and she sighed.

"You'll feel warmer soon." Tweeter brushed a light kiss over her forehead.

He allowed her to rest against him for ten minutes until the full-body shudders had lessened. Ren was expecting an update on DJ's condition. Tweeter had given a cursory report on her wounds during the snowmobile trip to the cave.

When he released DJ's body and wiggled out from under the comforter, she whimpered.

"Shh, sugar, I need to report in. After that, I'll clean your wounds and feed you. Then we'll snuggle until help comes. You have any allergies I need to know about?"

No answer.

Shit! He dropped to his knees by her side. He took her pulse. It was slow, but steady. Her skin was still too cool. Good news was, she was still shivering. But even the lesser shivering was causing her pain if the mewls and whimpers coming from her were any indication. The fact she was in pain was unacceptable.

He clicked on his headset. "Sanctuary, come in."

Ren's voice replied, "How's DJ?"

"She has a shallow bullet gouge on her left arm. She has bruises and scrapes and one deeper gouge on her left hip from falling rocks and debris. None of the injuries are currently bleeding or life-threatening. Getting her warmed up. She's been going in and out of consciousness, but that can be attributed to exhaustion and slight hypothermia. I'm going to clean her wounds, but need to know if she has drug allergies."

"Hold on a sec." After a short pause, Ren said, "She's allergic to penicillin. No other medical allergies listed on her military medical records. Lacey said to use the generic cephalosporin in the kit. No pain meds if she's unconscious. Could she have fractured anything?"

"Possibly. I'd feel better if we could take her to the hospital in Grangeville and get her checked out by a doctor."

"I hear ya, buddy. But we won't be able to get to you until this shit weather blows through."

"And when might that be?" Tweeter wouldn't be happy until DJ was x-rayed to rule out fractures as the cause of her pain.

"Twenty-four hours at a minimum. Probably more like thirty-six."

"Fuck." His angry tone caused DJ to whimper and move restlessly under her covers then just as quickly she stilled.

Ren relayed further info on the weather conditions and about Trey and Price's unsuccessful chase of the shooter, who'd turned out to have a partner. "The Varneys and DJ's father were confirmed to be in West Virginia ...so we have no clue who shot at you," Ren finished.

Dammit, he'd hoped the answer as to who'd shot at DJ would be the obvious one.

"The shooter wasn't interested in me, or he'd have had me." Tweeter had returned fire in the direction of where he'd thought the sniper was. There'd been no return fire in his direction.

"You sure?" Ren swore. "Forget that, of course, you're sure."

"Going to treat DJ's wounds now and try to get something warm inside her. I'll check back in once I make her more comfortable."

"Roger that. Out."

Tweeter pulled on sterile gloves and then placed sterile drapes under her hip and the wounded arm. He gave her a shot of antibiotics since he could see detritus in the hip wound and he wanted to play it safe. She moaned, but didn't rouse—that scared him and he didn't like the feeling. He needed to see her tropical blue eyes and hear her voice.

Wanting to get this over with so he could cuddle her, he began cleaning the wounds. As he worked, he pondered what the shooter's objective had been. An expert sniper could've easily killed them both. While the visibility had been somewhat bad, it hadn't been so bad that the shooter couldn't see them.

His conclusions? The shooter was either a really crappy shot, or the shots were … for what? Scaring them? Warning them off the perimeter areas? Plain old shits and giggles?

None of the reasons made sense or were acceptable.

Tweeter growled. No motherfucker shot at his DJ and got away with it. He'd find the bastard—sooner or later. Then he'd discover why.

DJ ROUSED TO CONSCIOUSNESS SLOWLY. She was warm and dry. Moving one of her arms, she discovered she was wrapped in something soft and heavy. She wiggled within the confines of whatever trapped her and moaned at the pain which shot up and down her left side.

"DJ?" Ace's voice came from her right.

She turned her head and found him watching her; his body aligned alongside hers. "Where are we?" She scanned the area around them and saw cabinets, some computer equipment, and stone walls.

He frowned at her question. "Don't you remember? We're sheltering in Cave A8." He placed a patch of some sort on her forehead. "Are you in pain? You can have something now that you're awake. You've been unconscious for a while."

"Mmmm. I'm achy, but I can handle it as long as I don't move too quickly." As she became more alert, she vaguely recalled key pads and retinal scans. Things before and after that were lost in the thick, pea soup fog filling her brain. She frowned. "I didn't get shot, did I?"

She would've recalled that, wouldn't she? She'd been shot before—in Afghanistan.

"A gouge on your arm. The wound on your hip was from falling rocks or something in the avalanche."

"Avalanche?" She closed her eyes and searched through the mess in her head. "Oh, yeah. Sniper. I had to squeeze into a hole in a rock. God, why is it so hard to think? To remember?"

"You've been through a lot." Ace's voice was comforting and she let it wrap around her senses and calm her. "Don't stress yourself. It'll all come back to you." He hummed under his breath as he pulled the patch off. "Good. Your body temperature is finally back to an acceptable reading."

"I had a fever?"

"No. You were hypothermic."

She sighed. "Okay. If I do get a fever, you need to know I'm allergic to…" She tried to lick her lips, attempted to swallow, but her mouth and throat were as dry as the Mojave Desert.

"Penicillin. Ren checked your medicals. I already gave you an alternative antibiotic. Your wounds had some debris in them. I didn't want to take a chance." He placed his hand under her head and lifted her, then held a bottle with a straw to her mouth. "Here drink some water. It might taste odd since I added electrolytes to it. Then I'll get you some juice or hot chocolate. Your choice."

She sucked at the water, made a face, and then pulled away and shook her head. "No more." She shivered. "Why do I feel so cold now?"

"Probably from inactivity." Ace cuddled her against him. He was like a blast furnace. "Want something to warm you up?"

"Besides you?" she asked and then blushed.

He chuckled and kissed her forehead. His lips blazing hot against her cooler skin. "Yeah, but you can have me, too."

"That sounds like a plan … but I'd like some hot chocolate also."

"You got it." Ace lowered her to the pillow, slid out from under a thick comforter and then tucked it back around her.

"How long have we been here?"

"A little over ten hours." He placed an extra pillow under her head and then moved away to what appeared to be a kitchenette.

Suddenly chilled, DJ burrowed further under the covers to escape the cooler air of the cave. Whoa, wait a minute.

What am I wearing? She struggled to look under the blanket and found— "Ace! This isn't my shirt and I don't have on any bottoms. What—"

Panic hit her with a force similar to the avalanche she'd just survived. While her forebrain was aware Ace was honorable and merely caring for her, her hindbrain had pulled up the violence from her past and screamed at her that men were beasts.

"DJ—" Ace hurried to her side. He knelt and reached to touch her.

She pulled away and immediately cursed the knee-jerk reaction.

"Are you scared of me?" Ace's blue eyes darkened with hurt.

"No. You're Ace. Not him." She tried a smile, and it must have been okay since his expression lightened a bit.

Slowly, cautiously, he skimmed his hand over her curls. His touch was gentle, comforting ... familiar. It felt ... right. She leaned into his hand.

"Don't you remember?" he whispered. "I had to cut off your clothes. They were wet from snow and sweat. The leggings were crusted with blood. After I warmed you up and cleaned your wounds, I put you in the shirt. And, yeah, I looked, but that's all. I'm a man, not a monk."

"I know you're a man," DJ stuttered, her cheeks burning. "That's the problem."

A look of sadness came and went on Ace's face.

"Forget I said anything." She petted his arm. "I know you did what needed to be done." She squeezed his arm. "Ace, I'm glad it was you with me when all this happened."

His expression brightened. "If it makes you feel better..." His voice was as smooth as warmed honey. "I was more concerned with treating your wounds and making sure you didn't get any sicker than you already were than checking out your body."

"Thank you ... I think." She wrinkled her nose. Now, she wanted to know if he liked what he'd seen.

Dahlia Jane, you contrary hussy.

"You're welcome." Chuckling, he stood and walked back to the counter where he resumed making her hot chocolate.

DJ took the opportunity to check out Ace from top to bottom as his back was turned to her. *Man, oh, man.* Her heart rate accelerated. Her breathing grew choppier. All bad experiences with the male sex vanished like smoke on the wind as she took in the picture he made.

Ace had always looked fit, but in his thermal underwear, she recognized just how muscular he really was. His body was that of a tri-athlete—all lean muscle with broad shoulders and narrow hips.

She swallowed—hard—and managed not to hum her approval. She'd never liked hulk-type men; they reminded her too much of Sean who'd used steroids to beef up for football, still used them if the pictures Dev and Andy had taken were any evidence.

Ace turned, and she moaned low in her throat before she could stop it. Lordy, lordy, the man was built … all over. The front view was even better than the rear. The tight thermal underwear displayed a nicely formed chest, a nice set of sculpted abs, and a large bulge at the juncture of his thighs. A bulge that grew even larger as he watched her staring at him.

DJ swallowed hard and decided not to ignore the obvious. "That looks painful."

"I'm not going to jump you." His voice was a low croon, akin to what he might use to reassure a frightened animal.

"I know that." She licked, then bit her lip. "What if I want you to—"

To do what, exactly? She wasn't sure. But she did know she was tired of being afraid … of being half a woman. Plus, Ace would never hurt her.

"DJ," Ace murmured, "you're injured. I'm under strict instructions from Lacey to keep you as quiet as possible until they can get the chopper here to take you to the hospital in Grangeville for x-rays on your hip and an exam by a doctor."

"Nothing feels broken." She wiggled. "Just bruised and sore."

"We'll let the experts tell us whether you've fractured anything or not. Ren insisted." Ace's lips thinned into a stubborn line.

"Pulling the boss card?" DJ shook her head. "Not fair."

"He has to clear you for training." He moved to her side, placing the hot chocolate out of the way, then he pulled over something to prop her up and helped her to a sitting position. "Here, drink this." He handed her the insulated mug.

DJ took the cup from his hands. Her fingers brushed over his. He inhaled sharply. "Ace? What…"

"Drink your chocolate." He stood. "We'll talk about *what* later—once I have you safely back at the Lodge." He moved to the counter and picked up another mug and then returned to sit by her side. "By the way, the shooter was after you. We need to address that. Who would want to scare or hurt you—and knows you're on Sanctuary?"

Thinking over his question, she sipped the chocolate and murmured, "Yummy, marshmallows."

"Thought you'd like those. You and your mom make S'mores in the fireplace each evening." He shook his head. "Now, I'm craving them, too."

"You should've said something." She stared into the mug. "We'd have made room for you."

"Nope, that's your alone time with your mom." He took a deep drink from his mug and swallowed. "Mmmm, that's good." Then he licked the marshmallow foam off his lips.

DJ's body tightened, remembering his kisses after he rescued her and how they'd taken her away from the cold and the pain. She was tempted to pull him to her and lick the foam off his mouth and then kiss him, sharing the taste.

"Answer the question, DJ." He turned, a frown on his beautifully sculpted lips. "Who would want to scare you? Take a chance at hurting you?"

"Sean Varney. His father. My father." She shrugged and wiped a finger around the top of her mug, removing the sticky froth. She stuck her finger in her mouth and sucked off the yummy goodness.

Ace's heated gaze zeroed in on her mouth. His nostrils flared. A quick glance at his crotch showed a small wet spot where his cock head was religiously outline by the tight fabric.

She took another sip to avoid moaning aloud. Now, she realized what the topic was he wanted to table until later. He was attracted to her, but had strong enough control to wait until she'd been given a clean bill of health.

"They were all in West Virginia. Ren checked. There has to be someone else," Ace said.

"No one else. I tried not to make enemies in the military. Couldn't whoever shot at us be one of SSI's enemies? After all, just one week ago, we had a battle at Ma's with some mercs y'all think MacLean sent to get Keely and Riley?"

MacLean was a former Defense Intelligence Agency employee and a traitor who'd blamed Keely and SSI for exposing him and forcing him to run. He was currently in the wind, but still managing to cause trouble.

"Then the shooter would've also shot at me. For all he knew, you were just my climbing buddy."

"I'm female and blonde like your sister. Also like Callie," she parried.

"You look nothing like Keely or Callie. Even a crappy sniper would notice that through a long-range scope." He shook his head. "No, the shooter knew who you were. All the shots were aimed at you. The avalanche was a side effect of the shooting and unstable snow conditions."

Ace was silent for several seconds, then snorted like an

angry bull. "Plus, Varney doesn't want you dead. He wants to kill you himself."

But she didn't plan on letting Sean kill her.

After several seconds of companionable silence, Ace stiffened and snarled. "There is someone who'd want to hurt you. Ben Crawley."

DJ inhaled sharply. "Yeah. I can see him blaming me. In his juvenile brain, I was the reason he got kicked off Sanctuary and later, fired." Men like Crawley always blamed others for their own bone-headed moves.

"Yeah, those reasons and because the rat-bastard had a hard-on for you from day one. You rejected him. You physically took him down in front of his peers. He didn't like that at all."

Ace clenched his hand around his mug until the tendons showed white. He clicked his headset. "Come in Sanctuary … Ren? … No, DJ's fine. You need to locate Ben Crawley. We need to question him about the shots taken at DJ."

His facial expression changed, grew more tense as he listened to whatever Ren said. She felt for her headset and muttered "rats" under her breath when she realized it was gone. She really wanted to know what put the glowering look on Ace's face. If he ever looked at her that way, she'd run as fast as she could in the opposite direction; that was, if she hadn't already expired on the spot. This man was definitely not the easy-going geek the Walshes had said he was.

"Roger that, Ren. Out." Ace tapped his headset and looked at her. "Let's get some sleep. You need rest to heal, and I'm bushed."

"No…" She reached across the short space between them and touched his chest. "What did Ren say?"

"DJ…"

"No, tell me. I'll just lie here and make stuff up and not sleep. Don't hide things from me."

Ace let out a harsh breath. "Crawley's dead. Another man, a trouble-maker well known to Idaho County law enforcement was found with him, also dead. The rifle was by the bodies."

"How did they die? From the weather?" She frowned when he shook his head. "Then who killed them?"

"That's the question Ren and Dan want answered. Whoever killed them, dumped their bodies at the side of the highway this side of Grangeville." He paused then added, "There was a note. It was addressed to you…" His lips twisted and his eyes blazed with anger.

"Tell me." She caressed his fingers.

He turned his hand over and cradled her hand as if it were the most precious thing he'd ever held, and she knew in that instant, this man would treat the rest of her just as gently and lovingly—if she allowed it.

"It said the note's author would collect later for getting rid of the men who tried to kill you." He raised her hand to his lips and kissed the tips of her fingers, then stared into her eyes over their clasped hands. "Seems you have a very deadly secret admirer, sugar."

No, that was wrong. The only men she'd met since she left the Army were good men, with Crawley being a major exception. There was only one man who wanted her in his clutches—

"Not an admirer, more like a deadly stalker. Sean's found me." She looked into Ace's stormy blue eyes. "He knows where I am. You said it, he wants to kill me himself. He has someone watching me, keeping me alive until he can get his hands on me. Ace … I'm scared."

"Don't be." He leaned over and placed a light kiss on her mouth, even the brief touch sent heated awareness through her body. "Whoever the note's author is, believe this—I'll never let anyone hurt you. Swear to God."

"Ace…"

His lips cut off anything she might've said. This time his kiss was longer, deeper as his tongue swept inside and tangled with hers. Any lingering cold in her bones vanished as his kiss set fires burning in her core, in her very soul. Just as she began to return the kiss, seeking to taste his mouth as he tasted hers, he pulled away. Like a chill wind, disappointment swept over her.

"Sleep, sugar." He helped her to lie down.

DJ didn't want to sleep. She wanted to kiss Ace and find out where it would lead. She turned to him and found exhaustion on his face. This wonderful man had rescued her, taken care of her, watched over her for hours—he needed his rest. She could wait.

Ace dimmed the lights with a voice command and settled next to her on the bedding and pulled the blankets over them both. He pulled her into his arms, his arm anchored at her waist. She felt as if she'd come home. It was a good feeling.

Looking back, she realized her reaction to Ace had been different from the beginning. Why had this man reached her and no one else over the last ten years?

It is what it is, Dahlia Jane. Accept it.

DJ let out a sigh. Ace's arms tightened as he murmured unintelligible words against her hair. She snuggled closer to his heat and drifted into sleep. She could get used to this.

CHAPTER 10

8 a.m., February 15th, Main Lodge, Sanctuary

"I need to get out of here." DJ glanced at the women sitting around the breakfast nook table.

Lacey, Elana, Callie, and Keely with Riley had joined her for breakfast. Her mother and Scotty were off doing … well, she didn't want to know what they were doing, since she suspected her mother was getting more intense foreplay than DJ had been. Ace, for once, was not hanging around like a gander protecting his goose.

It had been five days since she and Ace had been rescued from Cave A8. The trip to the hospital had been a non-event since the doctor proclaimed her fracture-free. Other than a few bruises and the two wounds, which were healing fine, she was as healthy as a horse. But in Ace's mind, she was a frail, gentle creature who needed tending or, at least, it seemed that way to her.

Since the sniper adventure, Ace had hovered. When he wasn't making sure she was safe, comfortable, or warm enough, he was kissing her. There were the quick kisses with a hint of tongue and maybe a sweep of his hand over her back or arm if there was a chance someone might walk in on them. When he was assured they wouldn't be disturbed, there were the longer, hungrier kisses with lots of tongue, while he held her close and touched her, stroking her breasts, back, and hips. She liked all his kisses, but especially the longer ones; those she craved—and wanted more.

In fact, last night as they'd made out on the couch in front of the Lodge's great room fire, she'd pleaded, "Ace, I want more."

"You're still healing." He'd placed light sucking kisses on her mouth, her chin, her ear lobe, and finally at a particularly sensitive spot on the side of her neck right below her ear.

"I'm fine." And, yeah, she'd whined, sort of, but he was driving her effin' nuts. Her clit had throbbed and her pussy had gotten wet. She might not have had a normal sex life over the past ten years, but she was well aware her body was preparing for intercourse ... preparing for him.

Ace had smiled and touched his forehead to hers. "I don't want to hurt or scare you. We can wait." Then he'd taken her mouth and French-kissed the heck out of her.

Maybe he could wait, but she damn well didn't want to. For the first time in her life, she was horny and wanted to experience an orgasm. Yet, the only man she'd ever trust to initiate her into true intimacy was too busy protecting her.

AARGH!

She was also stir crazy.

"Earth to DJ"

DJ looked across the table at Keely, whose eyes danced with amusement as if she'd read DJ's mind. How long had DJ spaced out? She was doing a lot of wool-gathering lately; mostly because Ace's kisses messed with her normally acute mind. "What? Did I miss something?"

"You said you wanted to get out of here ... so, where do you want to go?" Keely asked as she wiped Riley's breakfast off his face and hands. It looked as if more food was on him than in him. And why that made DJ's heart pang and her insides turn to mush, she didn't know.

This sudden gooiness over baby Riley she blamed more on her mother's words than Ace's actions. Her parent kept dropping casual remarks about what a nice man Ace was—and he was—and what a good uncle he was to Riley and how he'd be a good father. Of course, Ace had to share some of the blame since he was so danged nice and solicitous and funny and smart and … sexy.

Her normal D.O.A. libido had received a jump start. As a result, her biological clock was sending use-it-or-lose-it notices.

"Go? Anywhere." DJ flung her arms in a wide sweeping motion. "To a mall. A fast-food restaurant. Heck the county library. Just away."

"Well, you'd better make your escape before your keepers get back." Lacey laughed. "Tweeter hasn't been more than twenty feet from you since your sojourn in A8. And your mom has been even closer."

DJ groaned. "You all noticed that, did you?" Keely, Lacey, Elana, and Callie nodded in sync, big grins on their faces. Then DJ frowned. "I know my mom is with Scotty." *Still not going there on what they're doing.* "But where is Ace?"

"My brother, along with my husband and Vanko, flew to Boise to meet some clients about a job," Keely said. "Can't tell you what the job is yet, but you might be going on an intelligence-gathering mission soon."

DJ perked up. A mission was just what she needed to take her mind off other "things." "Really? Ren thinks I'm ready?"

"You were ready the day you started," Keely said. "The training period was to get you acclimated to SSI ways, not to improve your skill set."

DJ was complimented by Keely's words and proud of the confidence Ren was showing in her by considering her for a mission a mere two weeks after she'd come on board. It warmed her heart at how quickly she'd been accepted as part of the team, and a lot of the credit for that went to Ace. He'd showed her the ropes and constantly praised her skills to the other operatives.

"So…" Keely said. "Where do you really want to go?"

DJ shrugged. "Suggestions?"

"I could use some body lotion and shampoo," Keely said. "Want to hit the Center Mall in Lewiston and have a girl's day out? We could make it a full day and have a meal before we come home. The mall's about four-and-a-half-hours driving time, round trip. Once we hit Grangeville, it's all interstate. The roads should be clear, and there's no snow in the forecast for the next twenty-four hours."

"That sounds like exactly what the doctor ordered." DJ wasn't only excited to get away from Sanctuary, but also thrilled she finally had female friends to do "girl-things" with. Yeah, she'd had female friends in the Army, but many of them had families or boyfriends. Plus, she had little in common with them other than the job. For the first time in her life, she felt she was becoming the woman she was meant to be, more rounded with work *and* personal time. More in balance. It was a good feeling.

"You gals go. I'm still having lingering morning sickness." Elana did look peaked. "Riley needs a sitter since I overheard Scotty ask Nancy to help him do the monthly grocery shopping in Grangeville. They planned to make a day of it with lunch out and all."

"You sure about staying in, Elana?" Lacey asked. "I can stay and take care of Riley. You might feel better after an outing."

"Thanks, Lacey. I don't think I can handle that long of a trip right now. Even without the nausea, I need my afternoon nap. Riley and I can take one together." She grinned. "But I do have a list of things I could use if you wouldn't mind picking them up for me?"

"I'm going, but I warn you I might need frequent potty breaks," Callie said. Everyone laughed. "Give me your list, Elana."

"Then you can count me in," Lacey said. "Quinn's taking some of the corporate security clients out on the property for more war gaming and survival lessons. He won't be back until tomorrow. I could use a break away."

"Meet back here in an hour?" Keely suggested.

"That's great. Thanks. Y'all are the best friends a gal could have." DJ grabbed a can of Pepsi to up her caffeine level another notch or two and then headed to the suite of rooms she shared with her mother. If she was going to be out all day in the bitter cold, she needed to add more layers.

---

7 p.m., February 15th, Ma's Bar and Grill

DJ SCOOTED INTO THE ONLY BOOTH at Ma's which gave a clear line of sight to the front door, the diner's counter space, and the entrance to the barroom off to the side of the main dining area. Lacey followed her in taking the end of the curved booth. Keely was next to DJ and Callie sat on the other end of the booth, opposite Lacey.

Settling back against the faux burgundy leather, DJ sighed happily. "That was a long day, but fun. I've never bought so many things at one time before."

DJ had never enjoyed shopping so much. The fun company made all the difference. She'd bought more winter clothing and a one-piece swimsuit for the Sanctuary indoor lap pool and hot tub. She also managed to find some pretty clothes for her mother whose birthday was later in the month.

"Well, you didn't buy the bikini that looked so good on you." Before DJ could defend her position, Callie added, "So,

I bought it for you." The former model winked. "Tweeter will lu-u-urve it."

DJ picked up a packet of sugar and threw it at Callie who laughed as she batted it away. "I can't wear that," she protested. "Not all of us are former *Sports Illustrated* swimsuit cover models. Besides it has huge holes."

"My dearest DJ, they're called strategically placed cut-outs," Callie intoned in a snooty tone she must've picked up from a top fashion designer. "And you, my dear, have the perfectly toned body to show this little ensemble to advantage. It just screams *you*."

DJ snorted and shook her head, but she couldn't help smiling at Callie's silliness.

Callie giggled and added in her normal voice, "Seriously, DJ you looked *hawt* in it. That royal blue color was great against your skin tones. So ... I'm giving it to you and you're keeping it."

"Might as well give up," Keely said. "Callie's going through the hormonal need-to-mother-everybody part of her pregnancy. And she's right, my brother will love you in that suit. I wish I had long legs ... and a long torso. I'd have bought the fuschia-colored one. Unfortunately, those cut-outs would hit me in all the wrong places. It's hell being short."

Before DJ could respond to Keely's—and Callie's— nonsense about Ace caring what she wore, someone's cell rang. It wasn't hers since she'd turned hers off when they'd left Sanctuary, not wanting her mother or Ace to track her down and scold her for leaving the premises. For chrissakes, she was a security operative and a former Army pilot who'd been involved in secret missions in some of the most dangerous places in the world and they were treating her like a two-year-old.

Plus, her ring tone wasn't Saving Abel's *Addicted to U*.

Keely pulled her ringing cell out of the side pocket of her purse and answered, "Hey, big guy. Where are you?" She eyed the rest of them and smiled. "We're at Ma's. What do you guys want to eat? We'll order for you. We haven't even ordered drinks yet."

After some "hmming" and "sures," Keely handed the phone to DJ. "Tweeter wants to talk to you. It seems your cell is off." The little blonde winked, amusement in her sparkling green eyes.

DJ took the phone and before Ace even had a chance to say a word said, "Don't start with me, Ace. I had a wonderful day with the girls. I plan on having a scotch since I'm not driving and then a nice meal. How was your day?"

"Productive." Ace sounded amused. Then in a more serious, solicitous tone, he asked, "You feeling okay?"

DJ sighed and crossed her eyes at the smiling women who avidly listened to her side of the conversation. "Did I tell you not to start with me?"

"Sugar…" Ace growled, sounding a lot like his father and older brothers when he did so. Walsh males seemed to breed true. All of them were over-protective, bossy, macho-men, but also honorable and caring. A very attractive combination. "I asked, because I care, not because I'm trying to dictate to you."

The man read her too well. Plus, of all the men she'd met or worked with, Ace was the best, hands down, at letting her be herself. She needed to cut him some slack and—

Answer the man's damn question, Dahlia Jane. He cares … and so do you.

"I feel fine." His snort of disbelief had her admitting, "Okay, I'm a little stiff … but nothing a little yoga and a good night's sleep won't fix."

"Get Lacey to give you a massage when you get home." Ace chuckled. "I'd offer, but I like my balls where they're at."

Ace? Massaging her? With those long, supple fingers? Skin to skin? Her whole body flushed at the thought … at the images in her mind's eye. Oh yeah, she was definitely into the concept of Ace touching her and then she'd have the right to touch him back. After which, they'd kiss and move on to other more intimate touching.

Before she could edit herself, she said, "I didn't hear an offer."

At Keely's delighted trill of laughter, DJ shot her petite friend the finger and handed the phone to Keely before Ace could reply. She also ignored Lacey's poke on the arm and muttered "what offer?"

"I have no idea what you're talking about, big brother." Keely's eyes twinkled with suppressed laughter. "No, I won't hand the phone back to her. We'll see you guys when you get here." The little blonde ended the call and then stared at DJ. "So-o-o ... you like my brother?"

"Never said I didn't." In fact, she more than liked him. She also needed him to stop teasing her with kisses and light touches and take the sexual foreplay to the next level. The promise of what they'd be like together was tantalizing and had occupied far too much of her conscious thought—and her dreams—ever since their time in the cave.

Her face burned as a result of the avid looks the other three women shot her way. Studiously ignoring them, DJ focused on the menu and decided meat was what she needed at that moment. The rarer and juicier, the better.

"You've never said you liked him, either," Callie pointed out. "I ... we ... have noticed you observing Tweeter when he wasn't looking. You don't watch any of the other single men that way."

"We're working together, so, of course, I look at him."

Lame, really lame, Dahlia Jane.

"It's more than that so fess up," Lacey urged. "We won't tease you ... much." Then the older woman laughed.

"This is the kind of thing you share with your gal pals," Keely said. "Plus, I know my brother, and he likes you ... a lot." Keely reached over and covered DJ's hand where it was fisted on the table. "*A lot* a lot. I've never seen him this way before, not even when he was dating one gal at M.I.T. for two years."

"Was that the girl he dated after…" Callie paused, a slight pink flush on her high cheekbones. "…this might be the time to mention that Tweeter and I … um, were each other's first lovers." She hurriedly added, "We immediately decided we were better friends than lovers."

"You … and Ace?" DJ looked at Callie. Surprisingly, all she felt over Callie's disclosure was envy since Callie admitted it had gone no further. But the M.I.T gal? Her, DJ wanted to hunt down and disembowel. She had just the knife for the job.

Sweet Jesus, when had she gotten so territorial over Ace? Oh, yeah, it had been during the two days in the cave.

Callie nodded. "We were both tired of saving it, and we liked each other, but…" She scrunched her nose. "…the experience was uncomfortable. After all, we were practically raised together. Right after we 'did it,' he went back to M.I.T. with Keely and met up with … what in the heck was her name?"

"Buffy Smithson." Keely spoke the name as if it left a rotten taste in her mouth. "At least, Callie I liked. Buffy? Meh. She merely wanted to use my handsome, popular, so smart brother as an escort and fuck buddy. She never really cared for or about him."

"Fuck buddy?" DJ couldn't help the snarl in her voice. God, she was jealous of some female called Buffy from Ace's past. That was just wrong. Damn, the man had changed her whole attitude about men and relationships in less than two weeks.

"Yep. I guess my brother has some moves." Keely wiggled her eyebrows.

Callie and Lacey laughed like loons. DJ swallowed hard, wondering what other moves he might have besides his kisses. Since his kisses were earth-shattering to her equilibrium, how in the hell would she survive more?

"Buffy panted after Tweetie like a bitch in heat. It was embarrassing. The she-devil didn't like me. I lived with Tweetie, because I was underage during my first years in college. I was always," Keely used her fingers to indicate quotes, "'underfoot' as she called it. She was a stuck-up piece of work and not nearly good enough for my brother. I quite illegally, and damn proud of it, placed a bug on her phone and listened in on her conversations with her friends. She was always bragging about my brother's sexual prowess and how she had him twisted around her little finger."

"Bragged to others?" DJ couldn't help herself. "She actually talked about their sex life with her friends?"

"Yep." Keely nodded. "By the way, you're perfect for Tweetie. I approve. My whole family loves you. So, if you're scared about him hurting you, don't be. He's serious about you. If you can't feel the same way about him, then you need to let him down gently—and soon, before he decides to make his move."

Move? What kind of move? Sex? Or more? At that moment, she wanted it all, whatever *it* was.

Then she realized—"He's been making subtle moves for a while—and just now, he—" DJ blushed and scanned the faces of the women who looked at her with genuine affection. Then she singled out Keely. "I like your brother a lot— *a lot* a lot." Her use of Keely's exact words had all the ladies chuckling. "He's different. He treats me like a partner and not some dumb blonde bimbo with tits and ass. He ... gawd, this is awkward."

Lacey rubbed DJ's arm. "Go on, you can tell us anything. We won't tell Tweeter or Nancy, who, by the way, has shared with everyone she likes the idea of you and Tweeter together."

"My momma's talking about us?" DJ inhaled and then coughed.

"Honey," Lacey said. "Everyone's been talking about you two since the day after you arrived at Sanctuary. Tweeter doesn't usually participate in the training sessions every single day, all day. Other than his routine trips to check on the security arrays, he normally spends most of his time in the Bat Cave and, maybe, the gym after the training sessions are done for the day."

"And as for Nancy, she's an excellent observer. She came to me and asked about my brother's actions. I told her what I thought," Keely put in. "Even Ren said something to me about Tweetie's interest in you. Men are usually the last to realize what's going on in other people's relationships. So, fess up, what was the latest move my too-smart-for-his-own-britches brother made over the phone?"

"When I told him I was stiff after the trip and all?" The girls nodded, and Keely fluttered her fingers in a give-me-more gesture. "He suggested I ask Lacey to give me a massage, because he was afraid if he offered, I'd take him down." She kept Ace's balls out of the conversation.

"Ooooh, and that was why you replied in a sexy tone of voice that he hadn't offered?" Callie gave her two thumbs up. "Good response. I figure Lacey won't be giving you a full body massage this evening, because Tweeter is probably urging Ren to break land speed records from the air strip to get to your side."

The other women smiled and nodded. DJ stared at the menu which she'd crumpled in her fist. "We'll see. He might not even offer."

"Oh, he'll offer," Keely said. "You didn't hear yourself. If I were a guy, I'd frick-fracking offer. This calls for a drink." She looked around. "This place is packed. Cabin fever must've hit everyone within a fifty-kilometer radius. Who's going with me to the bar to order drinks? I know what the guys want. We can wait on them to order food."

DJ nudged Lacey with her thigh. "Move, please. Someone has to protect the midget. Callie doesn't need to get pushed around in the crowded barroom."

Callie smiled at DJ. "Thanks. I have to admit, I do feel more tired than normal. I'll take a 7-Up with a lime in it.

Would you bring some bar mix back? The baby and I are starving."

"Bar mix sounds good. Lunch was a long time ago. A bottle of Bud for me." Lacey got out of the booth. "I'll grab some chairs so the guys can sit on the other side of the table. The booth isn't big enough for all of us."

"Sounds like a plan." DJ exited the booth. She looked at Keely who'd scooted out after her so Callie didn't have to move. The blonde's head came to just below her shoulders. "Let's go, Shorty."

"Okie-dokie, Legs." Keely snickered and led the way, nodding to friends and stopping once to tell their harried waitress that three more were coming and to take her time getting to them. The waitress looked profoundly grateful.

As they entered the bar area, the noise volume suddenly dropped by half. Several men's heads turned their way. DJ was prepared to ignore the male interest since that was her normal response, but the looks from some men at two tables in particular raised the hairs at the nape of her neck. Their interest wasn't the usual male scoping out a female just for the hell of it; it was more darkly speculative and, for lack of a better word, evil.

DJ touched the gun holstered at her back and hidden by the loose, plaid flannel shirt she wore. She took the safety off by feel.

Grabbing Keely by the arm, she stopped the little blonde before she could go any farther into the bar. "Getting bad vibes here. Maybe you should go back. I'll place the drink orders and tell the bartender to give them to our waitress to bring to the table."

Keely looked at DJ. Her green eyes slitted like a cat's. "What's wrong?"

"Multiple asshole alert. The two tables at two o'clock." DJ pulled Keely to the side, out of the way of some men exiting the bar to the dining area. Then, keeping the two tables in her line of sight, she began to move them sideways toward the doorway to the dining area. "Six huge guys dressed in hunting camouflage and armed."

The men hadn't bothered to hide their weapons. She spotted the holsters right off.

"Let go of my arm. Need to ready my weapon." Keely tugged and DJ released her.

She and Keely continued to sidle toward the dining room. A fusillade of gunfire in the crowded bar and restaurant would result in a lot of injured and possibly dead innocents.

DJ wanted, at the very least, to take the potential clusterfuck outside.

"I recognize some of them. They're part of a local militia group that recently moved into the area. They're stupid, mean, and crazy. They've been causing all sorts of trouble. Dan isn't happy," Keely said *sotte voce*. "At Dan's request, Ren has had me looking into their backgrounds. Dan and Ren think these guys might have contracts of mutual support with Varney's militia group."

"No thinking about it. I'll guarantee they're in a mutual support treaty with Varney's militia. I can't get away from my damn father and his scummy friends."

When she and Keely were within a few feet of the doorway, the six men rose as one and began moving toward them. Oh hell yeah, they were very armed. She spotted knives and more than one hand gun per man—the defenders at the Alamo hadn't had that much firepower. God, she hated it when she was right.

"Not getting a good feeling about this, Keely. Let's peddle."

DJ turned taking Keely with her and came face-to-face with two more huge guys—she named them Sasquatch and Baldy—dressed like the ones coming up behind her and Keely.

In an instant, DJ grabbed Keely and hustled her to the bar so they'd have only the bartender at their backs. She chanced a glance at the bartender who had his hands in the air and a pissed expression on his face. One of the six guys had split off and now held a gun on him.

Eight armed bad guys and two armed women equaled clusterfuck in any language.

The barroom had gone completely quiet at the moves. It was as if everyone in the room held their breath, waiting to see what would happen.

"Shit," she muttered.

"Yep, that about sums it up. Ren is going to freak." Keely scooted behind DJ's body and said in a low monotone, "Sending an SOS to Ren. Our men will come in hot. So get ready."

Not sure they could wait that long, but DJ would stall for as long as possible.

"Problem, boys?" she drawled, addressing the five men in the center of the room and keeping the two who'd entered from the restaurant in her peripheral vision.

"Your daddy and Sean want you and your momma home, bitch." The speaker was one of the men in the center of the room. *Arrogant ass.*

As if she'd go anywhere with any of them on her father's say-so. As for Sean? How stupid did the man think she was? She'd never make it easy for anyone to take her to that rapist bastard. And if they dared to get near her sweet momma? She'd gut them and hang them up to dry.

Mentally counting to ten, DJ took one long, deep breath and then let it out. "Not gonna happen. Consider the message delivered. Now, you boys go back to your tables and let me and my friends eat and drink in peace."

"Can't do that, girl. We're not messengers. We're transport. You and your momma are going back to West Virginia," Arrogant Ass said. "Now, we can do this easy or hard. You don't want us to shoot up the place and take the chance to hurt some of these fine citizens, do ya?"

Yep, dumber than shit if Arrogant Ass hadn't realized that at least half the men in the barroom could take care of themselves and would take care of any innocent civilians. That probably several fine citizens had already dialed the local emergency number for the sheriff's office. Plus, she'd recognized several men from the last time she'd been involved in a shoot out with bad guys at Ma's. They'd nodded at her. She had backup, and they'd follow her lead.

Arrogant Ass had no fucking clue what he'd just bit off.

Movement at DJ's back.

Keely had removed DJ's gun and pushed it into her hand. The bastards weren't expecting her or Keely to be armed—that was her ultimate ace in the hole. But she'd still like to move this whole potential shooting match outside.

But how?

"I'm waiting, girl. Get your ass over here so we can go fetch your momma." Arrogant Ass gestured with his gun to a spot next to him.

"I'm fine right here. And I don't know where my momma is." And that was the honest to God's truth.

"Get ready," Keely murmured.

DJ inclined her head in acknowledgment as she shot Arrogant Ass a fake smile.

Obviously, Keely knew something DJ didn't. Whatever happened, they'd have to take out Sasquatch and Baldy, who currently blocked their way out of the bar. The two hadn't pulled their weapons yet, so that gave her and Keely a slight advantage. But still without a distraction, she wasn't sure how they'd escape eight men.

Then Callie entered the game.

"No one move." Callie's voice was loud and mean. "I'm tired, hungry, and my feet hurt really, really bad. So, if you move toward my friends, I'll drop you."

"Hey, I know you," Arrogant Ass drawled. "I jack off to the *Sports Illustrated* issues you're in."

"You really are as dumb as you look." Callie's sigh was exaggerated. "I figure you all know what expert-rated sniper means, and I'll admit to being expert-rated in long and short guns. If you don't believe me, check out the jacker's forehead."

Sure enough, a laser dot was centered on Arrogant Ass's forehead. When he moved, it moved. DJ didn't know where Callie was positioned exactly, but she had the men in the middle of the room covered for sure.

"But you're a super-model," Sasquatch said as he looked over his shoulder into the dining room. "Super models can't shoot worth spit."

Callie's answer was to shoot the floor right in front of Arrogant Ass's boot, forcing him to jump back. The red dot went back to his forehead within a split second. "I don't miss … ever."

One of the locals shouted, "That's for damn sure. She beats me at the local shooting range every damn time."

"Thanks, Zeke. Oh, and I'll add that I have enough firepower to take y'all down without taking a fucking breath. So, drop your weapons and put your hands behind your necks, fingers laced."

"Jesus, Callie's one mean bitch when riled." DJ had used the shock from Callie's threats to point her weapon at Sasquatch. "You got, Baldy, Keely?"

"Yep." Keely stepped to DJ's side. "The bartender, who's an off-duty deputy, got the drop on the guy covering him when Callie entered the picture."

Nothing like a beautiful woman with a loaded gun to shift the advantage to the good guys.

"Okay, assholes, here's the deal—" Using her gun, DJ motioned Sasquatch and Baldy toward their buddies in the center of the barroom. "We're gonna stand here until the law arrives. You all," DJ indicated the entire group with a sweep of her head, "will be going to jail."

Callie's shooting buddy Zeke and several other locals moved to relieve the militia men of their weapons.

DJ shook her head and tsked. "Now, don't you regret hooking up with my loser father and his asshole friends?"

Sasquatch elbowed the man frisking him out of the way and lunged for DJ. At the same time, three shots rang out, none of them hers, aimed at Sasquatch's buddies. Faith in her friends' abilities to contain the other bad guys allowed her to concentrate on her attacker. She used Sasquatch's forward momentum and weight against him by ducking and upending him. He hit the floor face first and slid into the bar. The top of his head hit the solid oak bar with a loud *thunk*. She stayed out of grabbing range and trained her weapon on the back of his head.

Baldy, Keely's target, lay on the barroom floor not far from where Sasquatch had landed; he was bleeding from his upper left chest. Two other militia men lay on the ground, bleeding from their thighs. One was bleeding profusely. Obviously, Callie had decided to wound and not wipe.

"Someone had better put a tourniquet on Arrogant Ass," DJ said. "Looks like Callie nicked his femoral artery."

"Didn't nick it. Shot it on purpose," Callie shouted as she entered the bar, her weapon trained on the militia men still standing. She looked like a *Field and Stream* cover model slash avenging angel. "Anyone else want to do something dumb?" She looked around. When no one answered, she said, "I didn't think so."

The outer doors to Ma's banged open.

"Keely!" Ren's voice boomed off the walls.

"That's my man." Keely smiled and yelled, "We're in here, big guy."

"DJ!" Ace roared.

Her heart sang—*That's my man.*

"I'm fine, Ace," she shouted, a wide grin on her face.

Weapons in hand, Ren, Ace, and Vanko entered the room on the run. Their angry male vibes preceded them. DJ swore the walls and floor vibrated from the excess of pissed-off testosterone levels.

They were trailed by six cops of the county and state variety led by Dan Morgan. He shot an annoyed look at her and Keely. "You ladies never leave us anything to do but cleanup."

"You're welcome," she and Keely said in unison, then looked at each other and laughed.

As the local law took over the prisoners, Ren came over, took Keely's gun and shoved it in his belt, and then picked his wife up and hugged her. "Jesus H. Christ, sprite. Can't you stay out of trouble?"

"Not my fault." Keely kissed his chin. "So get over it."

Ace came to DJ and rubbed her arm. His touch sent goose bumps over her skin. "You okay?"

She was now ... just because he asked.

After holstering her gun, she moved into him and twined her arms around his waist. His arms immediately went around her. She was tall enough to whisper against his ear without the others hearing. "I'm fine—but I wouldn't say no to a massage—"

Ace stiffened and tightened his hold. They were so close the bulge in his jeans pulsed against her lower abs.

"—and Lacey is refusing to give me one. Did you really mean it when you said you'd—"

He cut off the rest of her question by kissing her full on the mouth—with tongue, lots of deep tongue thrusts alternating with soft and hard nibbles of her lips. Just the way she'd grown to like it.

Ace's kiss was a statement, an act of claiming to the world at large—or at least Ma's world. She had no issues being publically claimed by him.

Relaxing into his warm, strong body, DJ moaned into his mouth, letting him lead her further into the recently discovered arena of passion. He shifted a hand to hold her head still for his kisses. His breath became hers, and hers, his. He slid his other hand down to cup her butt which he then kneaded as he pressed her lower body against his erection.

Countering his moves, she moved a hand to his ass and squeezed. Gawd, she'd wanted to do that ever since she'd seen him in his ski underwear at the cave. Yep, his bottom was as tight as she'd imagined—and biteable.

Ace pulled his lips from hers with a low, deep groan. His breathing harsh, he touched his forehead to hers. "Sugar, you really want me to—"

"Yeah." She sucked on his lower lip and then let it go. "But you'll have to be patient with me. I can't guarantee I won't freak. I haven't been naked"—the cave didn't count since she'd been unconscious for the no clothing part—"in a sexual way … couldn't … not since—"

She buried her face against his neck. Tears of frustration at her inability to talk about her past, at her failure to put it behind her, trailed down her cheek. "Damn."

"Shh, I understand." Ace cuddled her closer and spoke softly into her ear. "We'll start with the massage, lots of making out, and take it from there. If I scare you, you tell me. I'll stop."

DJ nodded, rubbing her cheek over his shoulder. "Your sister says you like me a lot."

"My sister knows me well," he muttered right before he sucked on DJ's ear lobe. She trembled. He'd nibbled on her ear several times over the last five days, and she really liked it. "I like you plus—"

"Ahem." Ren grinned at her from behind Ace.

DJ mentally groaned. Plus what? What had Ace been about to say?

Then she recalled where they were and the circumstances and buried her hot face against Ace's shoulder. He rubbed her back and murmured, "It's okay, sugar."

She shook her head, her curls catching on Ace's five o'clock shadow.

"We're all glad you two are bonding, but—" Keely, held closely to her husband's side, elbowed him and Ren grunted. "Watch the elbows, sprite."

"Well, then don't embarrass DJ."

"Sorry, DJ, but Dan needs to take your statement." Ren looked over his shoulder at the scene in the center of the bar. "And the prisoners were taking in your and Tweeter's actions with way too much interest."

Ace growled. "They can keep their fucking eyes off DJ. And what the heck went down here? They hit on you? Touch you?"

DJ could tell Ace was building up a head of steam, but wasn't sure how much she should tell him. She was fairly certain whatever she said would only make him madder and bloodshed would ensue. He might end up in jail.

She looked at Keely who shrugged and said, "He'll find out eventually. You might as well tell him now."

"Tell me what, Dahlia Jane?" Ace tilted her face up to his. He proved he could read her when he said, "I won't kill them. Dan and Ren won't let me, so fess up."

DJ took in a breath and rushed the words out on her exhale. "They were here to take me and momma back to Mingo County."

Ace's arm tightened and then he pushed her head back to his shoulder. He rubbed his bristly cheek over her hair and muttered, "Like hell they were." He released her and nudged her toward Ren and Keely. After which, he headed toward the militia men sitting on the floor, their hands cuffed behind their backs.

Shit, shit, shit.

DJ caught up with him before Ren could and tugged on his arm. "Ace … you promised."

"I won't kill them, just point out the error of their ways." He leaned over and kissed the tip of her nose. "Let go, sugar."

"No." She dug in her heels and tightened her grip on his arm. "I'm tired. I'm hungry. I never got my scotch. Plus, I strained a muscle"—*not*—"when I put Sasquatch on the floor." She angled her head toward the hairy behemoth, who had a huge cut on his face and a black eye from his rough landing.

"I want to eat and have that drink, give my statement to Dan, then go home and get that massage you promised me."

Ace turned and gripped her upper arms gently. "My home."

It wasn't a question, but she answered, "Yes."

"What about your mom?" He pulled her closer until they touched, chest to chest, stomach to stomach, and then he circled her waist with one arm and lightly ruffled the fingers of his other hand through the curls at the nape of her neck.

Home ... this is what home feels like.

DJ sighed and gave him her weight. "From what the gals said earlier, my momma will be ecstatic."

"I knew I liked Nancy." Ace cracked a grin as he scooped her into his arms and carried her into the restaurant side of the building. He called over his shoulder, "Dan, DJ needs to eat and rest. You have until the time we're done eating to take her statement after that I'm taking her home."

"Hey, macho man, put me down," she muttered against the side of his neck while she marveled at his strength. The only guys who'd ever carried her were men in her unit and that was when they had thrown her over their shoulders to get her out of the line of fire after she'd been shot. "I said I was sore, not crippled."

"Not putting you down. Like carrying you." He held her even more tightly against his chest. "Get used to it."

CHAPTER 11

Tweeter's house, same night

Tweeter opened the door to his house and with a hand on her lower back, ushered DJ inside. She moved so stiffly he was afraid she'd bolt like a fractious mare at any second—and he'd let her. She needed to know she could trust him—anytime, anywhere.

Closing the door, he moved to her side and left enough space so she wouldn't feel crowded. She breathed in rapid little puffs as she slowly scanned his open concept living-dining-kitchen area.

"Well, what do you think?" he asked softly.

She jerked and inhaled sharply before turning toward him. "Think? About what …?" Her voice sounded strained.

His gaze traveled to her hands which were clutched in front of her stomach as if she were protecting her body from attack. From him.

Shit. She'd gone somewhere else in her head. Somewhere not good. Damn, Sean Varney and all the other bumblefucks who'd treated her like a convenient piece of ass.

DJ had been fine after the confrontation at Ma's. She'd eaten and joked with the others and then had calmly given her statement to Dan. But as she'd sat next to him in the back of

Ren's Hummer on the way to Sanctuary, she'd become more and more withdrawn. Part of the tremors now traveling over her body and her pale color could be blamed on adrenaline drop, the rest was sheer fear. Probably fear of what she'd gotten herself into with him. Fear of the unknown. No matter how much she trusted him, how much she'd liked his kisses and touch over the last five days, the evidence was plain that she was now afraid of what he'd do to her … with her.

He vowed to be patient even if it hurt. He needed to show her he wasn't like the other fuckasses she'd come across.

"My place." Tweeter used the reassuring tone he'd used with a much younger Keely when she'd had nightmares. "What do you think of it?"

"It's very nice." Her voice still held a bit of tension. She moved away from him and into the room. Trailing her fingers along the back of his huge leather sectional, she added, "Masculine. Rustic with just enough modern tones to show your tech side."

DJ turned her head and looked at him. The stark fear was gone, replaced with a wariness. Her caution he could handle. Her fear, however, made him want to howl and kill someone.

"It's very you." She shrugged off her coat and tossed it over the back of the couch, then sat down and began to remove her boots.

Tweeter let out a breath he hadn't even realized he held. Okay, she wasn't going to run, but that didn't mean—"DJ, if you aren't ready, you need to tell me. I don't want you to be uncomfortable with me."

DJ scrunched her nose as she concentrated on removing her Army-style lace-up boots. "I know that…" She looked up, her fingers fumbling with the laces.

He was afraid to open his mouth. She might not be turning tail, but they were still a long way from him touching her skin. A massage didn't need to be sexual. Plus, he hadn't planned on moving his stealth courtship to the intercourse stage this soon anyway—just to the heavy petting stage and maybe include some of the cuddling they'd done in the cave.

"I want your hands on me, Ace." She pulled off one boot and turned her attention to the other set of laces. Her high cheek bones blushed rosy pink. "I also want to sleep with you, like we did in the cave." She looked up then. Her facial expression, serious. "That was the best sleep I've had in years. I felt safe with you."

Relief at her words almost drove him to his knees. She also missed the closeness they'd shared in the cave. She trusted him to protect her. She trusted him enough to want to sleep next to him, held in his arms—and that would be all he did until she told him otherwise.

DJ came to him and touched his arm. "Where will we do it? The massage, I mean." She looked so sweetly flustered he fell even more in love with her. She wanted him, but was still a bit shy and unsure.

Despite her age and life experiences, she was still an innocent when it came to personal relationships and sexual intimacy. He needed to keep that at the front of his mind.

DJ needed to be one hundred percent sure she wanted this … wanted him. Because once he claimed her, it would kill him to let her go.

"My bedroom?" Stripping off his jacket, Tweeter picked up her shearling jacket and then moved away to hang both coats in the mud room off the kitchen.

"That was a question, Ace," DJ shouted after him as she sat on his couch. "Don't you know? From what your sister and the girls said, you have light years more experience than I do in these types of matters."

Was that what had put the dread in her eyes earlier? His past sexual experience? Shit, what had those interfering women told her? Keely had to have been behind the "talk." God, had Callie told DJ they'd been each other's firsts? Probably. So, what had DJ thought? And should he ask her what the women had told her?

Combing his fingers through his shaggy hair, he felt as if he were about to walk a mine field, blindfolded.

Tweeter moved toward the couch. Instead of sitting beside her and pulling her onto his lap as he really wanted, he knelt in front of her. He took her cold hands in his and rubbed his thumbs over their backs. She lowered her head and stared at their joined hands. Now, her whole face was blush-pink and she tortured her lower lip with her teeth.

Shy and nervous.

"I want to make sure we're on the same page here." He shook her hands. "Look at me, Dahlia Jane."

She assessed him with a speculative look, then said, "The last weeks … have all been about you teaching me to trust you, haven't they?"

Her question startled him. He'd expected questions about his past sexual encounters, expected to defend his sowing of oats, and she pulled the rug out from under him and went straight to the heart of the matter. His woman had smarts and guts.

"Yes."

His response had her relaxing into his hold on her hands and sighing. Then she surprised him yet again by asking, "Why? I think I know, but I'm not all that good at reading men's intentions toward me. Well, not unless they're trying to kill or hurt me. Why do you want my trust?"

Such honesty and open communication deserved an equally honest and open response. If the strength of his feelings scared her off, then he'd have to start all over again in gaining her trust.

Faint heart never won fair lady.

Tweeter brought her hands to his mouth, then turned them over and placed kisses in each palm. DJ's hands trembled within his light grasp. He squeezed them gently. "I was utterly fascinated with you before you arrived in Idaho. When you strode around the corner of the gas station, the wind blowing your curls, your eyes glowing, the rifle in your hand, and the fierce look of a warrior on your face … I became even more so. After flying with you, training alongside you, climbing with you, sheltering in a cave with you … I've fallen even harder."

DJ said nothing, merely stared at him as if he were speaking in a foreign language she didn't comprehend. Her silence scared him.

Well, here goes nothing—

"Dahlia Jane Poe, I want to be the only man in your life. Want you to be the only woman in mine." He brought her hands to his lips again and kissed the backs of her fingers. "The last weeks have been about more than gaining your trust, they've been about me *courting* you."

DJ gasped and blinked rapidly. Several crystalline tears slid down her cheeks. He felt as if someone had punched him in the gut.

Jesus Christ, asshat, you made her cry.

Tweeter moved one hand and cupped her face to capture the wetness with his thumb. *Hell.* Had his honesty pushed her too far, too fast? Scared her? DJ held his heart in her hands. Just because he'd quickly become used to the idea of a *them,* she might need more time.

"Is it okay? That I'm … courting you?" He faltered. He'd just put his insecurity out for her to see, to stomp on if she chose.

Tweeter couldn't breathe, waiting for her response.

"Yes."

One small, precious word, and he could breathe again. His heart could continue to beat.

DJ rubbed her damp cheek against his hand. "I've met a lot of men during my time in the military." He growled. Her lips twisted upward then straightened as she looked him in the eyes, her expression now solemn. "Many of them were decent men … but, Stuart Allen Walsh, none of them ever came close to breaking through the defenses I'd built after I was raped."

DJ pulled the hand still holding hers to her lips and nibbled at the tips of his fingers. His heart stuttered at the gesture. This was his warrior-woman sweetly teasing him, trusting him to have a care for her affection.

"You, you miracle man, did it in less than two weeks." She leaned forward touching her forehead to his. "So, yes, it's very okay that you're *courting* me."

Tweeter's heart swelled with so much joy he thought it would burst from his chest. "You want to be *mine?*"

"Absolutely." She looked into his eyes and smiled. "Fate, God, karma, or whatever it was that led me to you sure as hell knew what it was doing, because I've never ached for any man as I do for you. Never felt I needed to be near one man so I could breathe and continue living. But—"

Some dark emotion crossed her face, then her expression went blank. She released his hand and pulled away from him. Now, she stared at her hands, clenching and unclenching them in her lap—and, worst of all, she was crying again. No sound, just tears streaking unchecked down her face.

Panic stole his breath and trampled the happiness that mere seconds ago had permeated every cell in his body. What the fuck happened? One moment she was with him, as in really with him, and in the next, she was gone.

What had caused her to retreat and put fear back into her eyes? Because the quick flash he'd seen in her eyes before she'd blanked out had definitely been fright.

"What is it? What are you afraid of?"

"Me." She sniffled. "Not you." She reached a hand toward him.

Tweeter surged off the floor and sat next to her on the couch. Slowly, gently, he pulled her shaking body onto his lap. For several seconds, she held herself stiffly, then let out a whimpering sigh and collapsed against him, allowing him to take her weight.

Thank you, God. Whatever was wrong—she wasn't afraid of his touch, of his comfort.

"Sugar…" He nuzzled the soft blonde curls lying on her forehead. "Tell me what's making you cry. Whatever it is, we'll handle it together. You're not alone anymore."

DJ cried harder at his words and buried her face against his chest. God, she was killing him with her tears, but at least she cried in his arms, where she belonged. He rubbed her back and muttered soothing nonsense as he pressed light kisses to the top of her head.

After several minutes, DJ stopped crying with only the odd hiccup now and then. She lay quietly in his arms, rubbing her wet cheek on his flannel shirt.

He was hesitant to set off another crying jag, but had to know what she thought was so wrong with her that she'd been driven to tears. "Can you tell me what's frightening you? I can't help if I'm in the dark."

She nodded, her face burrowed in his shirtfront. He had to strain to hear her words. "I'm not sure how I'll react to having s-s-sex. I-I-I want you. I d-d-do…" She gripped his shirt as if for emphasis. "…but am afraid I'll fr-freeze … and then you'll be…" She shook her head and burrowed into him even further.

"Be what?" He whispered against the side of her head. "Tell me, sugar."

"M-m-mad." She shuddered, inhaled sharply, and then sniffled some more. "Men get m-m-mad … and get … m-m-mean … when a woman says n-n-no."

Mean? Oh hell no.

Tweeter muttered "fucking fuckwit fuckers" under his breath. Tipping DJ's face up, he gazed into her drenched aquamarine eyes and soothed her flushed, damp cheek with his fingers. In a soft voice, he asked, "Someone other than Sean hurt you?"

She nodded, several more tears trailing down her cheeks.

He growled low in his throat even as he tenderly swiped away the wetness. "I need names, Dahlia Jane."

"Why?" Her forehead creased, and she stared at him with a perplexed look in her eyes.

Tweeter switched from stroking her cheeks to smoothing away the frown lines. Why she asked? Why the hell not?

"So, I can hunt them down. Teach them a lesson. Only mother-fucking, slime-sucking douchebags get angry or physical when a lady says *no* to sex."

DJ released her grip on his shirt front and moved one hand to cradle the nape of his neck. She proceeded to drive him fucking nuts by rubbing her thumb up and down the tense muscles where his neck joined his spine. The comfortee had become the comforter.

He hadn't realized he was snarling until she murmured, "Shh. Calm down, darlin'." He loved when she called him that in her West Virginian drawl. "I handled them. But the sexual harassment happened enough times I swore off attempting to date. Swore off all men ... until *you* came along."

He traced a finger down the elegant line of her nose and then over her lips. "I'm glad you took care of the fuckwits. I'm especially happy to hear you don't lump me in with them."

"You're in a class all your own." DJ hiccuped, a sound between a laugh and a sob. "Don't imagine bad things, Ace. Those other men never got far enough to hurt me physically. Not like..." Her voice trailed off. She visibly shuddered and moved back into Tweeter's arms, then laid her head on his shoulder.

Sean Varney. Tweeter filled in the blank. He had no problem making the fucker disappear permanently. His brothers had also indicated an interest in making that event happen. DJ would never have to know. One day Sean Varney would simply disappear. End of threat.

Tweeter rubbed DJ's back in slow, comforting circles and leaned his head against the top of hers. Her hair and skin always smelled like oranges and vanilla. He wondered if her skin tasted—

Rein it in, Walsh.

She was nervy, reliving past emotional and physical traumas—and he wasn't a beast.

He murmured, "I've been trying very hard to show you not all men are rat-ass bastards."

"And you've succeeded." She sniffed and then snickered. "I even like your macho-male over-protectiveness, just as long as you can accept that I'll want to protect you in return."

"Wouldn't want it any other way. I adore the fact you're a kick-ass kind of woman." He chuckled. "You've met my mother and sister, so you know Walsh men aren't afraid they'll lose their dominant-male-card just because their women are also bad asses."

"Yeah, I think I gathered that." She spoke against his shoulder. "So," and he heard the hesitancy in her voice return, "you aren't going to get mad or throw me out if I can only handle the massage and maybe some kissing and cuddling followed by sleeping—just sleeping—in your arms?"

"I won't get mad—and the only way you'll leave my house tonight is if *you choose* to go." He gave her a gentle squeeze. "Plus, the activities you listed are right in line with my stealth courting plan."

DJ raised her head and arched a brow. Her eyes held amusement. "Stealth courting plan? You had a plan?"

"Yep. Plans are good. We macho brand of geeks like plans." He winked and kissed her nose which had scrunched in an adorable way.

"So, what *exactly* did this plan involve?" she teased.

Tweeter let out a relieved breath that she wasn't angry.

"First step was to gain your trust and friendship in order to demonstrate I'm not like other men you've known. I then planned to move onto kissing and some heavy petting. After that, sleeping together and eventually making love ... at your pace. But the stay in the cave seems to have jumped the line for some of my plans since we slept together for two nights and some kissing has already occurred."

"Heavy petting?" She snicker-snorted in a cute feminine way and was so adorable he had to take her lips in a light kiss that quickly turned hot and heavy with lots of tongue tangling on both sides. They both were groaning by the time he managed to pull away.

"Um," DJ swallowed hard, "I haven't heard foreplay called heavy petting since high school. You did mean with bases and everything?"

Tweeter grinned. "Yep. I want you used to my touch and my body—and the intensity of my desire—before we get to home plate." He brushed soft kisses over her face. "When you see, hear, smell, and feel me, I want you only to think of pleasure."

"Oh my gawd," she breathed into his mouth just as he captured her lips for another kiss. After several seconds, DJ pulled away first this time, her breath coming in rapid gasps. "When I'm ready … have no doubt, you'll be the only man in my head. You've already given me pleasure by caring for me as you do. No man has ever treated me the way you do … as if I'm … special."

What the fuck? She didn't think she was special? What had been wrong with the men in her life?

He couldn't let one more second go by without saying— "You're more than special." He held her close and rocked her. "You're smart, strong, brave, loving, and so damn beautiful you make my heart hurt. On top of that, you're a kick-ass fighter, a crack shot, a damn good chopper pilot…"

CHAPTER 12

If Ace didn't stop being so sweet, DJ might start crying again. Before she'd met him, she hardly ever cried. His words, his care for her—and, yes, the passion he expressed for her in those words and actions—had liberated a gentler, more tender side of her that she'd buried deeply after the rape. As her mother had always told her, actions speak louder than words. Ace's actions screamed his feelings for her.

DJ reveled in Ace's gentle strength as he held her close. Inhaling deeply, his scent calmed her, smoothed over her jagged nerves. His low voice, reciting all the things he liked about her, set her heart pounding. And his kisses, both the soft ones he now pressed against her hair and the earlier more carnal ones, made her quiver and her pussy wet.

The man had wormed his way into her heart and mind—and she was more than happy with him being there. But she was still worried about the physical side of the relationship. No matter how patient he was willing to be, eventually he'd want more. And truth be told, her body wanted him, but could she handle anything more intimate than a massage?

Let's find out, Dahlia Jane.

She shoved lightly against his chest. He let her go, but didn't look happy about it. She got off his lap and sat next to him. Tracing the deep furrows on his forehead and around his mouth, she said, "Stop frowning. You'll get wrinkles."

He captured her finger and kissed it. "I liked you on my lap. Makes it easier to get to the heavy petting part of the program."

Again her body shouted "yes." Her nipples beaded tightly and her panties got damp. Yet her mind wasn't quite there. In her very limited experience, men lost control when they were aroused.

This is Ace ... not any generic man.

Yes, which was the only reason she was at this juncture in intimacy. No other man would've gotten this far.

At least keep your options open.

That was the plan—and the promised massage would be a good way to ease into other pathways to intercourse.

"DJ?" Ace studied her. The crease she'd erased on his forehead had returned. "Where did you go? Are you scared? We can always watch a movie or go to the Lodge and play pool."

"Shh." She placed her fingers over his mouth. "I'm fine right here. Plus, you promised me a massage." She leaned back and pulled her thermal top over her head, leaving her in her sports bra and jeans. "And I'm holding you to that promise."

Ace's gaze fixed on her breasts, or in this case, at what they were encased in.

"What the hell? Why do you bind your breasts like that? I cut one of those torture devices off you when we were in the cave." He stood and traced a calloused finger around the tight edges of her super-reinforced sports bra. The light touch sent a frisson of awareness down her spine and made her clit quiver. "You're cutting off your circulation. That can't be healthy."

DJ choked back a laugh at his description of her athletic bra. Heck, she didn't disagree with him, but until today's shopping trip, these were the only types of bras she owned. Callie'd had the same reaction as Ace and dragged her to the lingerie department at Macy's and made her buy more feminine bras. The ex-model had also promised to get her some nice designer bras, such as La Perla, through her industry contacts.

"Got used to wearing these for extra support in the Army— and to keep from calling unwanted attention to my breasts. Just haven't had the time or inclination to buy new ones." Ace moved closer and pulled her against his body. The erection she'd felt while sitting on his lap seemed to have grown. "If they're uncomfortable, lose the sports bras, please. If any guy says anything about your breasts or makes a move on you, you let me know. I'll handle it."

He slid his hands up her back. "Now, let's get this one off you. It might take me all night to soothe away all the marks this fucking thing put on your body." He tugged the sports bra over her head. As he examined her upper body, he shook his head, a frown on his lips. "Hell, that sucker had to have pulled on your neck and shoulder muscles."

Ace's observations were just another hallmark of his protective nature. He wouldn't even allow inanimate objects to hurt her.

"Yeah, it did. Callie and a clerk helped me pick out some new ones."

"Good for Callie." He massaged the marks on her shoulders.

Feeling a bit awkward, DJ crossed her arms over her breasts and looked anywhere but at the intense look on Ace's face. His expression was a mixture of lingering distaste for the marks the bra had made and pleasure at the sight of her breasts. Testing her mood, she found neither emotion bothered her. Both demonstrated he cared for her.

"Trust me?" Ace sounded uncertain as he focused on her crossed arms.

Startled, DJ looked up and found a worried look in her man's eyes. That wouldn't do. She dropped her arms and moved closer until she could twine her arms around his neck. "I trust you. Just a little shy."

Ace let out a sigh of relief and began to stroke her back, his thumbs kneading the lines caused by the bra. She moaned at how good his hands felt on her naked skin and how the motion caused her 36Ds to rub against his lightly furred chest. His chest hair tickled, aroused, and caused her nipples to tighten even more.

"That feels so good." Goose bumps scattered over her exposed skin. She leaned into him even more.

"It's supposed to." Ace kissed the top of her shoulder. "Let's get you lying down so I can work at these knots along your spine." He trailed a thumb down one side of her spine. She moaned. "I won't touch ... anywhere you don't want me to."

Ace brought his thumb up the other side of her spine. He kissed his way over her shoulder to nuzzle her neck and then hummed, the sexy purr of a large cat. "You feel and smell wonderful."

DJ heard truth in his words, heard the need he suppressed. He was trying so hard not to scare her. She wanted him so badly—her desire increased with each tender touch and caring word—but she was still worried she'd freeze at the wrong moment.

Take one step at a time, Dahlia June. Whatever happens, he'll treat you with care.

Yes, he would. She pulled away from his light grasp and gave him a shy smile, then turned to head toward the bedroom. "I'm leaving my ski leggings on. We'll start with my back and take it from there. If a back massage is all I can handle—"

"Then that's what you'll get. We're going at your pace. I'm looking for a relationship, not a one-night-stand."

His statement alleviated any last twinge of doubt in her conscious mind. And if her subconscious mind reared its ugly head, then Ace would handle it.

Ace followed her, moving as silently as a cat. His dad and brothers had done a good job, teaching him how to stalk quietly. So, she wasn't too surprised when his next words were whispered hotly across one bare shoulder.

"And you'll sleep with me." A statement, not a question.

She thrilled at the hint of dominance sheathed in a velvet glove.

"You can sleep in one of my T-shirts and your long johns. I'll wear my boxers. I want to hold you all night just like in the cave. Deal?"

"Deal," she whispered, but knew he'd heard her when he placed a nibbling kiss on her shoulder. She shivered.

"Thank you for your trust. It means a lot to me." He patted her jeans-covered ass. "Strip to your long johns, sugar. Grab a bath towel to protect the sheets from the oil and then lie on it, face down. I'll warm up some almond massage oil. Any scent you don't like?"

"You have choices?" She looked over her shoulder and blushed at the loving, appreciative look in Ace's eyes.

He grinned. "I have a sister who's into aromatherapy and holistic healing methods. She pushed some of her smelly stuff on me and, damn, if she wasn't correct. The stuff really works."

DJ chuckled. She could see Keely lecturing her brother and probably every other macho male on Sanctuary about the healing properties of herbs and flowers.

"No preferences as to a particular scent. However, I'm still sore and somewhat bruised from the avalanche. Some arnica would be nice."

"Arnica and peppermint—it'll be calming." He turned and left the room. She barely caught the words he muttered—"for both of us."

A rush of happiness warmed the cold, dark places inside where Sean had done a lot of damage. Ace wanted her badly, but he wasn't pressuring her as other men had. It had taken traveling the world and ten years, but she'd finally found the one man who could deal with her intimacy issues.

DJ stripped off her jeans, leaving her ski leggings on. Entering the large and very sumptuous granite-tiled master bath, she pulled a large bath sheet in charcoal grey off a heated towel bar. She re-entered the bedroom and placed it on the king-size bed. Lying on the towel, she moaned at how good the heated terry cloth felt against her tired, achy body. She luxuriated in the warmth for several seconds before propping herself up on her forearms to take in more details of Ace's bedroom.

An accent wall at the head of the simple steel-gray iron tester bed was made up of white and gray rock and was lit by hidden lights from above and below. The bed sheets were pristine white; the blankets and linen bedspread were various shades of gray. The floors were stained cement and had been warm on her bare feet. White rugs she'd once heard someone call "flokati" were placed on each side of the bed and in the small seating area off to the far side of the room.

The seating area was anchored by a stone fireplace centered in the middle of a floor-to-ceiling window wall; the view was of the rustic mountain landscape. The rest of the bedroom walls were dark-stained rough wood that reminded her of the tobacco barns she'd seen in her youth. The room's art and accent colors were all Native American in shades of reds, golds, blues, and greens.

The overall effect was both masculine and artistic. Everything was neat and clean, probably the result of being raised by a Marine.

"Like it?"

She turned her head to find Ace standing at the end of the bed, his gleaming gaze focused on her and nothing else.

"Just like the great room … it's you." Strong and intelligent, but also sensitive and intuitive. She angled her head toward the window. "We gonna put on a show for anyone just happening by?"

Ace's lips twisted upwards as he shook his head. He walked to the side of the bed and picked up what looked like a remote control, then aimed it at the window wall and pushed a button. A slight whooshing noise and blinds made of some sort of translucent, dark fabric came down over the expanse of glass on either side of the fireplace. Another push of a button and the fireplace flamed into life.

"Cool gadgets." She wrinkled her nose. "But people can still see through the fabric, Ace, because I can see out. It's taking every nerve I have to bare this much for you … not sure I can handle anyone else seeing me half-naked with you touching me."

"No worries, sugar. We can see out. No one can see in." Ace swept a hand up and down her back. He hadn't even started the massage yet and already her skin tingled. Once he really got going, she might just die from a surfeit of sensation.

"Never in this world will I let anything, anyone, or any situation hurt or embarrass you. You can take that promise to the bank." He leaned over and placed a kiss at the top of her spine as he traced a finger along the waistband of her leggings. He then used a thumb to knead the knots she hadn't even realized she had at the base of her spine.

DJ collapsed her arms and face-planted into the mattress. "Gawd," she sighed into the towel beneath her, "that feels good."

"I aim to please." He peppered kisses up her spine. The sensation made her giggle. He stole her breath when he placed a light bite at the juncture of her neck and shoulder.

The mattress moved as Ace climbed onto the bed. "I'm gonna straddle your legs so I can get better leverage. Is that okay?"

She smiled. Even now, he took the time to make sure she wouldn't freak out.

"I'm good."

"You're better than good." He pressed his jeans-covered knees against the outside of her thighs.

The sensation of something warm and oily hit her back. The contrast between the heated oil and her air-cooled skin made her shiver. Ace's touch as he began with long and light strokes up and down her back made her moan.

The scent of the peppermint and the lulling motion of Ace's hands almost put her to sleep. Then he got down to work, working out each and every knot along her spine. The feeling was both painful and sublime. She groaned. Sweet Jesus, she could get used to this.

"You hurting?" The question was whispered next to her ear.

"Hmmm. More." She arched upward onto her forearms and looked at him over one shoulder. His face was close. "Kiss me. Then could you work on my cervicals a bit more? My neck is still twinging from being stuck sideways in a hole in the mountain."

He smiled and took her lips in a light kiss which ended all too soon. "You good? I mean, have I triggered—"

She rushed to cut off that line of thinking. "No bad memories. Everything you do makes me feel wonderful." She closed her eyes as she prepared to savor every single second of his touch and closeness. "I'd tell you if it were bad." She plopped face forward on the towel once more. "You've got healing hands, Stuart Allen Walsh."

Even better, he was also healing her from the inside out.

"Neck and cervicals coming up. Let me know if my touch gets too aggressive." Ace began rubbing across the fiber of the muscles at the nape of her neck. It was painful, but it was a good pain. She could almost feel the lactic acid release as he unknotted muscles that had been hard and hurting for days … weeks … maybe even years from stress. Soon, she floated on a haze of what felt like an endorphin release, losing all touch with reality. She might've even lightly dozed.

Then he stopped and she groaned, "No-o-o-o. Feels good."

Ace chuckled and placed another biting kiss on the place where her neck joined her shoulder. "Let's put you to bed, sleepy head."

She opened heavy-lidded eyes and smiled. Ace wore a look of amused indulgence. Looking more closely into his eyes, she found banked desire. Her body reacted. Her nipples pebbled tightly. Her core clutched at emptiness that only he could fill. She wanted him, but was too tired to figure out what to ask for.

"Hey, sugar," he whispered. "Gonna put a shirt on you."

Her eyelids drifting shut, she managed to murmur, "Mmmm."

The sensation of being lifted and something soft and smelling of Ace pulled over her head registered in her foggy brain as floating on clouds. She was lowered to the bed and a light kiss brushed over her lips. She moaned, "Ace…"

"Hush, you're safe in my bed. I promise." Ace's lips nibbled over hers once more. She licked her lips, tasted him, and smiled. "We'll talk in the morning. Night, Dahlia Jane."

The world grew even darker behind her eyelids and she slept.

CHAPTER 13

DJ yawned and stretched as she slowly woke up from one of the best night's sleep she'd had since, well, since she'd last slept next to Ace.

Must be the sense of safety he provides.

She'd had years and years of sleeping in places that were unsafe or had the potential to be. She could really get used to this new experience.

"Morning, sugar." Ace pulled her back against his body so that her back met his front. Because he was only four or so inches taller than her, their bodies meshed perfectly. So much so, her back met his lightly furred chest and her butt made contact with his long, hard, and hot cock.

Ahhh, the much-vaunted morning wood.

Having worked alongside men, she couldn't avoid overhearing about this common biological occurrence. Men seemed to have no shame and liked to talk, and even brag, about their cocks.

Women, or at least the ones she'd met prior to coming to Idaho, didn't talk about their sexual arousal. Keely and her friends seemed to have no problem, talking about their sex lives and about the possibility of sex—hers with Ace—with nary a blush.

DJ had a long way to go before she could sit over lunch and discuss sexual urges and her newfound desire for Keely's brother. Hell, she had a hard enough time talking about sex with him—and he'd inspired all those urges.

Sexual intimacy was not for wussies.

So ... stop being a wuss.

"Morning." She buried the side of her face into her pillow and sought for some courage. Finally, she took a deep breath and mumbled, "Um, doesn't that hurt?" She wiggled her bottom against his erection which reacted by moving and nestling more firmly against the cleft of her butt.

Ace kissed the back of her neck. It was amazing how the mere touch of his lips at the top of her spine awakened the nerve endings at the apex of her thighs. Damn, the man was potent if the mere brush of his mouth could arouse her so quickly.

"If it does, it's not your problem. But I can truly say it hurts a lot less knowing you went to sleep in my bed and woke up in my arms. So all is good. A nice shower and my hand will take care of the problem."

She had a clear mental image of him, all long, lean muscles and naked skin glistening with water with his hand on his erection, taking care of the problem.

No, that was wrong. All wrong. If she was to be his, then he had to be hers. And she needed to start being the woman she wanted to be. She had to gut it up and ask for what she wanted.

"Um ... can I help with ... it? Not the shower, I mean..." She stopped and hid her face in her pillow and mumbled. "... well, you know what I mean."

Way to woman up and spit it out.

Now, that she'd made the offer, as tongue-tied as it was, what would she do if he accepted? She didn't have the first effin' clue about how to help Ace take care of his erection that didn't involve actual intercourse. Her stress titer told her she wasn't ready for home base just yet.

Goddamn, Sean for making her a sexual cripple.

Ace rolled her over until they lay face-to-face. Well, his face was against the top of her head since she was too humiliated to look at him.

He refused to let her hide and tipped up her chin. "Don't be embarrassed. That was the sweetest offer I've ever had." He kissed her heated cheek, then moved his lips over her face until he took her mouth in a deep, tongue-thrusting kiss that soon had her tangling her tongue with his and moaning in the back of her throat.

After a while, Ace groaned and then pulled his mouth from hers. He looked into her eyes and smiled. "That's better. Now the color in your cheeks is from our kisses—and the deer in the headlights look is gone from your eyes."

DJ shook her head and snorted. "Deer in the headlights? Hell yeah, I looked scared, because I was … am. I've never, ever helped a man with his … you know."

"I sort of guessed that." He rubbed his nose alongside hers. "That makes the offer extra-special."

DJ licked her lips. "I never even thought about offering … until you. Would you teach me … how to help with … it?"

Ace chuckled. "Sugar, it's called a cock or a dick or a penis—or in this instance, a full-blown erection."

She nodded. "Okay, can I help you with your full-blown erection?"

Ace touched his forehead to hers and breathed slowly for several seconds. He was going to refuse. For some reason, she felt bereft as if she'd failed as a woman. She was such a loser.

He raised his head and looked her straight in the eyes. "We'll start with you using your hands. That sound okay?"

Relief swept through her like wildfire. He hadn't rejected her, was willing to proceed at her pace and work with her fears and lack of experience. "Yes."

"Good." Ace sat up and pulled her with him. He propped pillows behind their backs to protect them from the cold metal headboard. "Now, sit close to me." She wiggled over until her left side hugged his. "I'm going to pull my cock out, then I'll show you what makes me feel good, okay?"

DJ nodded. Her gaze was glued to his boxers and the prominent bulge lying beneath the plaid flannel fabric. When he shoved his boxers down to his thighs, she took a deep breath and steeled herself against potential flashbacks.

When the past didn't swamp her with frightening memories, she was shocked—and relieved.

"You all right?" Ace cupped her face and angled her head until his fiercely protective gaze captured hers. "Breathe, sugar."

She blew out the breath she'd held and then took another. Covering his hand with hers, she patted it. "I'm fine. I haven't seen all that many cocks up close and personal." She examined Ace's erect penis. The head was somewhere between a red and a purple in color, very much like the plum it resembled. The veins on his shaft were prominent as they pumped blood to his erection. His shaft was thick and seemed really long … she reached with her right hand to test the size, then stopped.

"DJ, if this is bringing back bad memories…"

Leaning into him, she kissed his chin. "Surprisingly, it's not. I'm feeling almost as breathless and excited as the first time I took up a Black Hawk. May I touch it?"

"Sugar, this only works if you touch it." He took her cold hand in his oh-so-warm one and placed it on his cock. His penis jerked within her light grasp. "Go ahead, squeeze it. If I weren't already this erect, you'd start out lighter—but at this point, a firm grip is good."

She gripped it just as she would the Black Hawk's cyclic stick—hard enough to control, light enough to sense and adjust to changes in conditions. Her fingers barely enclosed his breadth. She gave the shaft a small squeeze. The shaft was firm, but responsive. The skin was like hot silk over steel.

"Harder." He placed his hand over hers and forced her fingers tighter around his penis. "There, that's good. I was half-aroused all night with your sweet scent surrounding me. Ready to come ever since your delectable ass snuggled into my cock. Your hand feels so good. But ... we need to take this lesson slowly, or it'll be all over before we've even begun."

Her confidence swelled. She'd taken him to the verge of losing his vaunted control by just being close to him. One thing she'd learned over the last weeks was Ace had an iron will. The fact she could pierce it gave her equal power in the relationship. It was only fair. He sure as hell had cut through all her defenses.

"Okay." She leaned forward and kissed his nipple. His full body shudder delighted her. Good to know his nipples were as sensitive as hers. "What next?"

"Now, you stroke my cock." He guided her hand up and down the seven or so inches—more on the "or so" side—in a slow, steady rhythm. After a couple of minutes of the tip-to-root and back motion, he urged their hands into a slightly faster, jerkier speed.

After a few minutes of the rougher handling, he stilled their hands and then guided hers to her mouth. "Put your thumb in your mouth and get it really wet." His voice was husky and somewhat breathless. Sweat glistened on his skin, clung to the golden-brown hair on his chest. He looked as if he had a fever. "Thumb, Dahlia Jane. Now."

Staring into his eyes, DJ sucked her thumb, tasting the salty muskiness of Ace's penis, and pulled it out. "What—"

"Wetter. My cock head skin is more sensitive than my shaft." He sucked her thumb into his mouth and made it even wetter. Then he took their joined hands back to his erection. "Use your thumb and sweep it over the top of my cock to spread the precum around."

Her thumb back under her control, she massaged the pearly white droplets over the dark purple head.

"Yeah, that's good." His voice was rough. "Now, stroke me again and add a swipe over the top of my cock with your thumb." He showed her what he wanted for two or three repetitions and then let her control the pace.

His breathing had grown harsher. He groaned each time she swirled her thumb over the top of his penis. The tenseness of his body spoke to the strain as he held back his need to take control from her and find completion.

From beneath narrowed lids, his wolfish gaze followed her hand on his erection. The blue of his eyes was no longer ice blue, but was the color of the hottest part of a gas flame.

His increased arousal fed the banked fire in her belly, which had begun to kindle after their first kiss of the morning.

"So fucking good," he growled. "Kiss me. Give me that hot, sweet tongue of yours."

DJ met Ace's mouth halfway. As they kissed, he covered her hand on his penis and urged her to increase the pace. Matching the rhythm of their joined hands, he thrust his tongue into her mouth like an invading army of one. There wasn't a single millimeter he didn't taste ... didn't claim.

With a growing confidence, DJ battled back, using her tongue to conquer his mouth, mark it as her own. He groaned and then inhaled, taking her breath into him, squeezing her hand more tightly around his erection.

Faster and faster their joined hands moved. DJ leaned into his body as if she were a magnet and he was her true north. As long as she had him in her life, she'd never be lost.

Suddenly, Ace stiffened and grunted, a long, low, nearly painful sound. For a split-second, their bodies—nothing in the universe—moved. Then he roared his climax into her mouth. He pressed their joined hands even harder around his cock, moving them faster and more roughly on his jerking penis.

Warm, silky fluid flowed over their fingers as his body spasmed and shook. And all the while, he kissed her as if she were the only thing holding him to earth.

If DJ could've bottled the feeling of joy she felt at that moment, she would have.

When he stopped coming, he broke off the kiss and gasped out, "God ... that was so fucking good." He hugged her to him and placed a sweet, almost innocent kiss on her swollen mouth. "The only thing better ... would be coming deep inside you."

His tender actions, his earthy words caused her body to throb, to clench, seeking something she wasn't sure her mind could handle yet.

Ace cradled her hand and gently rubbed the backs of her fingers with his thumb. "Was I too rough? Did I bruise your hand? Your fingers cramping?"

She pulled her hand from his and wiped it on the sheet, then wriggled her fingers. "My hand is fine ... the sensation feels as if I'd gripped my Hawk's cyclic stick in rough weather. Although your penis is much more responsive."

Ace chuckled. "Good to know."

She reached for the back of his head and ruffled her fingers through his hair. He sighed and leaned into her touch like a cat being petted. "Didn't that hurt? I mean, we were sort of rough there at the end."

"It was perfect," Ace said. "I haven't come so hard from a hand job in ... well, never."

She leaned against his arm. "So, I really did okay?" Yeah, she was feeling a tad bit insecure and somewhat adrift.

Ace hugged her. "If it had been any better, I'd have expired on the spot—but I'd have died a happy man. How did touching me, watching me come, make you feel? Anything scare you or—"

"No, nothing was scary once we got started. I liked making you feel good. It made me feel womanly and—" She hid her face against his neck and inhaled his deliciously sexy scent as she tried to explain the feelings that sizzled through her body, making her skin sensitive and her pussy ache.

"And what?" Ace murmured against her hair.

She looked up and found in his patient, loving gaze the strength to voice her needs. "I think watching you come made me horny."

Ace's eyes, mouth, his whole face smiled at her words. "That's a good thing, sugar. Now, what can I do to help *you*?"

She raised her mouth to his and whispered against his lips, "Do you have a suggestion?—Because I've never really had these exact sensations before."

"Never? Not even with your own fingers or a toy?" Ace asked.

She examined his face and was relieved to see no judgment, just curiosity. He always listened to every word she uttered with an intensity that was flattering. He'd demonstrated in actions and words again and again that he wanted to *know* her. Sometimes his regard was slightly scary, as if he knew even more about her than she did.

"I tried once with my fingers." She wrinkled her nose in disgust. "I wanted to see what all the hoopla was about, but got nowhere. In fact, it hurt."

"You were probably too tense. Too dry." Ace petted her back and cuddled her even closer.

She melted under his tender touch. He always made her feel better about herself, whether it was treating her as an equal during training or now as he took such care easing her into intimacy.

"How do you feel now? Is talking about finding your own pleasure making you tense? Erasing the feelings of arousal?"

DJ took a moment to assess her body … her feelings. "I feel as if I'm missing something. It's as if I need to release pressure, but don't know where the release valve is."

He kissed her nose. "I think I can help find that release valve. Trust me?"

"Yes." She twined her arms around his neck. "You've never let me down yet."

"And I'll try never to disappoint you." His expression was solemn as he made what sounded like a vow. "So ... why don't I start with some heavy petting to help you gain your release? We can do it in the shower where your skin will get all sorts of other stimulation." He winked, then let her go and got out of bed.

Ace came around to stand by her side of the bed and offered a hand. She took it and let him help her up. His hands went to the shirt she wore and paused.

Again he gave her time to make the decision to take the next step. Her body wanted him, so there was no decision to make. She couldn't take a shower and have him finger her to orgasm in her clothes, and she really wanted him to give her relief.

DJ let out a breath, covered his hands, and helped him pull the shirt over her head. She shimmied out of the tight ski leggings herself. She stood less than a foot away from him and watched as his gaze burned as he took her body in from head to toe—as a sensual smile curved the lips she loved to kiss.

"Beautiful ... you are so beautiful. Want to help me get rid of my shorts the rest of the way?"

DJ nodded. Ace brought her hands to his boxer briefs and together they pulled them down over his hips. She took a step back and eyed his nudity. She hummed in the back of her throat. Everything about his leanly muscled body shot sparks of awareness over hers. From his perfectly formed chest and abs with the light smattering of golden-brown hair to his long legs. He even had nice feet. He could be a cover model for *Fitness Monthly*.

As DJ did a return trip up his body, his penis stood at attention once again and seemed to reach for her.

"Ignore my cock. It has a mind of its own where you're concerned." He reached for her hand. "The way I feel right now, I'll probably spontaneously combust while getting you off. No touching needed."

"Really?" She intertwined her fingers with his and let him tug her toward the bathroom. He did that a lot—held hands with her even when they'd cuddled on the Lodge's great room couches and watched TV, he'd take one of her hands in his and hold or massage it. She liked the fact he seemed to need to claim even that small part of her.

"Yeah." He let go of her hand and reached in and turned on the shower. "My blood pressure went up merely seeing you naked. If this keeps up, I might have that heart attack I barely avoided when you helped me get off."

"Buck up, Ace." DJ snorted delicately. "You're much stronger than that."

"Don't know." He leaned over and held her head still for a kiss, a brushing of lips that had her hungering for more. She'd begun to crave the deep, eating kisses he'd given her over the last week. "You should be classified as lethal."

She loved that they could be together like this—him teasing her, her teasing back. She was one hundred percent comfortable with him. Even with last night's and this morning's sex play, the nudity, and the promise of more of both in the shower, she wasn't afraid. Though she would admit to being a bit nervous of the unknown. Yet, with Ace as her guide, she expected it would all be wonderful.

I am one lucky woman.

"DJ, look at me." She met his light blue gaze. "If you have a problem with anything, you call a halt."

"I will. I'm all right ... really ... just a little anxious." She rubbed a hand up and down his firmly muscled arm. "But I do need you ... only you."

His smile promised pleasure. "Then let's see if I can make you scream."

Ace scooped her into his arms.

She squealed and then laughed. "Put me down. I'm too heavy."

"Don't disrespect your man's strength, woman." He gently set her on her feet in front of one of the body jets and under one of the rain shower heads. With a wide grin on his face, he flexed his muscles for her.

Giggling, she placed a hand on one of his biceps and squeezed. "Nice guns. Glad to see my man is up for the job of lugging me around."

He leaned over and lightly bit her lower lip. "Let's see what else I can get up to. Turn around and lean back against me."

DJ turned and allowed Ace to pull her against his wet and warm body. His cock twitched against her upper buttocks. She laughed.

"What's funny?" Ace nipped her ear lobe.

"Your cock tickled me."

"My cock, like his master, adores you and wants to be as close as he can get to you," he growled. He placed an arm around her torso right under her breasts and the other, lower down around her hips. "Now, I'm gonna play with your breasts and your pussy. All you have to do is let me take your weight and feel. If I hurt you or—"

DJ took the hand near her breast and placed it over her nipple and then took his other hand and pressed it to her aching pussy. "I'll tell you if I get scared … but I won't. The only man in this shower is you. I want you to take this neediness away and give me my first orgasm."

"Thank you for your trust." He nibbled along her shoulder and an almost electrical sensation swept across her skin and raced to her clit at the speed of light.

Who knew her whole shoulder was an erogenous zone? But then everywhere Ace touched her seemed to light a fire in her belly and set her skin ablaze. Her body had been ready for this next stage since their time in the cave. It had simply taken her head awhile to get in the game.

After the shoulder nibbling, Ace started teasing her. A sweep of a thumb over her nipple. A tracing of a finger around and around her labia, always avoiding her clit which seemed to swell and throb more with each pass. Every touch made her tremble. After a minute or so, she felt the urge to move to meet his touches.

When he withdrew his fingers from her highly sensitized areas, she moaned, "Ace…"

"Did I hurt you?" His breath warmed her ear and made her shiver delicately.

"No…" He was taking it slow, gradually teasing a response from her as promised, but she wanted—"More. Ace, I need more."

"Like this?" He licked the side of her neck as he took a tightly budded nipple between his finger and thumb and pinched it.

The sensation rocketed straight to her core. He pressed a finger on the clitoral hood and wiggled it. She arched as a shot of molten pleasure had her squeezing her inner muscles. She sensed an orgasm was close, but still tantalizingly out of reach. "Oh my gawd. Do that again."

He did.

This time, the sensation was even stronger. Her insides clutched at … nothing. She needed something, anything, solid to help her over the edge. But she wasn't ready to accept his penis … yet.

Still, she ached and wanted—"More I need more." She panted the words and then turned her face to his, seeking his kiss, his tongue. At least her mouth wouldn't be empty.

Ace growled, "Oh fuck yeah." He took her mouth in a ravenous kiss as he increased the stimulation on her nipple, alternating between fondling and pinching. He plucked at her clit which seemed to have increased its size threefold.

DJ sucked on his tongue and moaned. She was drowning in the pleasure of Ace's taste, his scent, his touch. The sensory overload pushed her to an even higher peak, but still her body strove for a release that was always slightly out of reach.

She broke away from their kiss and groaned. "I can't … need …"

"I know what you need." He pulled his fingers away from her clit.

She cried out "no" and reached for his hand, meaning to pull it back to where the promise of pleasure lay.

He hugged her. "Shh … trust me."

DJ watched through a pleasure-induced haze as Ace adjusted the body jet and then turned her body, her clit, to meet the pulsing stream. When he added his fingers back to the mix, she went to her toes and braced her head back against his shoulder. "Ahhh, so good. Please … please…"

"Let go, sugar," he whispered against her cheek. "I've got you."

He spread her pussy lips and exposed her clit directly to the pulsating rhythm of the water and added extra pressure to the side of her swollen bud with a finger. She inhaled and, for several seconds, hung on a precipice, then fell. "Ace! F-f-fuck. Oh gawd, oh gawd … so good. Ahh. Fuck. Ace…"

As the pleasure swept over her like a training thunderstorm, she lost the ability to do anything but moan and feel. Her body shuddered out-of-control, and Ace anchored her in his strong arms. Her knees turned to jelly, and Ace didn't let her fall. As the torrent of pleasure began to wane, Ace fed the tempest anew with his fingers on her pussy, with biting, nibbling kisses along her shoulder and then up her arched neck.

When the water and touch on her pussy had become too much, Ace sensed it and turned her away from the jet to face him. Pulling her close, he urged her head onto his shoulder and petted her back, helping her come down.

"That was…" No words could really describe what it had been like, how it made her feel, or even what it meant to her, so she settled for. "…amazing."

"Good." He rubbed his cheek over hers. "This might sound abrupt—but I want you to move in with me. I promise not to push you any faster on the sexual front, but I want to be with you as much as possible. I want to sleep next to you every night and wake up to you every morning. I want to give you *amazing* every damn day until you're ready for more."

"Move in?" DJ managed to squeak out.

Just the thought of being with Ace everyday as they'd been last night and this morning made her deliriously happy. The weeks since she'd met him had been some of the happiest of her life. To take that joy to the next level, to live together as a couple—something she'd never even thought a possibility before—well, she really wanted it, but—"What about my momma … and the others? What will they think?"

"Nothing. We're adults." He hugged her tighter. "Besides, you already know my sister and the others won't be shocked—and Nancy likes me."

"Yeah, she does." DJ snickered. "If I move in with you, she'll start planning a wedding and knitting baby blankets."

"Fine with me." Ace began to wash her body as if he'd done it every day..

She let him care for her, drying her off and running a comb through her hair, and thought about his easy acquiescence to the idea of marriage and babies. Oddly enough, she wasn't freaked out, but she also wasn't ready to commit to either—just yet.

The cautious, cynical side of her nature, forged in the crucible of the night she was raped and tens years of flying into war zones, raised its ugly head and reminded her things could change for the worst in an instant. Living together for a while was a smart idea.

"You've been really quiet. If you aren't ready to move…"

She cut off his words with a kiss. "I'm moving in."

Ace's smile was brilliant as he returned the kiss. "Good. Let's finish getting dressed and then go grab some breakfast at the Lodge." He nibbled a trail along her jaw and to her ear lobe. "I don't know about you, but I seemed to have worked up an appetite."

CHAPTER 14

Morning, February 16th, the Lodge

DJ felt a tad bit self-conscious walking into the Lodge kitchen with Ace. But no one said a thing, not even her mother. Though there was a gleam in her eyes that portended a future conversation.

"Sugar, you sit here." Ace pulled out a chair at the large round nook table and seated her. "I'll bring you some food. What do you want?" He rubbed a hand over her shoulder and then massaged the back of her neck with his thumb as he waited for her answer.

Sensual awareness prickled over her skin still sensitized from the orgasm he'd given her with the same hand a mere hour ago. No man had ever paid such solicitous attention to her. She'd definitely been around all the wrong sorts of men to this point in her life. The way Ace treated her made her feel feminine and truly desired, even as he still respected her intelligence and strengths. He was proving to be a keeper with every second that passed.

But am I woman enough to seal the deal?

Only time would tell. Ace was being gentle with her now, but what if she couldn't ever—

"DJ," Ace whispered. "Why did you just tense up?"

She shifted in her chair to face him. Ignoring the sudden silence in the room, and she was sure the intent looks of the occupants, she grabbed his hand, pulled him closer, and then whispered, "Please be patient with me ... I'm a fricking hot mess because of—"

Ace brought her hand to his lips and kissed the backs of her fingers. "I'm not going anywhere. When I see something I want, I can wait. And, Dahlia Jane, I want you very much. Believe that."

"I'll try." She managed not to sob as relief overtook her.

"Don't try—do." He kissed her forehead. "Now, what would you like to eat?"

"Eggs. Bacon. Whole wheat toast." Climaxing seemed to have made her very hungry.

"You got it." He squeezed her hand. "Pour me some orange juice, please. I'll be right back."

Glad to have something to do, she pulled the pitcher of juice toward her and carefully poured two glasses and managed not to spill a drop even though her hand trembled.

Trembled? Her hand never shook. She could be in the middle of a war zone, flying her Hawk into surface-to-air fire, and her hand never faltered on the cyclic stick. But then, when she flew, she was in known territory and total control.

Being with Ace had her exploring a new world. Emotions she'd locked down and encased in ice were now loose. She felt a tad bit lost and out-of-control. The feelings were scary and exhilarating.

"DJ."

DJ turned toward Callie who sported a big smile. "Good morning, Callie. You look beautiful."

Not that the woman could ever look ugly. But between the morning sickness from hell and missing her husband, she had looked pale and tired since DJ had met her.

"I'm feeling beautiful, because I'm happy," Callie said. "My nausea seems to have disappeared overnight, and Risto is returning to Sanctuary today. He's missed me so much he's finally agreed to let me go back to Michigan with him."

Callie's husband had been worried about leaving his pregnant wife alone at SSI-East and a target for SSI's enemies. From the way Callie handled a gun, DJ thought the man was wildly over-protective. Yet all the SSI operatives with spouses were like that, even Ace was super-protective in his own way. Surprisingly, it didn't bug her as much as it might have with some other man.

"I know that was bothering you. I'm happy for you." She smiled at Callie.

"Here's your food, sugar."

DJ turned to look at Ace who placed her plate in front of her and then sat. She realized that even in the short time of knowing him, she'd miss him if they were apart for too long.

He wants me to live with him.

Just the thought filled her with delight and hope for the future. With Ace, she might have a chance at a normal family life, something she'd never even thought possible.

DJ wasn't ready to share her burgeoning feelings with anyone yet. But it looked as if that train had already left the station. She noted Callie looking from her to Ace and then back again. Callie's expression was one of happy approval.

"Um, Paul and Loren are stationed at SSI-East, right?" DJ asked no one in particular, hoping to shift attention away from her and Ace's new closeness.

It was Keely walking in with baby Riley and Ren who answered, "Yep. My Navy SEAL brothers wanted to be near water." Keely visibly shuddered. "Upper Peninsula Michigan has some damn cold water, even in the summer. Though Risto's island in the Cisco Chain of Lakes is beautiful. His grandfather was a famous architect, and the house he built there is amazing."

"You've been there?" DJ kept the new conversational thread going.

"Yep." Keely smiled across the table at her brother. "Tweetie and I helped Risto, who's no computer slacker, install a smaller version of the Bat Cave and then wired his island for the same 3-D security measures. This summer, we plan to help Big Earl wire his properties in Osprey's Point, the town closest to the island."

"You'll go with me, of course," Ace said, turning toward DJ. "You can hang with Callie and Tessa, Earl's wife. Earl has a helicopter I'm sure he'll let you fly."

Okay, so Ace wasn't going to let her, or anyone else, ignore the two-hundred-pound elephant in the room, also known as their more intimate relationship. He was sharing in actions and words they were a "couple"—and sharing it with the people closest to them.

Contentment swelled within her heart and soul. Tears of happiness welled in her eyes. She concentrated on buttering her toast as she struggled to regain control of her roller-coaster emotions.

"That sounds like fun." DJ swallowed hard and attempted to match Ace's nonchalant, forthrightness about their relationship. "Callie, wasn't Tessa the model you did those perfume ads with?" Callie had brought it up on the shopping trip when DJ was buying perfume. "You were light and she was dark."

"Yes, that's right," Callie said. "Tessa met Earl at my wedding to Risto. I'll give you all the details later. But let's just say, they're perfect for one another. She's like another sister to me—just like Keely, Elana, Lacey, and you are."

"Really?" DJ couldn't help it. The happy tears she'd managed to control earlier began to fall. And there wasn't a dang thing she could do about it.

Ace placed his arm around her shoulders and tugged her, chair and all, closer to him. He handed her a napkin. "Blow."

She took the napkin and wiped her eyes, then blew her nose.

"I'll take that." Her mother stood on her other side. DJ

handed the balled up tissue to her and whispered thanks. "I like him, baby girl."

"Me, too." DJ sniffed.

Her mother kissed her cheek, then patted Ace's shoulder before heading back to the kitchen where Scotty hugged her and then kissed her cheek. She looked so happy and relaxed in Scotty's arms, more so than DJ had ever seen her. The tears DJ had managed to halt began to fall again, but now they were tears of happiness for her mother.

DJ hid her face in Ace's shoulder. She hadn't realized until that moment exactly how much her mother had been worried about her, how much damage Sean, his father, and her own father had caused them both, and how heavy the burden of fear and hate had been all these years.

"DJ, you're killing me here." Ace rubbed his cheek over the top of her head. "You want to leave? Or, do you think you could try to eat something?"

She pulled away from his hold. He seemed reluctant to let her go, but he did. His concerned expression almost had her crying even more.

Enough with the water works, Dahlia Jane. You're worrying your man.

"I'm fine. Just hungry." She wiped her eyes with the back of her hand and gave him a smile, then chanced a glance around the table. Ren, Keely, and Callie looked at her with a mixture of concern and affection. "Hey, guys. I'm okay … really. Seems I'm catching up on all the crying I haven't done in the last ten years. Just ignore me."

The last time she'd really let go was the day after she'd been raped. It was that same day she'd vowed never to let anyone close enough to hurt her again.

"Then it's about time to let it all go," Ren said in a matter of fact tone. "Although I relate to Tweeter's feelings. I can't handle it when Keely or Riley cries. I want to fix whatever caused their unhappiness—or kill someone."

DJ chuckled when Ace growled out an "amen." She shoulder-bumped him. "Thanks, Ace. I'd feel the same way if someone hurt you and made you sad."

"I know you would. You're a warrior—my warrior." He tucked a curl behind her ear, then trailed his finger down the side of her neck. She felt the touch all the way to her clit. The man packed a sexual punch.

Ren cleared his throat. "DJ, you need to be at the planning meeting for an op we've been hired to do. Tweeter convinced me you're mission-ready. Although, it didn't take much persuasion." He winked. "We're waiting on Risto and Conn Redmond to arrive, then we'll start the briefing."

DJ turned toward Ace. "Really?"

He nodded. "You're perfect for this op. You'll see why when Keely presents it to the rest of the team. Trust me?"

"Of course I do." A warm glow suffused her body. He'd gone to bat for her.

Since she didn't know yet what the mission entailed, and it was obvious Ren wasn't going to let anything leak while her mother was in the vicinity, she asked the next most obvious question, "Who's Conn?"

Callie answered, a big smile on her face. "Conn is SSI's main contract operative based in South America. He also runs a safe house in Cartagena used by SSI operatives and various other intelligence agency assets. He was a godsend to Risto and me when I had to call on SSI to help me get out of Colombia safely."

DJ had heard some of Callie's story on the shopping trip, but hadn't caught the man's name. "He's a former Marine, right?"

"Yes," Ren said. "I worked with a lot of Marines when I was a Navy SEAL. I'm always open to hiring a former Marine, and Keely's dad and brothers send a lot of them my way."

"Plus, your brother's a former Marine," Keely pointed out.

Ren snorted. "Well, I couldn't help it that the Navy didn't want him."

"I'm so telling Trey you said that," Keely teased.

"It's nothing I haven't said to his face, sprite." Ren tipped Keely's face up for a kiss that appeared to involve a lot of tongue. Riley, sitting on his mother's lap, patted both their faces as if he wanted in on the action. His parents broke off their kiss and began peppering their adorable son with lots of loud smacking smooches.

Something warm unfurled inside her heart. She wanted that kind of love in her life—but only with the man sitting beside her. She turned and found Ace staring at her with an expression of such longing that she knew he was thinking along the same lines.

"It'll happen," he murmured in her ear. "One day at a time. We'll get there."

She turned her face and brushed her lips over his. He inhaled sharply then took her mouth in a searing kiss. She wasn't sure how long they'd been kissing when her mother stood over them and said, "Eat, children. Food's getting cold."

They broke apart and in unison said "Yes, ma'am," then began to laugh as they turned to their food. Cold food had never tasted so good in her whole life.

———

THE PLANNING OP TOOK PLACE in the library, a room DJ had used a lot since moving to Sanctuary. The decor was warm and cozy with the smell of lots and lots of books. The floor-to-ceiling shelves on three walls were filled with all sorts of books. She loved to pick one at random and then sit in a leather chair facing the fourth wall which was made entirely of glass and overlooked the mountain valley. She'd read until life intruded.

Today, the normally quiet-as-a-tomb setting was filled with the buzz of people. Ren and Keely sat on one of the leather couches placed perpendicular to the fireplace, which broke up one wall of bookshelves. Next to them was Ren's brother Trey; he held his nephew Riley who'd fallen asleep after his breakfast. On the sofa facing them sat Quinn Jones, Ren's right-hand man, and his wife Lacey plus Price Teague.

Tweeter led DJ to a club chair facing the fireplace then seated himself on the chair's arm. He placed his hand on her shoulder and gently rubbed as if he could sense her nervousness at her first mission planning session.

"We're still waiting on Callie, Risto, and Conn." Ren laughed. "That might take awhile. Risto dragged Callie off somewhere to interrogate her about her health and well-being. Conn is grabbing a quick breakfast. So feel free to get a drink from the table Scotty and Nancy set up for us."

"Do you want something?" Ace gave her a smile that she'd come to recognize was meant for her alone—it was intimate and loving.

"A diet cola, please." She smiled back.

"Be right back. Save my spot." He tapped the arm of the chair.

She watched him walk toward the window wall where a sideboard looked to have every kind of cold and hot beverage one could want plus cookies and muffins. Her breathing hitched and her heart fluttered as she realized this man was hers. Now, all she had to do was kick her past in the butt and conquer her remaining fears.

A mechanical sound drew her attention. The painting over the fireplace disappeared and a large video monitor appeared. Audio-visual? Well then, they must already have some intel to share since they had visuals. She wondered what kind of contract job they'd send Ace on. She hoped it was a soft, eyes-on-the-ground intel mission and not in the middle of a war zone. If it was the latter, she was happy she'd be there to cover his so-fine ass. She had a vested interest in Ace—apart from being his SSI teammate—in keeping him alive and healthy.

Chatter at the entrance to the library had her turning her head toward the sound. Callie entered the room clasped against a tall, superbly fit, dark-haired man who had danger and Marine written all over him. While he rubbed the slight baby bump she sported, Risto looked at his wife as if she were crucial to his very existence.

Next to them was a tall, tough-looking, shaggy-haired blond male. His dark tan set off light eyes that were framed in long, dark lashes. He was a little bit taller than Risto and looked as if he could hold his own in a fight. He also carried himself like a Marine. This had to be Conn Redmond.

Conn looked around the room and nodded at the others in turn. His sharp gaze then singled her out. He smiled and headed her way and had almost reached her when Ace appeared at her side and sat on the chair arm.

"Here's your drink, sugar." Ace's narrowed gaze was fixed on Conn. "Hey, Conn. Meet DJ Poe. She's taken. Find your own woman."

DJ didn't know whether to be affronted by Ace's caveman pronouncement or amused. Conn, it seemed, chose to be amused. He laughed.

"The good ones are always gone before I even get a chance to put my oar in the water." He smiled and winked at her, his teeth blinding white against his tropical tan, then offered his hand. "Nice to meet you, DJ. If the nerd doesn't treat you right, I have a lovely *casa* in Cartagena that needs a woman's touch."

DJ had the impression he'd used that line before.

Ace growled low in his throat. "Fuck off, Redmond."

She smiled at Conn as he gently shook her hand. "I appreciate the offer, but as Ace said, I'm currently taken."

Ace grumbled just loud enough for the three of them to hear, "Permanently taken."

Conn laughed again. "He's a lucky man." He let her fingers slip from his, then pulled up a chair and sat next to Ace.

"As tempting as it might be to eliminate the competition, I promise to cover his ass while we're working the op in Belize."

"Thanks, asshat." Ace slapped the back of Conn's head—hard enough for the man to wince even as he chuckled.

"Belize?" She straightened and unconsciously placed a hand on Ace's thigh. He covered her hand and held it in place as if he wanted the connection as much as she did. "What's happening in Belize? I haven't seen anything in the State Department updates." As part of an SSI operative's on-going duties, she read the daily briefings on what was going on in the world.

Belize, the former British Honduras, and still a British Protectorate, was a diver's paradise and an eco-tourist's dream vacation spot. There might be some drug activity—that was everywhere these days—but she'd be very surprised if there was any on-going terrorist activity in the small country.

Before either Ace or Conn could respond, Ren stood and addressed the room's inhabitants. "It looks as if we're all here. Vanko and Elana won't be attending. Elana seems to have caught a stomach virus on top of her morning sickness, and Vanko had to give her an IV to hydrate her."

Lacey inhaled sharply. "I hadn't heard. I'll go over and see if I can help."

Ren motioned her to stay put. "Vanko has it covered. Though this underlines the fact we need a doctor living closer to Sanctuary than the small, part-time clinic in Elk City and the hospital group in Grangeville."

"I'm working on it," Trey muttered, followed by a growl of frustration. "Fee will be here soon, if I have anything to say about it."

Keely had told DJ about Price's sister Fiona, who was an emergency room physician, currently working off her medical student loans in a small clinic in New Mexico. Trey had fallen for Fee when she'd visited Sanctuary after escaping an abusive relationship with a fellow physician in Detroit. Abusive assholes were everywhere, it seemed.

"Amen to that," Price muttered. "I don't like my sister living in that border town. Too much cartel business on both sides of the border."

Trey grunted, a dark look on his face. "Fee was actually happy to see me on my last monthly visit. Something's going on, but she wouldn't share." He took a sip of his coffee and frowned. "She even agreed to go out on a date on my next visit."

Fee and DJ had a lot more in common than the sexual violence in their past. Obviously, a stealth courting approach wasn't uncommon among the macho males of SSI. Poor Fee probably hadn't even realized yet what Trey was doing. Ace's wooing had been more effective and quicker than Trey's since DJ was close at hand.

A look of angry frustration crossed Trey's face. "I want to go back to Detroit and beat the shit out of the mother-fucker who hurt her again."

"You and me both," Price snarled.

"Hurry the wooing up, Trey," Keely said. "I have the Feds authorization to shift her student loan repayment commitment to our area of Idaho. All we have to do is set up a clinic on Sanctuary land with access to the state highway so locals can also utilize it."

Trey shot a grateful look at Keely. "Thanks, little sister. With the way you gals are getting pregnant, we need a doctor close by."

Ren coughed. "Okay, people, enough catching up. Let's get started. Keely will present the op since it was her contact at NSA who hired us. Conn, there've been some changes since I last briefed you."

"Changes?" Conn asked. "What fucking changes?"

Ace snorted. "You don't have to be my boy toy while I'm undercover. DJ will be my arm candy. You'll provide backup.

"Boy toy? I thought you were gonna be my bitch. We flipped for it, if I recall." Conn managed to avoid Ace's head slap this time. "I was so looking forward to sharing your bed, Tweeter."

"Never would've happened." Ace gave him the finger.

Conn didn't seem too upset about DJ being added to the team. She was sure of it when he leaned over to look past Ace and shot her a jaunty grin. "Guess I get to cover *both* your asses in Belize. Welcome to the team." He paused and his expression turned all business. "What exactly is your mission background?"

"Classified," DJ, Ace, and Ren said virtually at the same time.

Conn nodded. "That's good enough for me. Anyone who has a classified background—and don't we all?—is more than ready for this type of HUMINT mission." He turned to Ren. "Hell, boss, this will work even better. The men will be so busy looking at her, they wouldn't notice if Tweeter walked off with all their hard drives."

"Hard drives?" DJ looked at Ren, then Ace. "We're going to steal someone's computer hardware?"

"No. Conn was trying to be amusing," Ace frowned at the man, "and he failed abysmally. Keely will explain all. Conn was right about one thing. You'll be a big distraction, and it'll allow me to do my job without the bad guys breathing down my neck."

"And Ace's job is … what exactly?" DJ turned her attention toward Ren and Keely, who'd patiently waited with looks of amusement on their faces as Conn and Ace had traded quips and insults. Obviously, private security mission briefings were done in a much more relaxed environment than what she was used to in the military. She quite liked the give-and-take among the team and the teasing that still managed to convey respect.

"Right. Some mission background first," Keely said. "NSA has seen increased Dark Net activity recruiting hackers to compete in a hack-a-thon. The ultimate winner will then be offered a job by a reclusive, shady Brazilian businessman by the name of Sergio Manuel Lazaro a.k.a. Oraio. Oraio was formerly a minor player in South and Central American drug and weapons trafficking."

From what little DJ knew, the Dark Net was a private network which was utilized by people who wished their business dealings to be anonymous. To access parties on this shadow network, a person had to know the specific IP address. Lots of really bad people used the Dark Net. If this Oraio was recruiting a hacker in this milieu, he was up to no good.

"I take it Oraio's no longer a minor player?" DJ said.

"Exactly. In recent months, his increase in weapons sales in Central and South America has gone up five hundred percent. That's what bothers the intelligence community," Ren said. "Almost overnight, Oraio has become a player of gargantuan proportions. The DIA, CIA/NCS, Interpol, MI-6, and Central and South American intelligence agencies want to know—why now? NSA has been tasked to gather intelligence since Oraio's recruitment of hackers is in their wheelhouse. Later, we'll hand out mission dossiers so you can read the analyses from the different agencies looking into his past and present activities. Right now, Keely will show you the main players identified as working for Oraio."

Keely clicked on a remote and an image appeared on the screen above the fireplace of a red-haired, light-skinned male. He wasn't handsome, nor was he ugly. He was an everyman until a person looked into his smiling eyes and spotted the cold calculation hiding behind them.

"This man has been Oraio's front man ever since the Brazilian began his legal and illegal businesses. His name is Declan O'Riley. He's an Irish national with former IRA ties. Prior to working for Oraio, he often acted as a broker for other drug and arms dealers in every Third-World hellhole there is. He's survived this long, because he's lethal and cunning. Do not underestimate him. O'Riley has been taking the reservations and vetting the contestants for the hacking contest."

"So, Ace has been accepted to be in the contest?" DJ asked.

"Yes." Keely grinned. "They jumped at the chance to get the infamous Phantom a.k.a. Erik Slade to play with the other hackers."

"Phantom?" DJ looked at Ace whose cheeks had flushed.

"I'm considered one of the top hackers in the world and the Dark Net is my kingdom. Most hackers would love to say they went up against me and won. Most bad asses want my skills on their side. But I've established a reputation of being very choosy for whom I hack."

"This is what you do in the Bat Cave?" DJ asked.

"Yeah, when I'm not assigned to specific COMINT contract jobs or on-the-ground missions."

DJ nodded. "Okay, so we go to Belize, and Ace plays hacking games with the other hackers. What's his exact mission objective? Or, is this a fishing expedition? Do you expect the elusive Oraio to show up?" So far the mission sounded rather innocuous, even with the specter of O'Riley in the background.

"More of a fishing expedition," Ren replied. "The NSA wants any and all information about Oraio's operations. The Brazilian is supplying arms to many of our and our allies' enemies. During the hack-a-thon, Tweeter will have the opportunity to gain access to the Dark Net IPs of Oraio's trusted business associates since the hackers will be using Oraio's closed, secure network for the competition. Also, NSA is interested in who else shows up at the hack-a-thon so they can prepare dossiers on them and monitor them on the Internet and the Dark Net more easily. Many of the hackers who've expressed interest on the Dark Net recruitment site are ones NSA has on their 'of interest' list. Some of the hacker contestants might even be foreign operatives, friendly and not."

"Won't there be a danger of someone recognizing Ace as Stuart Allen Walsh and not this Erik Slade dude?" A frisson of unease slithered down DJ's spine and lodged like a cold lump in her belly. She leaned into Ace's side, seeking his warmth.

"Unlike Keely, I've kept a low profile since I left M.I.T. Also, I've been on the Dark Net for a long time, long before I went to college. So my alter ego is fairly well-established." Ace hugged her. "As Keely said, I'm sort of infamous." He grinned, a devilish look in his eyes. "The U.S. Government allowed me to hack into some classified areas that made the bad-actor hackers salivate. I've got me some serious street cred."

"Let you?" Keely snorted. "My brother's too modest. He hacked his way into all those supposedly highly-protected places. After which, he let enough out onto the Dark Net to prove he could do it. Tweetie and I then plugged the holes before anyone could take advantage of them. So, his infamy was earned, not given. He'll frick-fracking hack circles around the ones who've been granted a seat in Belize."

"Seems straight forward, but…" DJ looked around the room. "…what am I not hearing?" Or was she overreacting, because it was Ace whose butt would have a target on it?

"Nothing." Ren shrugged. "But any operation can go tits up. This is why SSI never sends anyone undercover without redundant backup. Since Tweeter needs to concentrate on his COMINT, and he tends to go into a fugue state when in front of a monitor, we needed someone to be close enough to alert him to danger. That would be you. Conn will be there to back up both of you and to keep any unexpected unfriendlies on-site honest. Plus, O'Riley has been rumored to kill people who merely inconvenience him."

DJ huffed. "Well, if O'Riley makes a move on Ace, then he'll be the one inconvenienced."

"Blood-thirsty." Conn laughed. "I like her." He looked at Ren. "Looks as if DJ has Tweeter covered, I might as well plan on diving and fishing."

"That's part of your new cover, Conn," Keely said. "We've rented a yacht out of Cancun. Tweeter has already let it be known he's sailing from Cancun to Belize with his new girlfriend and the yacht's captain."

Something primitive inside DJ stirred. *There be dragons here.*

"So, this could become a fishing expedition of another sort with us as live bait," DJ said.

"Exactly." Ren smiled at her as if she'd just aced a test. "The Phantom is extremely well-known. There *might* be other parties interested in *acquiring* his services. This way, we can draw out any such interested parties before you get to Belize. If there are tails and they prove to be a danger to you or the mission, then Conn can handle them."

Dragons, indeed. Ace had a larger target on his back than she'd thought.

Keely used the remote and pulled up another image on the monitor. "Here are some of Oraio's other known employees. They helped O'Riley run the Brazilian's business during his more reclusive years. This man, Alejandro Salazar, is his main negotiator."

The image showed a man in a tuxedo at some sort of society function. His darkly tanned skin had DJ guessing his heritage as Central or South American. He had a face the camera loved. But the expression in his dark eyes was that of a shark's. Every instinct she posessed identified this man as a sadistic predator along the lines of Sean Varney

DJ shivered and leaned even more into Ace's body warmth. He whispered against her ear, "What's wrong?"

She shook her head and was happy he didn't pressure her for an answer. She wasn't sure what she could tell him other than she planned never to have Salazar at her back.

"This is Oraio's enforcer, Alberto Rossi a.k.a. The Albatross."

The man was also dark-skinned and Latino. He had a disfiguring scar that diagonally bisected his face. He looked as if he ate babies for breakfast. He was another one she'd keep in front of her.

"Here are other known associates." Keely pulled up several more pictures. All of them ugly customers, thugs mostly. "I have reports on all of these men. Read them. Memorize them before you leave for Cancun next week. After arriving in Cancun, DJ, you and Tweeter will take a day or two and play tourist to attract the attention of any interested parties. Conn will cover you. After you board the yacht for the trip to Belize, you'll stop for a day and dive the Big Blue Hole. We'll be monitoring you over NSA-satellites and through hidden cameras and listening devices on the yacht. If someone's following you physically or electronically, we'll figure out who they are and their possible motives before you get to Belize."

"This means, once we're in Cancun, DJ," Ace said. "Our cover story starts. I'm your man and you're my arm candy. We'll stick together like glue."

DJ brushed her cheek against Ace's shoulder and murmured, "Oh, I don't think I'll have any trouble being your girlfriend."

"Oh, sugar, I'm counting on it," Ace muttered for her ears alone.

CHAPTER 15

One week later, Sanctuary

DJ moaned, "Good ... so good ... ahh... sweet Jesus..."
Tweeter chuckled as he continued to suck on her
swollen clit. He could say for a certainty that his warrior-
woman was now over her discomfort about letting him eat
her pussy.

"Ace ... oh my gawd!" One hand grasping at the sheets,
she lifted her hips toward his mouth and held his head to her
pussy with her other hand. He brought her to her third climax
of the evening—once with just his fingers and now twice with
his mouth.

Over the last week, he'd eased her toward this moment with
lots of kissing and petting-to-orgasm. She'd been reluctant to
let him eat her "down there" as she called it. Just two nights
ago, she declared it "unsanitary."

But this evening, after she'd had a girls' Happy Hour in
the Lodge bar area, she'd come back to his—now what he
considered their—cabin and given him the go-ahead. He
didn't know which of the women had told her to "go for it,"
but he was happy one or all of them had. He really liked going
down on a woman and giving her pleasure. It was even more
special since this was his DJ.

DJ loosened her grip on his head and now played with his hair as he lightly tongued her through the post-orgasm mini-spasms. "That was so-o-o good." She petted his head. "The girls were correct. I liked it. In the future, I'll never doubt your more superior knowledge of how to give me pleasure."

Tweeter smiled as he rubbed his unshaven cheek along her inner thigh and inhaled her musky scent.

"Are you sniffing me?" DJ leaned up on her elbows and stared at him. Her expression was priceless—a mixture of shock and awe.

"Yeah…" Slowly, he moved from between her thighs and then stretched out alongside her flushed, relaxed body. He'd learned early on that too quick of a movement, especially with him in anywhere near a male-superior position, freaked her the hell out. While DJ was doing so much better in the intimacy department, she still wasn't ready for full-on intercourse—and even when she was—he'd urge her to be on top until she grew accustomed to taking his cock inside her body. "…you smell like hot sex and taste so sweet. I could eat you up."

She turned to face him and traced his mouth with a finger. "Your lips are swollen." She leaned in and kissed him lightly, tasting herself on his lips. "Hmm, more earthy than sweet, I think."

Tweeter laughed and touched his forehead to hers. "Well, my taste buds think you're candy."

"Guess it's your taste buds that count then." Rubbing her nose over his, she took a quick nip of his lower lip. She brushed a hand down his torso. When she reached his throbbing erection, she clasped it in her fist and began to stroke him exactly as he'd taught her. With a week of hand jobs under her belt, she'd become an expert at giving him pleasure in this manner. "How do *you* taste?"

Ace moaned at the thought of her luscious, hot mouth on his cock. "Um, never tasted my cum, so I can't say. But…"

"Hush." She leaned in and swept another teasing kiss over his mouth. "I need to try this. You've given and given, and I…"

"Don't finish that sentence." Tweeter nipped her chin then licked the sting away. "I love what we have together … what we're progressing toward. There's no rush."

She frowned. "Maybe not … but I need to try. This is about you … me … us." She leaned in to teeth his ear lobe, then whispered, "Help me … please?"

Tweeter pulled away and angled her face toward his. The tears in her eyes pierced his heart and turned his resolve to protect her from her previous hurts to mush. He groaned. "Okay, sugar, but if you can't…"

"If I can't," she swallowed hard, "I'll stop and let you hold me. I like it when you hold me, Ace. I feel so safe in your arms."

And DJ was scared. Fear lurked in her eyes, darkening the normally clear aquamarine to stormy teal. His woman was strong, but past trauma was insidious and difficult to overcome. The fact she even tried after what she'd experienced demonstrated how much she trusted him.

Tweeter rolled over on his back and laced his fingers behind his head. "It might be easier this way, with you on top and between my legs. That way, you can move away more easily if you need to stop."

DJ nodded. Her eyes widened. Her pupils were so big he could only see a thin line of her irises. She moved slowly into position. Her formerly relaxed body was now tense and trembling. He wanted to call a halt, but the determination on her face kept him quiet. He couldn't insult her courage that way.

Once she was kneeling between his legs, she sat back on her calves and stared at his erection as it lay on his abdomen. She traced his length with a finger. His cock twitched.

She smiled, a slight curving of her lips, and glanced at him, a twinkle in her eye. "I think your penis likes my touch."

"Sugar, after this past week, my cock is addicted to your touch."

Her lips curved up even more. "So, what do I do?" She shot him an anxious look, the short moment of ease she'd found had vanished as quickly as smoke on the wind.

"Remember how I started by licking your pussy?" She nodded. "My cock also likes to be licked. Begin on the shaft and as my slit begins to leak, you can tongue the head."

"Okay." Fisting his shaft, she bent over and took a lick … then another until she was lapping at him as if his cock was a messy ice cream cone.

Tweeter held as still as he could, not wanting to startle her, but it wasn't easy. He fought against the urge to thrust.

"That feels so good." He praised her, then coughed to ease the strain in his voice. "You can add a squeeze or a stroke with your hand, if you want."

She nodded and alternated strokes of her hand with licks of her tongue. He moaned, and she smiled as she placed a kiss on the tip of his cock. When she swiped her tongue over his cock head, he groaned, "Fuck … that's good."

Encouraged by his reaction, his warrior-woman grew bolder and placed her mouth over his glans and took his shaft slowly into her mouth. The feeling of her hot, wet, silky mouth was intense and became more so when she hummed as she took even more of his cock inside.

Then he fucked up royally. He lost control and thrust his cock farther into her mouth.

DJ gagged and released his penis.

With a look of terror in her eyes, she scrambled off his body and then off the end of the bed. In her panic-stricken retreat, her legs became tangled in the comforter and she fell to the floor with a loud thud.

The sound hammered at his gut.

Tweeter surged off the bed, but stopped and then approached her cautiously.

Animal-like cries came from DJ's throat as she tried to scramble backwards, but the comforter inhibited her escape. The mewling sounds and the vacant look in her dilated eyes gutted him.

Walsh, why the fuck did you move?

"Dahlia Jane? Sugar?" He got down on his knees about two feet away from her and held his arms open. "Baby, it's me … Ace. I won't hurt you. Let me hold you. Please. Remember? You said you'd let me hold you if you got scared."

The awful sounds lessened to whimpers. DJ's breaths were shallow and far too rapid. Tendons on her hands shone white from the death grip she had on the comforter.

The past had her in its maw.

Tweeter roared silently, helpless in the face of an enemy he couldn't see … couldn't kill.

"God … sugar … please … let me … I need to hold you … protect you," Tweeter pleaded, knowing what happened in the next few seconds was crucial to the immediate future of their relationship.

DJ opened her mouth, tried to speak, but couldn't. She shook her head. Lines of frustration creased her forehead. She closed her eyes and held her breath, then exhaled a second or so later in one big rush.

"Ace…" she rasped. She opened her eyes and found him. "S-s-s-o sorry…" She shuddered, violently enough he could hear her teeth chatter. "Help me?"

Tweeter moved to her, pulled the comforter up and around her nudity, then tugged her into his arms and then moved her to his lap once he sat on the floor. He rocked her and peppered soft kisses anywhere he could reach without having to let her go.

"S-s-sorry…"

"Fuck … don't apologize. You have nothing to apologize for. You're not ready. I'm okay with that. Hear me? It's okay." He never wanted to hear those mewling cries or be the cause of the hell he'd seen in her eyes. If he had to start all over again with the wooing, he would. She was his to protect, even from him.

DJ nodded and burrowed into his body. She clutched at him as if she were afraid he'd disappear if she let him go.

She'd soon figure out he wasn't going anywhere, and if he did, she'd be right there with him.

Tweeter didn't know how long he sat on the floor rocking her before she sighed. Her breathing, back to normal. The rigidity in her body, dissipated.

Sweet blessed relief lifted a load off his chest. "Let's move to the bed, okay?" He kissed the side of her head and nuzzled her ear.

"Okay," she whispered. "Can I have something warm to drink. I'm so cold."

"You can have anything you want." Tweeter made sure she was bundled up and set her on the floor before getting to his feet. He quickly positioned some pillows against the headboard, then picked her up and placed her on the bed with her back cushioned against the pillows. He pulled the rest of the bedding on top of her to keep her warm until he could climb in next to her. "How about hot chocolate with some creme de menthe in it?"

She attempted a smile. "Sounds good. When you get back, will you hold me?"

"Planned on it."

"Good, because I need to explain…"

Tweeter placed his fingers on her lips. "No explanations necessary."

DJ shook her head and laughed, but it wasn't a happy sound. "Ace … yeah, I think I need to talk about this. I want to exorcize the monster in my head. I want you to help me get him out of there once and for all. Or, at the very least, bury him under better memories, so he can't keep me from living the life I want to have with you."

Each time she verified she wanted to be with him, his heart filled with joy to the point of bursting. The past week had been one of the happiest of his life. So, if she needed to share the demons in her head, he'd listen and do whatever it took to help her defeat them.

Tweeter kissed the tip of her nose. "Okay, you talk. I'll listen. I'll be back as soon as I get our drinks."

His would be scotch, straight, a double. He had a feeling he was gonna need the alcohol to deal with DJ's revelations.

EYES CLOSED, DJ HUDDLED UNDER the blankets and couldn't keep from shivering. She was so cold, inside and out, as opposed to earlier when she'd burned from the pleasure Ace had given her with his hands and mouth.

She cursed the frigid darkness which had surged from the depths of her mind and stolen the happiness, the closeness, she'd experienced from Ace's lovemaking—and it had been lovemaking and not mere sex.

Ace had told her again and again she was more than a sexual fling. He wanted a relationship with her. Simply recalling his words warmed her and helped slow the trembling.

He loved her.

Yeah, he hadn't used the L-word yet, but he demonstrated his feelings in a myriad of other ways. He'd also told her he wanted to make a life with her. If all that wasn't a declaration of love, she wasn't sure what was.

"You okay, Dahlia Jane?"

The way he said her full name—with such sweet affection and tenderness—made her melt even more. She opened her eyes.

Ace stood by the bed, still gloriously naked, with a concerned look on his face. He held a cup of hot chocolate in one hand and a glass of his favorite scotch in the other—a double from the looks of it. Ouch, she'd really done a number on her man.

Her man.

She especially liked the sound of that, since she'd never thought she'd ever have one.

"I'm better." When his eyes narrowed as if he didn't believe her, she grinned. He was so cute. "Really, I am." She threw back the bedclothes. "Crawl in, darlin'. You need to know what triggered my meltdown. It has to do with what happened that night. Together, we'll beat back the memories."

"God, I love you."

Her heart stuttered and she forced herself to take her next breath.

He'd said it. He loved her.

The truth of the words was evident. His tone had been husky and his expression so fraught with love that her heart ached trying to hold all the emotion contained in the words.

DJ focused on his face. She wanted to memorize how he looked at this moment. She'd then tuck the image away in a safe place in her mind and pull it out when her past threatened to drag her down.

Ace loved her—and she loved him.

Any lingering frost melted away.

Was it totally gone? Probably not. Evil never totally left, but it would always be checked by the strength of Ace's love and thrust back into the depths again and again until it lost its power to rise and take her over.

"DJ?" He was worried.

She smiled and opened her arms.

Ace sat the drinks on the bedside table. He crawled into bed and wasted no time in tugging her into his arms and pulling the covers over them.

Cocooned by his body and blankets, she snuggled against him and idly traced little patterns on his chest. She inhaled and let his scent permeate her pores and soothe her as it had done so many times over the few weeks she'd known him.

"Talk to me," he muttered the words against her hair.

"So-o-o, you love me?" Just saying the words thrilled her to her toes.

Ace tipped her face to meet his gaze. "Yeah. Can't help it. I fell for you the first day. You okay with that?"

DJ leaned in and kissed him, putting all her joy, her love into the act.

Ace groaned and took control, twisting his tongue with hers.

She whimpered, wanting more, and took it. She ran her fingers up his neck to cup his head and held him to her as she claimed every inch of his mouth as hers.

Ace clutched her to him as if he'd never let her go.

DJ hoped not. In his arms was where she wanted to begin and end each day for the rest of her life.

Finally, Ace ended the kiss. Leisurely, he placed light kisses over face as he murmured, "I take it that means you're okay with me loving you."

She laughed and tugged on his hair. "Yeah." She angled her head until she could look him in the eye. "Just in case you haven't figured it out … I love you, too."

"Thank God," he rasped out. Moisture welled in her man's eyes as he continued to cherish her with kisses.

"Thank God or who or whatever brought Dev to the pilots' briefing room that day, because that day set me on the path to you," she said. "I plan on loving you for a long, long time."

"That's good, since I plan on doing the same." He placed one last lingering kiss on her lips, then nudged her head onto his chest. "You still want to talk or go to sleep? We have an early day tomorrow with the flight to Denver to catch the charter flight to Cancun."

The Belize mission started tomorrow. That had been part of the reason she'd spoken with the gals earlier about oral sex. She wanted her and Ace's sex life to be another step closer to normalcy for many reasons, one of which was for the sake of their cover during the mission. She'd thought she could handle third base in the game of foreplay, but obviously not. So—

"Talk, please." She sensed the Stygian shadows creeping in, determined to take control of her conscious mind again. But Ace's love was too bright, and the darkness was swallowed by the light, defeated for now.

"Talk, it is." Ace handed her the hot chocolate and then grabbed his scotch and took a long drink.

She sipped at her cocoa. The warm chocolate felt good going down and then—"Whoa, that has a kick."

"I figured you might need a little extra alcohol to relax—plus it should help you go to sleep." He cuddled her against him, then rubbed his hand up and down her arm. "Why don't I start? I hit a memory trigger, didn't I? You were okay licking and sucking my cock until I thrust into your mouth."

He sounded so guilty.

"Not your fault. You couldn't have known." She heaved a sigh. "Because I didn't warn you. I figured since it was you and not … him, I'd be okay. I'd been doing so well … being with you. Guess I underestimated the power of past sexual trauma." She coughed, then took a sip of the hot chocolate and let the alcohol do its thing.

"He raped your mouth." It wasn't a question. The words sounded as if Ace ground them out.

"Yeah." She closed her eyes. "But … back then … I wasn't on top. I figured … well, you can guess what I figured." She inched even closer to Ace's body and let his warmth chase away the chills. "After beating me, he forced me … to my knees. Told me if I sucked him off, he wouldn't rape me."

"Fucker." Ace growled and tossed back the rest of his scotch and then slammed the glass on the beside table.

She petted his chest in soothing circles. "Obviously, he lied. And—"

"Shh, I can guess the rest." Carefully, as if he were afraid to spook her yet again, Ace took her cup and placed it on the table. He framed her face with his hands and held her gently as he looked her in the eyes. "I promise as long as I have a breath in my body, I'll protect you from Varney and men like him. I swear this on all I hold dear." Then he sealed his vow, her gentle knight, with a kiss that held all his love for her.

"I know." She covered his hands with hers. "My promise to you is I'll fight any man who tries to hurt me. I also promise I won't let the memory of what that asshole did to me hurt us. So-o-o, I want to try sucking you off again, but…"

"Not tonight." He urged her head back to his chest and rubbed his bristled cheek over her hair. "The fact you can still tolerate to be held and kissed by me is all I need right now. Well, that and your love."

And there was why she loved this man so very much. He was strong enough to protect her from everyone, even from herself. He sensed the memories were still too close to the surface. Ace read her better than anyone she'd ever known, including her mother.

"Love you so much." She kissed his chest and was delighted when his strong body shuddered in response. It was nice to know she affected him just as intensely as he did her.

"Love you back." He kissed the top of her head and then rearranged them so they lay on the bed. Her body still held protectively in his arms, her head resting on his chest. "Do you think you can sleep now?"

"In your arms? Always." She closed her eyes, and all she found in the darkness of her mind's eye was the image of Ace's face when he'd told her he loved her. Sleep stole over her as she replayed his words of love again and again.

CHAPTER 16

February 24th, Cancun, Mexico

Tweeter took DJ's elbow and then guided her across the open-air lobby. They followed the porter who had their mostly empty bags. Once they were checked into their private *casita*, he'd take DJ shopping for some resort clothes. The bags currently contained some survival gear and clothing, just in case they had to make an emergency escape into the Belizean jungle to rendezvous with Conn.

As they strolled through the lush lobby, he checked out the picture DJ made in the outfit Callie had given her from her personal wardrobe—much of which were couture clothes from her modeling days.

DJ looked like a sex goddess. The dress, what there was of it, was the color of a tropical sea with a halter top composed of fabric criss-crossing her gorgeous, full breasts and then buttoning behind her neck. Her toned back was left bare to the waist; the rest of the dress flowed over her hips to stop mid-thigh. There were no panty lines as the silky fabric lovingly outlined the luscious curve of her ass. He'd looked and so had every man they'd passed since they landed in Cancun and entered the hotel. But he'd be the only man who'd discover just what she had on under the sinfully sexy dress. And if the

Latin-lover-wanna-be they were about to pass didn't put his tongue back in his mouth, Tweeter would be very happy to cut the fucker off.

"Behave." DJ pulled him closer to her side and hugged his arm, which brushed the side of her breast. He almost swallowed his tongue when her nipple immediately peaked at the brief touch. "Stop growling like a hungry jaguar. The man's merely looking."

"He can fucking stop." Tweeter leaned over just enough to nuzzle her ear and mutter, "He's stripping you with his eyes."

DJ turned and brushed her lips over his chin. "Pot ... kettle?"

She had him there. "But I have the right," he murmured. "I sleep with you." He adored sleeping with her. She was a cuddler—and he liked going to sleep and waking up with her plastered against his body.

After last night, he was thankful she still wanted to be with him at all. Because DJ had a spine of steel and because his slow, patient approach had garnered her trust, he'd dodged the bullet after hitting one of her trigger points. He never wanted to see such a stark look of fear on her face again—and especially didn't want to be the cause of it.

This morning, she'd awakened him with her hand on his cock and her tongue in his ear. She was all teasing smiles and warm affection. He'd fingered her clit and suckled her breasts as she worked his cock with the confidence she'd gained over the last week. After mutual orgasms, they showered together just as they'd done each day since she'd moved into his cabin and then went to the Lodge to eat a hearty breakfast before their flights.

His woman was a survivor, but she also no longer had to work through her emotional trauma alone. Now that they'd declared their love for one another and committed to a life together—they had time to work out everything else.

"Ace…" DJ tugged on his arm and pulled him into a secluded, arched alcove. "I've been thinking about last night … I want to try again."

"Sugar—" He understood what she meant and was about to tell her he didn't mind waiting until after the op when she placed her palm over the front of his well-washed jeans and then squeezed the semi-erection he'd sported ever since his arm brushed her breast.

"No arguments. We're safe in this hotel, right?" She arched an eyebrow. She rubbed her hand down then up his crotch.

Clenching his jaw against a groan, he muttered, "Yeah." Well, as much as anyone was safe anywhere.

The *casita* he'd reserved was isolated by location and the surrounding landscaping. It also had a nine-foot privacy wall around a patio with a small pool. Plus, he planned to set up some Wi-Fi perimeter alarms that would work through his computer and the secure satellite connection he had through NSA. They could make love with the assurance there were no extra eyes and ears.

All of a sudden his neck itched. Shit, someone was watching them.

Tweeter'd had a similar twinge of *knowing* at the taxi stand outside the airport charter terminal. He'd signaled Conn, who'd preceded them to Cancun and was mingling in the crowd at the terminal.

Conn had singled out the watcher and was even now keeping an eye on the man, whom they presumed had been hired by someone to follow the Phantom.

Glancing at his phone, he noted Conn's tracker signal was at the front of the hotel. So, this could be the same tail and Conn was allowing the man some space—or it could be someone new. The sensation of being watched felt different and, if pinned down, he wouldn't be able to say why. It just did.

Either way, they needed to get out of the open and do so without raising any alarms in their watcher.

Making sure they were protected by the alcove stuccoed wall, he kissed her shoulder and took a surreptitious look around to see if he could spot anyone taking an unusual interest in them. "Have I told you how absolutely gorgeous you are in that dress?"

All he saw was thick foliage, stone columns, other *casitas*, and no one else.

DJ narrowed her eyes at him, but played along. Fuck, he loved smart women. She snorted, a cute feminine sound. "At least a hundred times. It's too short. I'm four inches taller than Callie."

"Yeah, all leg. Nice." He aimed a snarl and a nasty look at a sun-burned Nordic type in a Speedo who'd just exited a *casita* across from the alcove and stopped to ogle DJ. "I didn't appreciate her sending pics of you to Evan. Now he wants you and Callie to model for him."

After the skin cancer case waiting to happen passed by, Tweeter moved them back onto the tiled walkway which led to their *casita*. He wanted her safe, behind locked doors and all the protection he could muster before he called Conn and got a sit rep on the tail from the airport and to report what he'd sensed just now.

"I'm not the model-type, Ace." She hugged his arm against her breast again and his dick twitched in response. "I'm more your type."

"Damn straight," Tweeter muttered as he continued to scan the surroundings. Not only did his neck itch, the hairs on his arms raised. They were definitely being observed, and Tweeter couldn't see anyone. All he could think of was sniper, and the thought chilled him to the bone. He made sure his body was between DJ's and the wide open area where a shooter might set up his hide.

DJ placed her mouth against his ear. "Ace … is it the watcher from the airport?"

Tweeter pulled her to a stop as the porter, who'd gone ahead of them and waited for them to catch up, opened the door to their *casita*. "We'll talk once we're inside." He gently pushed her ahead of him into the dim coolness of the entry hall.

DJ frowned, then mouthed "fuck." He gave her credit. She hadn't looked around and gave their suspicions away. Also, her instincts were good. She'd cottoned onto their tail at the airport as soon as he had. Her question also indicated she sensed the difference in this guy. The new watcher was much better than their airport shadow.

DJ turned into his body, hugged him, and muttered into his neck. "I'm a loser."

"You aren't a loser," he murmured in a low monotone against her ear. "Let me do my thing inside and then we can talk freely."

DJ nodded and then laid her head on his shoulder, waiting quietly while Tweeter gave the porter a tip and took the key cards. But he knew her active mind was going back over every step between here and the airport.

"Come on, sugar." He nudged her farther into what was basically a one-bedroom cottage, a very luxurious one. "Let's check out the place."

DJ immediately split off and headed for the bedroom with her phone in hand. It was loaded with his and Keely's special app for finding electronic surveillance devices. "I'll check for *bed bugs*. These Mexican resorts get them all too easily and have a hard time getting rid of them."

Lips curved into a wide smile, Tweeter shook his head as he used his phone and swept the main rooms. He found nothing, but he hadn't really expected anything. The room reservation was made after they were on the private charter flight leased to Erik Slade. The yacht was a more likely target for alien bugs since he'd purposely bragged on some hacker forums on the Dark Net about bringing his new girlfriend down by private boat.

But again, anyone trying to bug the yacht would have to get by Conn, and that was an unlikely occurrence.

Quickly, he set up his security perimeter and fired up his laptop to make sure the system worked. Anyone breaking in would see a normal-looking laptop and not figure it for the mobile hotspot for an NSA satellite and an alarm system.

DJ came out of the bedroom and walked straight into his arms. "No bugs. Am I crazy or did it feel like a different watcher here than at the airport?"

"Nope. I read it the same way." He rubbed her back. "Conn will follow us when we go out and do the tourist thing. He'll spot anyone following, no matter how many."

"Yeah, and we'll deal with them if and when we have to." She stared at his chest and played with the buttons on his tropical shirt. "I meant what I said outside ... I want to pick up where we left off last night." She rubbed her cheek on his chest. "Plus, I want to slide into home plate before we board the yacht."

"I also want that," he said. "But ... I don't want you to feel pressured into doing anything. We'll have all the time in the world to take home plate once we're back in Idaho. I'd never forgive myself if I scared or hurt you, because you weren't one hundred percent ready."

DJ leaned her head back. Her eyes glowed with happiness and love. "You are an amazing man, Stuart Allen Walsh. But hear me—I want this. I can handle it. Your words of love, your commitment to me ... to us, freed me. The past can't hurt us. I refuse to let it."

Yeah, he'd called it—she was a warrior-woman ... and all his.

DJ looped her arms around his waist. "Right now, my main worry is you'll be ... disappointed. I've heard stories ... about you and Price ... about your sexual conquests."

Shit. Keely and her gossipy gal pals again. Why did women have to talk about other people's sex lives? Men just talked about their own, mostly for my-dick-is-bigger-than-your-dick bragging rights.

While he couldn't deny what DJ might've heard, he could blunt the effect somewhat. "Probably exaggeration as to my exploits. Most likely true about Price's. I don't have nearly the amount of experience he has, mostly because I had a later start. As I grew older, meaningless fucks were depressing. I soon figured out I wanted to connect with the woman I had sex with. Occasional hookups just didn't do it for me. I wanted a relationship."

"Well, you've got that now." She placed a biting kiss on his lower lip, then suckled it before letting go. "Deep inside, I always knew if I found *the* man who could deal with my past that I'd hang onto him with everything in me."

"Then we're good." Tweeter brushed his lips over hers. "Because I feel the same way about you." He took her mouth in a deep kiss, tasting her with his tongue and lips just as he planned on sampling her sweet pussy later. If the replay of third base went well this afternoon, then, tonight, after a romantic dinner, some rum drinks, and skinny-dipping in their private pool, he'd take her into home plate.

———

WITH CONN GUARDING THEIR BUTTS and watching for tails, Tweeter took DJ to lunch and then shopping. Now, they were alone in their *casita*.

"Going to catch some sun, Ace. I don't want to be pasty white if I'm gonna be your arm candy, especially in all those clothes meant to be set off by a tan."

Tweeter turned as DJ walked out of the bedroom. His jaw dropped. He started to speak, choked, coughed, swallowed, then managed to croak, "Where in the hell did you get that bikini? We didn't buy that."

The bikini he'd okayed for public consumption, after she tried on about a dozen, had more fabric and was basic black.

This one was bright blue with cutouts in what little fabric it had. It looked as if someone had taken a skimpy two piece suit and slashed it. The suit screamed "take me to the ground and fuck me."

"Callie bought it for me at Macy's in Lewiston." DJ exited the patio doors to their very private, thank fuck, pool area.

Blinded by the bright, tropical sunlight reflecting off the white limestone pavers, he didn't get a good look at the back of the outrageously sexy suit. It struck him he needed to check it out. He moved onto the patio.

DJ picked up a towel and spread it on a chaise, then lay on her stomach.

Fuck me. He almost swallowed his tongue. To save his life, he couldn't look away; his gaze was super-glued to the view.

The back of the bikini bottoms didn't cover all of her perfectly formed ass cheeks, didn't even come close. He swiped at his mouth, checking for drool, then forcibly closed his eyes and prayed to anyone who'd listen to give him the strength not to fall on her like some rutting animal and take her right where she lay. He'd worked hard over the last weeks to prove he wasn't a mindless animal. Hell, less than twenty-four hours ago, he'd frightened her with one small unintentional thrust of his hips. Leaping on her could erase all his progress.

But at the moment, his little brain didn't want to listen to reason. He'd devolved into a primitive male itching to claim his mate. His hard-on could drive nails into cement.

"You have this weird look on your face." Angling her head, DJ stared at him over the top of her sunglasses. "Are you in pain?"

Hell yeah, he was in pain, but not the kind she was thinking.

"You will *not* wear that suit on the boat or in Belize." He was pleased he managed to get all the words out, even though they were uttered through gritted teeth in the tone a ravening beast might use.

DJ pushed up further onto her forearms and shoved the sunglasses to the top of her head. "You don't like it." The corners of her lips turned downward. "I told Callie it didn't fit right, but she insisted I looked like a super-model in it."

Okay, now he'd put his foot in it. He'd made her doubt her beauty. Her self-confidence as a woman was something he, Keely, and the SSI women had worked on since DJ had arrived at Sanctuary. Nancy had noticed what they'd been doing and had taken him aside one evening right after she and DJ had arrived. She'd explained the circumstances behind why DJ possessed a low self-image. Al-fucking-Poe had only valued DJ as a tool to gain more power and took every opportunity to beat down her self-esteem as a way to control her. Then Sean "the bottom-feeder" Varney had raped DJ and made her feel even worse about herself.

Tweeter had to make this right. He couldn't let DJ believe she was anything less than beautiful in his eyes.

Taking a deep breath and praying he didn't mess this up, he walked over and knelt by the chaise. He cupped her chin and massaged her tense jaw with his thumb. She leaned into his touch like a kitten getting petted and that elated him—she liked his touch, and, damn, he liked touching her.

"Sugar, it's not that I don't like the suit on you—it's that you're every straight man's wet dream in that suit. You're gorgeous. That's why you'll wear it only for me." Tweeter took another breath. "And just to put you on notice, when you do, it won't stay on long, because I'll strip it off you and make love to you until you can't remember what day it is."

Mentally he groaned. *Way to go, Walsh. Threaten her with a physical attack, why dontcha?*

He held his breath—and prepared to grovel—as he waited to see how DJ would react to his Neanderthal garbage.

"Oh?" A mischievous sparkle entered her eyes making them look like back-lit sapphires. "Does that mean you want to make love to me right this second?" She stroked a finger down the front of his shirt then lingered over the conspicuous bulge in his jeans. "Your penis seems interested."

He exhaled. She wasn't scared. His gut said it was time to make a move. She was teasing and happy—and had opened the door to sex herself.

"I want to make love to you more than I want to keep breathing." He let go of her chin and removed the sunglasses from the top of her head, placing them on a side table. Then he cradled the back of her head in one hand, his fingers threaded through her soft blonde curls. "You okay with that? Do you want me to kiss and lick your pussy as I did last night? Bring you to orgasm?—Get your body ready to accept my cock?"

"Yeah…" She licked her lips as she gazed into his eyes. "More than I want my next breath." He laughed at her use of the same cliche. "All I could think about on the flight down was how happy I am … being with you. Then this afternoon, I saw the pleasure you took in shopping with me—in simply being with me. I felt your love every time you looked at me or touched me. It was fricking sexy when you used your body and fiery wolf eyes to protect me from all the men leering and making salacious comments." She leaned forward and whispered against his lips, "Yeah, I want you to make me completely yours."

Tweeter closed his eyes and muttered, "Thank fuck." He opened his eyes and then looked around the patio. He wanted to make love to her out here. The air was warm, but not hot. The scent of the local flora was exotic and added to the overall ambience.

But he didn't want DJ to get burned. There was a day bed situated under an awning that screamed outdoor sex. He silently thanked the hotel's decorator for thinking of everything an amorous hotel guest might want.

Tweeter stood, turned DJ over, and then scooped her into his arms. "Hold on." Her arms went around his neck as he carried her to the day bed perfectly situated in dappled shade. He lowered her onto it.

Her eyes glittering with arousal, DJ pushed up into a sitting position and began to remove her bikini top.

He stayed her hands. "No. Let me undress you."

She smiled, then dropped her hands to her sides. Her expression held no fear, only trust and love.

After Tweeter removed her top, which involved a lot of touching and kissing each satiny inch as her skin was exposed, he lowered her torso onto the day bed and then placed a kiss on the tip of her nose. His hands, seemingly with minds of their own, stroked up and down her naked upper half. Her breasts were flushed with her arousal. Her nipples had budded and were dark, dusty pink. Her skin felt like hot, warm silk under his fingers, and he wanted to feel it against his own nakedness.

"God, you're glowing like a sun goddess already." He traced a finger over her chest where she had tan lines from the criss-cross of the halter dress. "Maybe we should take this inside."

"No. I want you to make love to me out here." She trailed a slightly shaky finger down the middle of his chest where his shirt was now unbuttoned. He hadn't even realized she'd opened his shirt; he'd been too busy taking in every detail of her body. "I tan easily. Just walking the plazas and eating at that outdoor café built up my base even with a ton of sunscreen."

She was nervous, talking to cover it up.

Hell, he was anxious, too. What if he fucked this up? What if he went too fast and ... scared her again?

Stop being a pussy. She trusts you. She loves you. Take a breath. Take it a step at a time.

"We'll stay outside." Her happy sigh told him he'd made the right decision. "But I'm warning you now, I won't take chances with your health. I'll be putting your sunscreen on you each morning to make sure you don't get severely burned. The sun's stronger down here."

"No one's ever taken such good care of me before." She ran her fingers through his chest hair, avoiding his nipples. She was teasing him, and he loved the fact she felt safe enough with him to do so.

Tweeter sat on the edge of the day bed and continued to smooth his hands over her skin and fondle her breasts—accustoming her to his touch all over again. Her burgeoning pleasure was evident in her mewling sighs and moans and her nipples pebbling to even sharper points. The dark pink nubs all but begged to be suckled.

"Help me off with my shirt," he whispered against her lips. He wanted her to be an equal partner in their lovemaking.

DJ's eyes glistened with excitement as she slipped a few remaining buttons open on his shirt and then used both hands to spread the shirt open and down his arms. He shrugged it off and tossed it to the patio floor.

"I love your chest." She swept her hands over his chest, now stopping occasionally to pay attention to his nipples. His cock stirred in reaction.

"I'm glad." He leaned down and nibbled at the lip she so often tortured when she was nervous … and aroused. "I adore your chest." He cuddled a plush breast, perfectly sized for his hand, and rubbed his thumb over the turgid peak.

DJ arched into the touch even as she continued to sexually torture him by smoothing her hands over his chest in a firm, circular motion. He inhaled sharply, his cock shoving against the fabric imprisoning it, when she gently ground the heels of her hands into his nipples.

"You like that?" Her voice was low and sexy.

He grunted his answer and pushed his chest against her hands.

"Good. I like touching you." She curled up from the bed, thrusting her breast even more into his hand, and then teethed and licked the juncture of his neck and shoulder. "Mmm, I also like tasting you. You taste good. All clean and salty male." She looped her arms around his neck. "I love everything about you."

While DJ didn't really need Ace to protect her from whatever the world threw at them, such as the Latino men leering at her on the Cancun plazas or making sure she didn't get a sunburn, she *did* need him to lead in the bedroom. Even after a week of escalating foreplay, she still wasn't comfortable taking control of their love play. Someday maybe—but not today.

Most adult males wouldn't have put up with their slow pace, the tame high school heavy petting. But Ace had never complained or pressured her for intercourse.

Even last night, he hadn't gotten mad when she'd lost it and couldn't handle giving him head. Instead, he'd told her he loved her, held her in his arms all night with them curled around each other like sleepy kittens. And, today, he'd gone out of his way to give her a perfect afternoon just like any other loving couple might have experienced visiting Cancun on vacation.

"I love everything about you, too." Ace angled his head, skimming her body with his heated gaze. "Since I'm on the razor edge of coming, you need to let me arouse you more before you touch me. First, though, we need to remove the rest of that extremely naughty bikini so I can kiss every luscious inch of you and make you come."

"Ace," she whispered as she grabbed one of his hands and dragged it inside her bikini bottom to press against her mound. "I'm wet. I ache. It won't take me long to climax."

His nostrils flared at the news and the wolf-blue of his eyes all but disappeared with his extreme arousal. "Good."

He gently lowered her again to the chaise. Kneeling next to the chaise, he kissed his way down her body and then placed a suckling kiss on her stomach just above her belly button before he stripped the bikini bottoms down her legs. Her abdominal muscles contracted and her pussy got even wetter.

"Since I plan on making you come several times before you take my cock," he said, his voice a low rumble that traveled throughout her body and set her clit to vibrating. "I want you crazy ready when I slide my cock into you."

"Ace…" She whimpered as he nudged her legs apart and lightly bit an inner thigh. "Trust me, I'm already there." She raised a hand and ruffled her fingers through his shaggy blond hair, loving the raw silk feel of it. "Make love to me, darlin'. Make me fly."

"Planning on it. And I'll be there to catch you when you fall." Ace moved to sit on the side of the day bed and bracketed her upper torso between his bent arms. He leaned down to devour her mouth.

DJ twined her arms around his neck and tugged him closer. She turned her head away from his ravenous kisses just long enough to demand, "On me. Skin-to-skin. I want your weight."

He looked into her eyes, a look of concern on his face. "You sure?"

Once again, in the midst of passion, Ace was protecting her, putting her needs above his. Sweet Jesus, she'd put the poor man through the wringer over the last week. She vowed not to balk at the gate this time. This was Ace, her first—and last—lover.

"Definitely." She soothed the worry lines on his forehead with a finger. "The only man in this bed … in my head … is you. My man." She lifted her head and bit his chin lightly. "I want you rubbing that effin' gorgeous body all over mine. I want us to give each other as much pleasure as we can handle. I want *you* to be the only man who has ever and will ever make love to me."

"God, I want that, too." After placing a gentle, worshipful kiss on her lips, he stood and stripped off his jeans and boxers in one motion. His beautifully formed cock stood tall. The purpled head sported a silver drop of precum.

Her eyes widened at the sight and she forgot how to breathe for several seconds. It took all her resolve not to whimper at the thought of finally taking all that generous length and breadth inside her. And, yeah, she'd seen and handled his erection many times over the past week, and last night even had it in her mouth, but right now it looked to be larger than ever before.

DJ swallowed hard. "Ace…" She swept a finger up the length of his cock and smoothed the drop of precum over the extremely swollen glans. His penis moved and seemed to seek her touch once she removed it. "Um, I really don't see how it'll fit."

"Oh, it'll fit. But only after I pleasure you first with my mouth and stretch you with my fingers." Ace took her hand and placed it on the day bed by her head. "Let's see if we can get your mind on your orgasm and off the size of my cock."

Ace climbed onto the day bed and lay next to her. He began to kiss and fondle her body, from head to toe. There wasn't an inch of skin he didn't stroke or kiss. Over the past week, she'd become addicted to his brand of heavy petting. He'd never failed to make her feel good. But today, he put it all together like a symphony with all the sections playing together for the first time. He gave her so many sensations all at once that soon her arousal simmered under and over her skin.

Each time Ace swept a finger over her labia or her clit, she thrust her hips to meet his touch. When he suckled her breasts, she clasped his head to her and arched so he'd take more. He moved down her body, licking and kissing, setting small fires across her overly sensitized skin.

Finally, he settled between her legs and alternated licking and sucking her swollen labia with nipping and suckling her clit. The sensations crescendoed and she came like a final crash of cymbals.

DJ screamed, a breathless sound she'd never before made in her life. Her hips thrust upward and twisted, seeking … no, demanding Ace feed the flames consuming her.

Her man generously gave and gave until she collapsed, panting, quivering, and boneless on the bed.

Invading barbarians could've overrun the hotel grounds and she wouldn't have been able to move to defend herself. Ace had laid waste to her body and left her helpless against the onslaught as surely as Attila the Hun had Europe.

Floating in a hazy aftermath, she sensed a shadow come between her and the late afternoon light, then a weight settled over her. Just that quickly, she was sucked into the depths of the hell that was her past. She struggled and whimpered and felt the same helplessness her eighteen-year-old self had.

The weight moved. A susurrant white noise muffled the screams in her head. "DJ ... sugar ... come back to me." The whispered words, the gentle tone, were soothing, familiar, and stubbornly persistent, demanding she come back to the present.

Get your head out of your ass, Dahlia Jane. You scared your man again.

"Ace?" She reached blindly for him. He grabbed her cold hand in his hot one and kissed it. With his loving touch, her strength, her sanity, returned as if Ace had mainlined his energy, his will, straight into her body.

"Dahlia Jane? You coming back to me?" He rubbed his cheek over the hand he held and kissed it again and again. "God, sugar ... I'm so sorry."

At the guilt, the self-flagellation in his voice, she finally found her spine and opened her eyes. His dear face was white with shock, with guilt. "No reason to be sorry. It's me. All me. Can we try that again? I promise not to freak out this time."

Ace shook his head and opened his mouth, and she cut him off—

"Please?" She sat up, twined her arms around his waist and then peppered kisses over his chest. "Last night, you said we should try making love with me on top. Can we do that? To start? Then we'll progress to you on top?"

Ace stared at her, a piercing look as if he could read her thoughts. He must've found what he needed, because he nodded, moved out of her arms, then lay on the bed beside her. His wonderland of a body was now an open invitation for her to take.

DJ got to her knees by his side and looked him up and down. His penis was semi-erect, lying on his lower abs in its nest of golden-brown hair. She stroked a finger along the shaft, and it swelled instantly. Emboldened by the instant reaction to her touch, she fisted his shaft and bent over to give it a lick. She looked up and found Ace's hot blue gaze fixed on her. His expression said it all: he loved her and would let her take him however she wanted.

"Later, you'll finish teaching me how to suck your cock, yes?" She swiped her thumb over the precum leaking from the slit, then brought it to her mouth and sucked the silken fluid from it.

He inhaled on a hiss, then answered, his voice strained from arousal, from reining in his lust ... for her, "Yeah, but only if I'm sure you're ready."

"Oh, I'll be ready. But right now, my body is demanding I take you inside me." She licked another bead of precum, savoring the salty, earthy taste of him. "And, yes, I'm scared." He frowned and opened his mouth, but she hurriedly cut him off. "But I ache and need you more, I also want to stop being frightened."

"Sugar..." he whispered, "you..."

"Hush, darlin'." DJ half-laughed and shook her head. "This reminds me of the first time I jumped out of a helicopter in the mountains for heli-skiing training. I was so scared, but also exhilarated. Back then, I learned I just needed to jump, get it over with, and realize I could do it."

Ace chuckled. "I don't think I've ever heard initiating intercourse compared to heli-skiing before." He petted her thigh where it rested against his torso. "I love you, Dahlia Jane."

"I know," she leaned over and kissed his lips, "and I love you—and I will conquer my fears, because I need this intimate connection with you." She rubbed her nose over his. "Help me?"

"Always." He reached for her hips and assisted her to move into position over him. She braced one hand on his chest. "Let my cock ride your slit for now."

DJ wiggled and shifted until his penis nestled between her labia. She moved forward and back over his erection, her fluids making the motion easy and smooth. "Feels good. Like when you trace around my opening with your fingers, but more intense."

Ace had a look on his face that made her heart stutter.

"What's wrong?" she whispered. "Why are you staring at me like that?"

"I'm memorizing this moment. How you look. How you smell." He inhaled deeply and his cock pulsed against her sensitive, swollen lips. "How your skin feels touching mine."

Ace moved, one short undulation that made her moan. He squeezed her hips. "I want this moment engraved in my memory. Want to tell our kids about the day their mother and father cemented their love for one another. Well, the un-X-rated portions, of course." A naughty grin crossed his lips.

His words, his teasing, filled her with joy. "Take your time. I did the exact same thing the first time you told me you loved me." She caressed his chest and kneaded his strong muscled shoulders.

He was her alpha-geek. Her sweet, funny, fierce man. Hers.

"I never had those kinds of stories from my father. I know you did, because your dad told me and Momma all about how he'd met your mom. It was a wonderful, funny story made even more so since Molly kept interrupting to correct him. Then your brothers put in points your parents left out. I want that for our children."

"I want three kids." Ace massaged her hips and lower back.

DJ leaned down until she her lips met his. "I can do three. We'll be leaving off the condom, Ace. I've waited long enough to make a family of my own."

"God, I won't last," Ace growled. "Must take care of you first." His hips bucked under hers. The slide of his penis over her needy slit sent ripples of electricity over her body. He gritted his teeth and managed to regain control. "Get closer. I want my mouth on your breasts."

DJ moved her bracing hand to above his shoulder, bringing her breasts within easy reach of his mouth. She drove her hips forward and then slid back over his erection, feeding her growing arousal.

As Ace licked and suckled her nipples, he slid his hand between their bodies to play with her clit, lightly at first, then with more and more pressure.

The passage of time slowed as he built the need in her to explosive proportions. She kissed and nuzzled his face, neck, and shoulders as she continued to rub her pussy over his erection.

The ache within became even more demanding. Her body wanted his cock inside—and finally her mind was on board with it all.

"Ace?" Was that her voice? So breathless? So needy?

His response was a soothing murmur against a nipple and a testing of her entrance with a finger. "You're so wet, sugar. Ready to take that jump?"

She shivered and nodded. In her head—just to be safe— she began a litany: *This is Stuart Allen Walsh. Her Ace. Her love. Hers.*

"Put me in—only when you're ready." He placed his hands on her hips and helped her rise to her knees.

Ace didn't shove her down onto his penis. Didn't scream at her or call her a bitch or cunt or tease. He just … waited as if he'd hold her there forever … waited on her to make the call … with such a look of love and pride on his face.

His expression was all it took for her to take the leap. She circled his penis with her hand, guided the tip to her opening and then began to slide down onto him in small increments. His strong hands helped her control the movement. His loving, observant gaze never left her face. He wouldn't allow her to rush and hurt herself. At the first sign of distress or fear on her face, she knew, he'd pull her off him.

DJ smiled. The rightness of it all swept through her body, her mind, clearing out any lingering darkness.

"I'm okay, darlin'." She moaned as her pussy stretched to take even more of him inside—as she allowed the feeling of fullness and the pleasure of his heavily veined erection rubbing against the sensitive inner tissues to take over. Slowly, she spread her legs farther apart on the day bed as she sank ever further onto his throbbing erection.

Finally, he was fully seated within her body and she paused.

Bracing both hands on his chest, she lifted her hips slightly and then reversed. She moaned. "I like this. I feel your cock throbbing inside me. It's like controlling my Hawk."

"Yeah." Ace thrust upward, one quick movement, then subsided. "There's heavy turbulence coming, sugar. So, I need you to move and take control of the stick—or I might have to take over as second seat." He winked, but she could see the strain on his face, feel it in the reined-in strength underneath her.

"Get ready to fly, Ace. If you feel the need to take the controls, just do it." She began posting up and down on his erection, finding a speed that made him groan and increased her pleasure. But after a while, she realized—"I'm not sure I can come this way. It's there … on the horizon, but I can't get there."

"Maybe this'll help." Ace took control of her hips and moved them in a circular motion as he thrust upward. She groaned as his pelvic bone ground against her clit.

After several minutes of this hip action, she moaned and babbled as the sensations built and built until—nothing. It felt good, but she knew there was more—and she wanted it all.

"Ace!" She leaned over and clutched his shoulders, digging her nails in. "I need—" She attempted to drive her hips faster, but his grip on her hips held her back. "Something. Anything. Now!"

"I'll take care of you," he murmured against her forehead.

"Sooner, please." She rotated her hips and ground her mound against his pelvic bone, seeking more friction, a better angle … and got nothing.

Ace chuckled. "This'll help." He released one of her hips and moved his hand between them and began rubbing her clit.

"Fuck, yes. There. Harder." DJ buried her face at the juncture of his neck and shoulder and bit down.

Ace shouted and thrust his hips to meet hers as he increased the pressure on her clit.

"Awww, gawd." She threw back her head and arched her back. Her face raised to the skies, she let out a shrieking gasp. She pounded into Ace's hips faster and faster. Her body shook as if she were having a seizure of epic proportions.

Pleasure took over her body. She could only moan and grunt and gasp. As the ecstasy swelled and eddied, she babbled, "Oh, gawd … fuck, fuck … so good darlin' … gawd so good, so good … oh gawd, oh gawd … fu-u-uck…"

The sensations kept getting better, because Ace didn't stop. He kept thrusting his hips and playing with her clit. He curled up and licked and nibbled and sucked her breasts and neck and shoulders through what had to be half a dozen aftershocks.

While she'd enjoyed running the bases with Ace over the last week, taking home plate beat foreplay all to pieces. What made it even better was she could look forward to having this with him for the rest of their lives. Just that thought had DJ shooting to another, much stronger peak. She screamed, "Ace!"

"Awww, fuck." Ace roared and began jerking against her as his hot cum filled her.

DJ reached one more peak as his penis hit a highly sensitive spot on the inside of her vaginal wall.

"Sweet effin' hell. What was that?" She moaned as she clutched his shoulders to ground her. "What ... are you doing to me?"

"Loving you." He pulled her face to his and kissed her with strong thrusts of his tongue as, still connected, they rode out the post-orgasmic waves. She whimpered and luxuriated in the intimate kiss. Groaning, a deep sound that went straight to her clit, he pulled his mouth from hers and murmured, "Going to take you up again. Hold on."

"I don't think..." Her words trailed off as another orgasm came out of nowhere and stole her breath. For several minutes, maybe longer, she swore she had an out-of-body experience.

"So beautiful." Ace sucked her lower lip into his mouth and let it go with a distinct *plop*. "So fucking sexy. Love having your pussy squeezing my cock."

Ace ground his hips against hers. His erection was still hard enough to remain inside her. He hit the sensitive spot again and had her seeing stars and screaming his name over and over.

Finally, exhausted and climaxed-out, DJ collapsed on top of Ace. Neither of them moved for a long while. The sounds of their heavy breathing were broken only by the buzzing of bees and the trill of some exotic birds in the trees surrounding the *casita*.

Ace held her tightly against him, one arm around her hips, the other around her upper back. His cock still spasmed sporadically inside her.

Boneless and satiated, DJ hovered on the edge of sleep. Ace nuzzled her ear and said something that sounded similar to the buzzing of the bees. He chuckled then, pulling her off his body ... pulling his cock from her.

She mewled at the loss. "Ace?" She reached for him.

"I'm here." Now lying next to her, he tucked her against him. He peppered kisses over her face and neck, punctuating each touch of his mouth with an "I love you."

She arched her throat to give him better access and was shocked to find his touch and words could still arouse her. She'd figured she was all aroused out. She was so wrong.

When one of her legs cramped, she moaned.

Ace stopped kissing her and raised concerned eyes to her. "Did I hurt you? What's wrong?"

With a great deal of effort, she lifted an arm and shoved some sweaty hair off his face with shaky fingers. "No, you didn't hurt me. I loved every single second of your lovemaking. And once I get cleaned up, eat something, and catch my second wind, I want to do it again. But…"

"But what?" Ace moved back and began to check over her body. He touched her hips with a gentle finger and then swore, "Damn it, I left marks. You're going to have bruises."

"Good. Then anyone seeing them will know my man loved me well." She shoved his hands down lower, onto her right leg where her hamstring screamed for attention. "Rub."

He complied and it felt like heaven.

DJ smiled. She'd done it. She'd had sex with her man. The sexual trauma from her past had lost its smothering grip on her.

"Sugar," his voice was all grumbly, "when we're making love, you need to tell me when I'm hurting you." His talented hands kneaded the cramp out of existence, then went on to care for her other leg.

"You were giving me so much pleasure, the cramp didn't even register." She petted his arm in an attempt to soothe him.

Ace grunted. "Can't stand the thought of you in pain." He finished turning her thighs into limp noodles. "How's that?" As if he couldn't stop touching her, he began to knead her shoulders.

DJ closed her eyes at the feeling of bliss his hands on her body gave her. "Hmmmm. So good. You have great hands."

He snorted, and she opened her eyes to find him watching her closely, worry and love and lust in his eyes.

She grinned. "You also have excellent hip movement and lots of power. I especially liked the hard, fast, deep action at the end."

"Good to know since I fucking loved it." He patted her hip then aligned his body to lie along hers. "Everything okay?"

"Very okay." She stretched like a cat, brushing the front of her body against his ... preening for him. "Let's take a shower. Then you need to feed me. Later, you can show me variations of what we just did *after* you finish teaching me how to suck your cock."

His head braced on one hand, Ace stared into her eyes. He was reading her again. Smiling, he said, "Now, that's a deal I'll never turn down."

Ace rose and gathered her into his arms, which feat of sheer strength never ceased to amaze and thrill her. Her big, strong alpha-geek carried her into the *casita* and thoroughly washed every square inch of her body, giving her another orgasm with his fingers. He called it an appetizer. She couldn't wait to see what dessert would be.

CHAPTER 17

The setting sun cast shadows over the trendy shopping district. The heat of the day could still be felt radiating off the bricked streets. The cantina DJ and Ace had chosen had an outdoor bar and patio seating; it looked out over a square that featured a small burbling fountain in the center with large pots of colorful tropical flowers spaced all around the perimeter.

While the setting was gorgeous and romantic, DJ felt eyes on them through drinks and appetizers. Because the plaza was crowded with tourists, it was hard for DJ to single out who was focusing on them. While the SSI team had speculated someone might follow Ace, the reality made her nervous. Having just found the man with whom she wanted to spend the rest of her life, she wanted to protect him.

Right now, she felt about as useless as tits on a boar. Her arm candy outfit had necessitated leaving her hand gun back in the room. Yeah, she had a knife strapped to her thigh, but guns always trumped knives in an ambush.

"How many do you think are following us?" She idly ran a finger up and down Ace's muscled forearm with its smattering of dark blond hair.

Ace leaned into her and brushed a kiss over her cheek. "One, at least. My neck began to itch as soon as we left the hotel. Conn's been on us the whole way."

DJ casually looked across the square at another cantina and spotted Conn standing, his back to the bar, nursing a beer and watching the crowd. She didn't know Conn all that well, but could tell he was alert by how his gaze quartered the square. Some of her tension dissipated. Yeah, the former Marine had their backs.

Situational awareness. She and the men both had it. Hers was from her tours in third-world countries, and from being a female in a world where there were, unfortunately, a lot of male predators. Conn's was from being a Marine and from living in a South American country where the top dogs changed weekly. She wasn't sure where Ace had gotten his situational awareness; she didn't think M.I.T. taught it. Maybe it was bred into the Walsh genetics.

"Call me crazy, but I'm feeling more than one set of eyes. At first, I chalked it up to passers-by checking us out. But within the last few minutes or so, the feeling of being observed ramped up"—she kissed his cheek—"and not in a friendly oh-aren't-they-a-cute-couple sort of way."

"Passers-by wouldn't give me a second look. You were the one catching all the attention as we walked here." Ace leaned back in his chair and looked around as he picked up her hand and kissed the palm. "Case in point, I spy several Latin Lotharios scoping you out, but they aren't bothering to hide their interest—the fuckers."

"Ditto on some cougar-type females." DJ growled at a woman at the table next to them who was at that very moment licking her over-collagen-filled lips at how Ace's jeans hugged his muscular thighs. The woman, who had to be old enough to be his mother, inhaled sharply as DJ aimed a narrow-eyed glare her way and turned back to the slightly over-the-hill male sitting with her.

"Bitch," DJ muttered under her breath then turned to find Ace smiling at her. "What?"

"I appreciate your territoriality." He leaned over and gave her a full, on-the-mouth-with-tongue kiss that left DJ gasping for breath when he moved away. "Now, that should take care of the bitch and her man who's been eye-fucking your breasts since he'd slipped the waiter money to sit next to us."

"Now *that* I hadn't noticed." DJ rubbed her cheek over Ace's shoulder. "Do you think they're the ones who've been following us?" She looked at the couple, who were now focused on anything but her and Ace. "I don't get any bad vibes from them, just skeevy ones. If I were going to swing, it wouldn't be with people old enough to be our parents. Can I just say *ick*?"

Ace choked on his sip of beer. "Just for information purposes, I don't share. You're with me. I'm with you. That means no one else is welcome in our bed but our pets and kids—and the last two won't be there when I'm making love to my wife."

"Wife?" DJ inhaled a sip of her margarita and coughed until her eyes watered. "Did you…" cough "…just propose?"

Please, please, say you did.

Ace put his beer down and then turned her face toward his. "We love each other. I said I wanted three kids, and you didn't disagree. I figured marriage was understood."

He looked and sounded pissed. He was scared she was back-tracking.

DJ covered the hand cupping her face. "Ace, lots of people live together, make a family, and don't get married these days. I didn't want to presume—"

"Presume," he growled just before he took her lips in a hungry kiss, leaving her breathless. "I'm a Walsh. We mate and marry for life. You think you can handle that?"

Joy swept through her like wildfire. The man she loved wanted to marry and make a family with her. Yeah, he'd said as much before, but a proposal was concrete; it made it real. Images of little Aces tussling with their daddy and loving their mommy made her heart hurt with happiness. They'd have to have a little girl for Ace to love and treat like a princess. The world suddenly seemed brighter and filled with infinite possibilities.

"Yeah," she whispered. "And I can handle you."

"So that's a *yes?*" Ace's voice still held a hint of anxiety.

She opened her mouth, but couldn't speak; her throat, tight with too much emotion. So, she nodded, several times. Her answering smile was so wide it made her jaw hurt.

He smiled and leaned over to press a kiss to her lips, then whispered, "Thank you for making me the happiest man in the world. I'll make you happy, I promise."

Still unable to form a word, she nodded and kissed him back.

Ace settled her even closer against his side, then picked up his beer. "By the way, you can handle me anyway you want— and I'll love it."

Images flooded her mind at just how she might handle him—and he would handle her. She licked suddenly dry lips and took another sip of her margarita. Her mouth twisted into a slightly naughty grin as she anticipated what delights the rest of the evening might include. If anyone had told her she'd like sex this much, she would've laughed at them. But she craved sex with Ace.

The sooner they finished eating, the sooner they could return to the *casita*, get naked, and proceed to drive each other crazy with pleasure.

"Later, right now we're playing bait to lure out our watcher or watchers, so Conn can identify them." He kissed her exposed shoulder.

"Are you reading my mind again?" She took a passing look around the plaza. Whoever was watching them was still out there. She sighed and shoved lovemaking out of her head, for now. The op was important, and she wouldn't let the team down by not carrying her share of the load.

"Nope." Ace grinned as he toasted her with his beer. "You blush when you're thinking about sex."

DJ moaned. Damn her fair skin.

"Back to the being-watched feeling," Ace said. "The odd couple at the next table definitely aren't the ones making our necks itch. They were at the cantina when we arrived, sitting at a table on the other side of the patio. Let's see what our friendly shadow has to say for himself."

Ace pulled out his phone and hit a set of numbers. When DJ made a move to pull away, he tightened his arm around her shoulders. "Stay put. Snuggle closer, sugar, so you can hear."

"Sugar? I didn't know you cared, buddy." Conn's laconic voice was atonal to keep others from overhearing what he was saying, but came across the phone loud and clear. Although from the laughter and music in the background, DJ was fairly sure no one could hear what the man said even with a super-sensitive listening device.

Ace snorted into the phone. "You aren't my type, asshat. How are you finding Cancun?"

"Too crowded. Maybe we should go snorkeling sooner than planned. I can be ready at dawn."

Snorkeling was the agreed upon term for when Conn had confirmed the identity of the tail. He'd also just confirmed they had more than one watcher. DJ was happy to know her gut was working efficiently.

"Okay, my sugar baby and I will check out earlier than planned. She's looking forward to spending some time at a secluded snorkeling spot."

"I've got just the one all picked out," Conn said. "Nice and private." His tone had changed, grown grittier. The sound set her nerves on edge. Something about their tails had bothered Conn and that couldn't be good. "Besides making a new friend here, I ran across an old friend ... from my military days."

Conn knew one of their watchers? Since Conn had been MARSOC, that meant the "old friend" was highly skilled. DJ stiffened and Ace rubbed her shoulder.

"Anyone I know?"Ace asked.

"Indirectly. You have friends in common from back home. He's also very interested in the new friend I made. My military friend might try to contact you to catch up on old times."

DJ stiffened and forced herself not to search the crowd for anyone watching them too closely. Ace gave her a gentle squeeze. She sighed and then relaxed into him. They'd expected to be spied upon. It was good to know Conn had eyes on both men. She had no issues taking anyone out who might be a danger to Ace and their operation. If they had to, she was sure she and the guys could rig up a convincing accident. Lots of people died while boating alone in strange waters.

"If you talk to your friend, say hello from me."Ace had just given Conn the go ahead to take out Conn's acquaintance if the man became a danger.

Conn chuckled. "If I talk to him, I'll just invite him along for the trip to Belize. I'm fairly sure he knows how to dive. He recently spent a lot of time in Key West and on an island off the Bahamas."

Now, it was Ace who stiffened. "Fuck." His voice, now an angry rumble, he muttered into the phone, "Crocker's here?"

Crocker? The guy who kidnapped Elana and took her to the Russian *mafiya* boss? From the story DJ had heard, the man was supposed to be in a Federal prison for his crimes in aiding and abetting a traitor.

"Yeah." Conn's tone had also turned fierce. "Shall I offer to buy him a drink?"

"No. Leave him alone. If he does contact you, suggest you meet to catch up on old times and common friends."

"Gotcha," Conn said. "That's how I'd play it also. Have a nice last night in Cancun. See you bright and early tomorrow. I'll make sure the yacht is spic-and-span for your trip down the coast."

The yacht would be bug-free for their trip. Probably the last time they wouldn't be on someone's video or audio for the remainder of the op.

Don't think about it. Just pretend you're in a movie and the hidden cameras are filming scenes.

And that would be a porn movie.

Yet, there was no way, she'd go without sex with Ace now that she'd realized what she'd missed all these years. Plus, they were a couple—it was part of their cover.

"Sounds good, buddy. See you bright and early in the morning." Ace swiped the highly sophisticated phone off. The signal was routed through NSA satellites and scrambled so no one would be able to trace or decode the call in time to interfere with the op—if they even could break the encryption.

Ace turned toward her, a dark, glowering look on his face. "Shit. Could never have seen that coming in a thousand years."

"Is that the Crocker I think it is?"

Ace nodded, one short abrupt movement of his head. He was furious and no wonder. Sam Crocker was *persona non grata* at SSI.

DJ had heard the story from Keely. Crocker had tried to kill Elana for Syd MacLean, a DIA traitor. When MacLean fled the country, Crocker, a savvy survivor, switched sides and kidnapped Elana for a *mafiya* chief who wanted her.

Keely had also been a target of Crocker's and his band of mercs when he'd worked for MacLean. It made no difference to any male at SSI that Crocker had later attempted to protect Elana and had been injured while doing so. If he was in Cancun, some kind of deal had been made.

Unfortunately, in the intelligence community, men like Crocker had skill sets and knowledge that could be used; it was the "enemy of your enemy is your friend" credo.

"Do you think the Feds turned him?" DJ murmured against Ace's ear. Anyone looking would see a woman nuzzling her man.

"Maybe," Ace turned to mutter against her cheek. "When we get back to the *casita*, I'll call my sister. She'll know what to do. If Crocker's working on a black op for the U.S.—and even though he's a fucking douchebag—I don't want to screw it up."

DJ rubbed her nose alongside his. Ace wouldn't talk to Ren, because she suspected her future sister-in-law's husband would rush down here to take out Crocker's sorry ass even if it blew their current op.

"I need to know what this effin' douchebag looks like," DJ said. Because she was determined to protect her man's ass and needed to be able to identify any and all potential enemies.

"I can get you his military file tonight. If Conn recognized him, Crocker must not have changed his identifying features." Ace hugged her and placed a tender kiss on her lips before settling back into his seat.

The waiter placed their entrees on the table. After the man left, Ace cut into his grilled sea bass and muttered, "Damn. Crocker *let* Conn see him. For a reason. I figure you'll be meeting the man tomorrow when we drop anchor to go snorkeling. If he doesn't come in soft—"

DJ took several deep breaths as adrenaline set her heart to racing. Her body was ready to fight, but the enemy was still unseen. She forced herself to relax. What had started out to be a simple intel-gathering undercover op had suddenly gained the potential to turn dangerous.

"We'll handle it." Calmly, she cut and took a bite of her Tilapia, then hummed under her breath as the flaky fish melted in her mouth. "Does this mean the evening's planned entertainment is off?"

She had all this adrenaline pumping in her bloodstream and no danger to leech it off ... but sex could.

"Fuck no." He shot her a glance so scorching it could melt iron. "First, I'm buying you a ring. There's a jeweler on the way back to our hotel." He picked up her left hand and kissed her ring finger. "I want to mark you as mine."

DJ had no problem being marked as his. He was her partner, her soul mate, her lover. She would wear his ring with pride.

"Once we get back to the hotel," he continued, "we might have to cut the lovemaking back a bit, but no way am I losing my last evening of completely safe and private time with you. You just accepted my proposal of marriage and we're celebrating."

"I don't need much sleep." She smoothed her hand up and down his thigh under the cover of the table—then shifted it to the erection straining the placket of his jeans. "And I don't want this to go to waste." She gave his cock a firm squeeze before pulling away.

"Isn't it lucky I don't need much sleep either?" Ace winked. "We can nap on the yacht. It'll take a few hours to reach the snorkeling site."

"Sounds like a plan." DJ turned her attention to making her food disappear as quickly as possible. Suddenly, she was hungry for more than seafood.

Chapter 18

February 25th, on the yacht Titania

DJ lay on a lounge chair on the aft upper sundeck of the hundred-foot yacht which SSI had leased for the op. Ace and Conn were bonding over the state-of-the-art equipment on the yacht's bridge.

She stretched her arms over her head and smiled. Her sun-warmed body had a few twinges in little-used muscles, a result of yesterday's introduction to lovemaking. Her body hummed with the opposing mixture of satiation and need—she couldn't wait to see where Ace would take her next on the path to sexual discovery.

After they'd made love after dinner, Ace had teased her that she was loud, but then admitted he liked the noises she made. If screaming his name and invoking deities made him happy, she didn't plan on holding back. Later today, sex-on-board-a-luxury-yacht was definitely on her newly created sexual bucket list. It was a good thing the master suite on the yacht was well away from the bridge and the captain's cabin Conn was using.

Post-mission, she'd like to take a few days and cross off some more of the things on her list: sex on a secluded beach, sex while swimming in a cenote in the rainforest, sex in a

Jacuzzi, sex on the furry rug in front of Ace's fireplace, and anything else she could think of.

Ace's love had liberated her in a way she'd never thought would happen.

"You look happy…" The object of all her sexual desire sat down on the edge of her lounge chair. "And pleased."

"I am." She eyed him over the top of her sunglasses and licked her lips. *Yummy.* Ace looked *hawt* in his swim trunks and no shirt. His muscles were delineated even more by his tan, which seemed to have darkened to bronze since they boarded the yacht early this morning.

His hooded gaze gleamed as he scanned her length. A muscle in his jaw twitched. His hands fisted at his side as if he fought for control.

"You look…" Her skin felt scorched by his intense perusal. Her pussy grew damp and her core clenched. All it took was a "look" from him and her body prepared to receive his cock. "…predatory."

Slowly, he moved to cage her between his arms. He lowered his head and placed a single kiss in the cleavage exposed by her bikini. "I so want to take you below deck and make love to you right now." He sighed, the sound filled with regret, and shook his head as if shaking off the need. "But we're being followed, and he's not being subtle about it."

Ace sat up and petted her thigh. "Get up and put on more clothes. It's one thing to have Conn ogling your body, but I'll be damned if Crocker does."

She swung her legs over the side of the lounger and reached for the coverup she'd worn at breakfast. As she pulled the silk caftan over her head, she asked, "You sure it's this Crocker guy?"

Ace helped her smooth the voluminous, but diaphanous garment over her body and gave her hips a gentle squeeze. "He sent Conn a message, detailing the last mission they'd worked together in the Marines. So we know it's him."

"He's definitely not being secretive, is he? What could he want?" DJ frowned and turned to look aft and spotted a sailboat trailing behind them.

Worry and curiosity fought for supremacy in her mind over why Crocker would expose himself in such a blatant way. Curiosity won. If he turned out to be their enemy, they'd deal with it. Her gun and knife were in a bag on the floor by the lounger. Conn had also secreted several other weapons around the yacht and made sure she and Ace knew where they were. They were well-prepared to repel or eliminate an unfriendly guest.

The yacht's engines went silent. The sound of the anchor dropping was loud. The boat rode the waves gently. The sailboat Crocker captained under engine power stopped about sixty meters astern. Its anchor was also down.

"Whatever he wants. We'll know soon. Conn and I are fairly sure Crocker is one of Uncle Sam's minions and not Oraio's. Keely's research and analysis seems to confirm that conclusion also. It's a good bet our intelligence agencies aren't playing nicely with each other ... again. Fucking politics."

Upon arriving back at their *casita* last evening—and before she and Ace had made love—Ace had sent Keely an encrypted e-mail, asking her to dig deeper on Crocker and see if he could be working undercover. The best bets were either Crocker was an operative for the CIA's National Clandestine Service, which handles black ops, or he was a private contractor the U.S. had hired because they wanted deniability. SSI had done such contract work for the NCS in the past. Investigating Oraio's current bid to control the illegal trafficking of drugs and weapons in Central and South America was exactly the kind of work the CIA/NCS might contract out to someone like Crocker.

Ace moved to the stairs that led down to the swim platform. His gun was tucked in the back waistband of his swim trunks. She was happy to see her man wasn't taking any chances.

"He's swimming over," Ace said over his shoulder as he started his descent.

Swimming didn't necessarily mean Crocker wouldn't be armed; there were several highly dependable hand guns that could handle getting wet. Also, no Marine would swim in shark-infested waters without a good knife.

DJ pulled her Beretta out of the beach bag and followed Ace down the stairs as swiftly as her outfit allowed. Caftans sucked for freedom of movement, but she didn't have time to change. She wanted to be in position to cover Ace's ass.

"Has Keely found anything concrete to corroborate your guts yet?" DJ asked.

DJ would bet on NCS. SSI's employer on this op was NSA, which meant all the Defense intelligence agencies were in the loop. The CIA/NCS had never liked to share its toys with the other kids, especially the DIA. She'd been on several classifed military missions where the NCS operatives had screwed the pooch and had almost cost soldiers their lives because of inter-agency rivalries. *Asshats.*

"Ahoy, *Titania,*" Crocker called out as he treaded water about five meters from the stern of the yacht. "Permission to come aboard."

"You armed?" Ace shouted back.

"Diving knife."

Ace looked at DJ. A pleased smile curved his lips when she showed him her gun where she'd hidden it in the folds of the caftan. "That's my warrior-woman."

"I have a vested and very personal interest in you—so, of course, I'm protecting it. I want you to be around to father those three kids we talked about."

"Oh, I'm planning on it, sugar." He looked over her shoulder. "Conn, if shit happens, you're responsible for covering DJ."

"Will do, buddy." Conn tapped DJ on the shoulder. "Three kids?"

"Yep." She held up her left hand. Wiggling her fingers, she showed Conn a hammered silver ring set with a square cut, reticulated tourmaline in shades of green to blue. Ace had said the stone covered the complete blue-green spectrum of her eyes.

"Congratulations." Conn moved to stand by her side. "Let me cover Tweeter, sweetheart. You cover me. Crocker's a mean-assed fighter. Once, he took out a nest of Taliban snipers single-handedly with just his hands and some rocks."

Ace glared at Conn. "You don't think I can handle Crocker?"

"I didn't say that. I've seen you fight," Conn replied. "But I haven't seen DJ fight. So, I'd feel better if I'm between her and Sam's knife."

"I don't have to fight the man." DJ's gaze never wavered from the man now treading water at the swim platform ladder. "I can just shoot him."

"That'll work." Conn laughed and moved to her side, his gun in hand.

"Coming aboard, Walsh," Crocker shouted. "No need for all the firepower."

Ace's attention was also fully fixed on Crocker. He didn't lower his weapon. A decision of which she fully approved. She fingered the safety on her weapon, making sure it was disengaged. Only Conn lowered his weapon, but he didn't put it away.

"Come ahead," Ace shouted. "We can have a beer and chat."

"Sounds good." Crocker ignoring the ladder, pulled himself up onto the swim platform in a show of extraordinary upper body strength.

Sam Crocker was dark-skinned from sun exposure and had longish dark hair that lay in wet waves around his head. His eyes were a striking light gray, made even more noticeable by the contrast against his thick, dark eyelashes and tanned skin. He had a scar along his right jaw which served to make him look tough, but not disfigured. His sculpted body had numerous other scars—but one on his chest and another on his lower abdomen looked to be more recent; they were exit wounds. Someone had shot him from behind.

For several seconds, Ace and Crocker stared at one another. She rolled her eyes. Men and their posturing.

"You get the chest and gut wounds in the Keys when you covered Elana?" Ace asked, stepping back and letting Crocker walk farther onto the lower aft deck.

"Yeah." Crocker's face was a sculpted emotional wasteland, but his eyes burned like molten silver. "Fucking Russian gassed us, then shot me and left me to bleed out. Told me he wanted me to suffer for interfering with Demidas's woman. Heard the guy who shot me is dead—that little Elana knifed him."

"She did." Ace smiled, a devil's smile of satisfaction. "Knifed Zivon in the groin and then opened up his femoral. He fell into a grotto. Guy was bleeding out even as he drowned."

"Good." Crocker grunted and a smile very similar to Ace's twisted his lips. "I'll have to send her a nice gift and a thank you note." He nodded at the stairs to the sundeck. "We going to go up and talk about the potential cluster y'all are heading into? Or, we going to stand around here talking about my past sins?"

"Both, but we can do that while drinking the beer I promised you. After you." Ace stepped back and swept his arm toward the stairs.

Crocker snorted and nodded. "Yeah, you're a Walsh all right. Your pa was one of my trainers at LeJeune."

"Then you know he taught all his kids how to survive," Ace said. "If you'd ever managed to get close to my little sister, she would've gutted you without blinking an eye."

Crocker nodded. "Fuck, I know that. Y'all don't have the whole story—" He shook his head, strode to the stairs, and began climbing. "We need to talk about then and now."

Had Crocker already been in deep cover when the shit had gone down with Elana? It felt right, gibed with what DJ knew about how deep-cover operatives worked in the NCS, but she'd wait and see. This was Ace's show—it had been his sister marked for capture and death.

But her inquisitive mind had to know one thing—"Is all your sinning in the past, Mr. Crocker?"

Crocker, with Conn on his heels, halted his climb and looked over his shoulder. He scanned her twice before another kind of heat entered his silver eyes. "And who might you be?"

Ace started to move in front of her, then must've thought better of it and stopped. His high cheekbones were flushed and the look he shot her was filled with apology—and entreaty.

DJ understood the opposing forces fighting for supremacy inside her man—he respected her ability to handle herself, but he also wanted to mark her as his and protect her. Ace's whole body was tense, ready to maim or kill if Crocker made one wrong move toward her. She snorted. Anyone who thought her man was merely a computer nerd had never seen him when he went all alpha-male this way.

Since she loved both sides of his nature, she'd give him this one and moved to his side. Plus, she was close enough to protect Ace, if needed. A win-win.

A quizzical look crossed Crocker's face as he glanced between the two of them. Then his eyes gleamed with understanding. He shot a quick man-to-man look of approval at Ace, a visual thumb's up.

Men and their pissing contests, and she was the tree marked by her alpha-dog.

DJ coughed, drawing Crocker's attention, and pulled her Beretta from the caftan's folds, letting him see it. "DJ Poe, former Army Airborne, CW4. Now an SSI operative."

Crocker looked amused. "Hell, if you were mine, I'd be acting the same way as Walsh."

She growled under her breath, "Damn men…"

Crocker chuckled and shook his head. "All of you, relax. I'm on your side. *Semper fi.*" He turned his back and finished climbing the stairs.

Conn followed Crocker up. "Don't rush. I know the man. If he says he's on our side, then he is. He never broke his word, or his oath to protect the U.S., while he was a Marine. And from the Corp scuttlebutt I heard, even when he was hiring out, Sam and his merc team took the moral high ground on their contracts more times than not."

Which meant Crocker, DJ strongly suspected, hadn't really been all that independent. Plus, the man she'd just met didn't read as evil—and she'd seen evil up close and personal over the years, from her father to the Varneys to terrorists all over the world. Crocker read the same way the SSI operatives and the Walsh men did—honorable and loyal to their country, their teams, and their loved ones.

DJ turned to Ace. "So … we gonna trust him?"

"Yeah, for now. If we don't like his explanation about whom he's working for and why he's following us, we can detain him and have Ren send someone to pick him up."

"Do you think he might've been working for the U.S. when he hired on with MacLean?" DJ asked.

"Seems probable. Fucking CIA." Ace took her arm and steered her toward the stairs. "Let's go up and see what Crocker has to share. If the CIA has sent out NCS operatives to monitor this hack-a-thon, the intelligence agencies could be working at cross-purposes again."

"You don't think Oraio is a front for the CIA in Central and South America, do you?" DJ muttered.

Ace threw her a dark look. "God, I hope not."

TWEETER STEPPED ONTO THE DECK and found Crocker and Conn sitting at the small salon bar adjacent to the sun deck.

Crocker didn't look like a man who could've cold-bloodedly signed on to kill Keely. Plus, he'd protected Elana with his body. The wounds he'd suffered could've easily killed him.

The two former Marines were laughing over something as he and DJ joined them. He led DJ to a bar stool away from Crocker, then sat between them. He mentally kicked himself for almost fucking things up earlier. He knew DJ could protect herself—and him and Conn, if needed—so why had he gone all territorial on her?

Maybe because the man eyed her as if she were a tasty treat and he has a sweet tooth.

Yeah, that would be why.

"Who are you working for?" Tweeter asked. Might as well be blunt.

"Who do you think?" Crocker's eyes glistened with amusement as he raised the bottle of Corona to his lips and took a long swallow.

"NCS," Tweeter responded.

Crocker saluted him with the bottle. "Bingo."

"What was your mission?" DJ accepted a Diet Coke from Conn with a smile.

"Still *is* my mission." Crocker heaved a sigh and put the bottle on the bar. "Observation of Oraio's hacker tryouts. Note who all the hackers are and then attempt to turn whoever takes the job to play both sides and provide intel to the CIA."

"Plausible," Tweeter said. "Since the CIA would never in a million years think to ask the NSA and DIA if they already had an op in place. Just wouldn't do to share info. Typical stove-piping."

"Exactly." Crocker looked at Conn and waggled his empty bottle. "Think I could get me another one of these?"

"Sure." Conn pulled out another beer and handed it to Crocker. He also pulled out platters of sandwiches, fruit, and chips with dips from the bar refrigerator. He placed everything on the bar top. "Might as well eat."

"Thanks." Crocker saluted the man, then took a sandwich, bit into it, chewed, and swallowed. "Good stuff." He grabbed some chips and added them to his plate. "Yeah, as to the sharing." He snorted with disgust. "As boots on the ground, you and me are all well aware that the big wigs in intelligence are often short-sighted along with having bad cases of tunnel vision. Like that deal with MacLean, that shouldn't have gone down the way it did. I told my handler the fucker was gonna rabbit, but the political asshat wouldn't listen to me."

Tweeter listened to Crocker's explanation as he snagged a beer for himself and prepared a plate of food to share with DJ.

"You could've been tried for treason." DJ accepted the plate Tweeter handed to her.

Crocker shook his head. "Never would've happened. They have too much invested in my cover." He smiled for a split-second, then an almost haunted look passed over his face before he went blank. "Damn Dillman fucked up royally on the National fucking Mall. Forced me to improvise. Little Elana was a game-changer and then the op really went tits up fast after that. MacLean would be in a Federal penitentiary in solitary, awaiting trial for treason and a bunch of other just as nasty Federal crimes, if Dillman had followed orders."

"Were your merc team members also CIA?" Tweeter asked. Fucking CIA had run an NCS black op on U.S. soil illegally. SSI could use that for leverage in the future. DIA would jump all over it.

"Nah, while my cover was as a mercenary for hire, Dillman and the others thought they were working a real merc contract." Crocker reached for another sandwich as if he hadn't eaten for days.

"So, how did the Feds explain you being allowed to go free after the Keys?" Conn asked, shoving Crocker the plate of fruit and cheeses.

"They didn't. They couldn't acknowledge the op." Crocker laughed. "I *escaped* from the locked ward of a military hospital after the CIA conveniently let slip the info of where I was. One of my backup merc teams came and took me away in the middle of the night. I recuperated in Panama at one of my men's *fonda*. So, my merc cover is solid and has been polished somewhat. The intelligence agencies conveniently lost the reports of my brief incarceration and hospitalization. Yay, me."

Tweeter got the impression Crocker was somewhat disillusioned with his CIA superiors and his undercover career. Crocker's experience, skills, and third-world connections would be the kind Ren could use at SSI, but currently, his brother-in-law and Vanko wanted to kill the man.

Before he went out on a limb and spoke to Ren about potentially recruiting Crocker to do contract work, there was one thing he had to know—"To maintain your cover, would you have shot my sister?"

DJ touched his arm and squeezed, whether to calm him or in preparation to stop him from leaping at Crocker and strangling him, he wasn't sure.

Crocker's expression went stone cold. "It wasn't supposed to get that far, man." His voice was filled with anger, frustration, and maybe some pain. The man rubbed a hand over his face and blew out a frustrated breath. "I told you Dillman fucked up—then he fucked up again in Virginia and shot—killed—police officers. Man, I could've killed Dillman and that dumbass Peavey who followed the idiot's lead myself. Instead, I dumped their asses, and thank fuck, the cops saved me the trouble."

"Dillman always was an asshole." Conn shook his head. "Peavey was just stupid."

Crocker clicked his bottle against Conn's. "What he said."

"You didn't answer my question," Tweeter ground out. "Would you have killed my sister?"

"No. I don't kill or hurt women—ever." Crocker picked at the label on the bottle with his thumbnail. "My mission, my only mission, was to get positive proof that MacLean was selling out our spec ops units and contractors like SSI and providing weapons and advanced technology to groups we didn't want to have such. When MacLean hired me to kill your sister and made the deposit into my merc account, that was the first piece of solid evidence against him and my superiors felt it would've led to the rest of what they needed. But little Elana overheard the meeting with MacLean and the whole mission went in the crapper."

"Fuck! Crocker, the CIA … you … were acting illegally on U.S. soil." Tweeter shook his head.

Crocker looked up, eyes blazing silver fire. "Yeah, I know. But it made sense to keep the op inside the CIA. MacLean had already reached out to *me*. If the FBI had taken over, precious time would've been wasted, playing games on who'd run the op and them trying to substitute one of their own undercover people. Time we didn't have. That fucker was getting soldiers and undercover operatives killed in hellholes all over the world. He needed to be taken down. ASAP. Still needs to be taken down—hard."

"Amen, brother," Conn said.

Tweeter admired Crocker's zeal, but it might still be a hard sell to get Ren—and Vanko—to consider using Crocker as an asset. Though, if Keely and Elana hadn't been involved in MacLean's evil plots, Tweeter was certain Ren and Vanko would've played the game the same as Crocker had.

And that brought them to—"What's the deal? Why did you break cover now?" Tweeter asked.

"MacLean," Crocker replied.

"What about the fucker?" Tweeter asked even as an answer presented itself.

DJ voiced her own conclusions before he managed to offer his own. "Oraio is MacLean."

Crocker nodded, his face ruddy with anger. "Can't prove it … yet. But the guy shadowing you was one of MacLean's go-to mercs in South America. From my reconnaissance of the resort y'all are going to, the security there is made up of other guns-for-hire MacLean's used in the past. Also, I found it too much of a coincidence that the reclusive, never-before-seen-in-public Oraio is now man-about-town in Rio and in residence at his island off the Brazilian coast. What nailed it for me was the fact that Oraio has taken over the majority of the weapons and drugs contracts MacLean serviced while double-crossing the U.S. government. The circumstantial evidence and my gut agreed—Oraio is MacLean."

"Makes sense," Tweeter said. "He would've had his exit strategy and an established cover in place in case he had to run. But that still doesn't explain why you broke cover. You worried he'll recognize you and you need us to feed you intel?"

"Fuck, you really don't think much of me, do you?" Crocker glared at Tweeter, then he sighed. "But then, why would you?"

Crocker fixed his gaze on something in the distance. "I was following the tail who was following the Phantom, which I now know is you. The CIA figured the Phantom would take the contest and wanted me to approach and turn him so we could get the goods on Oraio. How the hell you've kept your secret?—I'll never know."

Tweeter grinned. "My sister and I are smarter than the fucking CIA bureaucrats."

Crocker snickered and saluted him with his beer. "Yeah, you are. Hell, if I'd known a week ago you were this Erik Slade guy, I would've notified Maddox and had you pulled off this op. I outed myself, because I *saw you* in the Cancun airport."

"You broke cover because of me?" Tweeter asked. "Why?"

"Because I figured MacLean's man would recognize you and let O'Riley know." Crocker blew out a frustrated breath. "Hell, man, I figured I owed SSI a favor, okay?"

Tweeter was momentarily speechless. Conn had been correct—Crocker had a bone deep sense of honor.

DJ asked the next logical question, "What happened to MacLean's, um, Oraio's, man?"

"I killed him after I made sure he hadn't identified you. Lucky for all of us, he was a lousy tail. He hadn't reported in or even sent O'Riley pictures of you, though he'd taken plenty."

Yeah, Crocker had acted selflessly. The pictures of the formerly reclusive Phantom could've have been identified as Stuart Allen Walsh if Oraio or any of his contacts had access to a U.S. government database.

"Won't that make O'Riley suspicious?" DJ asked, frowning. "If he doesn't hear from his man…"

"No worries, sweetheart. I made it look like a back alley robbery. Called it into the local cops anonymously from a throw-away cell." Crocker then shot Conn a wry grin. "After which, I made sure my Marine brother saw me, so y'all wouldn't shoot me on sight when I set up this meet."

Crocker's eyes went flat and darkened to gunmetal gray. "You need to fucking go home, Walsh. Oraio's people may not be able to hack, but they sure as hell can hire someone to run recognition software and find out who you are. What's even more disturbing is the tail confessed he was supposed to abduct you *before* you arrived at the resort. Oraio has a real hard-on to have you in his employ. You're walking into a bear trap, my friend."

"Can't stop now." When Crocker opened his mouth to make further arguments, Tweeter cut him off with a slash of his hand. "Think, man. You've already covered the death of Oraio's man with a plausible explanation. O'Riley *is still* expecting Erik Slade. If I don't show, he'll definitely smell a rat. He'd close the contest down and months of work on your and NSA's end would go down the fucking drain. We might never get someone else inside to get into Oraio's cyber-operations. If Keely and I could've hacked in off-site, we would've. We tried. Hell, every hacker in the NSA tried. Someone … I … need to be on-site to get into Oraio's closed network to mine intel and find the weaknesses."

"If they identify you, you're dead"—Crocker angled his head toward DJ—"and your girl, too."

DJ snarled, "I'm not a *girl*, and I'm damn hard to kill. I'm not gonna let anyone hurt or take Ace."

"Plus," Tweeter added, "I don't plan on being there long. Twelve hours tops." Logic said, now that their plan to abduct him failed, Oraio's people would try to recruit him before they'd kidnap him.

Conn who'd been quietly listening to their exchange addressed Crocker, "Will MacLean—shit, let's call him Oraio since that's who he is now—will he be on-site?"

"Hasn't been yet. Haven't heard any rumors to the effect, either. The bastard has to be recuperating from extensive plastic surgery. The long-distance photos I've seen of Oraio, look nothing like old Syd. Plus, the fucker's a coward. He wouldn't risk his own hide."

"NSA had never been able to get a picture of Oraio prior to his recent coming out," Tweeter said. "MacLean operated as Oraio for years through O'Riley, Salazar, and Rossi. The rumor in the intelligence community was Oraio had been scarred in a fire and that's why he was a recluse."

"Well, his front men have definitely been busy on his behalf in Belize." Crocker snagged a banana and peeled it. "Over copious amounts of alcohol at one of the local hangouts, I discovered O'Riley bought the resort two years ago in one of Oraio's Brazilian businesses' name. So, expect eyes and ears where you can't see them."

"That change in the resort's ownership wasn't in our dossier, so they must've buried the purchase under multiple layers of shell companies." Tweeter added, "We already expected the place to be bugged. I can disrupt them, if I need to, and make it look like a local network problem."

"Plus, if the op goes to shit and they identify Ace, Conn will be close by with a helicopter to pull us out," DJ added.

"I'll be closer." Crocker gave DJ a jaunty wink. "I have a camp set up just outside the resort grounds perimeter, eastside. If you need me, I'll come running and to hell with my fucking mission. The CIA and DIA should've worked together on nailing MacLean from the get-go. He was a Defense problem."

"That's for damn sure," Conn said. "I'll visit Sam's camp so I know where it is. I'll send you the coordinates over our secure feed so you'll have his exact location. And, Sam, if you need an evac, I can pull you out also."

"Man, if I need to bug out, I'll steal Oraio's Apache helicopter." Crocker grinned. "Always wanted to fly one of those bad boys."

"I'll need to know where the Apache is," DJ said. "Just in case everything goes tits up fast."

"Can't miss it, beautiful." Crocker laughed when Tweeter growled. "I know she's yours, Walsh, but she's beautiful." He turned his attention back to DJ. "The helipad is next to the tennis courts."

"I think we need to take a nice walk when we get there, Ace, to scope things out."

"We can fit it in right before the evening meal." Tweeter looked at Crocker. "I'll make sure Ren and Keely get the information you've shared and are aware of your presence. NSA needs to know we suspect Oraio is MacLean."

"And unlike the CIA, I know NSA will make sure the other intelligence agencies get a dossier on the whole mess." Crocker's statement dripped with sarcasm. "I really should've gotten out after the Demidas mess, found me a nice gal, and started a family. But MacLean was still out there. I really want that fucker."

"You can't want him anymore than SSI does," Tweeter said. "If we work together, we can take him down once and for all."

"Man, if you find out where MacLean is exactly," Crocker said. "I'll go in and put a bullet right between his eyes myself."

"If I find out where he is, one of my SEAL brothers will beat you to him." Tweeter grinned. "They've been itching to go after the bastard ever since he had his goons torture Keely."

"Yeah, I heard about that way after the fact. Read the report and saw the pictures of the warehouse where they held her. That was when the CIA—and I—got involved, even though it was on U.S. soil. The ramifications of MacLean's actions were global. He had to go. Plus, Keely was one of NCS's contract employees at the time. Say what you will about my bosses, they don't like it when their civilian COMINT and HUMINT operatives are hurt."

Tweeter examined the man's face. Everything in what he said and how he said it told him Crocker was telling the gospel truth. "Tell Ren that when you meet him. He might not take off your balls and shove them down your throat. Vanko, well, you might want to stay away from him for a while longer. You actually touched Elana. Ukrainians have long memories."

"Don't blame Petriv at all. If I had a woman and someone kidnapped and terrorized her with her biggest fear, I'd be looking for retribution, too." Crocker stood. "You need to be on your way. I'll lag behind y'all by an hour or so."

Crocker turned toward Conn. "There's a bar in the small village that built up around the resort. Let's say I meet you there mid-afternoon for a drink and then I'll show you where I'm set up. We can then reconnoiter the area around the resort together. You might see something I missed. I'm still trying to figure out why Oraio bought the damn place."

Conn stood and clapped a hand on Crocker's back. "Sounds like a plan. I'll bring you one of our headsets and give you our rolling frequency code, so we can stay in touch with each other.

"Sounds like a plan." Crocker turned away from Conn and toward Tweeter. "Good luck, Walsh. I hope you're as good and as fast as you think you are." Crocker turned to go down to the swim deck, then paused and spoke over his shoulder, "Keep in mind. These guys get even the hint you're more than you appear to be, you'll be dead on the spot, and neither Conn nor I will be close enough to stop it."

"We're aware. You watch your own ass," returned Tweeter.

"Always." Crocker waved and climbed down to lower aft deck, then dove off the swim platform and returned to his boat.

Tweeter turned to Conn. "Conclusions?—Is he on the up-and-up? My reading of him says yes, but you know him better."

"He is," Conn said. No doubt in his face or voice at all. "The man was an excellent Marine. If I stuck him, he'd bleed red, white, and blue." He paused and took a drink of his beer. "When he left the Marines, I was shocked. Thought he'd be a lifer. It makes sense now—he was recruited for NCS black ops shit by the CI-fucking-A."

Conn's confirmation settled any remaining doubts Tweeter might have had.

"Are you going to let Ren and Keely know you might already be compromised?" DJ turned to Tweeter.

"It's a very slim possibility, but yeah. No matter what I said to Crocker…" Tweeter took a drink of DJ's soda. "It's Ren's decision if the op's still viable."

And Keely would make Ren see reason. Tweeter was that good and that fast of a hacker.

"What if one of the other hackers recognizes you from somewhere?" DJ shoulder-bumped him. "I'd hate to have to shoot up a resort with civilians present and then steal an Apache helicopter the first night we're there."

Tweeter grinned. "You do what you have to do. Just promise me, you'll stay away from the Albatross."

Rossi had a sick history with women, and leggy blondes were his prey of choice. The women he pursued often ended up dead, or wished they were once the fucker was done with them.

DJ's eyes went blank for a few seconds. Dammit, was she having a flashback? Then she shuddered. Her eyes full of life once more, she laid her cheek against his arm. "I read his dossier," she said. "I saw the photos of his victims."

"Fuck, sugar, if you—"

"Shh." She rubbed her cheek on his arm. "I'll be fine. What Varney did to me has no resemblance to what this sick fuck did to his victims. Plus, I'm not helpless. He tries anything with me when you aren't around, I'll take care of it."

"Good." He rose. "You finish eating. Conn and I will go up to the bridge and get us moving again. Then I'll call Ren."

"I'll be sunning. Come get me when you're done." DJ looked at him through her lashes. "We can take a nap. I don't see us getting a lot of sleep once we're at the resort."

"If I do my job, we'll leave in the early morning hours tomorrow."

"That fast?" DJ looked surprised and pleased.

"I'm that good." He winked at her.

"Oh, I knew that, Ace."

When Conn laughed, Tweeter shoved him against the bar.

CHAPTER 19

After a short wilderness walk in the rainforest to scope out Crocker's hiding spot, DJ and Ace took a leisurely stroll by the tennis courts. Sitting on a bench, they pretended to watch the couple attempting to play tennis. There were more misses, than hits, and the woman giggled a lot. Since they were told upon check-in the whole resort had been rented out for the hack-a-thon, it seemed another hacker had brought his "arm candy."

"So? What do you think?" Ace whispered into her ear and while there took a little nuzzle and then a nip of her lobe.

"They both need lessons." The man had just swung and missed a ball she could've returned when she was four.

Ace chuckled into the curve of her neck where it met her shoulder. "Not them. I meant the other reason we're sitting here in the heat and humidity instead of taking a shower together."

She turned to give him a kiss and muttered, "It's a helicopter. I can fly anything with a rotor on it." She sucked on his lower lip then let it go. It was also loaded with some heavy duty ordnance. Once they'd completed their mission and were well away, they'd need to give the Belizean Defense Force a heads up.

273

"Itching to fly it?" She shrugged. Ace chuckled. "You so are."

"Yeah, but flying that particular bird means something went horribly wrong." She looked into his eyes. "I'd like to avoid a goat rope."

"We'll be fine. Not one of Oraio's men gave me more than a passing glance when I picked up my packet. I got more response from the other hackers when they heard O'Riley call me the Phantom." Ace pulled her closer and leaned his head against hers. "I think those two are drunk or on something. No one can be that bad at tennis."

"Um, I think it's foreplay," she replied.

"Why would you say that?"

DJ snickered. "You mean you hadn't noticed?"

"Noticed what?"

"Darlin', she isn't wearing a bra or panties. Her double-Ds are bouncing all over the damn place and she has a Brazilian wax—and I think I saw a tattoo on her butt cheek when she picked up her ball a second ago."

Ace whistled. "Damn, I didn't even notice. No wonder the guy's distracted."

"Yeah, he isn't even trying to hit her the balls so she can return them. She's playing along. Do you think she's a paid companion? Because that guy, bless his heart, has a face only his momma could love."

The guy was also middling height, skinny, pasty white and getting a sunburn fast, and had no muscle tone. And wasn't that superficial of her? He was probably very smart and nice. But since meeting and falling for Ace, she'd compared all other males to him, and they all ended up on the losing side.

"Now that you've pointed out the elephant on the tennis court." He rubbed his cheek over her hair. "I can say your breasts and ass are much, much nicer than hers—and real."

"Aww, thanks, Ace." She patted his thigh. "Now, tell me what's going on after dinner?"

"O'Riley has set up a lightning round hack to weed the lesser talents out before he explains exactly what Oraio wants to see in the later rounds from a potential employee." Tweeter grinned. "Plays right into my schedule, since I can mine what I need from the system while I'm doing the preliminary hacks."

"Why take a chance where people might catch you?" She frowned. "I thought you were going to get what you needed from the safety of our suite after the evening's fun was over?"

"That was the plan. But, according to the information packet, their closed network will only be live during hacking hours." Ace's lips twisted into a grimace. "Oraio and his people are smarter about closed networks than either Keely or I thought. Of course, back then we were under the impression Oraio was a clueless Brazilian businessman who needed cyber-help, not a former Defense intelligence officer who just needs a top-notch hacker."

"Well, hell." She settled into the curve of his arm. "Are we still on target for leaving before dawn tomorrow?"

"Yeah, as long as Oraio hasn't planted any traps in his programs. Most of what I need to find out will be obvious by merely accessing the closed network. Since closed networks are to hackers what catnip is to cats, I probably won't be the only hacker poking around. If more than one of us is trolling around in his network, there's a good chance Oraio will shrug it off."

"Or kill the hackers caught doing it," DJ said. A realistic possibility considering with whom they were dealing.

"Don't worry. I'd be surprised if they even caught a whiff of me in their system." He kissed the side of her head. "Once I have what I need, we'll bug out. Seen enough of the lay out?"

While they'd talked, DJ had taken in more than just the inept tennis players. "Yeah, the chopper maintenance crew may be A-type, but the security guards are lax."

The two men guarding the Apache and whatever else was in the hanger were smoking and playing with their cell phones rather than making security rounds and keeping eyes on their surroundings. She could take both of them out at once, if she had to.

"Yeah. My dad would have their asses on report." Ace eyed the building and the area around it. "They do have cameras, though."

"Not worried," DJ said. "If we have to use the Apache, we'll have other issues than security cameras."

Ace stood and gave her a hand up. "We'll be fine. Let's go check out the big shower and lie down before dinner." He guided her away from the tennis courts, his arm around her waist.

"But I'm not tired," DJ said.

"Neither am I." He squeezed her waist.

———

Dinnertime

THE RESORT'S DINING AREA WAS in a faux palapa-styled building open to the outside along two walls. The area was lit with torches that seemed to keep the mosquitos away, for which DJ was grateful. Her dress, what there was of it, revealed her shoulders, lots of cleavage, and her back. At least the outfit covered her legs to her ankle which protected her from vampire bugs and allowed her to carry a small gun and a knife strapped to her thighs.

As Ace seated her at their designated table, he kissed her bare shoulder. "You smell and taste like vanilla and lemons."

"So do you." She grinned up at him. "I'm stealing as many bottles of the resort's body products I can when we leave." She didn't bother to lower her voice since this was her role—the superficial piece of arm candy.

The other couple at the table laughed. The only other occupant was a single girl who was a picture of unrelieved black set off against white skin—black hair, dark brown almost black eyes, and black Goth-like clothing that made DJ hot just to look at her. The girl's nails were sensibly hacker-short and painted in a dark, blood red polish.

Goth girl stared at DJ as if she'd crawled out from under a rock.

The haughty expression struck a note of familiarity, but for the life of her, DJ couldn't figure out why. She was fairly sure she'd never met anyone who dressed that way.

The woman from the couple smiled. "I love the body products also. I've already put them in my case, hoping they'll give me more when they do the room tomorrow." She offered her hand to Ace who sat next to her. "I'm Bev Landry and this is my husband Jeff. Jeff is here to try out for the job. I'm just along, because I love traveling with him. He goes to such interesting places."

Goth girl rolled her eyes and muttered something under her breath that DJ thought sounded like "fucking plum." It didn't sound like a compliment.

Ace smiled and shook the friendly woman's hand. "Hi, Bev and Jeff." Jeff nodded. "I'm Erik Slade—"

Jeff gasped and looked impressed—and maybe a bit worried about making the cut.

Ace's fake name had Goth girl straightening in her chair and turning a piercing stare on him. The expression on Goth girl's face was shrewd and intensely perceptive, and it was one DJ had seen somewhere before. While DJ still couldn't remember who or where or when, she knew one thing, for sure—this girl wasn't as young as she wanted people to believe and she wasn't just another hacker.

"This is my fiancée, Dahlia. One name. She's an up-and-coming model." Ace smiled at DJ as if she were a goddess among mere mortals. The best thing about his adoring smile, was she knew he really felt that way about her.

"I'm Dawn Wilson," Goth girl offered in a cultured British accent that didn't gibe with her punk looks. "I haven't seen you in any magazines."

Even the name seemed familiar. If it wasn't her real name, it was damn close.

DJ gave Dawn a big smile. "Because I haven't actually been in one yet. The photographer Evan Moreau asked me to model for him. He discovered Calista and Tessa, you know?" Best to stick as close to the truth as possible. She fingered the bright turquoise silk of her dress. "Evan got me this Dolce & Gabanna dress from their new resort wear line."

Evan at Callie's request had overnighted it to the yacht. The photographer actually did want her and Callie to model for him after the other woman had given birth. Would never happen, but DJ could use it as part of her cover story.

"Really?" Dawn raised a very nicely groomed dark brow. "What kind of shoots? I do so like the fashion scene."

Well, that was a bald-faced lie. Dawn's tone said she could care less.

"For a new line of fragrances from a designer whose name I can't divulge at this point. Callie will be Venus and I'm to be Athena. Evan also mentioned a *Sports Illustrated* swimsuit gig. My darlin' doesn't want me doing that."

"Absolutely not. The only man who gets to see you nearly naked is me." Ace picked up her left hand and kissed her ring finger. Bev and Jeff smiled their approval. Dawn just looked slightly nauseated. "So, Dawn, what's your avatar? Mine's Phantom."

"Well, Phantom," Dawn smiled slyly, "I'm known as Queen Maeve."

DJ knew something of Celtic mythology. Maeve was a very powerful Celtic goddess, a warrioress, and—

"The king-maker," Ace replied. "I've seen your work. You're good."

But not as good as Ace, DJ concluded, since Dawn frowned.

"Yeah, well, I figure you have a few years on me, mate," Dawn replied, a snarky tone to her voice. "When I'm your age, we'll compare hacks."

Then Dawn teethed the tip of her tongue.

Bingo! The nervous habit brought all the puzzle pieces together. Dawn Wilson had also been her name while they'd worked together on a joint drug task force in Central America. Dawn had been on loan from Interpol, and DJ had flown Dawn and the rest of the team around the Darien Region. The petite Brit was close to DJ's age. While her hair was actually black, the things that had thrown off DJ's identifying her sooner were the shapeless clothes hiding a pocket Venus figure and the dark eyes. Dawn's eyes were a pure peridot green.

DJ had liked Dawn. The agent had to recognize DJ, because they'd been the only two women on that particular task force.

"Well, Dawn…" DJ picked up her water glass and saluted the other woman. "We'll have to talk fashion later. Maybe when you take a break during the hacking session.

"Maybe." Dawn returned the gesture with a can of Diet Coke. "But I won't be leaving my computer often. I want to win that job."

"We'll find some time. I'll be in the conference room all evening. My darlin' loves for me to massage his shoulders." DJ turned and kissed Ace's cheek. "His neck gets so stiff hunching over that dang computer. I'll just check on you, too, and bring you a drink and a snack since you're all by your lonesome. We can talk then."

"You are too kind." Dawn narrowed her eyes at DJ.

The Brit was pissed. Too bad. DJ wanted to know what the fuck the Interpol agent was doing here and if it was going to mess up SSI's op.

Ace looked between DJ and Dawn. Knowledge flashed in his eyes. He understood she knew Dawn. "My Dahlia is such a good little masseuse." He played with DJ's engagement ring. "She keeps me all loose and relaxed. Dontcha, sugar?"

DJ nodded, then blushed as Dawn muttered loudly enough for everyone at the table to hear, "I'll bet."

———

"Quick before O'Riley and the others get here." Tweeter murmured against her ear. To anyone entering the currently empty conference room, it would appear he was being amorous. "You recognized Dawn Wilson. Who is she?"

"Real name is Dawn Wilson. She's Interpol, on their drug task force. I met her in Central America when my unit was assigned to help the Panamanians in their fight against the narcotrafficantes."

"Well, hell."

"Yeah. I'll talk to—" DJ went silent. Her eyes widened with alarm and then she stiffened. "Fuck."

Tweeter turned and saw that Rossi had entered the room along several other people. The enforcer's black, hundred-yard stare was fixed on DJ. The Albatross had DJ's scent now and was on the hunt.

Rossi had first singled DJ out during dinner. He'd made his interest known by joining their table during dessert, taking the empty seat between Dawn and DJ. He'd ignored everyone else at the table and practically salivated over DJ.

DJ had sensed Tweeter's unease and had pulled his hand to her thigh, the one where she'd strapped her gun. The gesture had been her not-so-subtle way of reminding him the female was often deadlier than the male, especially his female.

"That man's evil." DJ shuddered. "I hate to admit it, but after reading his dossier back at Sanctuary, I had a tiny flashback to the rape."

Tweeter's stomach churned. He wanted to throw DJ over his shoulder and take her away from here—and fuck the mission. But while the action would make him feel better, doing so would belittle DJ's abilities and courage. He couldn't hurt her that way. She trusted him to believe in her.

Of course, the reality that she could defend herself didn't allay his need to protect her. Right now, his primitive side wanted to destroy the fucker for even breathing DJ's air.

"Can I just shoot him?" DJ turned toward him, a glint in her eye. "I could take a walk. The bastard will follow. *Bam, bam*. Two bullets, heart and head. He'd be food for the big cats this resort is named for."

"Don't even think of going anywhere alone." Tweeter winced at how overbearing he sounded. But just the thought of her, alone, in the dark, with no backup, threatened to drive him bat shit crazy. He caressed her lower back and spoke in a more pacifying tone, "Please … I want you within my line of sight or hearing all evening."

"Um, you can't go to the ladies room with me, Ace." She rubbed her cheek affectionately over his shoulder.

Thank fuck, she wasn't pissed. In fact, she sounded amused. Though there might have been a wee bit of chastisement mixed in with her teasing words.

DJ could gently scold him all she wanted, but the Albatross wanted her with a viciously sick hunger that everyone at dinner couldn't help but notice.

Even O'Riley had taken his man aside and had a low-voiced, nasty-sounding argument with a lot of arm waving and finger-stabbing-chest action. The intensity of the altercation had sent ice shards straight to Tweeter's gut. The two men had almost come to blows, but Salazar had calmed them down.

Tweeter didn't trust the slimy Salazar either. That S.O.B. was just as much of a predator as Rossi. Salazar also had a filthy rep with women, but coated it in an educated and well-clothed persona.

"Stay away from bloody-fucking Salazar also," Tweeter gritted out. "He's even more dangerous than Rossi."

"I know," soothed DJ. "The sly, charming ones are always the worst. Keep in mind, I'm armed. Plus, they think I have as much intelligence as a cotton ball. They might want to stay away from *me*, because I'd rather shoot them then deal with them."

Tweeter's sentiment exactly. He stiffened as someone attempted to sneak up behind him. Since DJ hadn't warned him or pulled a knife on the person, the person wasn't a threat. Then he smelled roses and musk.

DJ muttered, "Goth girl."

A light laugh came from behind him. She joined them and tapped a finger to her ear. He noted a small device, probably an amplifier, so she'd overheard their conversation. She played with one of her many earrings and plucked the small bud out and slipped it into one of the many pockets her over-sized clothing sported.

"I'm with DJ. We need to kill both the fuckwits before we leave the resort. Do the female portion of the world a favor." Dawn winked at DJ, then flashed her smart watch at him. He recognized the app on it as one Keely had designed and patented. It glowed "green." No listening devices were active nearby.

"So, has DJ told you how she knows me?" She lowered her voice to match his and DJ's. While there might not be any active bugs, they didn't need to have their conversation overheard by passers-by. Who knew who else among the many contestants or even hotel personnel might be spying for O'Riley and gang?

"Yes." Tweeter would let Dawn lead this conversation.

"I can guess why you're here. Probably overlaps with my intelligence-gathering mission. If we work together, we can get what we both need and leave sooner." Dawn shivered slightly. Then, loudly, for benefit of some of the hackers lurking nearby, she said, "I hate the bloody jungle. Can't effin' stand heat, humidity, or insects, not to mention big kitty-cats that would sooner eat me than not."

"I like the jungle." DJ picked up the conversational ball. "Earlier, we took a nature walk and followed a path into the rainforest. But you're right about the heat, it was like a steam bath. I much prefer my heat with ocean breezes such as we had on the yacht trip down from Cancun. But walking where there wasn't *one ... living ... person,*" her emphasis was to clue Dawn on the watcher in the jungle, "around was sort of exciting."

"Exciting? You are either very brave or stupid, doll. Lots of lovely predators of all shapes and sizes around here that love to eat silly little female humans." Dawn arched a brow and mouthed "which direction?"

DJ looked to the east. Dawn winked.

Tweeter snorted softly. "Watch it, ladies. Three of those predators are looking our way."

Rossi, Salazar, and O'Riley mingled with the contestants. The Albatross's rapacious gaze kept zeroing in on DJ as he worked his way across the room.

"If Dahlia wasn't so leggy and blonde, Rossi wouldn't be an issue ... the prick," Dawn muttered. "The only other centerfold material here is Olga, and she's Russian intelligence."

Dawn's gaze sought out the Russian. Tweeter recognized the woman as the one he and DJ had seen playing tennis earlier. "The vampire-pale guy with her is one of the leading hackers in eastern Europe," Dawn said. "Hell, he might even be a vampire for all I know. Anyway, poor git has no fucking clue he's being used to get Olga closer to Oraio's operation."

"Crap, Rossi is definitely heading this way." DJ turned toward Tweeter and planted a kiss on him that made his head swim.

The urge to carry DJ away from Rossi's vile presence hit him hard yet again. But he knew DJ would fight him every step of the way. She was a member of the team, and he couldn't forget it. If he did, she'd remind him with a punch to the gut or somewhere even more sensitive.

"If you aren't with the Phantom, DJ," Dawn muttered, "come find me. That fucker is nasty."

Tweeter's gut eased a bit and nodded at Dawn who, in turn, gave him a chin lift. The agent and he were on the same page.

"I can handle Rossi, but would rather not." DJ patted Dawn's arm and then slid one of SSI's ear bud receivers into the woman's hand. She wouldn't be able to talk to them, but could hear what was going on, if there was trouble. "After the session is over, maybe we can get a drink or a snack?"

"Count on it." Dawn turned to move away. "I need a lot of fuel when I'm hacking. In fact, I'm going to see if I can still snag one of those fruit tarts from the dessert bar and another cold soda before we start." She walked by Rossi who ignored her as if she didn't even exist.

"Dahlia, come." The fucking bastard held out a hand the size of a dinner plate.

"I'm fine right here, thank you." DJ's voice was so icy Rossi should've turned instantly into the Abominable Snowman.

The poster-boy-for-steroid-use ignored her cold tone and didn't move away. Instead, Rossi said, "Phantom needs to work." He reached for DJ's arm. "You leave."

"She stays." Tweeter pulled DJ into his side and anchored her there with an arm around her back, his other hand resting possessively on her stomach. He could feel her full-body shudder, but knew she was mentally present—and not in the past—when she covered the hand on her stomach and gave it a reassuring squeeze. "I need her to keep me focused. I worry about her if she isn't near."

"Is there a problem here?" O'Riley came up on Rossi's left and one of the other security men was on the hulk's right.

"Yes. This person is making moves on my fiancée." Tweeter made sure his anger was present in his tone and expression.

O'Riley wanted the Phantom so badly for Oraio, Tweeter could taste it.

O'Riley's demeanor might've read calm, but his eyes blazed with anger over the situation.

"I informed y'all when I registered that I need Dahlia with me. You agreed. This cretin needs to leave my woman alone."

O'Riley's pale face bloomed red and his mouth thinned. He turned to Rossi who was breathing heavy like an enraged bull, his black-pit-of-hell gaze fixed on DJ's cleavage. Rossi ignored everyone around them, but DJ. He licked his thick lips and began to move forward.

"Stand down, Alberto." O'Riley grabbed Rossi's left arm. The security guard snagged his right.

Rossi looked at his boss and snarled, "She comes with me."

DJ stiffened and gave a small cry. Her breathing turned shallow and rapid. Her eyes dilated.

Hell, she was on the verge of a flashback. He tightened his hold on her and crooned against her ear, "It's okay, sugar. I'm here."

Tweeter sensed her fighting the pull of the past. After a few seconds, she heaved a sigh, allowing her body to go limp against his. She petted his chest. "I know you are. I'm good."

Her pale face looked strained, but her gaze was steady and fierce. His warrior-woman had a core of steel. She'd defeated her demons again. Would've beaten them whether he'd been there to support her or not, because she was a fighter … a survivor. "Yeah, you are."

Someone came upon them from behind.

Tweeter readied himself to shove DJ aside and turn to face whoever had attempted to sneak up on them when the man spoke, "Is she okay?" It was Salazar.

"*She* can speak for herself. I'm all right." DJ's voice wobbled. She shot a dismissive look at a glowering Rossi, then snuggled even further into Tweeter's hold. Under her breath and against his shirt, she muttered, "Fucking assholes."

Tweeter had to bite back the smile threatening to take over his face.

"That man…" she waved an arm in Rossi's general direction while her face remained buried against his chest, "reminds me of an abusive ex. I don't like him."

DJ was definitely focused and playing her role as the helpless arm candy.

"Alberto will not bother you again," O'Riley promised. "Come on, boyo. Leave the lady alone. She has a man."

"He's not a man." Rossi snorted like the bull he resembled. "He's a nerd." The fucktard thumped his chest. "Me. I'm a man. Can protect her better."

That did it. Time to show Oraio's men the other side of Erik Slade's carefully crafted reputation.

"Excuse me, sugar. It seems I have to prove I'm man enough to protect my own."

Rossi would never heed O'Riley or Salazar when it came to DJ. The Albatross was a narcissistic sociopath. Rossi's dossier detailed how once he was fixed on prey, he didn't stop, whether they were people Oraio wanted to eliminate or a woman the Albatross wanted in his bed. The beast was fixated with DJ, so he needed to be taught that such an obsession was dangerous to his continued existence.

The only thing Rossi respected was force. Wasn't it handy that Tweeter had made sure his alter ego's background had all of his real-life skill sets?

Also, the demonstration would put O'Riley and Salazar on notice that acquiring the Phantom by force was not a smart idea.

Tweeter gently nudged DJ out of the way.

She grabbed his hand. "You shouldn't be doing this."

Rossi laughed. "See? Even your woman worries you are not man enough."

Tweeter eyed DJ, a smile in his eyes. "Is that what you meant?"

"Hell, no." DJ sniffed, then stalked to the side of the room and stood by Dawn, who'd re-entered and watched the scene with an expression of amused horror. "I don't want you to bruise your hands. You need them to get this damn job."

Salazar burst into laughter and O'Riley grinned. As he expected, Rossi charged. Using a Krav Maga move his SEAL brothers had taught him, Tweeter turned Rossi's mass and movement against him and sent the much heavier man flying into a table.

Rossi wasn't smart enough to stay down.

Thank fuck. Tweeter had a driving need to punish.

The Albatross shook himself off and then with an enraged roar, rushed at Tweeter once more. This time Tweeter grabbed, twisted, and tossed him over his hip. Rossi landed with a thud. Tweeter followed through by using every dirty street move his dad and older brothers had taught him. He kicked Rossi's steroid-shrunken pecker and nuts into his abdominal cavity and then put the man's thick neck in a triangle headlock. The move served to cut off oxygen to Rossi's pea-sized brain. When the fucking idiot was unconscious, Tweeter let go and Rossi's head thunked on the limestone floor.

Tweeter stood and looked around at the stunned crowd. DJ and Dawn smiled at him. He winked at them and said in a loud enough voice to carry to the hallway where even more people had gathered, "Dahlia's mine. Stay the fuck away from her." Finally, he turned to focus on O'Riley and Salazar. "Just because I'm a hacker, doesn't mean I'm not a man."

"Never said you weren't, boyo." O'Riley smirked. "I tried to tell the lad that my investigation into your background had turned up a multiple martial arts history, but the blighter didn't believe me. Now, he does. Later, would you show me the headlock variation you used?"

"Sure." *Not*—as in never. Well, unless he needed to use it to get O'Riley out of the way. "It's a submission move used in MMA, called an Anaconda choke."

"Very appropriate for the rainforest," Salazar responded with a chuckle. "Let's remove Alberto so the hackers can get to work." The man turned to DJ and bowed. "Be assured Alberto will not bother you or Erik again. Good evening."

Salazar's words were everything appropriate under the circumstance, but the man's eyes held heat and an intelligence missing from Rossi's.

Tweeter went to DJ, pulled her into his arms, and whispered into her ear, "Definitely stay away from Salazar."

"Planned on it." DJ leaned into him. "Hack fast, Ace."

"You got it." He kissed her forehead, then guided her back to his computer setup … right next to Dawn's.

"Your setup wasn't there before," he said to the Interpol agent.

"No, but it is now. I switched it while you were loudly proclaiming your possessory interest in DJ." She winked. "This way, we gals can hit the loo together and talk fashion."

"Appreciate it." Tweeter sat and booted his computer.

"You're welcome, not that DJ needs me to back her up. I figure she has her own special moves, don't you, doll?" As Dawn's fingers flew over her soft touch, customized key pad, she glanced at DJ.

"Why do you think that?" Tweeter asked as he set a program running to slither its way through the network. While his program did its thing, he proceeded to hack the Russian intelligence agency's secure network, his first test for the evening, one he could do in his sleep. So, he'd begin with shock and awe, then slow down and let his mole program tunnel into Oraio's systems.

"She thinks that, because…" DJ leaned over his shoulder and whispered, "…she spotted the small syringe of ketamine that Conn gave me. I pulled it from my evening bag and was ready to jab Rossi in the neck. I held back. I was glad I did. Watching you take that behemoth down was … exciting." She breathed the last word against his neck and then teethed the edge of his jaw.

Tweeter turned and kissed her, quick and hard. "I'll show you some of my better moves … later. For now, sit between me and Dawn and watch two hackers have some fun." He slapped the time clock like the ones used in professional chess tournaments to indicate the completion of a move, but in this case, a task.

Dawn paused and looked over at him, obvious shock on her face. "You already hacked into Russian intelligence and planted a virus?"

"Oh yeah." Tweeter trailed a finger down DJ's spine until it reached the silky fabric at her waist. "Been in before. Left a back door."

"Fuck me," Dawn breathed. "I think I'm in love."

"Mine," DJ said. "But I'm sure we can find you a nice guy."

Dawn laughed and shook her head. "Maybe I should let you. God knows, the guys I come across are twats."

"Twats?" DJ asked.

"Idiots," Dawn translated.

Tweeter liked the little Brit, and he could tell DJ did also. Maybe Dawn would like to become the second SSI female operative? He'd talk to Ren after their current op was done. SSI paid a lot better than Interpol and had much less bureaucracy. They could have Vanko, a former Interpol operative, talk to her.

O'Riley ran over and fawning ensued. If the Irishman had beamed any brighter, he could've done double duty as a fucking lighthouse. It promised to be a long, boring evening, but Tweeter would take boring as long as DJ was next to him, all safe and sound.

CHAPTER 20

Evening, February 25th

"Ace?" DJ called out for the third time. This time she leaned over his shoulder and bit his ear lobe.

The lines and lines of code on his monitor passed in a blur. Clearly, he understood all that gibberish, but she didn't. Give her a computer screen with maps, longitudes, latitudes, wind speed, air speed, and elevations—and she was fine. This?—not so much.

"Sec," he muttered.

Over the last few hours, he'd been in what she'd come to think of as a geek coma. She wasn't even sure if she'd walked in front of him stark naked, knelt down, and began giving him a blow job, he'd have come out of it.

He typed in a few more lines to the multitude of existing lines and hit "Enter." Then he turned and pulled her face to his and took her mouth in a nibbling, tongue-thrusting kiss. When he broke away, she was breathless.

"Thanks, I needed that," he rasped, his voice scratchy from lack of use.

Okay, the blow job might've pulled him out, but she bet just her naked wouldn't have. Might be interesting to test her theory some time when they weren't in public and surrounded by potential danger.

She sank her teeth into his lower lip and then let go. "You're welcome, but that's not why I wanted your attention."

Ace swivelled his chair and pulled her onto his lap. She threw her arms around his neck and rested against him. She massaged his neck as he rubbed her thigh. "You know you could cover my ass by sitting next to me. You don't have to stand."

"Yeah, but I want to be able to move fast." And reach her weapons quickly. Her long dress concealed the weapons she'd strapped to her thighs, but getting access in a timely manner wasn't something the designer figured into the design of his evening dresses. To remedy that fault, she'd undone the stitching on both sides so she could slip her hand through the seams and get at her weapons. Still not the fastest route, but better than not being able to access them at all. Her quick go-to backup was a Taser in her evening purse, along with her cell phone with Conn as number one on her speed dial.

"Well, I'm done. We can leave tonight after we've retired to our suite and things quiet down a bit."

Halle-fucking-lujah. Over the evening, the tension in the room had bloomed as the tests grew harder. Even nerds got intense and threw off their own unique form of testosterone. Even stronger vibes had come from O'Riley and Salazar. Their avid focus was on Ace; they had ever-growing hard-ons for his computer skills.

DJ wanted her man out of here—the sooner, the better.

Ace nuzzled her neck and took a little bite. "Why were you trying to get my attention?"

"I need to visit the ladies' room, and Dawn's willing to go with me." She turned and the other woman was laughing at them. "I sort of forgot."

He chuckled. "I like that I can befuddle you."

"I like you befuddling me. But if you can leave now—"

"Not just yet. Still need to play the game. O'Riley is supposed to sign off on the completion of the tests. No reason to make them suspicious now." Ace hit his time clock and looked over at O'Riley who nodded and then turned to say something to Salazar. "Come straight back here. I should be ready to leave by then."

"Okay." DJ got off his lap and kissed him on the lips. "Hold my place. I have plans for you once we're well away from here."

"What a coincidence—I have plans for you, too. The bedroom on the jet has our name written all over it." He slapped her on the butt. "Go on. Hurry back."

DJ joined Dawn, who still sat at her comp station a few feet from Ace's. "Ace is completely done."

Dawn whistled and rose. "The Phantom's good. You two going to retire for the night?"

"Yes. I have plans for that man."

Dawn laughed. "Doll, if I had a man like that, I'd have plans too." The woman led the way into the ladies' room and checked it out. "No one else here. No little bugs either. Let's take turns. I don't trust Rossi. He was eyeing me earlier after you were declared off-limits. Guess his bad reputation has had a chilling effect on the local female population, and he's willing to settle for the only single woman available even if she's a little dark wren."

"Dawn, without all the gunk..." DJ entered the stall. "You're striking."

"Tell the blokes that, would you? Most men never notice small dark birds when they can have leggy blonde goddesses."

Since they were alone and bug-free, DJ asked the question that had been bothering her ever since she recognized the agent. "I've seen you without all that gunk. You're very pretty. In fact, I'd call you a delicate beauty, striking with porcelain skin, green cat eyes, and thick, silky hair. Is that why you layered on the Goth makeup—to deflect male attention?"

"Yeah, even geek types get handsy." She entered the stall as DJ went to the sink. "But I'm still not in your league. You could be the model you're pretending to be."

"Have no desire to stand around and have people take my picture." DJ would rather shoot herself than model. "By the way, Ace has four brothers. I've met them. Very nice guys. They're just like Ace, strong and intelligent, but without the computer geek side. Interested?"

Dawn exited the stall and joined DJ at the sink. "Really? Okay, maybe—we'll see. Ready to go back? I still have another three tasks to finish on my hacking for the evening. Not all of us are the Phantom."

DJ laughed. "Well, you know more than I do about computers. All that stuff looked like nonsense to me."

They walked back into the conference room. DJ looked around and her gut roiled. Forcing herself to breathe through the overwhelming sense of dread, she turned to Dawn. "Do you see Ace?"

"No." Dawn's answer was terse as they approached Ace's computer station. "His computer's still here. No self-respecting geek leaves his computer on and unlocked for another geek to mess with."

"Yeah." DJ looked around. "Plus, he wouldn't leave without me." Even more worrisome, she didn't see O'Riley.

"I know. That man loves you. Even if you weren't covering his ass, he'd be covering yours. My gut is screaming bloody murder." Dawn frowned. "Bloody fucking hell. Salazar just entered the room from the back service hallway. I do not like the smarmy look on the fuckwit's face."

DJ looked over her shoulder. Salazar headed their way. She turned to face Dawn and then leaned into the smaller woman and pressed a small card into her hand. The Brit slid it into one of her pockets. "Those coordinates lead to a man named Sam Crocker. He's CIA. Tell him what happened. He knows how to get in touch with Ace's and my backup—if I can't."

"Okay, doll." Dawn patted her arm and then said loudly for Salazar's benefit, "I'm sure there's a good reason why your man isn't waiting for you."

DJ sniffed. "He promised to stay right here." She turned away from Dawn and faced Salazar who reached for her hands. She wrung them together in front of her to avoid having her movements restricted. Plus, she didn't want the sleaze-bag touching her.

"Erik is not missing, Dahlia." Salazar practically purred. "We are hammering out our agreement with him." DJ didn't like Salazar's slimy tone of voice or the slight smile on his face. "We are suspending the rest of the tests. Erik is obviously the best hacker present, and my employer very much wants the Phantom to agree to be on his team."

The latter was most likely true, but Ace wouldn't have left the room willingly. He definitely would've put off talking employment since he hadn't planned on hanging around for the rest of the contest. So, the hammering-out-an-agreement language was Salazar bullshit. Her worst fear was they'd figured out who Ace really was and even now were torturing him for information on how compromised Oraio was.

Chill, Dahlia Jane. You're guessing. Go with the man. Deal with him. Then get your man back.

"Where he is?" She blinked at Salazar and managed to squeeze a tear, from undiluted anger, not fear.

"No need to cry, lovely one." *Gag.* Salazar gestured toward the exit to the service hallway which ran behind all the conference rooms. "We'll go to the room we are using as an office and you can see him."

DJ nodded, then turned to Dawn and hugged her. She muttered against the woman's ear, "Ace and I have trackers. Get to Crocker."

"Okay, doll. See you later." Dawn gave her a squeeze.

DJ turned and walked on Salazar's left side, maintaining enough distance so she could defend herself, if needed. Her mind kept wandering to what they might be doing to Ace.

Get your head in the game, Dahlia Jane.

This was a search-and-rescue operation. She'd done hundreds of those in war zones. She needed to get her mind wrapped around the current mission and stay on task. Whatever had happened in the past or was happening now, she had no control over. What happened in the next few minutes and beyond was totally under her control, and her actions would take her one step closer to completing her mission—getting Ace back.

She refused to fail.

Her head back in the game, she slipped her left hand through the slit in her dress and touched the knife in its scabbard. The motion further helped to center her and strengthen her resolve.

Hold on, Ace. I'm coming.

As they walked the lengthy, deserted hallway, she took slow, deep breaths and readied herself to move quickly and decisively when the opportunity arose. Her senses became hyper-aware to every breath and motion from the man beside her and to their surroundings.

They were alone. There were no resort employees around. No security guards.

Salazar had come for her without backup, thinking he could easily handle her. He was cocky and that would be his downfall.

When they reached a rear exit to the outside, she stopped. "I thought we were going to where Erik is."

"We are. The room we're using as an office is in a *casita*." His tone was impatient.

He was also lying. If Ace were in a *casita* on the grounds, she'd eat her Beretta.

"Mr. Salazar, I apologize for my earlier upset when I didn't find Erik waiting for me. I really don't need to be there while my fiancé does his business thing. Why don't I just go and wait in our *casita*? He can come to me when he's done signing contracts or whatever."

Salazar grabbed her upper right arm in a tight grip and man-handled her through the doorway. "No, no, Dahlia. You must come with me. Erik is being very unreasonable. He is refusing to sign anything without seeing you first. He thinks my friend Alberto has you."

"Why would he think that?" She allowed him to drag her along, while still managing to keep her body away from his as much as possible.

Her left hand hovered over her thigh. Her Taser was unreachable in her purse slung across her chest and lying between her and Salazar. Even if she could get to her gun on her right thigh, it was too noisy to use this close to the resort.

"Because we told him so. He wishes to see that you are unharmed."

DJ heard the implied "for now" he left off.

One thing she knew for sure, Ace's cover was still intact. Somehow, O'Riley had subdued him in a room full of people and taken him away. Now, Oraio's people were using threats to harm her as leverage to get the Phantom to work for Oraio. The only bright spot in all of this was they needed Ace healthy enough to work for them, so they wouldn't hurt him so much that he couldn't. Still, she wouldn't be at ease until she had him safely by her side.

DJ never should've left him. But then neither one of them would've expected Oraio's men to make such a move in a room full of potential witnesses.

A bruising grip on her arm, Salazar hustled her along a stone path illuminated by landscape lighting. This path led to the back of the resort property. It was the same route she and Ace had taken earlier today. There were no buildings past the helicopter hanger, just groomed, lush landscaping that gave way to thick jungle. Once in the jungle, she and Ace had found and followed a beaten-down path for quite a ways on their reconnaissance of the area. There were no obvious structures in the jungle either.

When they were about eight meters from the back of the resort's main building, she pretended to stumble. "Oww. My ankle."

Listing toward the ground, placing her body even farther away from Salazar, she pulled her knife. As her captor turned toward her and tugged at her right arm to keep her upright, she swung her left arm in an arc. The momentum of her thrust and his off-balanced body posture allowed her to shove the blade up, under his rib cage, and then twist the knife in his chest cavity, ripping through his lung and into his heart. His sharp inhalation of pain and shock was relatively quiet in the noisy jungle.

As his grip on her weakened, DJ shoved Salazar away. Laboring for breath, he fell to the ground. With shaky hands, he grabbed at the knife, but failed to dislodge it as his life faded away. His eyes held shock. Bloody foam came from his mouth, then he went limp in death.

The smell of his bowels evacuating overpowered the night-blooming tropical flowers lining the path. DJ swallowed hard against the nausea rising in her throat.

A potent emotional cocktail swept through her, freezing her in place, messing with her head. Satisfaction at slaying an enemy. Regret for taking a life. Fear that before the night was over she'd take even more lives. She shivered so hard her teeth chattered as she hugged herself, trying to hold herself together.

Her skin was cold and clammy in the hot tropical night air. Her vision blurred. She was slipping into shock—but the creak of the main building's rear door brought DJ abruptly back into the now as adrenaline surged into her bloodstream.

She moved off the path and hid among some giant ferns. Going for the more silent option, she left her gun holstered and fumbled her Taser out of her purse. Whoever had followed them, she'd take him down quickly and then find her man.

"You can come out, DJ."

DJ peered through the fern fronds and found Dawn standing over Salazar, studying him with a wrinkled nose and thinned lips.

"Bloody hell, doll." Dawn looked around and then spotted her. "You don't mess around."

Relief at seeing Dawn had DJ going weak for a split-second, then she rose and joined the petite woman.

"Let's hide him before anyone else happens by." DJ picked up Salazar's arms and began to pull him off the path and under the ferns. Dawn helped by dragging one of his legs.

"Check him for any weapons we might be able to use," DJ said. "I'm not pulling my knife out of him." The blood had mostly been contained inside his chest cavity, and she planned to keep it that way. As far as she could tell, she only had a bit of blood splatter on her hand and arm. She wiped that off with some dewy fern leaves.

"Here's another knife," Dawn handed it to her. "You need this gun?" She held up a Glock.

"No." She slipped the knife into her scabbard. "Why'd you follow us?"

Dawn shrugged. "Since I had to go out this way to get to that Crocker person anyway, I thought I would lag behind and make sure Salazar wasn't just bringing you out here to shag you."

"Thanks. I wasn't expecting good things to happen when he led me to an outside exit either." DJ replaced her Taser in her purse and retrieved her phone. First, she signaled Conn with the code for FUBAR, then pulled up Ace's tracker signal. "Shit. Ace is well off the resort property and in the jungle proper. They must have a well-hidden facility, because Ace and I saw nothing out there but trees, rocks, and cenotes."

"Well, let's go get him and get the fuck out of this place. My makeup is melting." Dawn pulled at her eyes and tossed something away. "Hate fucking contacts." Her pale green eyes glittered like cat's eyes in the low-level path lighting. "What are you waiting for?"

DJ looked back toward the resort, warring obligations tearing her apart. She wanted to get Ace away from O'Riley before the Irishman realized Salazar wasn't coming, but Ace would want her to cover their asses on their presence here. The stuff in their suite wasn't important and had nothing that could identify them. Ace's computer, however, was a dangerous piece of evidence to be left behind.

"Dammit. I forgot about Ace's laptop." She looked into the jungle in the direction of Ace's signal and then again at the resort and then said, "Fuck it."

Phone in hand with the tracking app live on the screen, she turned and moved quickly away from the building at a lope, thankful she'd worn flats to dinner. "By the time anyone can break the encryption, Keely and Ace will have changed it."

Dawn trotted alongside her on the path, which was just wide enough to hold two people side by side. "No worries, doll. I sort of removed his hard drive and mine." She patted a buttoned pocket on the leg of her baggy black pants. "Hope he'll share his intel with Interpol."

"He will." DJ's phone vibrated. She pulled up the text. "Good news. Conn is already on his way in response to my SOS. He'll meet us at the coordinates of Ace's GPS signal. Bad news is, he'll have to land the chopper farther away from the coordinates than he'd like. He'll have a hike to meet us."

"Then we'll just have to get your Ace and then hike to meet up with this Conn person," Dawn said.

DJ switched back to the tracking app. She stopped and then turned slightly south. In the filtered light from the full moon, she could see an area that was more trampled than most and looked as if some branches had been trimmed away. Not a groomed path, but one used a lot. It headed off in a direction she and Ace hadn't explored.

"Ace is two hundred meters, southwest of this main path. The app indicates he's below ground." Fear skittered down her spine, then she mentally got a hold of herself. He wasn't dead since his tracker would cease working if his heart had stopped.

Was he buried alive to scare him into signing on with Oraio? Was he chained up in some cave, hurt and in pain?

Stop torturing yourself. Make a plan to get him out.

DJ looked at Dawn whose expression was grim. Most likely, the Interpol agent was mentally running much the same scenarios as DJ.

"Okay, if he's being held underground, that means there might be only one way in and out. Much easier for them to defend," said DJ. "We'll need more firepower than the two of us have. We need Crocker now. He's just east of here. We can't wait on Conn."

Dawn held up a cell phone with a GPS program on it. "I'll get the Crocker bloke. I programmed in the coordinates you gave me. Give me the ones where we need to meet you."

DJ took Dawn's phone and programmed Ace's tracker coordinates into it and handed it back.

"You going to do the smart thing and wait for backup?" Dawn asked.

As much as DJ wanted to rush into where they held Ace and free him, she knew that was the surest way to get both of them killed. "I'll wait. I'll reconnoiter the area. Find the entrance. Make note of the security measures." Which translated to, take out perimeter guards to make ingress and egress easier.

"Take the fuckwits down hard, DJ." Showing Dawn knew exactly what DJ planned on doing while the agent made her way to Crocker's camp. "Me and this Crocker bloke will be back soon. At least, I'm dressed for tromping through the jungle."

DJ grimaced at the long skirt, now torn and dirtied. "That can be fixed." She used Salazar's knife to cut off the dress at her knees. She tossed the extra cloth into the underbrush.

Dawn laughed harshly. "That'll work. I'll be back as soon as I can."

"Be careful," DJ said.

Dawn waved a hand before she blended into the jungle.

DJ wished she were wearing all Goth black and motorcycle boots like the petite brunette, but arm candy didn't get to look like a punk rocker. She wished she had something to darken her exposed skin so she could blend into the jungle more easily. She'd use dirt, but was concerned about the poisonous insects that lived in the jungle floor detritus. She wouldn't do Ace any good dead.

Ignoring the branches pulling at the remnants of her designer silk dress and scraping her exposed skin, she moved into the undergrowth to lessen the chance of someone spotting her pale skin on the rough pathway. She had her knife in one hand.

With her inborn sense of direction leading her, DJ moved as swiftly and steadily as the terrain and filtered moonlight allowed toward the coordinates on the tracker. She'd placed the cell phone with its tell-tale lit screen into her purse slung across her chest. As she moved around trees and clambered over limestone rock formations, she pulled the phone out several times to make sure Ace's tracker hadn't moved.

The night jungle was noisy with bird calls, insects buzzing—and wasn't she glad Ace had insisted on refreshing her DEET before the open-air dinner—and the coughing cries of jaguars hunting a meal. She also kept a close lookout for snakes of both the two-legged and reptile kind.

When she stopped once again to check coordinates, she smelled a sign of humans. Cigar smoke. A raspy cough of a heavy-duty smoker sounded like a gunshot in the night jungle and alerted her in which direction and approximately how far ahead the smoker was.

Had to be a perimeter guard—a careless one at that. Her Army trainer would've put any soldier on report who gave his position away by something as stupid as smoking.

DJ stopped moving and hunkered down. Motionless, she slowed her breathing, ignored the dive-bombing insects, the skittering of some small creature she'd disturbed, and focused all her senses in the direction of the cough. There it was again. Now, she spotted the glow of the thick ash on the end of the man's cigar as he moved closer to her position.

Before eliminating the guard from the equation, she needed to confirm he was alone. The knowledge that with each second she and the others delayed was one more second that Ace was held in captivity twisted her up inside and made her want to howl. Then the words of one of her drill sergeants came to her: "You don't rush in and throw a teacup of water on a fire. You wait for your team and pour gallons of water on the fucking fire."

Still it was hard to sit still.

He's alive. Oraio needs him alive and able to work.

That fact was the only thing that kept her somewhat sane. If they'd hurt him, she'd go Rambo on their asses.

Hell, who was she kidding? She'd go Rambo on their asses for daring to take him from her. She hadn't gone through her whole life, waiting for the perfect man, to lose him to a bunch of criminal assclowns.

The guard hacking up his lungs walked her way.

Come to momma.

Every sense and her gut told her he was alone—for now. She clenched and unclenched the hilt of her knife and waited.

The guard came closer. Now she could see his face in a beam of moonlight. It was Rossi!

The Albatross carelessly balanced an AK-47 in one arm as he used his other hand to hold his cigar to his lips. Though totally inept as a guard, the bastard was huge and wouldn't be easy to take down without a fight. Plus, she had no idea of how many other perimeter guards might be on patrol and how far apart they were spaced. She needed to take him down as fast and as quietly as possible.

She'd be taking a huge risk, but the Albatross had to be eliminated from the equation. Not only because he was between her and getting Ace back alive, but also because he was an abomination and a danger to all women everywhere.

DJ didn't fool herself. Rossi wouldn't go down as handily as Salazar. Her knife while the more quiet method was more dangerous for her. There was a lot of fat and muscle to get through on Rossi's torso, and she didn't think she could easily hold him and manage to slit his throat. The man was a beast and could easily turn her weapon against her, using his superior strength.

The best weapon for the job would be the Taser. Yeah, it was noisier, but far less so than a gun. She'd seen Tasers take down far bigger guys than Rossi. He'd be helpless and then she could use her knife.

Even as the alternatives flew through her mind, her body prepared for battle. The adrenaline rush had her heart pumping. She took deep breaths to focus her mind and to oxygenate her blood for the burst of energy she'd need to take the bull of a man down. She slipped the knife back into her thigh scabbard and carefully pulled the Taser from her purse.

When Rossi was less than a meter away from her, he paused, looked around, then unzipped his pants and aimed his cock into the undergrowth. His back was mostly to her. He was as vulnerable as a man could be at that moment.

DJ aimed for a fleshier part of his back and shot. Rossi must've sensed something since he turned just as she depressed the trigger. The barbs missed his huge back. One barb lodged in the biceps on one arm; the other barb missed him completely.

Rossi's roar of rage sounded like that of a grizzly bear on a rampage. The electrical shock while enough to piss him off and cause him some impaired motor skills hadn't taken him down.

Shit, shit, shit.

As she rose, DJ dropped the Taser and pulled her knife, then lunged for the angry, disoriented giant. She leapt onto his back and wrapped one arm around his thick neck and hung on as he twisted and turned in an attempt to dislodge her. She sliced at his chest and arms; his blood coated her skin. But he only fought harder.

Her attempt to cut off his oxygen wasn't working. His neck was too thick, and she had a hard time keeping the needed pressure on his carotid. She couldn't slice his carotid since every time she raised her knife, he moved and threw off her aim.

However, thank you Jesus, she got enough pressure on his throat to mute his shouts of rage. Now, he merely snorted and snarled as he used his one good arm to attempt to pry her arm off his neck.

In one violent motion, she was thrown to the ground. She fell on her back, momentarily stunned, as the jungle swam in and out of her vision above her.

Stay conscious. Stay conscious.

With a harshly muttered "fucking bitch," Rossi staggered over, then fell on her. He covered her like a living avalanche. For a second or a minute or maybe longer—she couldn't tell she was too busy attempting to breathe—he lay on top of her, his fetid breaths coming in ragged gasps. His weight was intolerable. She wanted him off her ... now. Then his cock, still exposed from his interrupted call of nature, moved over her mound thinly covered by the remnants of her dress and a silk thong.

A dark whirlwind from the depths of her mind took her over. The past became the present. The Belizean night jungle became the banks of a West Virginian creek on a hot summer night. Rossi's hips moved and became Varney's.

A mewling cry made it past her lips. Her stomach heaved. She went still beneath the mass moving on top of her, hiding in her mind. Her body frozen into inactivity just as it had all those years ago.

When Rossi used his one good arm to tear open the bodice of her gown and grab a breast, she turned her head to the side and retched.

Rossi cursed and moved away from her. She could now move her arms. Could catch a breath. Could think again.

Fuck this. Fuck the past.

Ace needed her. She refused to be a victim, and she sure as hell wouldn't let a specter from her past cause harm to her Ace.

As Rossi knelt over her, his feral gaze took in her torn gown and her now-bared breasts. She used his distraction and swung up her hand still holding the knife. Praying she could do enough damage to take the big man down, she shoved the blade under the ribs and into his chest cavity as far as it would go and then ruthlessly twisted.

A look of surprise on his face, Rossi grunted as he grabbed for her knife-arm, but he couldn't hold on. Her arm was too slippery with his blood as it ran down from the wound in his torso. From the amount of blood spilling from around the knife's entry point, she'd hit one of the heart's arteries.

Face pale with shock and pain, Rossi began to weave from side-to-side.

DJ let go of the knife and found enough energy to shove him, just as he tilted. She managed to wiggle out from between his thighs as he tipped over, away from her. When his body hit the jungle floor, she swore she could feel the vibrations, just as she might from a giant tree being felled. She lay for a second or two, silently crying from a mixture of pain and relief and gasping for each and every breath.

Too close. That was too fricking close.

Finally, she pushed shakily to her hands and knees and crawled over to his motionless body to make sure he was dead. She reached for his thick neck with a trembling, bloody hand and found no pulse. She struggled to her knees and then sat with her butt on her calves and took stock of her condition and the situation.

Bad news: Her dress was a wreck, more off than on. She was covered in Rossi's blood. The knife she'd taken from Salazar was now lodged in Rossi's body, and there it would stay. She still hadn't freed Ace.

Good news: She was alive and not injured as far as she could tell. She still had her gun in its thigh holster. Somehow, her purse had stayed around her neck and her cell was safely inside. The tracking app still registered Ace at the same coordinates. There was one less bad guy between her and her man—and she'd have backup soon.

Steadying herself, ignoring the scent of death, she searched Rossi's body for weapons. Thank you, Jesus, he had two knives, one which went straight into her thigh scabbard. His handgun was a Glock, and she took it from his holster and tossed it into the underbrush. She didn't think he'd rise from the dead or become a zombie, but she was spooked enough by the encounter with him, she wasn't taking any chances. She spotted his AK-47 where he'd dropped it when she'd first shot him with the Taser; the assault rifle she'd take for later use.

The gods of all warriors everywhere must've been watching over her, since she hadn't heard any shouts of alarm or been overrun by bad guys. Either her fight with Rossi had been more quiet than she'd thought, or the other guards weren't in the area yet. Or, they were as inept as the ones patrolling the hotel. She hoped for the latter, but expected it was a bit of the first two and a lot of luck.

As she weaponed up, Rossi's blood on her body was already attracting bugs which were not at all dissuaded by her guaranteed waterproof, twelve-hour DEET. She needed to get the blood off her as soon as possible. Mostly because she couldn't fricking stand it. The coppery smell and the stickiness made her sick to her stomach. An even more important reason was the fresh blood would attract even more dangerous predators such as the jaguars that reined supreme in this area of Belize.

A gurgle of flowing water reached her ears. It sounded several meters away and in the direction of a rock outcropping.

It was away from the general direction in which she needed to go, but she also needed to wash the blood off. She walked on steadier legs than she deserved for all she'd been through; the adrenaline in her system was still doing its job.

The burbling stream came from the rock outcropping and had created a small pool or cenote. The whole area was rife with limestone caves and such crystal clear bodies of water.

Ace was somewhere in one of those caves. She still needed to find the entrance and secure it before Dawn and Crocker arrived.

DJ placed the extra knife, her gun, the AK-47, and her purse on a limestone ledge and waded into the shallow edges of the pool still dressed. The water was cool and crisp and felt good on the scrapes and bruises she'd collected so far. She used a fern leaf as a wash cloth and wiped away the sticky blood as best she could. She prayed her bug repellant was as waterproof as advertised, but wouldn't hold her breath.

After getting out of the pool and wringing the water out of the silk fabric, she tied her bodice together. It was then she began to shake, so hard she sat down with a plop and a splash on a limestone shelf near the edge of the cenote. She hugged herself and rocked in place. Her teeth chattered, not with cold, but from the effects of adrenaline overload and, she wasn't too proud to admit it, the emotional aftermath of killing two men up-close-and-personal.

Her emotions swept over her like a tornado outbreak, tearing, twisting, and battering her insides. Relief, regret, fear, guilt, and never-ending worry—the same emotions that had swamped her when she'd killed Salazar.

She gave herself a few seconds to breathe and process, then she'd bury the emotions getting in the way of her mission. Once she freed Ace, they'd go home. Later, he'd be there, in their bed, to hold her and help her deal with any lingering emotional aftermath of what she'd done to get him back.

Her erratic emotions finally locked down, she strapped her handgun onto her thigh, checked the knife in the scabbard on the other thigh and then picked up her purse and other weapons from the limestone ledge. She checked her cell and the app to re-orient her position, then set off, all senses alert for more guards.

DJ silently snickered. She could just imagine how she looked. Dolce and Gabanna had probably never imagined their resort wear accessorized with weapons and the enemy's blood. Her mental laughter smacked of hysteria, and she realized she wasn't as calm as she'd hoped.

Breathe. Concentrate. Get your ass in gear.

Good advice. Now all she had to do was follow it.

Gradually, the urge to laugh faded away. She relocated the faint path Rossi had been on before leaving it to take a leak. This path looked to be circular and was most likely the path worn down by the perimeter guards.

How long had it taken her to eliminate Rossi and then clean up? Five minutes? Ten? Fifteen?

However long, there could be another guard along soon. DJ couldn't be too cautious.

From the GPS coordinates, she was currently about twenty-five meters away from the place Ace was being held underground.

A rustling to her right had her hiding under another giant fern. Once again she stilled, barely breathing as she merged with her surroundings.

"Rossi! *Pendejo!*" A rough male voice called out. "*Dónde estás, rosquete de mierda?*"

She translated—*Where are you, fucking faggot?* She recognized it as Peruvian Spanish slang.

From what she'd overheard during her short time at the resort, Oraio was an equal opportunity employer; the majority of his hirelings came from all over South and Central America with the few odd Europeans like O'Riley. She'd taken lots of photos while playing dumb blonde tourist. Later, the intelligence community could go nuts identifying them.

The guard hunting Rossi approached, not at all quietly or carefully. Sweet Jesus, Darwinism at its best.

Girding herself for another close and silent kill, DJ deep-breathed to pull as much oxygen into her body as she could; she wanted to take the man down as quickly and decisively as she had Salazar.

"Rossi!" The man continued to walk and yell.

DJ remained where she was. He could come to her. There would then be one less *pendejo* between her and Ace.

He was close and getting closer. She was ready. Her fingers tightened on her knife, but her gut screamed at her to wait … to make sure no other guards were close by.

Rossi's solitary walk in the jungle might've been a one-off instance—a cigar and pee break.

One man was easy to take down. Two would be doable, but necessarily noisy. She was too close to the entrance now to risk being overheard.

Another set of footsteps approached at a run. She slowly exhaled, happy to know her situational awareness was on point.

The second man joined the first guy and rapid Peruvian Spanish ensued. The salient parts she could understand told her the new man had also been looking for Rossi. The two discussed whether to report the missing Rossi or cover for him. It seemed Rossi was known for going MIA when forced to be on guard duty. O'Riley had been pissed at Rossi and this had been his punishment. The first guy was Rossi's brother-in-law. If the situation hadn't involved the love of her life being held and possibly abused, she would've found the duo's dilemma amusing.

Now she just found it effin' inconvenient.

Taking them both out at once without shooting wasn't feasible. Nor could she overpower two males in complete silence even using the knives she had.

When they decided to cover Rossi's ass, she let out a silent sigh of relief, especially since the brother-in-law left to continue his patrol around the security perimeter. The second guy moved away to guard what turned out to be the cave entrance behind some bushes.

First, she'd take the entrance guard out and then wait for Rossi's brother-in-law to circle back around and take him down. The count would be three guards eliminated, giving her and her backup team better odds at a successful extraction.

Steeling her nerves to take yet another man's life, she slithered through the underbrush and took out the next obstacle on her path to freeing her man.

Hang on, Ace. I'm coming.

TWEETER WAS FINALLY ALONE. HE hadn't been alone since regaining consciousness from whatever drug O'Riley had injected into his neck. He was still pissed as hell he'd gotten caught off-guard. To give the Irish devil his due, O'Riley had been slicker than shit at subduing and kidnapping a man from a room full of people.

As Tweeter had slipped under the influence of the drug, he'd noticed one person who'd realized what was going down— Olga, the Russian undercover operative. Sitting on the other side of Dawn's station, she'd seen what was happening, but hadn't raised a finger to help. He'd remember her and let Ren know she was on SSI's shit list. Keely would have fun outing the woman on social media and ruining the woman's career and life.

Since drugging and kidnapping potential employees weren't positive employment negotiation tactics, it seemed Oraio and his minions could give a shit about a cooperative hacker-employee. As Crocker had discovered from the tail he'd killed, Oraio's people had planned all along to kidnap and coerce the Phantom to work for Oraio, most likely using the carrot-and-stick method of incentives.

Unfortunately, Tweeter had brought along his own stick. O'Riley had used it, by threatening to turn Rossi loose on DJ.

Tweeter probably shouldn't have shouted all the Marine insults he knew at the Irishman. How was he to know O'Riley was gay? Marines liberally used the word "faggot" with a bunch of other equally non-PC words to taunt their buddies.

O'Riley, however, had taken offense and beat the crap out of Tweeter—and enjoyed it. The sadistic pervert.

Worried about DJ having to deal with the likes of Rossi and Salazar, Tweeter now worked furiously on the bindings on his wrists. There was a trick to getting out of flex-cuffs, but he'd never gotten the hang of it. He'd pay more attention the next time Loren or Paul tried to teach him.

Right now, his wrists were slick with blood and he couldn't feel his fingers. He also had bruised ribs and a very sore jaw. On top of those minor injuries, he was still recovering from whatever the Irishman had injected into him and wanted to hack up his guts.

At least, DJ had been absent when the take-down occurred and would have a fighting chance to stay free. Even though O'Riley had gleefully informed Tweeter that Rossi had DJ, he hadn't really believed it. Yeah, he'd gotten mad, because the idea infuriated him, but the Irishman hadn't mentioned Dawn. The Interpol agent would've lifted more than a finger if someone had tried to make off with DJ. Logic said, both women were free and even now making plans to come get him.

Of course, O'Riley could've piped gas into the ladies' room or shot the women with tranquilizer darts as they exited. Stone cold fear chilled him to the bones, and he went motionless as he fought to beat back the dread.

Jesus H. Christ. Stop making up horror stories. The Irishman was lying.

He growled and pulled at the flex-cuffs with renewed force.

DJ was resourceful and a warrior. She'd have gone on high alert as soon as she realized he was gone. In his heart and mind, he could almost feel her anger and determination to get him out. If she hadn't already closed in on his position, she was on her way—and she wouldn't be alone.

Taking a couple of deep breaths, which helped abate the lingering nausea, but not the hammer-and-anvil headache, he managed to get his racing heart rate down as much as the pain and adrenaline in his system would allow.

His vitals back to within acceptable ranges, he looked around to see if there was anything lying around he could use to cut the cuffs off his wrists. The cave walls were smoothed by centuries of water erosion. No jagged edges there, dammit.

His tracker should work up to one hundred feet below sea level. He probably wasn't that far underground. This rock being a porous limestone and not a more solid rock like granite should allow the signal to reach his rescuers.

But if he could manage to escape before DJ came running to his rescue, he'd feel a lot better about the situation. It would be too easy for O'Riley's people to trap DJ and the others underground.

"Mr. Slade." At least his false identity still held, or he might've been dead by now.

O'Riley came to stand in front of him. "My employer is looking forward to making your and your lovely fiancée's acquaintance. Once Dahlia arrives, we'll be leaving for Oraio's private island."

"I told you, I'd work for Oraio voluntarily if Dahlia was released—and I was shown proof she was safely back home. She doesn't deserve forced servitude, because I made the lousy choice to interview for this fucking job."

Tweeter relaxed into his bonds in anticipation of being hit again. O'Riley liked to hit people who couldn't hit back.

"Oh, I put that offer in front of Oraio, but he's seen a picture of Dahlia and decided he would love to have her as a house guest—for his use."

Tweeter saw red at the threat to DJ and snarled. "You fucking pecker-headed faggot."

O'Riley smiled as he punched Tweeter in the gut. Once. Twice. Three times. The Irishman wiggled his fingers. "Your fiancée will be here soon, then we'll see how cooperative you plan to be. By the way, Oraio's willing to let you have conjugal visits to keep you happy."

O'Riley turned and left.

Tweeter growled and re-attacked the flex-cuffs.

CHAPTER 21

A click came over the receiver in her ear. Someone with an SSI headset was approaching. DJ stood up and a crashing wave of relief washed over her when she spotted the shaggy-haired Crocker close on Dawn's heels. The two of them came loaded for bear, considering the weapons they carried.

Until that moment she hadn't realized how apprehensive she'd been about heading underground with only Dawn at her side. Yeah, the Interpol agent was cool-headed and competent, but Crocker was big, mean, Marine-trained, and war-tested. When going into an unknown and dangerous situation, a Marine was always welcome.

Crocker glanced at the pile of weapons next to DJ's feet and then looked her up and down as if checking her over for injuries. His approving smile showed brightly in the darkness. "Little Bit said you were armed with only a knife, a Taser, and your handgun, but it looks like you found yourself an arsenal. Good work."

DJ shrugged. "Three guards. Three sets of weapons and ammunition."

Dawn bristled at his side like a pissed off cat. "I keep telling you the name is Dawn," she snarled, then added, "Crock-of-shit."

Crocker chuckled. "Honey, I've been called worse." He then gave Dawn a once over that told DJ the man was curious to discover what was under all the Goth camouflage. "I'll grow on you."

"Like some disease-ridden fungi," muttered Dawn as she bent over and picked up one of the assault rifles and checked it over in quick, efficient movements, then slung it over her chest to partner with the rifle she already carried. She adjusted the additional rifle so she could bring it up to firing position quickly. She went back for one of the guards' Ruger, slightly big for the smaller woman's hand, but she didn't seem to mind as she checked it out and set it in the ready position, then stuffed it in one of her big pockets.

"Damn, that's sexy. Love me a woman who knows her way around a weapon." Crocker picked up the last assault rifle and the extra ammo and added them to his weapons, leaving one for DJ.

"As interesting as the dynamic is between you two, we have a job to do. I'll be happy to offer my services as referee later."

"Not needed," Dawn replied, "because I'll never cross this man's path ever again."

"Now that hurt, sweetheart." But Crocker was smart enough to leave it at that.

"Okay." DJ held up a communication device she took off one of the guards. "Been waiting to hear a call. But so far, nada to or from the underground. This means no one is missing Salazar or the guards I took down ... yet."

Dawn held out a hand. "Maybe I can find another frequency they're playing on. They probably have agreed upon rotating frequency codes to make it harder for outside parties to come across their chatter."

"I wouldn't bet on it." DJ knelt down and stared at the entrance to the underground lair, approximately five meters in front of their current position. "The perimeter guards were really lax. The first guy"—she aimed a look at Dawn—"Rossi … was smoking. I took him out."

Dawn gasped. "You took down the Albatross? With what?"

"Taser, then knife." DJ wiped a hand down her tattered dress where Rossi's blood stained the turquoise silk. It served as a reminder she'd survived, he hadn't. "The guard on the cave entrance wasn't paying attention either, and the other guy just walked into my knife. It's been about ten minutes since I took out the third guy. I haven't heard a peep out of their com units, and no one has come to check on them or arrived from the resort."

"Stupid gits. You did the gene pool a favor—" Dawn played with the device and all she got was a bunch of static and then nothing. "They also didn't bother to recharge their equipment." She tossed the unit into the undergrowth. "Where did Oraio get these jokers? The security detail at the hotel spent more time trying to get into the maids' knickers and scrounging food from the kitchen."

DJ stood and looked over at the entrance. A metal door had been painted to blend with the rocks around it. "The guards' stupidity gives me hope any other guards inside will be just as careless."

"O'Riley won't be," Crocker said. "I've read the CIA file on him. Come across his type before. He cut his eye teeth on guns and learned security protocols at his IRA mother's knee." He nudged past DJ. "I'll go first. I'm wearing body armor." He looked her up and down, then aimed the same thorough once-over at Dawn. "You two aren't."

DJ nodded. Dawn said nothing, merely stared back, an obstinate frown creasing her forehead.

Crocker noticed. He sighed and shook his head. "We're going in hard, Little Bit. DJ's proven she can kill, can you?"

Dawn smiled, a really nasty twisting of her lips. "Bloody right I can. We can compare kill lists once we're out of here. You're just lucky we're on the same side, or I'd prove it to you now. So ... lead on, MacCrocker."

DJ had to smile. These two were like cats circling each other, their fur all ruffled and hissing.

"No talking once we're inside. Sound carries in caves. Use one click for everything's okay and two clicks for trouble and need backup." He handed DJ a full headset to replace her ear bud. "Dawn synced it to SSI's frequency so Conn will be able to hear us and us, him."

DJ nodded, placed the bud in her ear and then situated the microphone over her ear, aligning it along her jaw. "Testing," she whispered into the mic, then tapped.

"Gotcha," Crocker murmured into his headset and tapped back. "You hear me?"

"All green here," Dawn said.

"Green here also," DJ confirmed.

Waving them back, Crocker approached the door, his gaze always moving, checking the surroundings, particularly around the entrance. After stopping, he listened for several seconds, then signaled them forward as he opened the door.

The squeak it made sounded loud in the jungle night. All three of them froze and began looking around, listening for any response to the noise.

After about thirty seconds, when nothing jumped out at them shooting, Crocker entered the darkness beyond the gaping hole in the rock wall, signaling "hold" with his hand.

DJ and Dawn waited by the doorway. When the single click came over their receivers, they moved into the relative darkness of a large cave anteroom lit with a few butane-powered lanterns. Dawn shut the door behind them.

Crocker wasn't there, so they waited. Both of them constantly scanning for trouble of the two-legged kind.

When Crocker reappeared from one of the four tunnels off the main area, he shook his head and then signaled he'd take the larger tunnel and indicated DJ should take a tunnel to the left and Dawn, to the right.

Quickly, it became clear that DJ's tunnel dead-ended and was used for storage. She took several pictures with her cell phone of the boxes of weapons and ammunition with labels indicating they'd come from several Central American military bases. There were also boxes packed with plastine bags of what looked to be pure cocaine. After documenting her findings, she went back to the main entry cave where she found Dawn emerging from the right-hand cave. The other woman shook her head. DJ clicked once and received an answering click. She and Dawn entered the larger tunnel.

They found Crocker hiding behind a stack of boxes, similar to those she'd found in her tunnel. He either heard or sensed them, because he motioned them forward. DJ settled on one side of him and Dawn, the other.

Their view was of a large, well-lit cave. Two men were occupied, measuring and packing a white powder into packages, exactly like the ones she'd discovered in the left-hand tunnel. Cocaine.

A sibilant hiss of indrawn breath, Dawn rustled on Crocker's other side. Obviously, this was what Dawn's assignment had been all about—finding this source of cocaine, connecting it to Oraio, and shutting it down.

Crocker placed a hand on Dawn's shoulder in warning. She nodded. The product wasn't going anywhere, and Dawn had both her and Ace's hard drives to assist in finding evidence connecting this distribution center to Oraio.

Now was all about getting past these men and finding Ace. It had been just under an hour and a half since she'd last seen him—and another minute, even another few seconds, were too long to wait.

DJ tugged on Crocker's sleeve and showed him the tracker app on her phone. Ace's location was straight through the cave in which the two men were packing drugs and into a tunnel on the other side. He nodded and gave her a smile that could only be described as unholy. They were on the same page.

Slit two throats. Move through the tunnel. Take out anyone who wasn't Ace.

Crocker tugged on Dawn's sleeve. He pointed at DJ and himself, then at the two men who had no idea how close to meeting their maker they were. He sliced his finger across his neck. He signaled Dawn to stay put.

The Interpol agent's lips thinned, probably pissed at being left out of the action, but she nodded, then pulled her knife with one hand as she held the Ruger in her other. She'd back them up.

It was the right call. DJ had no doubt Dawn could kill, but she was short. Silencing two average-height men while holding them to slit their throats took leverage the smaller woman didn't have.

Knives in hand, DJ and Crocker prepared to move out from cover.

Dawn clicked twice.

DJ and Crocker turned to look at her. She pointed to where the cave walls met the cavern's ceiling. There were cameras disguised to blend in with the rocks. They blinked every few seconds.

Shit. Live video-feed.

O'Riley might have lax guards, but he made sure to have security cameras focused on the drug operations.

Dawn held up a finger, asking for a second. She pulled a device from one of the many pockets on her baggy pants and aimed it at one of the cameras. She smiled and punched in a few things on the small box. The blinking lights went out. She was jamming the signal.

DJ prayed glitches were routine in the damp cave, or that the people watching the monitors were asleep at the switch. If not, there'd be more than throat-slitting going on.

Using the boxes stacked along the perimeter of the large cave, she and Crocker moved until they were behind the two men. The cameras were still dark, so the jammer was doing its job. It was now or never.

DJ angled her head and indicated she'd take out the slightly shorter, skinnier guy on the left. Crocker gave her a thumbs up.

In full synchronization, they moved as if they'd practiced the maneuver together hundreds of time. Before the men even realized they were under attack, she and Crocker had their hands on the men's mouths and their heads tilted back. The struggle was a non-event, because she didn't hesitate to slit the throat of her man. Crocker was right there with her on his.

The smell of death surrounded her. She dropped her victim and stepped away. In the closed space, the hot coppery smell of blood and the smell of their bowels evacuating made her gag.

Grabbing a bottle of water off the work table, Crocker thrust it at her. She took several gulps and managed not to hurl. She nodded her thanks and grabbed a roll of paper towels, tore some off before handing the roll to Crocker.

Focusing on getting to Ace, she shoved the death of yet another man to the back of her mind as she wet the towels and then wiped her knife and then her arms. Most of her victim's blood had spurted forward, but there'd been no way to avoid the hot mess on her hands and arms.

Crocker tapped her shoulder. She turned. His face was expressionless, but his eyes held respect. He used a moistened towel to wipe some spatter off her face. The care and thoughtfulness of the gesture touched her.

He angled his head at the tunnel and mouthed "you ready?"

She nodded. His kindness, his steadiness, helped center her. Whatever he'd done in the past in the name of his undercover work, she'd just become Crocker's—no, Sam's—biggest supporter.

Dawn had already moved to take up a position guarding the entrance into the drug operations cave. She looked over her shoulder and muttered in her headset, "Get moving." She settled behind some boxes and had her assault rifle up and ready to defend them.

DJ and Crocker hurried toward the tunnel leading to Ace's tracker coordinates. Her assault rifle slung across her back, DJ shoved her knife in its scabbard and pulled her Beretta. Close up work didn't call for assault rifles. Crocker held a Desert Eagle; the big gun looked small in his large and very capable-looking hand.

Again, Crocker insisted on taking the lead and entered the tunnel which, unlike the others, was man-made and lit by low-level lighting strips along the floor. DJ followed on his heels.

They came to a spot where the tunnel curved obliquely. Light shone around the bend in the tunnel, indicating a larger and well-lit space was near.

Crocker signaled a halt with his hand, then slithered along the wall like a two-legged snake to take a look. He retraced his steps and urged her back down the tunnel, almost to the drug operations cave where they had little chance of being overheard.

He muttered into the headset. "Walsh is there. Middle of cave. Conscious. Beat up. Flex-cuffs, hands and ankles. O'Riley and another. Shoot to kill?"

Anger tasted like acid in her mouth, felt like a raging fire in her veins. She wanted to rush in there and tear O'Riley limb-from-limb for hurting Ace.

But on the heels of the fierce flood of protective anger came a frigid wash of reality. Ace was alive and would be freed soon. So, she needed to calm down and take a look at the bigger picture—at what would be best for SSI and the world-at-large.

Syd MacLean a.k.a. Oraio was smart, slippery, and had had years to plan multiple exit strategies. Oraio had merely been MacLean's first choice. Whatever they did here today would force MacLean to react.

Best bet? He'd go underground in order to save his ass and protect his ill-gotten gains and take on another identity. Finding him again would take a lot of hard work plus another freakish bit of luck. Until he was located once more, he'd continue to operate his criminal enterprises.

Conclusion?—"We need O'Riley. For intel purposes. MacLean could be in the wind after this."

Crocker stared at her for a second, then nodded. "Take out the minion … hard. Care for your man. I've got O'Riley."

DJ wasn't insulted. It was the best use of resources. Plus, once Ace was freed and had a weapon, they could help Crocker, if needed.

"Let's go," Crocker said.

They flowed down the tunnel and then into larger cave. DJ shot her man in the head before he could even react. The crack of her shot echoed off the rock walls. Crocker engaged O'Riley several feet away from Ace.

His gaze on Crocker and O'Riley, Ace grinned with what looked to be holy glee and then turned his head, looking for her. He took in her appearance, frowned, and struggled against his bonds. "Any of that blood yours?"

"Nope." All DJ's distress and fear for him vanished. He was alive, and his first concern had been for her. God, she loved this man.

As she ran toward him, she quickly categorized his external damage. Black eye. Bruised jaw. No other noticeable external injuries. When she reached his side and saw his wrists, she added severe lacerations and bruising from trying to get loose from the tight cuffs.

DJ pulled her knife and moved behind him to cut off the wrist cuffs. "Hold on. This is going to hurt." She pulled his arms away from the chair back and sliced through the bindings.

Ace hissed and moved his arms around to his front. "Fuck. Shit. Fuck."

DJ growled low in her throat, wanting to hurt O'Riley really badly. It was probably a good idea that Crocker was handling the fucker. Massaging Ace's shoulders and neck, she glanced at the fighting men.

O'Riley appeared harried and out of breath as he stumbled and cursed at Crocker. Crocker made no sound. The Marine was brutally toying with the smaller man, sort of like a large cat playing with its prey.

She turned her attention back to Ace and moved around to his front, going to her knees to cut off the equally tight ankle cuffs. She placed a hand on his thigh, still so angry she wanted to spit, and ordered, "Stay put." She then massaged his calves to get his circulation going.

"DJ…" She looked up and found Ace's wolf-blue gaze, filled with love, smiling down at her. "Thanks…"

"He took you. Hurt you. I…" She shook her head. The words were clogged in her throat. Emotions slammed through her. Anger. Relief. Guilt.

"Shh. I'm okay. Really." He rubbed a gentle finger over the lip she'd bit the hell out of since she'd found him missing. "Let's get out of here. Got a gun for me?"

"Yeah." She stood and offered him one of the guards' Glock. He took it and stood without assistance, then swayed slightly.

"Ace…?" She reached for him.

He waved her off. "I'm okay. Whatever drugs they gave me are still wearing off." He swept a hand down her back and patted her butt.

"What else hurts?" She scanned him and wished she had x-ray vision.

"Not much … they needed me functional."

She nodded and turned to look at Crocker. "Stop playing with the man, Sam. We need to bug out."

Crocker nodded and tossed O'Riley to the ground so hard the thud echoed off the rock walls.

"Where's Conn?" Ace asked as he put on the headset she thrust at him.

They gave a wide berth to Crocker as he restrained O'Riley. She was happy to see Crocker pulled the flex-cuffs really tight.

"He's on his way. I sent the SOS as soon as I'd taken care of Salazar. Dawn went to get Sam, while I followed your tracker's signal. Dawn's covering our asses and listening in."

As she leaned over to kiss Ace's un-bruised jaw, a click came over DJ's headset. "What is it, Dawn?"

"That Conn guy is outside the main cave entrance. Tell Crock-of-shit to hurry it the fuck up. I could've had O'Riley knocked out and trussed up like my great-gran's corset by now. I need to get my team in here to secure the contraband. Plus, I want to start to work on that data Walsh mined from Oraio's system."

"Roger that." She turned to look at Crocker. "Dawn…"

"I heard what Little Bit said. Girl needs to learn to chill." Crocker picked up the unconscious Irishman in a fireman's carry. "You okay, Walsh?" He looked Ace over with a keen eye. "Need any medical attention before we bug out?"

"I'm good." Moving with what looked to be his normal masculine grace, Ace picked up an extra assault rifle leaning against the wall and palmed some stuff off a small side table and slipped it into his pocket. "Let's go. I need a beer." He came to DJ's side and placed a hand on her lower back. "My computer?"

"Dawn pulled your and her hard drives. She has them." DJ rubbed her cheek on his arm. Happiness at being with him, knowing he was okay, helped keep the post-adrenaline drop from knocking her on her butt. "I sort of promised you'd share the results of your hacking with her."

He nodded. "Least I can do for her taking your back."

When they entered the drug operations cave, Dawn looked relieved to see them—and her appearance was slightly less Goth. She'd brushed her hair back and gathered it into a high ponytail, exposing her elegant bone structure. Somehow, she'd wiped off the makeup that had begun to streak and melt in the heat and humidity. Her fine-grained, porcelain skin glowed in the light and her green eyes looked brighter.

Crocker's sharp inhalation from behind DJ had her smiling. *Yeah, she's very pretty, isn't she, Sam?*

"Jesus, Little Bit, you clean up nice," Crocker drawled, his Southern accent exaggerated by some strong emotion.

"Shut it, Crock-of-shit." Dawn's tone was crisp and clipped. "I don't have the time nor the inclination to listen to your bloody nonsense." As she talked, she moved into the tunnel leading to the cave's main entrance. "Someone's trying to bollocks up my jamming. I've managed to keep them blocked, but we need to leave, or we'll all end up on Oraio's version of CCTV."

DJ and the others followed. Ace leaned over and muttered, "Little Bit. Crock-of-shit?"

She snickered and covered her microphone. "I think they like each other."

Dawn opened the door to the outside and peeked out. She brought up her weapon. "Describe Conn."

"Tall. Blond shaggy hair," DJ said as she and Ace hurried to the entry. She looked out and found Conn standing not too far from where she'd left the bodies of the guards. He had his hands up and a big shit-eating grin on his face. "It's Conn."

Dawn lowered her gun and exited into the small clearing near the cave entrance. "Righto." She aimed a smile at Conn. "Sorry. Reflexes."

"No problem. Good ones to have." Conn winked at Dawn, then looked past her toward DJ and Ace. "You okay, Tweeter? Area's secure for the moment if we need to do a med check."

He looked at Dawn, Crocker, and DJ. "Whoever took down the Albatross and the other two ugly customers did damn good work."

"That would've been DJ," Crocker said, saluting her. "Couldn't have done better myself."

Ace stared at her and whispered, "You okay, sugar?"

DJ looked at him. He winced. He probably could read her horror over having to kill lurking in her eyes ... read her lingering distress over his safety. "I can't talk about it now."

"Later then," he whispered.

She nodded. Yes, later, she'd tell him all. He would hold her in his arms, with her head on his chest, the beat of his heart pounding in her ears, and his warmth surrounding her.

Ace addressed Conn, "As I told Crocker, I'm fine. Nothing a drink and TLC from DJ won't fix. Where's the chopper?"

And just that quickly, attention was deflected away from her. Yes, she loved Ace very, very much.

"One klick straight west of here in a fallow field," replied Conn as he turned and led the way.

"Damn, I really wanted to fly that Apache," teased DJ, in an attempt at lightening the mood.

Ace shot her an ornery grin. "Me, too. We'll have to visit Dad, and he can get us some air time in one."

Her arm intertwined with his, DJ rubbed her cheek against Ace's shoulder and inhaled deeply, allowing his scent to seep into her soul and calm her even more. "Sounds like a plan."

"Conn," Ace called out. "What should we expect between here and the chopper?"

"Area's clear of bogies. Terrain's too rough to patrol. Didn't see any lookouts." Conn spoke over his shoulder. "Looks like they might use the field for landing small planes. But didn't see any signs of recent activity."

What kind of candy-assed soldier was she? The danger wasn't over yet just because they'd freed Ace.

DJ stiffened, then looked around and sensed … nothing. Nothing but the jungle and its normal inhabitants. They were safe, but, damn, she needed to stay alert in case that changed.

Proving yet again her man could read her, Ace leaned over and murmured, "It's okay to relax. Let me be on alert now. You've carried more than your share of the team load today."

"But…" Ace cut off her protest with a quick, hard kiss.

Let your man worry, Dahlia Jane. He needs to care for you now.

"Probably where they fly the drugs out of." Dawn added her two cents to the conversation that had continued among the Interpol agent, Conn, and Crocker.

"Drugs?" Conn asked.

"Yeah, cocaine." Dawn carried her rifle as if it were a familiar accessory. "Interpol will be swooping in as soon as I can borrow a secure line."

"Interpol? Bloody fecking hell." O'Riley cursed and tried to wiggle his way off Crocker's shoulder.

"Wanna get dropped on your head, you pecker-headed douchebag?" growled Crocker.

DJ loved Marines and their blunt way with words.

Ace released her arm and moved forward. He pulled out of his pocket whatever he'd picked up in the cave. "Let me take care of the ass-clown. Hope this gives him as much of a bitching headache as it gave me." He injected the Irishman with something from a syringe, which Ace capped and then slid back into his pocket. "You okay carrying dead weight for a klick?"

"Don't insult me, Walsh." Crocker juggled the now-limp man into a slightly different position and began striding forward again. "I've carried packs heavier than him for ten times that distance."

Dawn muttered, "Bleeding fucking giant, he is." Her gaze fixed on Crocker's ass.

"I heard that, Little Bit, and stop looking at my ass." Crocker aimed a sideways glance at Ace. "What the fuck did you give him? He went out like a light."

"Whatever he gave me." Ace shrugged. "I'm betting ketamine. I have an effin' headache."

"No beer for you." DJ put her arm around his waist to give him support just in case he needed it—and because she wanted to touch him.

"I'm getting a damn beer." He sounded so grumpy ... and cute. "The adrenaline has flushed most of whatever it was out of my system." As they followed Conn and Crocker with Dawn bringing up the rear, Ace leaned over and whispered into her ear. "And you're gonna be a card-carrying member of the mile-high club as soon as I get cleaned up after we're in the air."

DJ's face turned red. The heat spread to the rest of her at the speed of light and pooled in her pussy. She needed to lie with him and make love as much as she needed to breathe, but—

"Ace, we need to get you checked over medically, make sure you're okay." DJ would've liked to strip him in the cave to search for other injuries, but they'd needed to get out of there and away from the area surrounding the resort.

"I'm not injured, sugar. But if you want to do all the work, I'm down with that. One way or another, we're making love on that plane."

The fierce determination in his voice, the hunger in his eyes, convinced her sex was going to happen no matter what she said. So, she answered, "I can do that."

And with him naked and under her, she could kill two birds with one stone: making love to him and checking him out for injuries. One thing DJ was excellent at was multi-tasking.

CHAPTER 22

February 26th, early morning, en route to Idaho

The SSI jet had been fueled and waiting on them when Conn had landed the helicopter at the international airport outside of Belize City. Price had flown the jet to Belize yesterday evening and had remained on stand-by to fly them out at the completion of the mission. Currently, Price flew the plane so Tweeter could have some down-time with DJ. They both needed it after the rough ending to their mission.

After taking a shower on the jet, getting his cuts and bruises tended to by DJ, and inhaling a beer and a roast beef sandwich, Tweeter relaxed into the leather love seat with another beer in hand. DJ was snuggled closely against his side, her head on his shoulder.

A feeling of satisfaction for a successful mission settled over him. The NSA now had a road map into Oraio's closed network and a list of IP addresses for his trusted parties in the DarkNet. Rossi and Salazar were dead. When they made the scheduled stop for fuel in Dallas, O'Riley would be turned over to operatives from the DIA for interrogation. DJ had managed to take pictures of all the hackers auditioning for the position of Oraio's go-to hacker for NSA's further investigation. Most importantly, no one on the SSI team had been severely injured.

While Tweeter's short period as a captive hadn't been fun, it hadn't been traumatic. He'd never doubted DJ would mount an immediate rescue. He was proud to have her as a teammate and even happier that she was his lover and soon-to-be his wife.

"Will we see Conn again?" DJ massaged his chest through the t-shirt he'd thrown on after cleaning up.

After flying them to the Belize City airport, Conn had hopped a commercial flight to Cartagena.

"Probably," Tweeter said. "Lately, we've used Conn quite a bit for intel gathering. Unfortunately, Central and South America are evolving into hot beds for international terrorism on top of the already prevalent drug trafficking."

Tweeter kissed the top of DJ's head, her hair smelling of the citrus-scented shampoo stocked on the jet. The shower gel was also scented with citrus; the fragrance mixed with her own unique musk made him want to eat her up. Soon, he'd take her to the jet's bedroom and do that very thing. Right now, he had the sense she wanted to talk.

"Well, I liked him." She cuddled closer and brushed a feather-like kiss over his bruised jaw. "I also liked Dawn. She'd be a great addition to SSI. I think Ren should approach her about a job."

He was happy to hear DJ was on the same page about the feisty little Brit. They could approach Ren together about making Dawn an offer. She might not take it, but they wouldn't know unless they tried.

Dawn had met her Interpol team as soon as the chopper had touched down. The little

Brit then hopped right back onto another helicopter to fly back to the *Gato Grande* resort to take down the drug operation and confiscate the weapons and anything else she could claim was used in the drug trafficking operation. The Belizean government was also sending troops to secure the resort, which would most likely be seized as an asset of a criminal enterprise.

"Did you happen to see where Crocker went?" Tweeter tipped her face to his.

Crocker had disappeared before Tweeter could propose the possibility of him doing contract work with Conn for SSI in Central and South America. There was no use going to Ren and making an argument for such a working relationship if Crocker wasn't even interested. Tweeter was positive Ren and Vanko would eventually get over Crocker's role in the threats to Keely and Elana once Crocker's undercover status was made clear.

"I think Sam followed Dawn back to the resort." DJ grinned. "Did you see her slap him across the face after he said something to her right before she met up with her team?"

Tweeter raised an eyebrow. "No. Missed that. I was too busy making sure Price sneaked O'Riley aboard the jet before the Belizean government swept in. It was nice of Dawn to tell the locals we were assisting Interpol with their Drug Task Force op." The little Brit's explanation kept things legal under international law and kept SSI's role in the matter low key.

"Dawn thinks well on her feet," DJ said.

"I agree. That's why I'd already planned on mentioning her to Ren." DJ smiled at him and he kissed the tip of her nose. "Did you happen to hear what Crocker said to earn a slap?"

"Part of it. I can guess the rest." DJ rubbed her hand over his thigh covered only by a much-washed pair of sweat pants. She then trailed her fingers up his thigh, took a sharp turn at the junction with his hip, then covered his erection, which she gently squeezed.

Tweeter inhaled sharply at the pleasure. "Sugar, you're surely tempting the beast."

His semi-erection had become full-blown as soon as she'd joined him in the very small shower stall to check over the damage to his body. She'd refused to believe him or Price when they'd told her he was fighting fit. His hard-on hadn't flagged since. Only one thing would make it go away, and he wasn't even sure climaxing would solve the problem for long. He was fairly certain he could spend the next two days making love to DJ and still not assuage his need for her.

"I know." She winked. "You and Price were one hundred percent correct. You're definitely up to the sort of physical activity I have in mind." She fondled his bulge before pulling her hand away.

He loved that DJ had grown more comfortable with lovemaking and could even tease him about their sex play. Considering her past trauma, she'd come a long way in the weeks he'd known her. He was a very lucky man to have earned her trust and her love.

"Now, finish your beer. That big old bed will wait a bit." She rubbed her cheek against his arm.

While DJ seemed relaxed, it was obvious she was still decompressing … still dealing with their mission and what actions she'd taken to rescue him. Before Dawn had left with her team, she'd taken a few minutes to pull him aside and tell him exactly how DJ had taken out Salazar, Rossi, and three others with knives. He'd seen her shoot one of his captors.

The knowledge that DJ had been forced to make six up-close kills threatened to take him to his knees. With immense courage and steely determination, his warrior-woman had done what needed to be done in order to free him and preserve their mission. No one with a solid core of morality, male or female, could brush aside taking that many lives easily. There was always a mental and emotional cost.

So, if she needed more downtime to cuddle, tease, and process, then she'd get it. Whatever the aftermath this mission might bring, be it nightmares or delayed PTSD, he'd be there to share it with her. His dick could damn well wait until DJ signaled she was ready to make love with him—however long that might take.

"Back to Crocker and Dawn. What did you overhear?" Tweeter raised the beer to his mouth and took a sip.

Whatever she'd heard set her to giggling like a teenage girl. Tweeter smiled and shook his head as DJ smothered her laughter against his chest.

"The part … I heard…" She snicker-snorted until tears leaked from the corner of her eyes. "…was Sam … saying s-s-something about Dawn having his b-b-babies." DJ turned her face into his chest again, clutching at his shirt, and giggled even harder.

Tweeter choked on his sip of beer, then coughed.

DJ sat up, eyes and mouth smiling, and helpfully patted him on his back. "Went down the wrong pipe?"

"Yeah. Sugar, you can stop beating on me." Tweeter put his arm around her and pulled her back into the curve of his body. "I'm shocked she only slapped him."

"It had some power behind it, too." DJ smoothed a finger over Tweeter's cheekbone, then swept over to his ear, tracing it, then back to his cheek. If he'd been a cat, he'd have purred. "Sam had a nice red splotch right about here." She tapped his cheek and then shifted the finger to trace along his jaw. "I think … she sort of likes him … in a love-hate sort of way."

DJ moved her hand from his face and trailed it down his chest over his stomach to his thigh, resting it really close to his throbbing cock. Distracted, she began to knead his leg. "It's also why I concluded Sam was heading back to the resort. I think he wanted to back her up—or get her phone number."

Hell. She was going to kill him, petting him that way. He gritted his teeth and reined in his need. She needed to talk … to relax.

"Ace…"

He almost swore out loud when she stilled her hand right over the erection tenting his sweat pants.

"…maybe now that we know Sam's a good guy—"

"Sort of good guy." Tweeter inhaled sharply as she swept a thumb over the top of his cock … once … twice … then stopped. He'd survived O'Riley's not-so-tender treatment, but this sweet torture might drive him over the edge into insanity. He wanted to be inside her right the fuck now, but she had to make the move.

"What do you mean sort of a good guy?" she asked. "He's working for our side."

"Yes, but the CIA is his employer, and so Crocker's often forced to do bad things, even if they're for the right reasons. His wings are tarnished."

"Like an archangel?" DJ arched a brow as she began to fondle his cock once more. "I believe Ren and Vanko will get over their issues … eventually."

Which again affirmed how much he and DJ thought alike.

"Elana and Keely won't hold a grudge once they realize Sam was doing his job and they were in no real danger from him," she said. "Plus, I'm betting Keely already knows all about his undercover missions."

Tweeter forced himself to hold onto his bottle of beer and fought the urge to grab DJ, throw her to the floor of the main cabin, and make love to her right then and there.

"Probably," he replied, his voice husky from his extreme arousal. "When we present our post-mission report, we can recommend using Crocker as a contract employee and suggest that he live and work in Colombia with Conn. Conn, I know, would be more than happy to have him. Marines stick together."

"Can we make a recommendation about Dawn in this report?"

DJ's cheeks were flushed. Her eyes dilated with her own simmering arousal. Thank fuck, she wanted him, too. All he needed was a word or a gesture that said she was ready to go to bed and make love.

"Yeah." As Tweeter thought about what DJ had told him about the couple, he frowned. "We'll just have to keep her away from Crocker so she doesn't emasculate him."

"Darlin', you obviously weren't paying attention to the sizzling emotions between those two. Of course, I saw them interact more than you did."

DJ untied the drawstring on his sweats and freed his cock—*Finally!*— and began to handle him exactly the way he liked with long, firm pulls and a twist over the top.

"After she slapped him…" DJ smoothed the precum over his glans before resuming her stroking. "…Dawn stood in the open cabin door of Interpol's helicopter and followed Sam with her eyes until he disappeared into the terminal building. She wasn't staring daggers at him, either."

"How was she looking at him?" Tweeter hated to do it, but he stilled her hand on his cock. If she kept petting him, he'd come before she ever took him inside her body. And this first time, he needed to be surrounded by her tight, hot channel … needed the bonding the intimate connection provided.

"As if Sam was an all-you-can-eat buffet and she was starving." DJ ended her sentence by pulling her hand out from under his and sliding it under his tee to torment his nipples.

"Sugar," he drawled, "you've let the beast out now, for sure."

"That was the plan." She looked at him from under her lashes, a naughty grin on her lush, pink lips. "If you recall, I promised I'd do all the work." She moved her hand down his torso and back to his cock and squeezed the base of his shaft. His cock leaked a drop, then another of precum. "I always keep my promises."

Tweeter set aside his all-but-forgotten beer and then slid his hand inside the opening of the terry cloth robe DJ had put on after their shower. She was completely naked underneath. He sought and tweaked an already pebbled nipple, then cuddled the plush breast in his hand.

"That feels so good. More." She lay her head on his shoulder and pressed nibbling kisses along his tense neck muscles. She resumed fisting his cock and finished each up-stroke by skimming her thumb lightly across the tip.

"More?" he murmured huskily. "Something like this?" He shoved open the front of the robe and then bent her back over his supporting arm so he could take a rosy bud into his mouth. Suckling the nubbin, he massaged her breast.

DJ let out a low moan. "Yes-s-s … so good."

After a minute or so of his brand of breast worship, DJ shoved at his chest. Tweeter immediately stopped, worried he'd moved too fast.

That thought was instantly proven erroneous when she pulled his t-shirt up. Even before he helped pull it over his head, DJ was brushing light kisses over his chest while combing her fingers through his chest hair. He sucked in a breath, then hissed with pleasure at the sensations gliding over his skin, down his spine, and coalescing in his already hard-to-the-point-of-pain cock.

"I love you, Ace. I'm so happy you're safe…" Her breath hitched slightly. The emotion in her voice pierced him like a sword. His capture had affected her more than he'd realized. "…and here with me now."

He caressed the back of her head as she dusted kisses over his chest, his nipples, and then down onto his abs. "I love you, Dahlia Jane. I never doubted, not for one single second, that you'd come for me."

DJ paused in her kissing exploration and looked up, a fierceness coupled with joy in her eyes. "There'll never be a time when I don't come after you." She bit one of his nipples lightly. Her lips twisted into a naughty grin, she said, "Since I get to do all the work, does that mean I get to be on top?"

His cock jerked and leaked at the thought of her above him, her breasts bouncing, as she rode him for her pleasure—and his.

"Oh hell yeah." Tweeter lifted her face to his and nibbled at her lips. The light kiss meant to be an appetizer became more of a feast as it soon turned hot and heavy.

Breaking away, they both were breathing hard. Tweeter's balls were so tight and heavy it wouldn't take much to make him explode. His cock leaked precum like a sieve. If they didn't move to the privacy of the bedroom now, he'd pull her over him and let her ride his cock where they sat. He needed her that much.

"We better take this to the bedroom—or Price could walk back to get coffee or check on the prisoner and get an eyeful."

DJ smiled, a mysterious womanly smile that made him hungrier for her, if that were possible. She rose and held out a hand. "Then come with me to the bedroom. I promise to be gentle."

"DON'T BE TOO GENTLE, SUGAR. I don't break."

DJ wasn't too sure about that. Ace and Price could assure her all they wanted, but the bruises on Ace's face and body had to hurt.

Yet, his penis was harder than she'd ever felt it—and had to pain him even more. So, she'd make love to him and be as gentle as she could while doing so. When they made it home later today, they'd be taking a trip to the hospital in Grangeville for some x-rays on his ribs and jaw. She wouldn't take no for an answer. He was hers to protect, even from himself and his warped male machismo.

Holding his hand, she tugged him into the jet's bedroom. Ace closed the door behind them and locked it one-handed.

He winked. "Just in case, Price gets nosy." He pulled his hand from hers and dropped the sweat pants to the floor. Even with ugly bruises on his tanned torso, his lean, strong body pleased her. He was alive, here, and—

Mine.

DJ slid off the robe and tossed it on a small chair. Licking her lips, she walked toward her man, showing off her body for his pleasure. His ice blue gaze burned over her, causing her body to ignite in response. His massive erection jutted from his body. He was so hard the veins were starkly delineated on his thick shaft.

Her bruised warrior really needed her—and she wanted his cock inside her where it belonged. She loved this man with every bit of her being. She coveted the closeness their lovemaking would bring and the reaffirmation they were alive.

Anticipation of the pleasure to come had her swallowing hard, but, for some reason, she was also nervous, hesitant. So, she babbled.

"Is Price a voyeur?" DJ pulled the linen coverlet down to the end of the bed, then plumped and replumped the pillows against the headboard. Normally, she could fricking care less about pillow arrangements.

"Not really."Ace's high cheek bones were flushed with his arousal, but his tone was terse when he added, "If he saw you naked, even accidentally, I'd have to hurt the man. So it's better we don't tempt him with easy access."

He paused and in a gentler voice, said, "Don't be nervous, sugar. If you're not ready, I'm happy simply being close to you, holding you."

DJ looked at her man, one who'd shown—continued to show—infinite patience with her foibles. His loving, but troubled gaze followed every move she made ... reading her. His body was tense and unmoving; he held a tightly reined control over his desire. It was clear through his words and actions if lovemaking was going to happen, she had to initiate it.

And she wanted to make love with him more than anything in the world. So, what the hell was wrong with her?

Aftermath, Dahlia Jane. What did you decide in the Belizean jungle about aftermath?

Ace would help her through it. She'd never have to deal with new or past traumas alone again.

What are you waiting for? Take care of your man, Dahlia Jane, and then let him take care of you ... later.

"I want you very, very much." DJ patted the soft sheets. "Sit down right here, so I can take care of that enormous problem between your legs."

"Problem?" He moved a hand to his cock. Instead of pumping it as he sometimes did, he squeezed it at the base ...

hard. He was holding off his climax—for her. "Yeah, and it's an ongoing one. Especially since my cock seems to get in this condition whenever you're near."

"All you ever have to do is find me, and I'll take care of it and you. Always." She took his free hand and pulled him toward the bed. "Now, come and let me make love to you."

With a masculine grace, Ace climbed onto the bed and then reclined against the pillows she'd plumped. He showed no signs of discomfort or pain from his ordeal.

Ace held out his arms. "Come here."

DJ climbed onto the bed from the bottom. As she crawled toward him, putting a sway into her movement, his heated blue gaze made her feel sexy and loved. She stopped by his thighs and then sat up. Swinging one of her legs over to straddle his thighs, she rested her butt on his legs.

Ace captured her breasts, one in each hand. She leaned over him as he pinched and rubbed her nipples. They were so tightly budded she swore they couldn't get any tighter, but amazingly, they did. The pleasure/pain sensations mainlined directly from her breasts to her clit.

"That feels so effin' good." Her arms braced on either side of his body, she pressed into his touch, getting closer so she could claim his mouth.

No passive partner, Ace sucked her tongue into his mouth and deepened the kiss, swallowing her moans even as she swallowed his growls and grunts.

His erection lay between their torsos. The tip reached just under his navel and her stomach undulated over it as she moved into him. His precum streaked her belly, feeling cool on her heated skin. Every so often his cock jerked as if it were impatient to get inside her.

Reluctantly, she broke off the carnal kiss and retreated. They both gasped for breath.

Adding to her breathlessness, Ace still held onto her breasts, fondling and squeezing. He eyed her as if she were essential to his very existence.

DJ sat back on Ace's legs once again. She grasped his penis with one hand and pumped his shaft. When she gently thumbed his glans, spreading the moisture around the tip, his strong body shuddered.

His eyes half-closed, he groaned low in this throat. "Have mercy on me."

"What do you need?" She sat up and knee-walked farther up his body until she could guide his cock to her slit. "This?" She rubbed the head in her juices.

"Fuck yeah." He circled his thumb over the hood of her clit. "How does that feel?"

DJ inhaled sharply as a piercing stab of pleasure had her pussy clenching. "So good." She shifted her hips forward seeking more of his touch.

"What kind of ride do you want?" She circled her hips over the top of his erection. "Long and slow? Hard and fast? Or blow job followed by a hard, fast ride to finish?"

Stilling her hips, she took his erection firmly in hand and waited.

Ace arched into her hand. "Sugar, if you put your lips or your pussy on my cock—I'll blow right then and there. I'm too close for anything long and slow."

"Hard and fast it is." She seated the tip of his erection into her swollen opening and took him inside her with one quick downward shove of her hips.

They both gasped.

"Fuck that feels good," growled Ace as he grabbed her hips, holding her to him as if she might escape.

DJ agreed whole-heartedly. Pausing a mere second or so to allow her body to adjust to his breadth, she felt his cock throb in time with the pulse beating at his throat.

"You good?" He stroked his thumbs over the curve of her hips.

"Oh hell yeah." She shimmied atop him and he swore under his breath. "Once I take you fast and hard, I plan to start all over and do you long and slow."

DJ arched her back and just luxuriated in the feel of him, hot and pulsing inside her. Yet, the connection was more than physical; it was also a union of souls.

"I'm yours. Do whatever you want to do to me." He slid his hands up her torso to cup her breasts; his thumbs played with her nipples. "Ride me, Dahlia Jane."

Beginning slowly, she moved up and down on his steel-hard erection. With each downstroke, she tightened her inner muscles around him and ground her clit over his pubic bone. It felt so damn good. So perfect. So right.

"Faster." Ace groaned the words as she completed yet another downstroke. "Fuck me. Take what's yours."

"Mine." DJ stared into his stormy blue eyes and increased her speed.

Grabbing a butt cheek in one large hand, Ace curled forward and suckled a nipple while tormenting and teasing its partner with his free hand. When he scraped her aching bud with his teeth, the sensation was like a lightning strike straight to her clit. She threw back her head and mewled. Her core gripped his cock even harder.

"Fuck. Damn. Let's do that again," Ace growled against the nipple he pleasured. He teethed the bud once more, then moved back and forth between her breasts, sucking and pinching and nibbling. The sensations crescendoed and now pounded at her core, building a pressure which threatened to destroy her once it was unleashed.

Faster and faster she rode him until she gasped for every breath. The world began to fade away as her reality narrowed to one end-game—to climax.

Ace released her breasts and lay back against the pillows. She whimpered at the loss of his mouth, his touch on her breasts, but moaned when he firmly grasped her ass with his big hot hands and began moving her even faster up and down his cock.

"Look at me," he growled out. She opened her eyes. His fierce, loving gaze was fixed on her as if she were the sexiest woman in the world. "Come for me, sugar."

He moved one hand and used his thumb to apply a firm, circular motion on her clit and—

"Ace!" she screamed as she soared. Her control over her body was gone, vanquished in an explosion of white-hot pleasure. All sense of time and space ceased to exist. She floated in a bubble of pure bliss. The only thing holding her to this place and time were Ace's hands and his cock.

Ace was now the one in control. It was he who steered their pleasure course as he gave her everything that was him—his protection, his love, his body.

Her orgasm was soul-shattering as Ace continued to take her higher. So high, she might never come down to earth. But she wasn't afraid, because he was with her.

As spasms traveled over her body, Ace grunted and pumped his hips, hard and fast. He ground against her clit, building the pressure within her once more.

When she thought she could handle no more, he pulled her hips down and held her against him as he roared his own completion. At that moment, she became his anchor as he roughly thrust into her, his hands gripping her hips as if he never wanted to let go.

As his hot seed flooded her, she gasped through another orgasm. Her exhausted body bent over his, her hands gripping his shoulders.

When all was silent and calm once again, Ace pulled her more fully onto his chest, urging her head to his shoulder with one, big, shaking hand. At least, she wasn't the only one affected by the earth-shattering orgasm. He held her to him, his grip both firm and gentle.

Her heart still racing, she relaxed onto his body, his penis still inside her, and kissed the underside of his jaw. Her body moved up and down as his chest expanded and contracted; it felt like floating on a gentle ocean surf.

Then she recalled his bruises. Her weight had to be hurting him. She tried to sit up.

"Stay put." He pulled her down.

"No, Ace, I'll hurt you—"

"No, you won't. You can't. I want to hold you close. I don't want to pull out." He kissed the top of her head. "We're working on making a baby today. After we pass O'Riley off in Dallas to the DIA agents, I'll be telling Price to set a course for Vegas. We're getting married as soon as possible." He paused. "You on board with that, sugar?"

He sounded almost … anxious.

Was she okay with it? She'd already told him she'd marry him. She wasn't getting any younger and she loved holding Keely and Ren's son. She knew having babies would make going out on SSI missions harder, but she also had built-in baby sitters and a man who'd share the load and not hold her back from doing her job once the children came along.

"Yes. To all of it." She smiled into the juncture of his neck and shoulder as he muttered "thank God" against her hair. Then she stiffened. "Ace! I want my mama there—in Vegas."

DJ raised her head and found the smiling eyes of her man.

"Ren and the others will bring Nancy to Vegas." He kissed the tip of her nose. "Every girl needs her mom at her wedding. Keely will get my family there. So, no worries. We'll get a suite at the Bellagio and practice getting the wedding night perfect while they're all gathering."

"I love you." She peppered kisses all over his face. "You get me."

"Yeah, I do," he whispered against her lips. "And now I've also gotten you." He bucked his hips against her. His penis was hard once again and pulsed with life inside her. "Now, shall we try long and slow?"

"You got it, darlin'." DJ began the motion that promised to shoot them to the stars once again.

———

"Tweeter! Answer the damn com!" Price's impatient voice broke through the pleasant post-orgasm haze in Tweeter's head. Making love to DJ was hands down the best pain medicine and muscle-relaxant in the universe.

He didn't want to answer the intercom, because it would involve moving. DJ was asleep, lying bonelessly on top of him. His semi-erect cock, still inside her. After she'd ridden him slow and long, they'd been too tired to move or even clean up. He'd had just enough energy to pull the covers over them, then joined DJ in sleep.

His internal clock indicated they hadn't been asleep all that long.

DJ needed her rest, dammit. So did he. He had a wedding night to practice for.

"Walsh, stop fucking your woman and answer the damn intercom!"

Tweeter gently pulled DJ off his cock and then moved her to lie next to him. She moaned and snuggled into his side. He turned away from her just enough so he could slap at the intercom mounted on the wall by the head of the bed.

"What the fuck, Price?" he said, trying to keep his voice as soft as possible. "We're trying to sleep."

"Ren called. We're diverting to West Virginia."

Tweeter sat up. "What happened?"

At his peremptory tone, DJ jerked against him. Awake now, she placed her arm over his waist, her hand on his stomach, and rested her front against his back.

"DJ's mom was kidnapped off the street in Elk City by some militia types." DJ stiffened against him; her whimpered cry, muffled against his back. He patted the hand on his abs. "They shot Scotty."

Fear-based adrenaline raced through Tweeter's bloodstream, wiping out any remaining fog in his head. "How badly was he hurt? Did they hurt Nancy?"

"Scotty's fine. He took a bullet to the upper left chest. It missed everything crucial." Price snorted. "The old salt wanted to go after Nancy himself. Ren said the doctor had to sedate Scotty. Nancy wasn't hurt from what the witnesses told the sheriff's deputy."

Tweeter let out a relieved breath when he heard Scotty would be okay. But his concern for DJ's mom twisted him up inside. Nancy might not have been hurt, but she had to be terrified.

"Price, how could this have happened? When did it happen?" DJ's voice was emotionally charged.

Tweeter turned and pulled her against his side. The look on her face—one of bewilderment and fear—made him want to howl and then rend and tear the fuckers who put the look on her face.

"As to how? No one figured anyone would try to take Nancy in broad daylight with an armed man at her side. As to when. Less than ninety minutes ago. Ren didn't contact us until they were sure Nancy had actually been taken out of state. The FBI has already been alerted as has Homeland Security since this is being classified as a home-grown terrorist act because of the militia involvement. Your mom's necklace tracker is working. Keely is following it in real time. The kidnappers are still in the air."

Price took a breath. "Ren will give you a full sit rep as soon as you call him back. I've changed course. We'll fly into the closest air strip to Red Bone that can handle this jet. Our ETA is two hours. We're closer than the assclowns flying from Idaho. If everything goes smoothly, we could even beat them to West Virginia."

"That's good. Thanks, Price," DJ murmured. She was so pale, Tweeter was afraid she might fade away.

He reached for her, pulling her across his lap, and then cuddled her chilled body against him.

"She'll be so scared." DJ shivered. Tweeter pulled the bedclothes up even further until she was cocooned by his body and the blankets. "So worried about Scotty."

"They won't have her long. I promise." Tweeter rubbed his cheek over her hair as she cried almost soundlessly against his chest. He felt so helpless when she cried. "Price … DJ and I'll get dressed. We'll call Ren back. Then I'll spell you in the cockpit so you can eat and catch a battle nap."

"Roger that. I could use a cup of coffee ASAP, if you get a chance in the next few minutes or so."

"You got it, buddy." Tweeter hit the intercom off and rocked DJ. "We'll get her back."

"I know, but…"

She looked up. Her wet eyes held a feral look. His warrior-woman was coming alive right before his eyes. Nothing kept her down for long.

"This is gonna end this time." Her words were a vow. "Momma deserves her new life. I'm making a life with you. So my effin' father and his fricking pals need to be history."

"I agree." He cradled her jaw and wiped away the few tears left on her cheeks with the edge of the sheet. "But we need to let the law handle their punishment."

"I know." The initial panic and fear in her eyes was gone and replaced with icy rage. "But if my fucking father has hurt her, I'll handle him."

"And I'll help you." Or, he'd just handle it. He wouldn't allow DJ to kill her father. She might not want to acknowledge it, but the act would destroy something inside her.

Tweeter placed a tender kiss on her lips, then touched his forehead to hers. "Promise me. Whatever our operational plan ends up being, you'll be careful. I don't want Sean Varney getting his hands on you."

"Ace, I can only promise to be as careful as I can." DJ traced her fingers lightly over his black eye and bruised jaw as if reminding him unexpected shit happened. "If Sean gets in my way, I will take the fucker down with my teeth and nails if I have to."

Yeah, she could do it. But he had a really bad feeling about this clusterfuck and planned never to let DJ out of his sight. Nancy's kidnapping was all about luring DJ to within Sean Varney's reach—and the fucking plan was working.

CHAPTER 23

Mid-Day, February 26, Appalachian Regional Airport, Williamson, West Virginia

Emotions under a tentative lock-down and her mind focused on the job ahead, DJ sat next to Ace as he landed the SSI jet at a regional airport built on reclaimed strip mining land, eight nautical miles east of Williamson, West Virginia. This airport was much closer to Red Bone than the Mingo County Airport and would cut their driving time in half.

The weather service chatter droned in her ears as she worried her lower lip. Conditions were deteriorating. Currently, there were streaks of snow on the asphalt strip. The snow would remain until the wind blew it away or it melted. There was no snow removal, no maintenance of any kind, at this unattended airport.

While the runway was manageable for now, even more snow was in the forecast with strong winds and accumulations of more than three inches.

Worried about what the conditions might be like later, DJ asked, "How does this jet handle a short runway in bad weather?" Then she gasped out, "Hell, is that a bear?" She pointed to the right of the plane as Ace taxied to the tie-down area.

"Yep. Big fucker, too." Ace adjusted to avoid a collision with the running bear. His hands were steady on the yoke and he didn't even blink at the wildlife that could've damaged the expensive plane. "Never know what you're going to see in small rural airports. As for the jet, let me and Price worry about it. We've flown in and out of a private strip in Elk City in some fairly dicey snow conditions. We know what this baby can handle."

Ace pulled into a space next to another plane, a Cessna, in the process of being covered by a tarp and tied down.

"Ah, Loren and Paul beat us here. Good. They're supposed to bring us winter clothing and gear." He turned toward her. "Risto took Callie back to Michigan with him. She sent some clothes for you."

"When did you talk to Risto and the others?" DJ took off the headset she'd used to monitor the weather conditions. She'd be glad to get some winter-weight clothes that fit better than Ace's jeans and long-sleeve t-shirt. She was already feeling drafts where his clothes were too big.

"When I relieved Price in the cockpit while you were cleaning up." A warm glow in his eyes told her he was recalling why she had to clean up.

Their lovemaking seemed as if it had happened days ago instead of hours. The news about her mother's kidnapping and Scotty's injury had dampened the satisfaction in a mission accomplished and the happiness of having Ace safe and sound in her arms. Adding to her emotional roller coaster were the obstacles tossed into the path of getting to her mother quickly. The lousy weather across the southern U.S. had forced them to stop for fuel en route to West Virginia in Mobile instead of Atlanta. While there, they'd had to wait to hand O'Riley over to someone from the DIA, flying in from their originally planned stop in Dallas. So, instead of beating the kidnappers' to West Virginia, they were now about three hours behind.

Her tissue-thin control over her emotions shredded as a feeling of pure dread feathered over her skin like a thousand spiders. Was her mother in pain? Was she scared? Was she even alive? Unlike the implanted trackers which operated using the body's natural electricity, her mother's tracker was in a necklace; she could be dead and the tracker would still send signals.

There's no reason to kill her.

There'd also been no reason to beat DJ and her mother all those years, but her father had done it anyway.

Worrying was useless and a waste of energy. DJ forced the damaging thoughts out of her head and stood. "I'll wake up Price." The other man had opted to take a battle nap after the refueling stop in Mobile. "And open the cabin door so Loren and Paul can deliver our gear."

Being former SEALs, Paul and Loren had probably brought enough weaponry and communication equipment to mount an invasion of a small country. She'd also spotted a large HumVee parked in the tie-down area. It looked to be a military vehicle, and she had to wonder what favors Ren, or Colonel Walsh, had to pull in to get it delivered to this small, out-of-the-way Appalachian airport.

"I'll just finish my post-flight checklist." Ace looked at the airport layout. "With no mechanical or fuel services readily available, I'm not taking chances with our best way to get out of here quickly."

"Good thing we topped the tanks in Mobile," DJ said.

"Yeah, we'd play hell getting quality jet fuel out here in this weather." Ace grasped her hand and gave it a squeeze. "We have more than enough fuel to get us the hell out of West Virginia and to Lexington. We can spend the night at a Lexington airport hotel and take care of—"

"My momma if she's been hurt. I'm praying hard he hasn't hurt her."

But when had prayer ever helped? Her father was bone-deep mean. He liked preying on the weak. Though, the fact her mother had survived all those years and gotten DJ away from him proved who the really strong person was in the Poe family.

Bending over, DJ rested her forehead against Ace's and breathed him in, let his mere presence strengthen her. She didn't have to fight the upcoming battle with her father and the Varneys alone. Yeah, she could've done it, but it was nice to have backup. It wasn't a sign of weakness to lean on a partner, especially when that partner was the man who loved you as no one else ever had.

"I love you," she whispered. "You complete me."

"And I love you, but you know that." He leaned back. His gaze traveled over her face and settled on her mouth. "Dahlia Jane, you're going to bite a hole clean through that lower lip if you don't stop fretting."

He pulled her closer to him and placed a light kiss on the lip she'd been worrying ever since Price had told them about the kidnapping. So much for thinking she had her emotions under control.

"Nancy's a strong woman. She'll know we're coming for her. She'll do whatever she did to survive the bastard for all those years to keep herself as safe as possible."

DJ cradled Ace's lean jaw. "I'm glad you're here to cover my ass in case I fuck up. This is too personal, and I can't seem to keep my fears from rising to the surface."

"You won't fuck up. I have complete faith in your ability to act and react under stress. You rescued me after all." He patted her bottom. "But, yeah, I've got your ass covered. The rest of the team will cover both of ours."

"I know," DJ said. "I needed to let you know I was feeling kind of shaky." Especially coming so close on top of Ace's rescue from O'Riley's clutches.

"My mom always said 'a burden shared lightens the load.' Of course, she usually pointed that out when one of us kids wasn't carrying our weight in chores." He winked.

DJ chuckled despite her roiling emotions. "Still applies, though."

Ace gently kissed her one last time and then turned back to the controls. "As soon as I finish this checklist and we tie down and cover the jet, we'll go get your mom and kick your father and his assclown friends' asses."

"Damn right we will." DJ left the cockpit.

———

Outside Red Bone, West Virginia

THE SMOKE COMING FROM THE chimney of her childhood home was the only sign of occupancy. Not even the motion detectors on the exterior security lights seemed to be working. The power had to be out, and her father was too damn cheap to run the generator he had in a shed near the back of the house.

However, the chills chasing down her spine and settling in her belly warned her something was … off … about the whole scene. The tracker in her mother's necklace indicated she was inside. Yet, the cabin not only looked, but also felt empty.

DJ edged closer to Ace, appreciating his warmth and the solidity of his body. His keen gaze examined the house as if he could see through the walls. If he spotted anything out of the ordinary, he wasn't talking.

To be truthful, she didn't want to hear what he thought about the cabin. Just as she'd been with Dev and Andy, she was embarrassed that he saw where she'd come from. While Ace liked and respected her mother, her mother was an angel who'd risen above the life Al Poe had put her through.

But DJ was another story—she had more than her mother's blood running in her veins.

The reality of DJ's origins sat in front of her and was further underlined by the actions of her father and his lowlife friends. This place—Al Poe—would always be part of who she was.

Thanks to her mother, DJ had gotten away before her father's abusiveness had tainted the good her mother and teachers like Mrs. Binkley had instilled within her.

Still, deep inside her lurked the shadows of her beginnings in Red Bone—dwelled the remnants of the angry, scared girl who'd never understood why her father hadn't loved and protected her.

Now, as those dark childhood memories and insecurities surfaced, she had Ace's love to dispel the shadows and warm her soul. She rested her head on Ace's shoulder, watched the house, and impatiently waited for their next move.

"Coming in." Loren's voice came over the headsets they all wore.

Loren and Paul moved like dark wraiths through the knee-deep snow, keeping to the trees so anyone who might be watching from the cabin couldn't easily see them.

Price had remained with the Hummer hidden in a copse of trees near the entrance to the road leading to the cabin. If anyone approached, he'd let them know.

The dark-haired Walsh twins hunkered down next to their younger brother.

"Sit rep," Ace said.

There was no doubt who was in charge of this rescue operation. Her man had taken the reins of leadership from the time they'd met up with Loren and Paul on the tarmac. After the time she'd spent with the Walsh family, she'd had some concerns his older brothers wouldn't cede to Ace's leadership, but they had with only a couple of raised eyebrows between them.

"No one moving around inside that we could see," said Loren. She knew it was Loren, because his eyes were green. Paul's were blue. Other than that distinguishing feature, the twins were the same height and approximately the same weight. "The fire's banked in the main room's fireplace. No vehicles parked out back or in the barn."

"Did you see any signs around the house of coming and going since this last snowfall?" Ace asked.

"None," Paul replied this time. "What tracks there are have been filled with fresh snow. Same as we saw on our approach to the cabin."

"That means no one has been in or out since shortly after they landed in West Virginia with Nancy." Ace turned to her. "You think your father would leave your mom locked up all by herself for that long?"

"He's done it before." DJ's stomach churned at the thought of her mother trussed up like a Thanksgiving turkey, cold and alone in the dark. "The last time I was here, he had her stashed in the unheated attic bedroom." She stood and dusted the snow off her pants and coat. "Or, it could be her necklace is here and she's not."

Ace uncoiled from his kneeling position, then took her hand and gave it a gentle squeeze. He didn't let go. Somehow he sensed she needed his touch. "Let's make sure she isn't here."

"If she's not?" Paul asked as he and Loren followed them across the large open area to the front porch.

DJ answered, speaking into the headset, her voice carrying only as far as her microphone, "Then we travel a couple of hollers back toward Red Bone and pay a not-so-neighborly visit to the Varneys. There, we might need all that firepower you brought. Varney always has his militia home boys in residence."

"Man, I'd love to kick some militia butt." Loren sounded elated. "Haven't had a good fight since we kicked South American drug-lord-minion butt in Osprey's Point."

"Hoo-rah." Paul high-fived him.

DJ shook her head at the twins' glee over a potential firefight. Personally, she'd rather sneak in and get her momma out before any shooting occurred.

So far, they hadn't seen or heard from the FBI or Homeland. Obviously, her mother wasn't the Federal agencies' priority or they would've come here first. Most likely, the Feds, were using her mother's abduction as an excuse to get into the Varneys' compound and find evidence to make a case for terrorism.

DJ suspected the two agencies were setting up in front of Varneys' place and playing whose political penis was bigger than whose. As far as she was concerned, the Feds could stay out of her way until after she had her mother back.

Upon reaching the porch, she stooped down, lifted a board, and retrieved the front door key. When she went to put the key into the door, she noticed—"It isn't locked." She glanced at the men surrounding her.

"Isn't that normal?"Ace asked. "Rural folks often don't lock their doors."

"Not in my memory. My father always had cash or drugs or moonshine stored under the cabin. He wouldn't leave it open for any yahoo to come in and rob him."

Loren and Paul had gone instantly alert, raising their guns ready to respond to whatever they might find inside. She pulled her Beretta.

Gun in one hand, Ace nudged her gently to the side. "Let's not be in front of the door when it's opened," he muttered.

Loren stood to one side of the door as Paul turned the handle and shoved the door open from his position on the other side. The door slammed into the wall behind it; the sound of the wood hitting wood was like a crack of thunder.

Nothing happened. No booby-trap explosion. No shots. No yelling. The only sound was of the wind whistling through the pines and the crackle and pop of the dying fire in the cabin's fireplace.

Loren addressed DJ over his shoulder. "Is your father or his buddies smart enough to use a delayed, motion-activated booby trap?"

"Don't know. Probably not." She inhaled deeply and smelled wood smoke and—death. "There's something dead in there. Ace—" She couldn't keep the tremor of fear, the panicky gasps, out of her voice.

"Let Loren and Paul go first." Ace pulled her into his side with his free arm and covered his brothers' backs.

Before Ace had finished speaking, Loren went in high and Paul low.

Loren's terse "fuck" had DJ breaking free of Ace's hold and rushing into the cabin.

At first, she couldn't process what she saw. When she did, she realized the bloody pulp on the floor was her father. Her first reaction was sweet blessed relief it wasn't her mother. Then guilt followed quickly and like acid ate away at her gut. Tears filled her eyes as a sense of loss squeezed her heart. Her father was dead—and she'd never learn why he hadn't loved her.

Choking back tears, she took several deep breaths to calm herself. The overpowering smell of blood and raw meat exacerbated her already chaotic emotions.

As memories swamped her, her vision began to fade and her surroundings receded. Images streamed across her mind's eye. The terrified, abused little girl crying as she hid in her attic bedroom. Her pa killing the kitten DJ smuggled into her bed. Pa hitting her when she'd tried to stop him from hurting Momma. Him sneering at DJ and refusing to let her attend her grade school graduation. Pa denying her offers of college scholarships without telling her. Him telling her she was a useless female and he should've drowned her at birth.

DJ cried out in a thin, wavering voice, "Pa … why…" then finished under her breath, "…didn't you love me?"

She was so cold … alone … unloved.

"Sugar, wherever your head is at right now, you need to come back to me." Ace pulled her boneless body into his arms. He held her high against his chest, rocking her like a child. "I've got you, Dahlia Jane. Hold onto me, baby."

His words—her Ace—reached her through the emotional sludge dragging her into the past. She moved her arms. It was as if she swam through molasses, but finally she managed to place them around Ace's neck. She buried her face against his neck and breathed him in. He was her safe haven in a chaotic world.

She kept breathing him in and, gradually, the world centered on its axis once again.

Bracing herself emotionally, she raised her head and looked at the body once more.

"Gawd…" she whispered. She'd seen worse in war zones, but … the body was almost unrecognizable. There were just enough identifying marks to verify it was her father.

DJ looked at Ace and then at Paul and Loren. The men wore similar grim expressions. "Why kill him now? And where's my momma?"

There was no doubt in her mind who'd killed her father—either one of the Varneys had or they'd ordered it done.

"I'll search the house." Paul's voice said he doubted he'd find anyone, but he'd make sure.

"Falling out of thieves?" Loren's suggestion mirrored her thoughts.

Ace set her on her feet, but kept a supporting arm around her waist. The trio stood in silence, listening to the sounds of Paul checking out the cabin. His search didn't take long; the cabin wasn't all that big and her mother obviously wasn't here or he would've shouted the news by now.

When Paul entered the room, he held up the tracker necklace. "She's not here." He went to stand by his brother and stared at her father's body as if it would give up its secrets. "Looks as if he really pissed somebody off."

"Yeah," DJ sighed. "He was good at that."

"For whatever reason he was killed," Ace said. "The whole situation comes back to what the Varneys' want now—and wanted when DJ was here before."

"Revenge." DJ leaned into Ace. "They want revenge for what I did to Sean."

Ace hugged her. "Maybe your father stepped up and argued against taking on SSI to get you. Maybe he finally decided he wanted no part of what the Varneys had planned for you."

DJ shook her head. "Don't make him out to be that smart or honorable. My father was a self-centered bastard. Whatever caused the breakdown in relations, it revolved about what he wanted. He'd never put himself out there to protect me or Momma. After all, we're useless women, only good for one thing."

The emotional pain from years of her father's abuse and rejection rose with a vengeance. DJ let out a howl and struggled to get free of Ace's hold. She wanted to run and scream—hit something until her fists were bloody. She needed to rid herself of the lingering, hurtful shadows in her mind and soul.

But Ace wouldn't let her move away. He held her tightly and pressed kisses against her neck and cheek, all the while muttering words of love.

Exhausted from unleashing years of pain and hurt, she slumped against him. Her bleary-eyed gaze on the body, she whispered, "To him, I was a commodity—used goods, at that."

Ace growled and shook her. "You aren't used goods. If I ever hear you talk about yourself like that again, I'll ... Hell, I don't know what I'll do, but you damn well won't like it."

God, he was so angry. He hadn't even gotten this mad when Crawley had tried to put the moves on her during training.

"Ace, I..." She shook her head. "Sorry."

"Dammit, woman, you should be." Ace rubbed his cheek over the top of her head. He stroked her back. She wasn't sure whether it was to soothe her or him, probably a bit of both.

DJ allowed herself a few seconds to find her balance. Ace's words and touch helped her quickly shove the past back where it belonged. She wasn't that helpless little girl any longer. She was a woman—Ace's woman—and that made her stronger than ever before.

"I'm okay now." She looked up and found only love in Ace's eyes. She chanced at look at Paul and Loren and found looks of support, no pity.

"Yeah, you are." Ace smiled at her as he said the words, but in the next second, his expression turned cold with determination and banked anger. "The Varneys won't stop until you're dead at their hands. That isn't going to happen."

DJ looked into her man's eyes and found the Varneys' death. "Then let's go put the bastards out of business permanently and get my momma back."

Tweeter studied DJ's face as she turned the Hummer onto an unpaved, snow-covered narrow road, which led to a back way into the Varneys' compound. He'd let her drive, because she knew the area and because it gave her a concrete task on which to concentrate. After her emotional collapse, he wanted to give her duties to keep her mind in the here and now.

Since they'd left her family home, she'd been quiet … pensive. Her expression, a blank mask. She'd done what he'd expected and buttoned up her emotions, but they were still there, lying under the surface, roiling and boiling. As with any trauma, it would only take the right trigger to set those destructive emotions loose once more.

At this point, Tweeter was worried that trigger might be seeing Sean Varney again—or, worst case, finding Nancy dead.

In the midst of her earlier meltdown, a vacant look had turned her aqua-colored eyes to silver. In that moment, she'd been completely helpless, unable to move or defend herself.

Tweeter didn't want her that vulnerable while on enemy territory. He'd like to leave her with the Hummer while he and the guys went in and did what needed to be done to get her mom back. But his warrior-woman was back in full force and she'd fight him over such an order.

The reality of it was, he and the guys needed DJ and her knowledge to sneak onto the Varneys' property and then into the main house without alerting the men living in the compound.

Could they do the rescue without her? Yeah, but at a greater risk of injury or death to one of them or even Nancy.

But, goddammit, every protective instinct Tweeter possessed argued against taking her along. He couldn't allow her to expose herself to danger if her head wasn't one hundred percent in the game.

Tweeter was team leader. He had to make the call.

"DJ…" He spoke softly. "Sugar … you okay?"

Several moments of silence settled over the Hummer's interior. He was afraid she wouldn't answer and, thus, force him into a making a unilateral decision that could harm the trust she'd placed in him.

DJ pulled the Hummer into a small clearing and shut the motor off, then turned to look at him. Loren, Paul, and Price were quiet in the back, but he felt the heaviness of their focus on him and DJ. For several seconds, it seemed as if no one took a breath.

Then DJ heaved out a sigh filled with so many emotions, he wasn't sure he could identify them if he tried. "Ace, I'm fine." She shook her head. "No, erase that. I'm operational. I'll be much better once I have my momma back. That's my lodestone. I swear … I won't let this team down."

"None of us would blame you if you wanted…" Tweeter shut up when she placed her hand on his thigh.

"I know." DJ squeezed his leg. "I hated my father with every fiber of my being, but…" She inhaled and let it out slowly. "…no one should have to die that way. The ones who killed him deserve whatever justice is meted out."

Her eyes blazed with an inner fire and her voice grew savage. "My momma loved that man once. My biggest concern right now is being strong for her—getting her free and then helping her deal with his death. Sean Varney is a piece of shit and has no place in my head—ever again. Same goes for his father."

The atmosphere in the vehicle lightened. His brothers and Price had seen what he saw—a female warrior staking her right to go to battle.

Tweeter brushed a thumb over her bottom lip. "Everyone on Sanctuary, plus the entire Walsh clan, will help your momma deal with what happened."

DJ kissed the pad of his thumb. "I know, and I'm so damn grateful to have you…" Then she turned to look at the three men in the back. "…all of you helping me through this."

"Wouldn't be anywhere else," Loren said. "You've been family ever since Dev and Andy adopted you."

DJ smiled at Loren, then looked at Tweeter. "I'm ready to kick Varney butt. How about the rest of you?"

A chorus of "hoo-rahs" was the response.

As they unloaded the back of the Hummer, DJ outlined the approach to the property and where the danger would most likely occur. Tweeter noted that Paul and Loren looked impressed as they listened attentively. Price winked at Tweeter. Price had the advantage of working with DJ during her weeks of training back in Idaho.

DJ waved a hand toward the west. "There's a trail through the woods which leads to a crag with a five-hundred-meter drop, overlooking the Varneys' compound. Using this route, we'll avoid the front gate security and the majority of perimeter alarms. There won't be cameras. The country is too rugged. Plus, we'll be on public land for most of our entry. The state refused to let Varney fence his property where it abuts public lands."

"Good thing we brought climbing gear," said Paul.

"Never knew a SEAL yet who didn't plan for all contingencies." DJ's lips tipped upward briefly. "We could've made it down without it, but rappelling will be faster."

Price interrupted, "Heads up, team. You should've just received a text from Ren."

Tweeter and the others pulled up the text on their phones. "Looks like little sis pulled in some favors. We're now working for Homeland, which is partnering with the FBI and the West Virginia State Police."

"The Feds will run interference at the front for us. We're authorized under federal law to gain entrance to the Varneys compound to find kidnap victim Nancy Poe and secure her safety and the safety of any other innocent civilians." Loren continued to paraphrase the lengthy text message. "We're also to feed real-time intel to the State Police SWAT teams and Homeland agents, so they can enter and seize weapons, drugs, and any or all other evidence of terrorist/criminal activity."

"Well, that takes the illegality out of anything we have to do," muttered Tweeter.

"I want to be in and out before the fireworks start," DJ said. "Ed Varney's men won't give up without a fight. This has the potential of being another Waco."

"Let's avoid that if we can." Tweeter hit a number on his phone and put it to his ear. "Ren … we're on the move. Entering across public lands from the south. We'll feed intel to you and you feed it to the Feds." Tweeter listened for a bit. "Roger that. Out."

Tweeter shut the call down and made sure his phone was on vibrate, then placed it into an inner zippered pocket. "Ren said ATF has joined the party and is currently playing nicely with the Staties and the other Fed teams. FYI, ATF has an informant inside the compound. He's going to try to maintain cover, go to ground, and stay the fuck out of our way. His picture has been sent to your phones. Check it out. We don't want to kill a good guy."

"The undercover agent have any intel for us about what we might find on the grounds?" DJ asked.

"Some." Tweeter stayed next to DJ as she led the way to the crag. "There are weapons and munitions in a large pole barn on the south side of the property. The informant reported he saw the Varneys bring in an unconscious woman. They took her to the main house. He can't tell us exactly where in the house."

DJ's mouth thinned at the news of her mother, but her stride never faltered as she picked her way over ground only a mountain goat could love. "I've been in that house many times. Ed was big on his people eating and drinking together. There are two floors and a basement. Lots of entry points. We can easily get in and out without the Varneys ever knowing we were there, especially if our law enforcement friends make a big stink at the front gate for us."

"How many men does Varney have in the compound?" Paul asked as he walked and fondled his rifle.

"No exact number given," Tweeter said. "Best guess from the area locals who were interviewed by Homeland, about thirty. Paul, we'll find you some high ground once we're in the holler so you can cover our asses with your sniper rifle."

"Got it, baby bro," Paul said.

"Assclown!" Tweeter slapped Paul on the back of the head.

Loren laughed. "Showed you, twin.

Tweeter snorted back a laugh as Paul flicked a pine cone at his twin. "DJ, Price, and I will breach the house. Loren can cover us on the ground."

"Works for me," Loren said.

Price nodded.

Tweeter swatted DJ on the butt. "Get us down there, sugar."

CHAPTER 24

DJ stood at the base of the five-hundred-meter mountain wall and pulled off her climbing harness. The last man down, Paul, would clear away any signs of their ingress. They still had another decline of about thirty meters to traverse through trees and knee-deep snow.

"I can see why we can't get Nancy out the way we came in." Ace came up behind her, pulled her back against his chest, and gave her a hard squeeze. "So, the exit plans you discussed?" She nodded. "Where are those resources ... exactly?"

DJ looked out over the holler. The compound's buildings were lit up like the Las Vegas Strip. "See the building on the northwest side," she pointed, "the one with the large dark space next to it?"

"Yeah. What is it?" Ace said.

The other men had gathered closer and looked to where she pointed.

"That's where Ed always kept a helicopter. He used to have a Bell jet helicopter. I figure he still has something similar. If not, there's a lightly guarded side gate behind that building and we can just borrow a four-wheel drive and crash it through the wooden gate. Let the Feds do clean up."

"Our main objective is the two-story Victorian house in the center of the compound." She turned to Paul. "Since I'm sure there's a chopper down there, if you take up a sniper position on that ledge over there," she pointed at an overlook on her right, "I can hover and pick you up on our way out of here."

"If there's no chopper?" Loren asked.

"We'll drive our 'borrowed' vehicle back to the Hummer and one of us can tend the lines so Paul can climb up to us." DJ began walking down the slope, picking her way around trees and watching her footing. The deep snow covered all sorts of holes and rocks that could cause a fall. "Never left a man behind, ever."

"Either way works for me." Paul's steady voice came over the headset as he made his way laterally to the position she'd pointed out.

After several minutes of silence, Paul reported in. "More than adequate view from this elevation. I have lines of sight on all the buildings at the back of the property and the rear view of the main house. Also, the hanger building. Have an oblique angle on the main gate and the guardhouse. I'll set up. You'll be covered by the time you reach the end of the tree line."

"Roger that," Ace said. "You handle all direct communications with Ren and any joint communications he sets up with the Feds and the State Police. Give us a heads up on what we need to know."

Paul came back with a "roger that." All was silent once more but for the wind whistling in the pines, the crunching of snow under their feet, and the team's breaths over the headsets.

Once they hit the floor of the holler, DJ moved through a heavily treed area that led into the compound itself. They then wove their way between a few out-buildings, some empty, some used for storage. About halfway toward their goal, she signaled a halt and knelt down among a thick stand of pines.

"Guard," she muttered into her headset. "Barracks."

Ace placed a hand on her shoulder, indicating he understood. Loren slid out and shadowed the man. They waited and watched to see how many other guards were on patrol in the area. DJ didn't want to take anyone down and have an alarm sounded too early. If they could sneak by the man, that would be best.

A minute, maybe two went by. All she could think of was how much damage a man could do to a woman in that short space of time, especially to a woman as petite as her mother.

Loren moved back to Ace's side. "Only the one."

"Confirmed," Paul's voice came over the headset. "Loren's guy is now at the outer perimeter and heading in a clockwise patrol pattern. I see one other man on the opposite side of the compound also proceeding clockwise. Heads up. Five minutes. Feds knock loudly on the front gate."

DJ stood and hurried forward, using the landscaping and buildings' shadows to hide their progress. Her goal was the pool house which would give them cover to wait for the distraction the Feds would provide. After they'd passed the last set of barracks, she breathed a sigh of relief. So far they'd managed to avoid a fight in which they would've been outnumbered and outgunned.

She signaled another halt and crouched behind some shrubbery. The pool house was in sight.

A flash of memory hit her out of the blue. *The annual pool party for Varney's men and their families. She was sixteen. She'd really blossomed since the previous summer. She wore a red two-piece swimsuit. She garnered far too much male attention.* That had been the summer Sean Varney really noticed her—and began to stalk her.

A dark vortex of emotions enveloped her, sucking her down so fast she gasped for breath—then Ace's scent, his light touch on her arm, broke through the maelstrom threatening to swallow her reality. She closed her eyes and shuddered as she quickly shook off the past.

Opening her eyes, she turned and found the men motionless, alert—and waiting for her direction. The fact they trusted her, especially after her meltdown at the cabin, heartened her.

Back on task, she studied the approach to the pool house. They had to cross a wide open, well-lit area to reach the safety of the building itself. This would be the most exposure they'd encountered since they entered the Varneys' land.

DJ silently thanked whoever had cleared off the pathways and cement patio around the pool house. At least, they wouldn't be leaving any obvious tracks.

After several seconds of observation—and as her mental timer counted down to the Feds diversion—a certainty settled into her gut. They were alone and still undetected. She rose and motioned the men to follow her. Hunching low, she ran across the open space. She flattened herself against the side of the pool house in the shadow of the overhang. The men followed, one-by-one, moving swiftly and silently.

She opened the unlocked door and slid inside. The team followed on her heels. There was light coming through the many windows from the security lights dotting the compound, made even brighter by the reflection off the snowy landscape and the white cement patio. They'd need to stay low, below window level, so as not to be seen by any passing patrols.

"We should be safe here while we wait for the diversion. We also need to time the foot patrols around the house." DJ duck-walked toward the windows facing the rear of the house. The distance from the pool house door to the house was around nine meters, less than thirty feet. "From here, you can see the brick balustrade which marks the steps down to the basement entrance."

Ace knelt next to her. Loren and Price were on the other side of him. The men surveyed the objective.

"Let's go over our roles," DJ said as she spotted a guard walking a security perimeter around the main house. She set the timer on her watch to mark the timing between patrols. "Price?"

"Once we're in the basement," Price said. "I'll go to the first floor, clear the back of the house, and then secure the rear entrance for our egress."

"I'll make sure y'all get inside the basement safely. Deal with any guards who might happen upon you," Loren said. "Once you signal you're in and hunting, I'll make my way to the hanger and check on our transport. If there is no chopper, I'll secure ground transport and advise where to rendevous."

"I'll search for Nancy with you," Ace said. "I'll clear the second floor. Take out any second floor guards. Rescue your mom if she's up there. If she isn't, I'll come downstairs and back you up."

Paul's voice came over the headsets. "I'll relay intel and also cover your entry and exit of the house."

"Two men have passed by at approximately thirty seconds apart. If that's their spacing, I should see another one"—DJ looked up from her watch—"right now."

A guard walked by, smoking a cigarette, his rifle cradled in his arms.

"Thirty second intervals. We all can't make it down to the basement door and inside in that short of a time frame," Price said.

"DJ needs to go first. I'll go second," Ace said. "Price, you come once we indicate we're in. Paul … we're counting on you to give us the wider, bird's-eye view on guards coming up on our asses so Loren can take them down, if needed."

"Roger that," Paul said.

"Then we're set. Now, all we need is the diversion promised us. They're late." DJ looked at Ace, was reassured by his steely calm, and became calmer herself as if by osmosis.

"Typical bureaucracy. Probably arguing over which agency gets to use the bullhorn. DJ, keep your headset on," Ace said. "If you run across the Var—"

Paul cut off what DJ was sure would've been a "do not engage" order. "Lights just went brighter at the front of the property." The former SEAL sounded as if he were reporting a boring golf match. "The barracks y'all passed just lit up like Rockefeller Center at Christmas. Men on the run. Loaded for bear. Wait to make your move."

"Roger that," DJ said. "We'll let them pass. Re-verify the house patrol timing."

"On that," Loren said as he lifted his wrist, ready to time, as he stared at the back of the house.

"With the increased threat level, they might move Nancy," Ace said.

"No, they won't. Ed Varney won't run. He'd lose face with his followers. But he does have hidey-holes," DJ said. "Though, he might increase the inside guards. So … watch your asses."

The men grunted at her warning. She couldn't help but grin. If acknowledgment grunts could sound insulted, theirs had.

As the real action neared, a sense of preternatural calm settled over DJ. Her vision and hearing became more acute. Her perception of the surroundings became more intense until she saw and heard not only what was there, but could intuit what might be there. These were the same feelings she had when flying a Black Hawk into the danger zone. She called it her mission-sense.

At that moment, she was zeroed-in on the target.

After about twenty men ran by without giving the pool house a glance, she and the others waited for Loren's report on house perimeter guards' timing.

"Shit," Loren muttered. "Still one man every thirty seconds."

"Figures," she said with disgust. "Varney would have his most reliable men protecting his ass in the house."

For damn sure, Sean wouldn't be at the front gate defending the compound. Both Ed and his son valued their hides too much to take on the Feds one-on-one. That's what they had all the men surrounding them for.

In a way, she was glad. There was an ugly part of her that wanted to confront the Varneys.

After one guard passed, DJ stood and nudged Ace. "Get ready. The sooner we get in there, the sooner we can leave—before the Feds overrun the place."

Ace cracked a grin. "Don't want to stick around and deal with government paperwork?"

"Hell, no." She led the way to the door and paused before opening it, checking that the last guard had passed around the far corner of the house. "Had enough of that in the military."

Mentally ticking off thirty seconds in her head, she ran toward the cement and brick wall that bordered the steps to the basement. She made it into the stairwell before Paul's voice came over her headset. "Guard turning the corner of the house. Keep down, guys."

DJ crouched in the darkest corner at the bottom of the stairwell. The guard walked by the entrance without stopping, without looking down. Not that well-trained. Guards should look in all directions on patrol, including up and down.

"Tweeter's on the move," Paul said. "Action at front gate has escalated. Varney's men are now shooting at the Feds."

The sounds of automatic weapon fire echoed off the surrounding mountains and buildings like rolling waves of thunder. World War III militia-style had come to Appalachia.

DJ needed to get inside the house. The Varneys would use anything and anyone to protect their own skins. Her mother was the perfect hostage to hide behind which was why DJ wanted her out of the middle of this clusterfuck sooner rather than later.

She turned to open the door, then stopped. *Shit. Damn. Fuck.* There was a coded alarm on the door. She could smash it, but that would definitely announce their presence.

This was a job for Ace. She turned to look up as he came down the steps as stealthily as a jaguar. She indicated the alarm system on the door. He pulled a small set of tools from a pocket and began working on the box, a penlight held in his mouth so he could see.

She covered his actions and the tell-tale light by placing her body between him and any danger from above. Her Beretta aimed upward, she worried her lip with her teeth and prayed the next guard was as lax as the last one had been.

"Guard approaching," Price reported. "Are you in?"

She clicked twice for no.

"Roger that," Price said. "Loren and I will hold and cover from the pool house until you are."

Ace snorted, a low disgusted sound. She looked over her shoulder and found him still working on the alarm, his long, supple fingers flying over the small box's innards.

"DJ!" Price's voice again. His tone held a warning. "Next guard is checking high and—low."

She sensed Ace stiffen for a split-second. She reached back and patted his hip. Holstering her weapon, she moved up the stairs.

Ace's "fuck" came across her headset as a feral snarl, but he didn't stop working on the door.

Stopping two steps from the top, she used the brick balustrade to hide her presence until the last possible second.

"He's two meters from the opening," Price said. "Go at my diversion."

At the sound of glass breaking, DJ flowed out of her cover and was on the man whose attention was on the pool house. Simultaneously, her hand went over his mouth and her arm, around his neck. One quick, adrenaline-fueled jerk and his neck was broken.

Her knees buckled as she took the man's body weight. He wasn't much bigger than she was, but dead weight and her position at his back threw her off-balance. Just as she was about to drop the body and reposition to drag him into the shrubbery, Ace relieved her of the man's weight and boosted him over his shoulder.

DJ turned and moved back into the shelter of the stairwell with Ace and his burden on her heels.

The basement door was open and no alarms. *Thank you, Jesus.*

"Next guard is rounding the house," Paul reported in this time. "Battle at the front gate has ceased for the moment. The Feds pulled back and are waiting for you guys to give them the go-ahead to enter. They want intel on what to expect and an all-clear from your side of the mission."

"Roger that." DJ moved into the basement and shifted to the side so Ace could enter. "We're in, Price."

"Roger that," Price responded. "I'll be over as soon as the next guard passes."

Ace dumped the dead guard behind the door, out of the way, and then closed the door just short of latching it.

"Moving out as soon as Price is down the steps," Loren said. "Paul, any action at the hanger?"

"Doors are open. Lights are on. Some activity. I see two men inside." Paul paused. "There is a helicopter. It's a Black Hawk with an External Stores Support System. Whoo-wee. The Varneys sure upgraded from a Bell."

DJ was ecstatic to hear about the Hawk. With the ESSS, they'd have extra weaponry to help cover their escape and assist the Feds, if needed. She moved even farther into the dimly lit basement. The little girl inside her heart wanted to run upstairs and find her mother. The soldier in her head kept her in the basement, following the mission plan. Pulling a small flashlight from her pocket, she aimed it around the dark corners of the room.

The basement contained lots and lots of boxes with military markings. She used her knife to pry open one of the boxes. *Shit.* Then another. *Double-shit.* Then she moved to some of the other ones.

Ace came to her side and examined the contents, then muttered, "Fuck."

Yeah, that about summed the situation up.

"Paul … advise the Feds there are enough military explosives in the main house's basement to take out a small city," Ace said. "Looks as if Varney had plans to blow something up. A big something."

"So conveyed," Paul responded seconds later. "ATF appreciates the intel. They didn't know."

The ATF undercover agent obviously hadn't gotten into the house, or these were recent acquisitions.

She and Ace waited with knives in their hands. Movement sounded on the exterior steps. Both stiffened. The door creaked open. Ace waved her back and began to move forward.

It was Price, and he had a man over his shoulder.

"Why the fuck didn't you click?" Ace growled. "I could have gutted you."

"Had my hands full." Price delivered the line in a don't-mess-with-me tone as he dumped the man he carried on the floor next to the other guard's body. He turned and shut the door.

"Another guard?" DJ looked at the body. He wore no coat.

Price nodded. "This one came from inside the house. Fucker must've heard the window break just as the fracas at the gate began to wind down. Loren and I double-teamed him. Not sure how long we have before someone notices some guards are missing."

"Paul, we're heading into the house proper." DJ looked at the men who gave her short, abrupt nods, knives in hand. "We need some more distraction from the Feds."

Paul's almost ghostly "Roger that" came across their headsets. Then he ordered, "Move it."

DJ followed Price and Ace up the steps. Price led the way into the back hallway and then into the kitchen. So far, they'd seen no one. In fact, the whole place felt empty. For once, she prayed her instincts were wrong. Her mother had to be somewhere in this house.

A knife in one hand and gun in the other, Price signaled his intent to clear the rooms at the back of the house, which were mostly live-in help's quarters and an office, if she recollected correctly.

Ace headed up the back staircase to the second level. He'd demanded that assignment since it would be the most likely place to hold a prisoner.

DJ had been okay with his choice since her gut told her otherwise. A feeling she'd chosen not to share with Ace.

Sean and his father would keep their hostage close to hand in case they needed her to save their butts. That meant the main level.

DJ ghosted through the butler's pantry and then used the servant's door into the formal dining room. Evidence of a recent meal was scattered over the large dining table's surface. She edged her way around the walls and toward the main hallway that ran from the front door all the way to the back of the house with rooms branching off each side.

"No one in the back of the house, main level," Price reported. "Need any help, Tweeter?"

"No," Ace replied. "Second floor is clear. No guards. No anyone. Secure rear door, Price. I'm heading to main floor."

"Roger that," Price replied.

Desperation and, she'd admit it, fear threatened to drive DJ to her knees. Where were the Varneys and her mother?

A flash of memory from that summer when Sean had really noticed her the first time streaked across her mind's eye. An incident she'd blocked about that pool party. Sean had cornered her ... in the pool house. He'd taken her down a hidden staircase to a basement that connected to the main house by a tunnel. She'd gotten away by escaping through the main house basement.

"Basement," she clipped out. "Tunnel to pool house."

"Wait on us," Ace growled. His feet pounded overhead.

DJ had already taken off, running toward the stairs to the basement. Once there, she took the steps two at a time and then went straight to the wall where the tunnel entrance was located and shoved boxes out of the way. The door blended into a faux landscape painted on the wall. She slid her knife into its scabbard and pulled her gun. She found the latch, pulled, and tore through the door.

Into the arms of Sean Varney.

"Gotcha, bitch." Sean hit her arm, hard, numbing it and causing her to drop her gun. He then put her in a choke hold.

For several seconds or minutes or an eternity, panic gripped her. It was just as it had been all those years ago. The bigger, older Sean manhandling the younger DJ. She couldn't catch a full breath. Her grunts of exertion mingled with wheezing and mewling cries. She fought him, but made no progress.

Ace's growl came across her headset. "Goddammit, Dahlia Jane. Fight." His furious and pissed-off order broke through her flashback.

Her mind back in the present, and backup on the way, she used every dirty trick she knew to loosen Sean's hold so she could take a full breath. She also managed to slip her knife out with her left hand and started stabbing at anyplace she could reach on the fucker. The scent of her nemesis's blood was the sweetest smell.

"Fuck!" roared Sean. With steroid-enhanced strength, he threw her against the cement wall.

She hit the surface so hard her knife flew out of her hand. Momentarily stunned, she slid down the wall, landing on her butt.

Sean kicked her in the side, hard enough to move her away from the wall. "Bitch, I'm gonna mess you up."

Over her headset, Ace bellowed, "DJ!"

The anguish in his voice focused her. She shook off the pain and concentrated on garnering her strength to stay alive until help arrived. Without taking her eyes off Sean's florid face, she used her peripheral vision to searched for the knife. And there it was … just out of reach.

"Like hell you will." She pulled in a full breath, then rolled toward and snagged her knife. She used her body to hide the weapon.

Sean lumbered over to where she lay and bent over as if to pick her up. "You'll beg me for death."

In one smooth, but painful motion, she turned and rose to her knees. In a maneuver she'd perfected over the last few days, she swung her knife arm in a short arc and plunged the knife up and under Sean's ribs and twisted. A gush of blood leaked from around the knife. "Don't think so."

The stunned look on Sean's face as he fell forward was the most gratifying thing she'd ever seen. Then his dead weight knocked her over and trapped her beneath him before she could move.

Shit.

TWEETER MET UP WITH PRICE at the stairs to the basement. The sounds of DJ's rasping breaths and pained grunts came over the headset. She was fighting for her life against a man who outweighed her by over a hundred pounds—and he wasn't there. He'd never been so scared in his whole life.

At Varney's snarled "fuck" and "bitch, I'm gonna mess you up," Tweeter yelled, "DJ!" He practically flew down the steps and landed heavily at the bottom. He spotted the shifted boxes and the partially open door.

A heavy thud—the sound of a body hitting something hard—shot shards of ice straight into his heart. "DJ!" He ran for the opening to the tunnel.

Price snagged the back of his jacket. "Hold up, man. You won't do her any good dead. I'll go in low."

His fury all-consuming, Tweeter shrugged off Price's hands and went in high. Price cursed viciously, but followed him in, going low.

The scene would be fixed in his mind forever. Varney's hulking body on top of DJ's. Neither of them moved. Blood seeped from between their bodies.

"DJ!" Tweeter shoved his gun in his holster and ran to pull the bastard off her. "Please, be alive. Goddammit, Dahlia Jane. Talk to me." With almost super-human strength, he lifted the fucker off her and tossed him aside.

"C-c-can't…" A low moan and a wiggle of her legs. "…breathe."

Thank God, she was alive.

"Sure you can. Take it slow, sugar." Tweeter knelt by her side. He examined her with gentle fingers. Nothing obviously broken. The blood wasn't hers, thank fuck. Her eyes were open and oriented; her gaze fixed on him as she still struggled to breathe. "One little breath at a time, baby."

"Shit … ass … hole … weighed … a ton." She panted with each word. "He's dead … right?"

Tweeter turned and looked at the body he'd tossed like a bag of garbage. The hilt of her knife was buried so far in the fucker's torso, he could barely see the tip of the handle. The front of Varney's shirt was blood-soaked. "Yeah. He's toast."

"Good." She took another breath. "Up … please." She tried to sit up.

"Hold on a sec." He stood and pulled her to a standing position and then held her against his body, facing him. Once again, he ran his hands over her precious body, rejoicing in the fact she was warm and breathing and in his arms.

When she inhaled sharply and winced, he probed more carefully. "Where does it hurt? I didn't feel anything broken. Is some of that blood yours? Did he cut you?"

"Just bruises. No and no." She looked around as she rubbed her throat. A frown creased her forehead. She tapped her headset. "Price? Sit rep."

Tweeter kept his arm around DJ as they moved down the tunnel in the direction Price had headed.

"Nancy's not here." Price met them as they entered the pool house basement. There were three women and an older man huddled in the corner of the room, looking scared out of their minds. "The servants said Ed took Nancy and headed up into the pool house."

"Shit," DJ moved to the stairs. "He'll go for the helicopter."

"Loren … sit rep." Tweeter said. "Ed Varney could…"

"Under control here. Fucker waltzed in here. I took him down. Nancy's physically fine. Varney's tied up. The chopper is all ours," Loren said. "Watch your asses on the way here. Some of Varney's men are trying to leave. Paul's putting the fear of the sniper into them."

"Paul…" Tweeter followed DJ up the steps. He wasn't letting her out of his sight again today—maybe never again. "Tell the Feds there are four civilians under the pool house and that there's an underground tunnel connecting the basements between it and the main house."

"Roger that. Feds are trying to breach the gate and aren't having much success. Seems the asshats have piled multiple vehicles and other crap up against the entrance," Paul said. "Loren says the Hawk is armed with Hellfire missiles. Feds are asking for help in gate-busting."

"Tell them we'll take a run on the gate once we're in the air," Tweeter said.

"Roger that," Paul said.

Once they were above the ground, Tweeter wrapped an arm around DJ's waist and held her back until Price caught up with them. "We go together."

She nodded. "Sorry. Want to see my momma. She has to be so scared."

"I know. Hold on a few more minutes." Tweeter brushed a kiss over her cheek. "You okay to run?"

DJ seemed to be favoring her one side and hip. Bruises were already forming on her throat where the bastard must've choked her. He really wished Sean was alive so he could kill the fucker again.

"Yes." She looked over her shoulder at Price. "The servants know to stay hidden until the shooting is over?"

"Yeah," Price said. "Ready to go when you are."

Tweeter handed DJ his backup gun and palmed his. "Let's go."

Taking the lead, he made sure DJ was between him and Price. He heard her harsh breaths as she ran. He checked over his shoulder and saw only stoicism on her face. His warrior-woman would never complain. She could have serious injuries. As soon as they were safe, he'd strip her down and check over every blessed inch of her.

A shot whizzed by his arm. Before he could take out the man who'd popped up out of some bushes, DJ had shot the bastard in the head.

Head in the game, Walsh. Get her safe first, then worry about her injuries.

"Get down," Price yelled as he dragged DJ with him.

Tweeter dove and rolled, taking a shot at the man Price had seen. Another one down.

Another man ran at them and then fell as a large caliber sniper round took off the top of his head. *Score one for Paul.*

"You're clear for a few seconds," Paul said. "Go, go, go!"

Tweeter pulled DJ from Price's hold and to her feet, then holding her hand, ran like the wind. Price, on their heels.

An AK-47 slung across his chest, Loren motioned them into the hanger. "Get in the bird, DJ. Get her ready to go." He then reached and snagged an assault rifle from a rack by the door, tossing one to Tweeter, then another to Price. "Give me some cover so I can pull the Hawk out of the hanger."

The tow tractor was already hooked up. Thank fuck, the hanger opening was broad enough to handle the Hawk's rotors in their fully extended position.

"I'll call the bogies as I see them," Paul said. "The rats are trying to leave. Imagine that." A pause. "Heads up. Group of four coming from your left."

Tweeter and Price took positions up on either side of the door and laid down fire to dissuade anyone from approaching the hanger and the tarmac immediately outside it. Paul added sniper-fire brand of dissuasion from his position.

Even more gunfire sounded from the front of the compound where the more loyal—or crazier—militia men were still defending the compound and holding the Feds at bay.

Loren pulled the Hawk onto the tarmac as quickly as the tractor could move.

"Ready to fire her up once the tractor is clear." DJ's voice was cool as a cucumber. "Get on board, guys."

Tweeter hopped into the cockpit and strapped into the co-pilot seat, pulling on the headset for intra-cabin communications. "Fire her up, sugar. Loren's clear."

Loren left the tractor off to the side. Price moved out from the hanger door, laying down suppressive fire. The two ran for the Hawk's open cabin door and jumped inside.

DJ started the rotors. Varney's militia men fired at the chopper. Hooked in, Loren and Price returned fire from the open cabin doors. DJ took the Hawk up fast and made a wide defensive swing to take them away from the threat on the ground.

Once they were away, DJ turned to look at him. "All systems are green including weapons. I checked—this Hawk is loaded with a full complement of Hellfires and a set of .50 caliber machine guns."

She looked at him, her gaze suddenly anxious. "Take over, please. I need to check on Momma. I gave her a quick once-over, fastened her into a seat, and put a headset on her, but," she touched Tweeter's arm, "I think, she's in shock."

Nodding, Tweeter took control of the Hawk. "Take care of her."

DJ smiled and kissed his cheek. "Love you so much." Then she moved to cabin.

"Loren. Price," Tweeter said. "Be sure you're hooked in good. The ride is about to get trickier. Going to send a little hellfire down on the fuckers."

Loren chuckled. "We're good, bro. Go for it."

"Paul," Tweeter cruised around the perimeter, far out of the range of anything the militia might throw at them. "Let the Feds know they need to get the fuck away from the gate. We'll come and pick you up once we open Varney's front door."

"Roger that," Paul responded.

Tweeter flew a wide arc over the mountains surrounding the holler and then flew an erratic pattern along the boundary until he got the all-clear to take his run and fire the missile. Price had come to take second seat while Loren closed and secured the cabin door and then strapped in.

"Feds are clear. Bad asses have been warned. Their response was gunfire," Paul said. "Take out the gate, brother."

For the second time in less then a day, a warm sense of accomplishment swept through Tweeter's mind. Nancy was rescued and safe in her daughter's arms. Bad guys were caught or dead. A potential home-grown terrorist threat had been foiled. And Tweeter would be marrying DJ, the woman he loved more than life itself; well, he'd marry her after they waded through the red tape from today's action. All in all, a damn good day with one thing left on his mission to-do list.

Coming at the compound gate from the front, he lined up the shot and sent the missile.

"Yippie-kay-yay, motherfuckers!"

"MOMMA, DID THOSE PIECES OF bull hooey hurt you?" DJ ran a hand over her mother's soft, messy hair as it curled around the headset. There were dark circles under her mother's eyes and several bruises on her arms and wrists. She'd make sure her mother was thoroughly checked over once they got to a hospital.

"I'm okay." Her mother tried to smile, but failed. "They shot Scotty." Tears flowed down her cheeks. She sobbed out, "He tried to protect me. There was so much blood." She wiped at a stain on her jeans.

"Scotty's going to be fine, Momma. Ren said so. The poor man's more worried about you." DJ hugged her mother's frail body and managed not to wince when the action jarred the area Sean had kicked.

DJ took a deep breath and decided, bruised not fractured. She'd be getting checked right alongside her mother. She'd seen the grave look in Ace's eyes when he'd examined her in the tunnel, and she wouldn't protest. He needed to know she was A-okay as much as she needed to know her mother was all right.

"Baby girl, they … killed your pa." Her mother's eyes held regret and sorrow for the man she'd married, not for the man into which he'd evolved.

Her mother shuddered violently. Oh God, no—

"They killed him in front of you?" For some reason that made her madder than anything. "I'm so sorry you had to see that."

"And I'm sorry he was never a good father to you."

"Well, I had the best momma, so that made up for it." DJ kissed a pale, bruised cheek. "Now, try to rest."

Her mother leaned into her and let out a sigh, then fell asleep like a little child exhausted from a too-busy day. But a mere minute or so later, she startled at the sound of the Hellfire being fired. "What's that?"

Cuddling her, DJ said, "Nothing to worry about. Just Ace taking care of business. Go to sleep. You're safe."

The mission over, DJ drifted on a sea of satisfaction and happiness. She, Ace, and the team had done it. They'd rescued her mother and taken care of a nasty nest of vipers. Soon, she'd be married to Ace, the man who loved her for who she was, who let her be strong when she needed to be, and who supported her when she required it.

The sound of the Hawk going into a hover roused her from a battle nap. She was aware of Loren opening the cabin door and lowering a harness. Paul's voice joked with his twin as the cabin door closed once more. She opened her eyes and smiled. Paul winked at her and covered both her and her mother with a blanket. He strapped in opposite them. Everything was now really all right. The team was all on board. She dozed off again.

DJ roused again a bit later when Ace slid next to her and put his arm around her. He nuzzled and kissed her ear as he tucked the blanket more securely around her shoulders. "Just lean on me. Rest. When we get on the jet, I'll tuck you and Nancy in bed. We'll stop in Lexington to get you both checked out. Ren has already gotten us hotel rooms and informed the Feds where they can find us for a debrief."

"What about Varney?" She yawned and looked over at the man who'd terrorized her mother. He was unconscious, courtesy of the drugs Ace had liberated from O'Riley, cuffed, and strapped into a seat.

"Homeland is sending agents to pick him up at the airfield where we left the jet."

"Good" She turned and kissed his chin. "When we're at the hospital in Kentucky, you need to get checked out, too."

"If that makes you happy…" She nodded. He smiled. "… then I will. I don't want you to worry. We have a wedding to arrange."

"Plus a wedding night and a honeymoon to anticipate," she reminded him. "I love you, Ace. I want to spend every day and night with you for the rest of my life."

Ace cradled her face with both hands and caressed her cheeks with his thumbs. He peppered kisses over her face until he finally lingered over her mouth. "I love you, Dahlia Jane. I'm the luckiest man in the world since I'll spend the rest of my days by your side and get to hold you in my arms each and every night." He sealed his words with a reverent kiss that soon turned deep and hungry.

When he broke off the kiss, DJ sighed and nestled her head on his shoulder. "Love you so, so much." She yawned. "So tired. Sorry…"

"Sleep, sugar." He rested his cheek on the top of her head. "I've got you. I'll never let you go."

DJ went to sleep, his vow resonating in her soul.

Epilogue

"A suite? I thought you were kidding when you said that." Standing at the floor-to-ceiling window, DJ tore her view away from the dancing fountains in the front of the hotel and found her husband—just thinking the word made her happy—at the door as he tipped the bellman.

A huge smile on his face, Ace walked to join her at the window. She watched his smooth, sure gait and was relieved to see he wasn't showing any lingering effects of his time in Oraio's hands.

Since the ER doctor in Lexington had found only bruising and no fractures from her altercation with Varney, she anticipated a wedding night filled with lots of sex and cuddling and making plans for a short honcymoon before returning to Idaho where the SSI and Walsh families planned a reception for them.

"Only the best for my beautiful wife." He held her head still with a hand at the nape of her neck and placed a gentle nibbling kiss on her lips. She moaned and deepened the kiss by threading her fingers in his hair and pulling his head closer. Rubbing her lower body over the rock-hard erection tenting his pants, she teased his lips open with her tongue. He groaned deep in his throat and ate at her mouth.

Ace pulled away, his breathing harsh, but his touch as he swept a finger down the length of her neck was gentle. "You know, later, if you want … you can have a ceremony with the dress and all the trappings. I didn't want to wait to make you completely mine."

She studied his face. He was worried he'd let her down. Since she'd never entertained any dreams about a big wedding—and she'd wanted to be his wife just as much as he wanted to be her husband—she hurried to reassure her man.

"I adored our wedding." She kissed his chin. Laying her head on his shoulder, she petted his chest. "It had everything that was important. You. Me. A legal license. My momma. Loren, Paul, and Price as witnesses." She giggled. "I loved the Liberace impersonator who performed our ceremony. The pictures will be something to show our kids. We'll tell them that their daddy loved their mommy so much he couldn't wait to marry her. And that's what's most important to me—your love."

She leaned back and then gestured around the suite. "That you took the extra time to arrange all this? Makes me the luckiest girl in the world."

There were flowers in each room of the suite. A cart with champagne, strawberries, and chocolates. And, most surprising, Agent Provocateur bags that had proven to contain a decadent silk nightgown and robe plus other delicate, beautiful undies she'd never have bought for herself. She was betting Callie had a hand in the lingerie surprise.

"So, who cares about a formal wedding?" DJ cuddled closer and traced circles around his nipple through his shirt. "I have you."

"I'm the lucky one." He covered her hand on his chest and rubbed his other hand up and down her back. "You tired?"

His thick lashes covered his partially closed ice blue eyes so she couldn't read him well. His expression was closed and his tone wasn't at all sexual. He sounded concerned about her well-being. This was so not the amorous new husband she'd anticipated for her wedding night.

Of course, less than twenty-four hours ago, he'd hovered and growled as the ER doctor had examined her. He'd scrutinized the chest x-rays, looking for any sign of a fracture, and practically cross-examined the radiologist about the accuracy of her diagnosis.

"No, I'm well-rested." She'd slept in his arms at the airport hotel in Lexington and then napped on the SSI jet on the way to Las Vegas. "Why?"

DJ pulled her hand out from under his and walked her fingers up his chest to cup the back of his neck, then ruffled her fingers through the hair curling there. Pressing her body against his, she placed a kiss where his shirt lay open at his neck.

Now, her tone was definitely sexual. It seemed as if it had been weeks since they'd made love on the plane after leaving Belize.

Tonight was her one and only wedding night, and she wanted to celebrate the fact—and the fact they were alive—in the most basic way.

"I thought you might want to go shopping or maybe try your luck at the tables." He moved a hand to knead her bottom. His erection pulsed where it lay between their bodies.

Seriously? She looked into what she could see of his eyes and found a hint of a mischievous twinkle. The tease.

"Well ... I do need clothes." She bit his lower lip and then licked away the sting. "Eventually. Right now, I want to take a shower ... with you." She licked up the side of his neck and teethed his ear lobe. His sharp hiss made her smile. "I might need help getting really, really clean. Are you up for the task, Mr. Walsh?"

"Oh, Mrs. Walsh..." His voice was a deep growl that reverberated over her skin and burrowed deeply in her pussy. "I think I'm just the man for the job." He turned her toward the bedroom and then patted her ass. "Lead the way, sugar."

"First one naked and in the shower gets oral sex?" DJ said.

"I'll take that challenge." Ace stripped off his shirt and shucked his pants as he stalked her through the large suite.

Over her shoulder, DJ eyed his long, muscular body and his hugely erect penis. She sighed happily. He was hers—and she had it in her mind to drive him out of his.

When she reached the bedroom, she purposely took her time shedding her clothes. She wanted to go down on him first, knowing he'd more than return the favor later in bed.

By the time she'd stripped and reached the luxuriously appointed marble bathroom, Ace was in the steam shower with his hand on his cock, stroking the deeply red shaft with its plum-colored head. His wolf-blue eyes burned for her.

"I win," he rasped.

"Oh, I think, we both win." DJ entered the shower and nudged him to the built-in bench. "Sit. Let me take care of you."

Her husband sat on the edge of the bench. She sank to her knees and took over control of his erection with one hand and cuddled his heavy balls with the other.

"Put this under your knees. I don't want my lovely wife bruised more than she is."

"You are so good to me." DJ took the folded towel he handed her and then knelt on it.

"I want to be even more good to you. What about your pleasure?" Ace stroked wet hair away from her face as she took a gentle swipe over his penis's engorged head to remove a single silver drop of precum. Another droplet quickly emerged to replace the one she'd tasted.

DJ peeked at him through her lashes. "Oh, you can take care of me ... later. I have this fantasy of you making love to me from behind while I'm naked against the window and looking out over the Strip."

His cock jerked in her hand. She smiled. "You like my fantasy?" She took a long, slow lick from the base of his shaft to his glans, then swirled her tongue around the head.

"Fuck, yeah." He cupped the back of her head, threading his fingers through her short curls. "Take me inside, sugar. I need to feel your hot, hungry mouth around my cock."

DJ moaned at the desire in his voice, a male hunger that was only hers to slake. She took his length inside her mouth in small increments.

"Fuck, baby. Don't tease." Ace threw back his head, a grimace of pleasure and pain on his face. The muscles in his throat strained as he swallowed hard and let out a groan. His fingers tangled in her hair, pressed her forward—urging her take more and more.

DJ moved her hand from his balls to brace herself on his leg, halting the inexorable forward movement. She mewled around his cock.

Always in tune with her, Ace loosened his grip on her hair … went motionless. "Sugar, you all right?" he whispered, his breaths harsh and rapid. The pulse point at his throat beat rapidly, indicating the intensity of his arousal. His erection throbbed just as wildly within her mouth.

But he waited—for her.

DJ slowly released his penis and licked her lips. "I sucked in too much, too fast." She winked and took a teasing swipe over the purple head. "I'm still on a learning curve."

He smiled. All his love was there, in his expression. "Just take what you can handle. Everything you do to me feels good."

She nodded and took several long licks, then traced the veins on his shaft with the tip of her tongue. Precum pooled in his slit and then dripped over his glans. Tonguing the slit, she then took the head into her mouth once more and slid down his shaft, then retreated. Eventually, she found a rhythm and depth that was comfortable for her—and made her man moan.

"That's good. Fuck, so fucking good." He held her head as if he was afraid she would stop. This time, though, his fingers were more loosely tangled in her hair.

DJ had no desire to stop. She wanted to suck him dry, then let him take over the sexual play and make her scream with pleasure.

Hollowing her cheeks, she applied stronger suction as she slid her lips up and down his thickness. She used her hand to add more sensation to his shaft and moved her other hand back to squeeze his balls gently.

He groaned. His eyes closed, he threw his head back. "God, so close. So fucking close. You gonna to take my cum?"

She hummed and nodded.

"Faster, sugar. I don't break."

Increasing her speed, she bobbed up and down on his cock, using her tongue to add another sensation.

"Fuck!" Ace roared, stiffened and then came and came. With a light touch, he held her head to his cock as she swallowed his cum. Held her there until a final full-body shudder indicated he was done.

"You, my lovely, talented wife, are amazing." He finger-combed her curls as she let his spent cock slide from her mouth.

Hot water pounding on her back, DJ sat back on her heels and smiled happily at the picture he made. He leaned back against the tile wall, his knees sprawled wide. His expression was relaxed and held the look of a large, fully sated cat—a lion accepting his due from his lioness.

And just as quickly as a lion, he pounced.

Grabbing her by the waist, he pulled her up to straddle his lap. He positioned her legs around his waist and then placed his hands on her hips to hold her in place. "I love you ... my most beautiful wife."

"Back atcha ... my most viral husband."

A hard protuberance poked her stomach. She looked down and found him fully erect. "Again? That was fast." She grinned.

He shrugged. "You breathe. I get hard." He nipped her shoulder as he took a breast into one hand and swept his thumb over the bud. "You on my lap? Guaranteed to make me harder than titanium steel."

"What about my window fantasy?" She squealed as he lifted her until her pussy was over his cock.

"We'll get to it," he promised. "Now, put me in and ride me, wife."

"Bossy much?" she teased as she placed the head at her swollen opening and took him in slowly, still amazed at how good it felt to have his stiff, throbbing penis inside her sheath.

"No, just dying to be inside you." He squeezed a hip and bent his head to the breast he'd captured. "As long as I'm breathing, I'll always need you."

"Always sounds nice." DJ sighed and began the up-and-down motion that would take her to heaven. Knowing that when she fell, Ace would be there to catch her—each and every time.

~THE END~

About the Author

Monette Michaels is the pen name for a multi-published author of suspense/thrillers, scifi romance, and paranormal romance. She also writes paranormal romance under the pen name Rae Morgan. She's been married to the love of her life for far longer than she cares to remember. Her home is in Central Indiana.

You can visit her website at
WWW.MONETTEMICHAELS.COM

Sign up for her newsletter:
HTTP://EEPURL.COM/KKGXJ

Facebook:
WWW.FACEBOOK.COM/AUTHORMONETTEMICHAELS

Twitter:
HTTP://TWITTER.COM/MonetteMichaels

Pinterest:
HTTPS://WWW.PINTEREST.COM/MONETTEMICHAELS/

Author Bibliography

Writing as Monette Michaels:

Fatal Vision
Death Benefits
Green Fire
Vested Interests
Blind-Sided (with Janet Ferran)

The Virtuous Vampire,
A Gooden and Knight Mystery, Case File #1

The Deadly Séance,
A Gooden and Knight Mystery, Case File #2

Eye of the Storm,
Book 1, Security Specialists International

Stormy Weather Baby,
Book 1.5, Security Specialists International

Cold Day in Hell,
Book 2, Security Specialists International

Storm Front,
Book 2.5, Security Specialists International

Weather the Storm,
Book 3, Security Specialists International

Storm Warning,
Book 4, Security Specialists International

Prime Obsession,
Book 1, The Prime Chronicles Trilogy

Prime Selection,
Book 2, The Prime Chronicles Trilogy

Prime Imperative,
Book 3, The Prime Chronicles Trilogy

Prime Claiming,
a Prime Chronicles Short Story

WRITING AS RAE MORGAN:

DESTINY'S MAGICK,
BOOK 1, COVEN OF THE WOLF SERIES

MOON MAGICK,
BOOK 2, COVEN OF THE WOLF SERIES

TREADING THE LABYRINTH,
BOOK 3, COVEN OF THE WOLF SERIES

NO SECRETS,
BOOK 4, COVEN OF THE WOLF SERIES

EARTH AWAKENED, A TERRAN REALM BOOK

ENCHANTRESS

EVANESCENCE

"ONCE UPON A PRINCESS,"
IN AIN'T YOUR MAMA'S BEDTIME STORIES